A PLUME BOOK

# THE TWO LIVES OF
# MISS CHARLOTTE MERRYWEATHER

Award-winning author ALEXANDRA POTTER was born in Yorkshire. Having lived in Los Angeles, Sydney, and London after university, she finally decided to settle where the sun shines and now lives full-time in Los Angeles. She has worked variously as a features editor and subeditor for women's magazines in the United Kingdom and now writes full-time. Please visit her website at www.alexandrapotter.com.

---

### Praise for
### *The Two Lives of Miss Charlotte Merryweather*

"This feel-good novel is a *Sliding Doors*–style romance."
—*Glamour* UK

"Warm, funny, and hope for us all that there are such things as second chances." —*Company* (UK) 4-star review

"A quirky, hilarious read, sure to get you in touch with your younger self." —*Candis* (UK) Book-of-the-Month Selection

"This novel has a satisfying ring to it, pulled happily along by the charm and honesty and both Charlottes."   —*Daily Mirror* (UK)

"[A] fun, feel-good novel . . . an escapist treat."   —*Sainsbury's*

### Praise for *Me and Mr. Darcy*

"Unexpectedly charming . . . *Me and Mr. Darcy* offers a *Pride and Prejudice*–appropriate surprise . . . it turns out to be one of the wittier of this summer's offerings, not to mention sharp and sad in its observations about what spinsterhood, identity, and aging look like for women in 2007."   —Salon.com

"[*Me and Mr. Darcy*] takes the reader on an extended daydream with an appropriately pleasant ending."   —*The Indianapolis Star*

"Pure candy for the imagination . . . Ms. Potter has worked literary magic with the creation of *Me and Mr. Darcy*."
                                                        —CoffeeTimeRomance.com

### More Praise for Alexandra Potter

"Nobody does it quite like Alexandra Potter."   —*Daily Mail*

"Feel-good fiction full of unexpected twists and turns."   —*OK!*

"Funny, romantic . . . [a] tale about what might happen if all your wishes suddenly came true."   —*Daily Mirror*

"Fantastically funny."   —*Elle*

ALSO BY ALEXANDRA POTTER

*Me and Mr. Darcy*
*Do You Come Here Often?*
*Calling Romeo*

# The Two Lives of
# Miss Charlotte Merryweather

## Alexandra Potter

A PLUME BOOK

PLUME
Published by the Penguin Group
Penguin Group (USA) Inc., 375 Hudson Street, New York, New York 10014, U.S.A. • Penguin
Group (Canada), 90 Eglinton Avenue East, Suite 700, Toronto, Ontario, Canada M4P 2Y3
(a division of Pearson Penguin Canada Inc.) • Penguin Books Ltd., 80 Strand, London WC2R 0RL,
England • Penguin Ireland, 25 St. Stephen's Green, Dublin 2, Ireland (a division of Penguin Books
Ltd.) • Penguin Group (Australia), 250 Camberwell Road, Camberwell, Victoria 3124, Australia
(a division of Pearson Australia Group Pty. Ltd.) • Penguin Books India Pvt. Ltd., 11 Community
Centre, Panchsheel Park, New Delhi – 110 017, India • Penguin Group (NZ), 67 Apollo Drive,
Rosedale, North Shore 0632, New Zealand (a division of Pearson New Zealand Ltd.) • Penguin
Books (South Africa) (Pty.) Ltd., 24 Sturdee Avenue, Rosebank, Johannesburg 2196, South Africa

Penguin Books Ltd., Registered Offices: 80 Strand, London WC2R 0RL, England

Published by Plume, a member of Penguin Group (USA) Inc. Originally published as *Who's That
Girl?* by Hodder and Stoughton, Great Britain.

First American Printing, April 2010
10  9  8  7  6  5  4  3  2  1

Ⓟ  REGISTERED TRADEMARK—MARCA REGISTRADA

LIBRARY OF CONGRESS CATALOGING-IN-PUBLICATION DATA

Potter, Alexandra.
    [Who's that girl?]
    The two lives of Miss Charlotte Merryweather / Alexandra Potter.
        p. cm.
    Originally published as: Who's that girl? London : Hodder, 2009.
    ISBN 978-0-452-29588-9
    1. Young women—Fiction.  2. Americans—England—Fiction.  3. Experiential learning—
Fiction.  4. Identity (Psychology)—Fiction.  5. London (England)—Fiction.  Chick lit.
I. Title.
    PR6116.O89W58    2010
    823'.92—dc22                                                          2009052026

Printed in the United States of America
Set in Adobe Garamond and Centaur • Designed by Eve L. Kirch

PUBLISHER'S NOTE
This is a work of fiction. Names, characters, places, and incidents are either the product of the
author's imagination or are used fictitiously, and any resemblance to actual persons, living or dead,
business establishments, events, or locales is entirely coincidental.

*For Beatrice*

# The Two Lives of
# Miss Charlotte Merryweather

August 20, 1997

Dear Diary,

Woke up with such a terrible hangover. Last night my new friend Nessy and I went to that new pub called the Wellington. She and I have been hanging out a lot, and it was a blast! We drank a bottle of Cava before we went out since we could only afford to buy one drink each. I saw Billy Romani, the British musician. God, he's so gorgeous, but of course he doesn't even know I exist . . .

I guess I'm slowly getting used to living here in England, although I still feel like a clunky American. I can't believe it's already been nine months! Sometimes I wish I could walk down the street with an I SWEAR MY MOTHER IS BRITISH T-shirt. I miss the States, but am loving my new job at the magazine—the people are really cool and I'm learning a lot—next stop *Vogue*! Well, we can dream . . . I called Dad from work and wished him happy birthday— he loved his card and present!!! I think he's adjusting to life in the UK. I arranged to visit Mom and Dad again next weekend—I miss them. At least their new "home" is close to London. Well, it's two hundred miles, but that's not far when I think of the distances in the States.

It's super hot again. At lunch yesterday Nessy and I sunbathed in the park. My tan is getting amazingly deep. She couldn't stop talking about Julian, her new boyfriend—they've only been on a few dates but she's already completely in love! Thank God for Nessy—I can't imagine what things would be like here if I hadn't met her.

Well, anyway, must go get ready. I'm going to a party tonight and am wearing my new miniskirt from Topshop. My new favorite store! Can't wait, it's going to be so much fun!!!

## iCal

**August 20, 2007**

6:00 a.m.: Wake up.

6:15 a.m.: Personal trainer.

7:30 a.m.: Check e-mails.

8:00 a.m.: Leave for office. En route make and return calls.

9:00 a.m.: Arrive at office. Track news stories.

10:00 a.m.: Send out e-mails about clients to a number of media outlets.

11:00 a.m.: Work on tomorrow's pitch with potential new client.

12:00 noon: Lunch meeting with journalists from *Daily Standard* et al.

2:00 p.m.: Return to office. Finish work on Melody account.

3:00 p.m.: Write press release.

4:00 p.m.: Connect Johnny Bird, West End hairstylist, with new editor of *Cuts* magazine for a quote and interview about his new shampoo line.

5:00 p.m.: Write that press release!

6:00 p.m.: Work on the award application for Healthy Waters account.

7:00 p.m.: Dinner with Miles.

10:00 p.m.: Review schedule for next day and prepare.

11:00 p.m.: Read new chapter in *Finding Yourself Made Easy*.

12:00 midnight: Go to sleep.

# Chapter One

*Woosh-woooosshhh-woosh-wooooshhhh.*

Ah, what total bliss. Listening to the waves gently rolling in on the deserted beach—*wooosh*—their white frothy peaks caressing the empty stretch of sand, before rolling back out again—*woooossshhhhh.*

In and out they flow. It's like the most wonderful lullaby. Relaxing. Soothing. Calming. My mind is drifting. My body is floating. I'm in a deeply peaceful place of serenity—

*BEEP-BEEP-BEEP-BEEP.*

Holy Christ! No, I'm not. I'm in my apartment in London. It's Monday morning. And I'm being jolted awake by the piercing drill of my alarm clock.

Heart thumping, mind racing, I roll over in bed, lift up my aromatherapy eye mask, and peer anxiously at the time: *six a.m.* My stomach lurches. God, is that the time already? I have a session with my personal trainer booked before work; I have to get up.

*BEEEEEPPPPP!!!!*

Like, now.

I hit the OFF button and throw back my sheets. I just bought these sheets. They're made from one hundred percent organic unbleached cotton, which the saleswoman assured me would help my allergies. I have a ton of allergies, which admittedly is embarrassing because it makes me sound like one of those trendy annoying women who wear Crocs and think it's cool to have a wheat intolerance, but I *genuinely* have them. Really, I do.

Anyway I thought I'd give the sheets a try. That said, I'm not sure if they're helping—my eyes start watering the moment I recall how much I paid for them.

My electronic nemesis is now silent but for a moment I can't rouse the energy to move. Arms and legs outstretched, I lie starfish-wide on my mattress, my eye mask still on my head, the humidifier in the corner puffing out little clouds of steam. My sound machine continues playing in the corner. It's set to "Relaxing Ocean Lullaby" to help aid restful sleep.

In addition to the allergies, I'm also a very bad sleeper. Just terrible. I find it so hard to switch off. As soon as I close my eyes all these niggling worries start running around in my head like so many millions of ants.

I tried counting them once, like they tell you to do with sheep, but it had the opposite effect. Instead of making me fall asleep, it made me wide awake with fear and I ended up staying up that whole night watching cosmetic-surgery-gone-wrong shows on TV. Not only was I exhausted the next day, but I now have these weird nightmares about vaginal rejuvenation (trust me, there is such a thing as too much information).

Lately I can't help but wonder if it might help to allow myself more than five hours of sleep a night. It was nearly one a.m. last night when I finished reading the chapter in my new book, *Finding Yourself Made Easy*, and turned out the light. But then all the most successful women survive on hardly any sleep, don't they? I'm always reading articles about Madonna getting up at four a.m. to do Ashtanga yoga . . .

A yawn rips through me. Maybe just this once I'll treat myself to another five minutes in bed. I mean, another five minutes isn't going to hurt, is it?

I reach for the duvet and am just curling back into the fetal position when I feel a twinge of doubt. Actually, on second thought, better make it two minutes. I've got a busy week ahead of me. Tomorrow I'm meeting with a potential new client—Larry Goldstein, cosmetic dentist to the stars in L.A., who is opening a new flagship store here in London. He's looking for a new public relations firm to help launch it. *Mine*, I hope.

I feel a flutter of pride. I still can't quite believe I have my own company—Merryweather PR—which, according to a recent mention in the business section of the *Telegraph*, is "*a London-based boutique public relationships company. Specializing in health and beauty, it was formed three years ago by Charlotte Merryweather* (that's me!), *PR expert and experienced journalist, who prides herself on giving each client an individual and personal touch*"—

Which reminds me. I have to check to see if this potential client has any personal dietary restrictions. Only last week I made a reservation for some clients at this trendy new sushi restaurant that has a month-long waiting list (in order to get a table I had to beg, plead, and bribe the restaurant with the promise of a dazzling mention of their menu in all forthcoming press releases) only to discover when we arrived that one of the female clients was pregnant and couldn't eat raw fish.

My flutter of pride is quickly swamped by a familiar pang of worry.

Okay, screw the extra two minutes in bed. Make it one.

Oh, and I can't forget to write my financial adviser back. As a responsible woman in my thirties I have to think about savings and retirement funds. Apparently my shares in Southeast Asia are looking healthy, but my pension isn't performing well. All fascinating stuff—if I had the faintest clue what he was talking about.

*Fifty-five seconds . . .*

Which is why I need to order a couple of those books off Amazon called things like *Investing for People Who Thought Dow Jones Was an Economic Theory until Very Recently*, or whatever.

*Fifty seconds.*

Miles, my boyfriend, says it's really important to plan for the future. He's a property developer and he's always talking security and investments. In fact, last week when we were in bed I zoned out in the middle of a conversation about lease-to-buy mortgages and imagined myself making out with Jake Gyllenhaal.

Actually, I've been doing that a lot lately . . ..

*Forty-five seconds.*

But that's normal. Everyone fantasizes in relationships. I know, because I read that in one of my self-help books too. We've been together for eighteen months and we have a great relationship. Okay, so the sex isn't always mind-blowing, but sex isn't everything, is it? When I was younger sex was, of course, very important—but now that I'm older there's so much more to think about.

*Forty seconds.*

Like my dry cleaning. I *have* to remember to pick up my dry cleaning.

*Thirty-five seconds.*

And grocery shopping. I shop at this really cool organic supermarket where I once spotted Gwyneth Paltrow by the King Edward potatoes. Unfortunately it's very expensive, a banana's like £2.50 or something (that would be five dollars!). I can't help it. I still think in dollars sometimes. Highway robbery! But I really do try to eat a healthy, well-balanced, organic diet. Except for this week—I was too busy and so there's nothing in the fridge.

Well, actually, that's a lie. There's the rotting vegetables and mesclun greens that have gone pretty wilty. That's the problem with buying organic. In fact to tell the truth, I usually end up throwing it away and going out to eat.

*Thirty seconds.*

Which reminds me. I promised I'd cook dinner tonight for Miles. Actually "cook" is a slight euphemism for emptying prewashed organic rocket salad from a bag and pricking the plastic sleeve of porcini risotto from the supermarket's "restaurant range."

I'm a huge fan of those ranges. All right, so they're a bit pricey, but they're *so* worth it. I mean, have you ever made risotto? It takes *eons*. All that hullabaloo about stirring in vegetable stock every five minutes, until your carpal tunnel is killing you and you're drunk from polishing off the white wine that was predestined for the risotto. (Well, you have to do *something* while you're stirring, it's so goddamn boring.)

Then, to add insult to injury, it still turns out lumpy and tasteless and you have to spend weeks eating it because it's like magic porridge and what started out as just two cupfuls of arborio rice is now enough to feed an army . . .

My mind is racing at its usual hundred miles an hour, and I roll over and hug my pillow to my chest.

*Twenty-five seconds.*

On second thought, I don't have time to go food shopping. We'll have to eat out instead. But that's okay. It's a good excuse to try that new restaurant at the bottom of my street. *Gastropub.* It opened a few weeks ago and I've been dying to go.

*Twenty seconds.*

Oh God, and now I've just remembered: it's Dad's birthday today.

My heart sinks. Mom left me three messages on my machine last week to remind me. And I *still* forgot. I haven't even sent him a card. He'll be so upset if he doesn't get a card in the mail. Last year I sent him an e-card, and when I called him his voice was all small and Mom had to get on the phone and make overly cheerful conversation about the neighbor's new extension—

*Fifteen seconds.*

My stomach clenches. Okay, Charlotte, don't stress. You'll get that funny bumpy rash on your chest and you'll have to wear turtlenecks all week and look like Diane Keaton in *Something's Gotta Give*. I'll call Interflora and get an express delivery. So what if he's a man, everyone likes flowers, right? I'll just ask for manly colors or something.

*Ten seconds.*

Do they *have* flowers in navy blue?

*Five seconds.*

Okay, that's it. Time's up.

I pull myself up on my elbows and take out my mouth guards. I grind. Well, I do according to my dentist. He says if I don't wear them I'm going to end up with teeth ground down to little stumps and I'll look like Shane MacGowan from the Pogues!

Well, he didn't *exactly* say I'd look like Shane MacGowan, but that's only because he doesn't know who Shane MacGowan or the Pogues are. And anyway, that's beside the point. I still had to have them made and they cost over a thousand pounds. That's nearly two thousand dollars! Vanessa, my best friend, thought I was crazy. She says I should have spent the money on a vacation because I just need to relax.

Honestly, I love Nessy, but she's the one that's crazy. *A vacation?* Like I have *time* for a vacation.

And anyway, I do lots of things to relax. For example, I do Pilates. Well, okay, perhaps *do* is a little bit of an exaggeration. I did it once and fell asleep during the mat exercises but I have every *intention* of doing it regularly. And I take baths with scented candles and lavender oil and a glass of chilled sauvignon blanc. Admittedly I haven't taken one recently, in fact these days I'm more likely to be found dashing in and out of the shower with a Bic razor, but still. *Plus* I even have that lovely relaxation CD that my mom sent me.

Somewhere. Tucked away in a drawer probably.

But I'm definitely going to listen to it when I have a minute . . .

Okay, so I wouldn't go as far as to say I'm *relaxed* really, but who is these days? I run a company. I have a mortgage, and responsibilities, and lines around my eyes to take care of. I mean, it's not like I'm twenty-one anymore.

And thank goodness.

Back then I was newly arrived, renting a room, working in a dead-end job, and always broke. Now I have my own successful PR company, a lovely apartment in a leafy part of West London, and one of those new convertible Beetles. I eat out at restaurants and can afford to shop for designer clothes and take luxury vacations.

Not that I actually do, of course, as I never have the time. But I'm just saying.

I even have my own personal trainer.

Speaking of whom . . . Dragging myself out of bed, I swap my warm fleecy pajamas for my gym outfit and hurry across to the window. Pulling back the curtains I can see that it's still pitch-black outside, and for a moment I pause to stare into the silent, sleeping street.

I'm thirty-one years old and I have the life I always dreamed of.

The doorbell rings, interrupting my thoughts.

"Coming," I yell loudly, and rubbing the sleep from my puffy eyes, I dash for the door.

# Chapter Two

An hour later, after running around the park and doing about a million jumping jacks, Richard, my personal trainer, is jogging me back to my place. Richard used to be in the army and likes to push me really hard.

Unfortunately I don't mean "push me" as in I'm on a swing wearing a floaty dress and going "weeeee," but as in me facedown on the pavement gasping for breath while he barks at me to do another fifty push-ups.

"Okay, Charlotte. Why don't we sprint the last hundred meters, huh?"

In moments like this I like to reflect on situations in which British accents lose their charm. But Richard has already zoomed ahead of me, all six-foot-three of solid muscle in his racing-back vest and tiny black shorts. I grip my hand weights and lurch after his receding figure, which is springing buoyantly along the concrete on his powerful calves.

"C'mon, no slacking. Fill those lungs. Lift those knees. *Hup, hup, hup, hup.*"

I swear Richard has the biggest calf muscles I've ever seen. Apparently, when he was in the army, he would run hundreds of miles with a backpack that weighed more than me. Which I always find a comforting thought. Just in case I were to collapse and need to be carried home one day. Or something.

I finally catch him up as he waits for me outside my apartment. "See you, same time Wednesday." Still running in place, Richard slaps me heartily on the back and I nearly fall over.

"Same time Wednesday," I reply cheerfully, smiling brightly and opening my front door.

"Now don't forget to stretch out those muscles," he yells, grabbing his elbows and effortlessly throwing in a little bit of over-arm stretching.

"I won't." I smile, giving an enthusiastic wave, before disappearing inside.

Where I collapse on the hall carpet.

I do this three times a week. When I was younger I used to be such a slob, but now I'm older and wiser and know it's really important to keep myself in shape. Although right now "in shape" isn't *exactly* the phrase I'd choose to describe how I'm feeling. *Exhausted* resonates. Or *in agony*.

With sweat pouring down my face I lie spread-eagled on the floor like a chalk drawing at a murder scene and concentrate on catching my breath.

Of course there are some mornings when I'd love to sleep in, but I also love being able to fit into my jeans. Plus, like Richard says, cardio is essential to maintaining a healthy heart. I rest my hand on my heart protectively. It's hammering so hard in my chest it feels as if it's going to explode.

Not that it's going to, of course. I mean, hearts don't just *explode*, do they?

I take off my heart monitor and look at the digital display. Gosh, that's kind of a lot of heartbeats per minute, isn't it? I feel a prickle of anxiety. And I am really breathless . . .

Scenes from all those *ER* episodes come rushing back, you know, the ones with a patient on a gurney and a handsome doctor yelling, "Clear!" as he grabs the defibrillator and slams two massive electric shocks into their chest—

My anxiety cranks up a notch. Oh my God, I'm not *really* having a heart attack, am I? And on my dad's birthday!

At the thought I clutch my chest in horror. If I die he'll never be able to celebrate it again. Instead of spending it at the local pub with his friends, he'll have to spend it kneeling at my graveside, grieving the loss of his beloved only daughter . . .

Charlotte, stop it! I get ahold of myself. Don't be so ridiculous. You're *supposed* to get your heart rate up, that's the *whole* idea. You've just been exercising. And exercise is good for you. Hoisting myself up from the hallway carpet, I catch my reflection in the mirror. My face is covered in bright purple blotches, I have bloodshot eyes, and my hair is plastered to my head in a sort of sweat helmet.

Wow. Sexy.

Well, anyway, I can't stand around here all day; I need to get ready for work. Automatically I check the time on the clock on the side table. I have lots of clocks. Vanessa's always teasing me by calling my apartment Switzerland because I have so many—but no matter how hard I try, I always seem to be running late.

Tugging off my sweaty gym things en route to the bathroom, I jump into the shower.

Once toweled, I do my customary and quite vital morning checklist.

Makeup? Perfect, yet "natural." *Check.*

Blow-dry? Super straight, yet flippy on the ends. *Check.*

Outfit?

Standing in front of the full-length mirrors in my walk-in closet, I do a twirl from side to side, checking out my black pencil skirt and funky blouse. It has to be professional yet hip. Street yet chic. Cool yet . . . what's the word? Ah, yes, polished.

I frown at my feet and slip on a different pair of designer heels. Much better.

*Check.*

I hurry out of the bedroom and start racing around the apartment collecting my things.

Laptop? I don't go anywhere without my iBook. Not even to the bathroom. Well, you never know when you might need to Google something. I sweep it up from the table, snap it shut, and tuck it under my arm. *Check.*

Briefcase? My eyes fall upon it. Perched on the sofa, bursting with tons of documents that I need to read and sign. ASAP. *Check.*

Yoga mat in case I get a free window later? (Yeah, right.) *Check.*

BlackBerry? Shit, where is it? Oh, right, yes, in my hand. Of course. *Check.*

Bluetooth earpiece? Um . . . I quickly retrace my steps . . . I came home from work last night, talked to Miles, tried to meditate . . . ah, there it is—balancing on the Buddha I had shipped all the way from Bali. *Check.*

My heart has recovered, by the way. I knew it would, of course. I was just having a teeny panic episode. I do that sometimes, especially if it's anything health-related, but I'm just being careful. Better safe than sorry, that's my motto.

Unfortunately my doctor doesn't share my attitude. He seems to think I'm a hypochondriac or something. Only last week I had this funny-looking rash on my chest and when I Googled my symptoms they were exactly the same as this flesh-eating bug you get from the Amazon. Okay, so I haven't "recently traveled to the Amazon" as he put it, but there was no need for him to get so grumpy. He didn't send me to the hospital for tropical diseases or anything! Just told me it was probably my eczema flaring up and told me to rub on some E45 Cream.

Which I did, and it went away, but still, it *could* have been a flesh-eating bug.

With a throng of bags hanging off each shoulder, I leave money for the cleaner and rush out the door. Then rush right back in again when blinded by the bright sunshine.

Sunglasses? My eyes sweep across the side table in the hallway on which stands a lamp, a white orchid, and several framed photographs, catching for a moment on one taken at my graduation from Stanford.

Mom and Dad are standing next to me, looking very much the proud parents. They look pretty much the same now as they did then, although Dad's got a bit less hair now, and Mom was going through her pearly-lipstick stage, but I'm barely recognizable. I'm wearing the traditional black gown and my flat square cap is balancing precariously on top of my hair, which is long, dark, and scrunch-dried to within an inch of its life. Unlike being blow-dried straight into a bob and colored honey blonde every six weeks like it is now.

This was also taken before I discovered tweezers and thus I have two thick black caterpillars where I now have two perfectly arched eyebrows, not to mention, I'm wearing so much black kohl around my eyes I could give Amy Winehouse a run for her liquid eyeliner.

And that smile! I peer closer at my crooked front teeth, which are now straightened, thanks to braces in my late twenties—my payback for refusing to wear my retainers when I was a teenager—

I'm distracted by my sunglasses, which I spot behind the photo. Grabbing them, I put back the picture—*check.*

Glasses in place I hurry down the steps and beep the lock on my Beetle. The lights flash and I tug open the door. Damn it. Another parking ticket, I curse, snatching it up from under my windscreen wiper and throwing myself into the plush cream leather interior. Stuffing it in a side pocket along with all the other tickets, I turn the ignition and shift the gears. The engine roars into life.

God, I love my car. It's really powerful and has all these little extras, like heated seats, satellite navigation, and a dashboard that lights up at night like a cockpit. The day I got it I was so excited. I remember just looking at it, parked outside my apartment, all shiny and gleaming and brand new, I couldn't believe it was mine.

Though to tell you the truth it's not as much fun as I thought it would be since you can't drive faster than 20 mph in London, I reflect as I pull out of my parking space and immediately hit rush-hour traffic.

In fact, you're probably quicker on the train.

My BlackBerry suddenly springs to life in my hand, ringing shrilly. I glance at the clock on the dashboard: it's not even eight a.m. "Hello, Merryweather PR . . . yes, wonderful to hear from you. Yes, now as we were discussing, about that contract . . ." Clipping on my earpiece I quickly switch into work mode and start fielding calls.

❧

Twenty minutes later, I'm running late. Traffic is terrible, worse than usual. It has to be the Olympics. There's a huge urban development program going on in London at the moment and they've started demolishing all these old buildings in preparation for 2012. I read in the paper something about how it's one of the biggest and most complex visions ever in sheer size and scope: "Dig, Demolition, Design" they call it. But it's not just limited to the East End of London. Apparently the whole city's being regenerated. There are even plans to build this amazing, state-of-the-art design center not far from my office, and they're digging up thousands of tons of earth for the foundations. "A feat of engineering" the *Evening Standard* called it.

A great hulking hole in the ground that's making me late is what I call it, I seethe, still edging along at a snail's pace. I drum my fingers on the steering wheel, feeling the ever-present knot in my stomach tighten a notch as I glance at my watch. Shit. I start running through my diary in my head. I've got a huge week ahead of me and so much to do this morning. Just then, I see a sign that makes my heart sink: ROADWORK AHEAD: FOLLOW DIVERSION. This is all I need, a detour! Now I *really am* going to be late.

I follow the cars as they merge into one lane and begin crawling through the bright orange traffic cones. I mean, seriously, can we go any slower? I glance at the speedometer. I'm going less than *five* miles an hour! At this rate I'll get to the office by—I try doing the calculations in my head—oh God, I don't know, but it's going to take forever.

Painstakingly slowly we take a left and start weaving down various side streets until finally I see what looks like a main road ahead. Hopefully we're nearing the end of the detour, I pray, spotting a set of traffic lights. And they're green! *Come on, come on, come on.*

Cars in front of me are filtering through.

*Almost there, almost there, almost there . . .*

I edge forward, bumper to bumper. And now the lights are turning to amber. I try to squeeze through—

They change to red.

Grrrrrr!

Thwarted, I stop dead. Feeling the pressure building I sit hunched over the steering wheel. Okay, come on now, Charlotte, just relax, I instruct myself sternly. Getting all stressed out isn't going to make you go any faster, is it? Let's just do some relaxing, some breathing. Like we do in yoga. Closing my eyes, I flare my nostrils and take a deep breath. *In and out. In and out. In and—*

Oh, fuck it. I snap open my eyes. Well, I'm sorry, Shivanyandra or whatever your name is, but this is useless. I'm going to have to call Bea and see if she can rearrange my schedule, I'm supposed to be on a conference call in fifteen minutes. Desperately, I snatch up my BlackBerry. But just when I thought it couldn't get worse . . . it has.

*No reception.*

Great. Just great. What am I doing to do now?

Chucking it down in exasperation, I glance back at the lights: they're still red. Jesus. These might just be the longest lights in history. Distractedly, I let my eyes drift along the road, taking in my surroundings. There's a newsstand on the corner, people waiting at the bus stop, a grungy tanning salon that looks like it's been there for years. Actually, now I think of it, it has been there for years.

I haven't been paying attention, but now I realize where I am. I used to drive down this road every morning to work when I first moved to London. Only back then, I used to drive in the opposite direction, I reflect, wondering how long it is since I last came down here. My memory flicks back.

Mom had decided to move back to England to care for Nana after she got sick. When we found out she wasn't going to get better, Dad got a transfer with his company and joined her. I could have stayed behind in the States, as I'd just finished college, but going to England seemed like such an adventure!

At first I was sad to leave my friends, but all I could think about were boys with sexy British accents. And thanks to Mom being British I have dual citizenship, so it wasn't long before I found myself a job and moved to London. I was only twenty-one. God, it seems like another lifetime. Like another person.

Thinking back, my gaze floats across the intersection. Opposite a line of cars are waiting and my eyes fall on the car at the front. It's an old Beetle, just like the one I used to drive back then. Oh my God, how funny. It's almost identical. The same funny tangerine color with the boxy little grille and rust around the headlights. It's even got a green and white WWF sticker like I used to have, peeling off on the windscreen. I glance at the driver.

And my heart stops.

Oh my God, she looks just like me!

Me when I was twenty-one.

She's singing along to the radio, scrunching her dark, curly hair in the rearview mirror just like I used to. She's even wearing a red and white T-shirt like the one I always used to wear . . .

What the—?

I stare in amazement as the lights change and the Beetle drives toward me. *Beeeeeeeeeeeeep.*

The honking of a horn snaps me out of my daze and I slam my foot on the accelerator. The engine promptly stalls. Crap! Flustered, I quickly turn the ignition. Only I'm all fingers and thumbs and I can't get it to start and now several cars are honking their horns and— Suddenly the engine fires into life.

With an embarrassing screeching of tires I speed away from the light, my mind whirring. I can't believe how much that girl looked like me when I was younger. The resemblance was uncanny. If it wasn't impossible, I'd almost think it *was* me. Goose bumps prickle on my arms and I give a little shiver. God, that was the weirdest thing . . .

Ahead I see a sign looming—END OF DIVERSION—and feel a rush of relief. My phone beeps from the passenger seat and I scramble for it. Hallelujah! I've got a signal. Plus five missed calls. Perfect. Okay, enough of this nonsense. Back to the real world. And slamming my foot on the accelerator I speed-dial the office.

# Chapter Three

By the time I arrive at the office I've taken nine calls, replied to two e-mails (surreptitiously while stuck in more traffic—well, I don't want to get *another* ticket, do I?), and put in a rush order with Interflora. Unfortunately, they don't do navy blue flowers. In fact the woman sounded quite puzzled when I asked, but they had purple, which is practically the same as navy blue.

Well, sort of.

As I charge through the door, my assistant Beatrice is waiting for me with an outstretched cup. This is how she greets me every morning: double espresso with a splash of soy milk. I'm on the phone with a journalist and, without stopping, I throw her a grateful smile and sweep it up like a runner in a relay race. After two years we've perfected the pass. We don't spill a drop.

I continue across the office, my stiletto heels clicking on the floor (polished cement, very de rigueur, in fact the whole office is totally cutting-edge; in the PR world appearances are everything). ". . . So I'll send over the new product for you to try, I'm sure you'll want to feature it in the magazine . . . oh, right, you want the *whole product line as well*?" Honestly, journalists can be so greedy.

"Absolutely. I'll get them sent over right away!" I say cheerfully.

Reaching my desk I snap my cell shut, sink down into my chair, and drain the espresso in one desperate gulp. I'm so fuzzy-headed before my morning coffee, I can't think straight, let alone *see* straight. Which of course totally explains that weird incident at the lights.

"Morning," chirps Beatrice, hugging a file to her chest and giving me a beaming smile.

Beatrice is always hugging files to her chest. Not because she's actually working on anything in the files, but because it's an attempt to hide her impressively large breasts (or "bosoms" as she likes to call them), which she inherited from her grandmother, the duchess of something or other. Along with a double string of pearls, a substantial trust fund, and a little "bolt-hole" in town.

The little bolt-hole being a ginormous penthouse apartment in Devonshire Square, W1, which is one of the poshest areas in London.

Honestly, Bea is so incredibly aristocratic I should hate her, but she makes it impossible by being one of the nicest people I've ever met.

"Hi, Bea, thanks for the coffee." I smile gratefully.

"Good weekend?" she says brightly, striding over to me and un-looping my bags, which I'd forgotten were still hanging from my shoulders. Deftly, she puts each in its place.

"It was okay, I had so much work to catch up on." I shrug, thinking back to yesterday, which I spent at the dining room table surrounded by paperwork while Miles played squash, which seems to be pretty much how I spend my weekends these days.

Plonking my elbows on a pile of papers I rub my forehead. I can already feel the beginnings of a tension headache. "Any messages?"

"Larry Goldstein's assistant called to confirm your lunch tomorrow at the Electric in Notting Hill," she begins, peeling off Post-it Notes. "Sally Pitt, the editor of the Lifestyle section of the *Daily Standard*, called. They want to interview you for an article they're doing on women who have it all . . ." She throws me an excited look. "Oh, and Melody called. Several times in fact."

My stomach knots. Melody is a famous TV presenter, who recently had a baby, shed about a truckload of weight, and is now making a fortune sharing her "secret" through her DVD, books, TV series, and her new line of prepackaged healthy meals, *Easy without the E-Numbers,* which we do the PR for.

"She's a little upset about the Sunday paper." Beatrice produces a copy of one of the tabloids. On the front page is a photograph of Melody stuffing her face with a large Big Mac and fries. The headline "Secrets and Fries" screams across the front.

"Ah, yes." I pull a face. "I saw that."

"Actually I think her exact words were . . ." Beatrice peels off a Post-it note and begins reading earnestly, "'Fucking furious, I want to fucking kill the fucking News of the Screws.'"

Despite my anxiety, I can't help smiling. With Bea's cut-glass accent, it's like hearing the queen blaspheming. Honestly, posh people shouldn't swear.

"I can imagine." I nod, spreading the paper across my desk and ignoring the knot in my stomach as it tightens.

Melody might be the nation's darling, all sweetness and light and toothpaste-ad smiles, but away from the cameras she's got a temper worse than—well, think of someone with a terrible temper, and it's worse. Much, *much* worse.

"Do you think she 'supersized' it?" says Beatrice, peering over my shoulder at the photograph. Beatrice just watched the film about the man who lived on McDonald's for a month and can't stop going on about it. Bea's like that. She watches movies about five years after they came out. It's the same with everything, music, fashion—

I take in Bea's outfit. She's wearing her faithful twinset, a knee-length skirt in gray tweed, opaque tights, and black flats she's had forever. Oh, and don't forget the pearls.

Actually, on second thought, I'm not actually sure what she's wearing was in fashion even five years ago.

"Does it matter?" I shrug, rubbing my temples. My headache is really starting to throb. "Supersized or not, she's launching her latest diet book, *Just Say No to Junk,* next month," I remind her. "And we're currently doing the promotion on her new range of *Easy without the E-Numbers* soups."

Beatrice frowns. "Hmmm, yes, that is slightly unfortunate."

Beatrice has a knack for understatement. Being a small, boutique agency we have only a few accounts—I take care of the large ones, while Beatrice deals with the smaller ones—and Melody's range of products is one of our biggest and most profitable. The last thing I need is for a paparazzi photograph to jeopardize that by discrediting her platform as a health and fitness guru.

"It's potentially a disaster," I murmur, shaking out two acetaminophen from the family-sized bottle I keep on my desk, and flicking on my computer. The screen comes awake and I quickly start typing into Google.

Beatrice grips harder onto her pearls.

"Golly," she says in a hushed voice. *"A disaster?"*

A bunch of articles pop up on my screen and I click one of them.

*"Potentially,"* I correct her, quickly scanning through the article. After a moment's pause I look up at Bea. "Call her agent and tell them we're going to put together a press release saying she's hypoglycemic."

Beatrice throws me a puzzled look.

"In other words she has low blood sugar."

Her face floods with recognition. "Oh, what a coincidence!" she whoops, galvanized by this piece of information. "So does Mummy! She can't go anywhere without her Ritz crackers! Once she forgot them and her levels dropped and she fainted. Right at the feet of Prince Philip . . ." She pauses as she sees my expression. "We were in the royal enclosure at Ascot at the time," she explains. "It caused quite a scene. Poor Mummy, she was terribly embarrassed . . ." She stops talking and shakes her head as she remembers. "Perhaps you should tell Melody about Ritz crackers. Probably a lot less calories than McDonald's," she advises, sagely.

"Beatrice. She's not really hypoglycemic."

She looks at me blankly, then it registers. "Oh . . . I see . . . gosh . . . you mean it's all a *ruse* . . . " she says, her voice lowered.

I nod and keep typing.

"Gosh, Charlotte, you're so clever. That's why I love working for you!"

People are often fooled by Bea. They dismiss her as a ditzy blonde, rather like I did when she first came for an interview, out of breath from running from the tube with her hair all over the place and a ladder in her tights. But in fact she's super brainy and behind that dumb blonde persona lies an academic genius. This is a woman who studied applied mathematics and double majored in physics at Cambridge University and in her spare time solves geometric equations, "just for fun."

To be honest, she's totally overqualified for the job. We're the same age and she should be working in some lab somewhere, doing something mind-bogglingly scientific. But she insisted she really wanted to work in PR, and was incredibly enthusiastic. Plus she also has the poshest voice I've ever heard, which in the world of PR is invaluable. Bea's cut-glass accent opens doors that my American one never could.

We work as a team. A sort of bait and switch. I make the deals, get the contracts, and take care of our clients, but Bea is the first point of contact for the press and media. And for that, her knack for sounding like the queen is priceless.

"Good morning, Merryweather PR," she trills as the phone starts ringing. "Which publication are you calling from? The *Telegraph*? Oh, how thrilling! My grandfather was the editor there for many years."

*See what I mean?*

After rescuing our *Easy without the E-Numbers* account from imploding, the rest of the morning slips away in the usual hive of activity: making calls to journalists, writing press releases, conference calls with clients about their accounts. One minute it's nine a.m. and I'm trying to think of something sexy and fabulous to say about a new dandruff shampoo, which is part of the new line by Johnny Bird, a West End hairstylist.

And the next minute it's nearly one and I'm being tossed about in the back of a cab on my way to a lunch meeting at the Wolseley, a fashionable restaurant in Piccadilly. Usually I drive, but today I thought a cab might be quicker. Plus, more importantly, it means I can catch up with some work on the way.

I hang on to a strap to steady myself while reading an e-mail that's just popped through to my BlackBerry. Scrolling down with my thumb I'm about to start typing a reply when my mobile starts ringing. I have a BlackBerry and a mobile. The BlackBerry's for business, the mobile's for personal calls. Normally I switch it to silent during the day, but I must have forgotten. I dig it out and glance at the screen. It's my parents.

Oh, shoot. Dad's birthday. I was going to call as soon as I had a free minute.

The knot in my stomach twists even tighter.

The thing is I'm still waiting for that free minute.

"Hello, Charlotte Merryweather speaking," I say, out of habit, before I can stop myself.

"Oh, so you *are* alive!" laughs a voice dryly.

"Oh, hi, Mom," I say innocently, trying not to think of all the voice-mail messages she's left on my phone the past week. "How are you?"

"Didn't you get my messages?" she demands, refusing to be sidetracked into pleasantries.

"Um . . . yes, but I—"

She doesn't let me finish. "Well, let's just hope me and your father never have an emergency," she continues tetchily. "We'll be dead and buried before they can get hold of you."

I roll my eyes into the phone. My mother loves melodrama. It's all the soaps she watches.

"I mean, what's the point of having a phone if you never answer it?"

"I was probably in meetings," I proffer weakly.

"I called you at home this morning. You still didn't answer."

Honestly, you'd think my mother was a prosecution lawyer, not a school secretary.

"I must have been out. My trainer came at six."

"Six *in the morning?*" she says, sounding shocked.

"Yeah, I ran five miles."

*"You ran five miles?"* Her voice has gone all high-pitched. "Oh, Charlotte," she gasps anxiously. "Are you sure you're not overdoing it? You should give yourself a lie-in sometimes."

*A lie-in?* God, I can't remember the last time I let myself sleep in.

Oh, actually I do, it was the morning after my big twenty-fifth birthday party. Which wasn't that long ago.

*It was seven years ago.*

"And are you eating properly? You can't exercise on an empty stomach."

Suddenly Mom's switched from prosecution lawyer into concerned-mother mode.

"Yes. I know," I lie.

My empty stomach gives an angry growl and I silence it by gulping down the Starbucks that I grabbed before I jumped in the cab.

"Because there was an article in the *Daily Mail* yesterday and it said vegetarians lack . . . hang on a minute . . ." There's the sound of rustling papers. "Here it is . . . 'essential minerals and vitamins' . . ."

"Ridiculous!" I exclaim, rooting around in my handbag and unearthing various vitamins and packets of health supplements. I'm forever buying different types. Only last week I read an article about ground-up apricot kernels. Apparently you can live to be a hundred if you eat them in the right quantities. Unscrewing the lids I swallow a handful.

Unfortunately the quantities are so large you'd have to live to be a hundred just to have enough time to eat all the darned things.

"A cooked breakfast, Charlotte, that's what you need."

"I don't have time to be eating a cooked breakfast," I reply a little impatiently.

"Well, you know what they say, 'All work and no play makes Jack a dull boy.'" She clucks, disapprovingly.

I roll my eyes again. "I bet Jack was successful though," I can't resist muttering.

My mom is always telling me I work too hard. Which is true. I *do* work too hard, but that's just part of running a successful business. Mom doesn't understand. She never wanted a career. All she wanted was to get married and have a family. For her a job was just a job. A way to earn a bit of "pocket money" as she puts it. But then she's always had Dad to look after her financially. It's different for my generation. *Better.*

At least I like to think so.

"Did I tell you, Marion just had a third grandchild," replies Mom, ignoring me pointedly.

Yes, three times, I think, as I drain the last of my Starbucks.

"That's great. Send her my congratulations!"

"Her daughter's your age you know," she persists. "Remember, Caroline Godfrey? That Christmas we came to visit Nana you were both angels in the Christmas pageant."

And that's another thing my mom does. Tell me all about her friends' daughters and how they're all giving birth like rabbits. Populating the village they all in live in with lots of bouncy, rosy-cheeked grandchildren. While her mean, selfish daughter lives two hundred miles away in London, having personal training sessions and being a vegetarian. Worse still, she *isn't even married.*

Speaking of which.

"How's Miles?"

Uh-oh.

Let me translate. "How's Miles?" in mother-tongue means, "Has he proposed yet?"

To be fair, it's not just Mom who does this. Miles and I have been together for eighteen months and everyone assumes he's going to propose. And everyone assumes I'm going to say yes. After all, why wouldn't I? He ticks all those boxes found in those glossy women's magazines: he's handsome, successful, loyal, reliable, *and* we never argue. In fact in the whole time we've been together we've never once had a fight. Which is great, isn't it?

Only sometimes there's a part of me that wouldn't *mind* the occasional argument. Like I say to Miles, just because we're a couple doesn't mean we're not allowed to have different opinions. In fact, it might help add a teensy-weensy bit more excitement to the relationship, a bit more *va-va-voom;* after all, making up is so much fun. . . .

But anyway, like I was saying, I can't think of a single reason *to* say no.

Not that I'm trying to, of course, I'm just saying.

"He's great. Is Dad there?" I say brightly, swiftly sidestepping the subject. "I want to wish him happy birthday."

"Oh, yes, hang on, he's just getting the post."

I wince. There goes my stomach again.

"David, luv, it's our Lottie," she calls loudly, then lowers her voice conspiratorially.

"You did send him a card, didn't you?" she hisses.

"Um . . . actually, I've sent flowers instead," I say brightly.

"Flowers?" she repeats blankly, taken aback. "For your *father*?"

"Why not? Dad loves flowers," I say defensively. "He's always gardening."

"Well, I suppose so. . . ." She trails off doubtfully, and I can tell she's wishing I'd just sent a Hallmark card and a new pair of socks like a normal daughter. Huge bouquets being delivered to Mr. Merryweather will no doubt cause a stir in their tiny village. They live in Nana's old house, which is in the middle of really beautiful countryside in the Yorkshire Dales. Full of pretty little pubs, and sheep, *and villagers who want to know all your business.* I can hear Mom now, explaining to the locals. "They're from his daughter. She lives in *Lundon,* you know."

Which, in tiny villages in the north of England, is explanation enough.

"Charlotte!"

Dad's hearty voice appears on the line, and I feel a warm glow. Ours has never been an easy relationship—we're both pretty stubborn. My teenage years were spent engaged in a perpetual battle over how loud I could play the Smiths. (Me: very loud. Dad: turn that goddamn noise off, it's music to slit your wrists to!) Yet despite our differences (or should that be similarities?) we're still incredibly close—in fact our birthdays are just a few days apart.

"Hi, Dad, happy birthday," I say, smiling and wedging the phone under my chin. We're coming up to the restaurant and I want to quickly touch up my makeup before my meeting.

"Thanks, sweetheart, I haven't opened my cards yet," he replies cheerfully.

Guilt stabs. Dad will love his flowers, I just know it, but still.

"So what are the big plans for today?" I ask, changing the subject.

I open my compact and tilt it to the light. The dark shadows under my eyes loom into view.

"Oh, you know, a little of this and a little of that. What about you? When are you going to come visit?"

"Soon," I reply, dabbing furiously with my Touche Éclat highlighter. I don't like to look as if I'm wearing too much, so this morning

I just went for the natural look. Just primer, light-diffusing foundation, concealer, powder, bronzer, a slight blush on the apples of my cheeks, a slick of mascara, lip balm—

You know, the irony is you have to wear an awful lot of makeup to look natural.

"You say soon every time," he grumbles. "We haven't seen you since the holidays."

Middab I pause. Has is it really been that long? I think back to my mad dash up the M1 on Christmas Eve. I hadn't been able to get away before. Melody was launching a new line of diet shakes in the new year and Beatrice had been out sick with the flu, so I'd been working around the clock, doing everything myself. Most of Christmas Day was spent at my laptop trying to finish a press release and then I was back in the office the next day.

"I know, I'm sorry, Dad. Things are just a little hectic, that's all. I had to work all last weekend on a big deadline, and this week I'm pitching for a new account . . ." I give up on my dark circles, click my compact shut, and stick on my sunglasses instead. "I promise, the first free weekend I have I'll drive up with Miles. You can see my new car, you'll love it, Dad, you can take it for a spin—"

"Hmmm, yes, I read an article about one of those new VW Beetles in that magazine you got me. . . ."

I can feel Dad softening. He adores tinkering around with cars, lifting up the hood, admiring the engineering.

"Whereabouts, luv?" the cabbie interrupts over the speaker.

"Hang on a minute, Dad." I look up to see the restaurant looming up before me. "Anywhere here's fine . . ." I reply, leaning forward on the edge of my seat so the driver can hear me, before being suddenly thrust back as the cab swerves into the curbside and comes to a shuddering halt. Flung across the backseat, I quickly gather together my things.

"Sorry about that," I gasp into my phone as I clamber out onto the pavement. "Thanks, if I could just get a receipt." Passing the

driver a tenner I catch sight of myself in the cab window and immediately set about smoothing down my hair. "You were saying," I continue, switching back to Dad.

I'm quite an expert now at having two conversations at once. At
first it used to freak me out and I'd get all muddled, but now I've
grown used to it.

"Well, as long as you're okay," he says, placated. "We just miss our
little girl, that's all."

I feel a wave of affection. *Little girl?* In four days I'll be turning
thirty-two. In eight years I'll be forty!

Okay, I really shouldn't have had that thought.

"I miss you too, Dad," I reply, hurrying up the front steps. "But
you don't have to worry about me, honestly." Pushing through the
glass doors my heels clatter into the marbled lobby.

"And you're happy, aren't you?"

I spot a couple of large mirrors on the wall next to me and begin
immediately checking out my reflection. "Of course I am," I say
distractedly.

Out of the corner of my eye I see a couple of the journalists I'm
meeting pulling up outside in a cab. My nerves jangle. I always feel
like this before one of those lunches. This is where I do a little presentation of a new product we represent, and it's my opportunity to
get press and promotion. As much as it's dressed up in lunch and
wine and chitchat, there's a lot of pressure on me.

"Look, Dad, I'm going to have to go—"

"Oh, right, well, off you go then, it was nice speaking to you."

I feel a clench of regret. We've barely spoken. But it's like that
nowadays. When I was younger I would sit on the phone for hours,
talking about anything and everything, but now I'm lucky if I can
snatch five minutes.

"I'll call you tonight," I say hastily.

"Well, okay, sweetheart. Have a good day."

"I will. You too, Dad."

I snap my phone closed, but for a moment I can't bring myself to move. My mind returns to my conversation with Dad, and for a moment I think about what he just said. Am I happy? I mean, *am I?*

"Charlotte!" I come to and turn around to see a woman in her early fifties. It's Katie Proctor, a journalist I've known since my days as a freelance writer. Grinning widely, she gives me a big perfumed hug. "Oooh, are those new shoes?" she gasps, pointing at my feet. "They're adorable."

I feel a beat of pleasure. "I didn't think you were coming." I smile, kissing her on both her blushered cheeks. "You never RSVP'd!" I throw her a mock look of disapproval.

"I know, I'm terrible." She rolls her eyes guiltily. "Do you forgive me?"

If it was anyone else, I'd be thrown into a panic, but Katie is more a friend than a work colleague. "Of course. How are you?"

"Parched! C'mon, let's go have a drink and catch up. . . ."

She links arms, and as we enter the bar I grab hold of myself. Honestly I don't know what's got into me today. The other journalists start arriving, and, plunged into a cacophony of air-kissing, introductions, and ice-cold sauvignon blanc, I pin on a bright smile and get to work.

Of course I'm happy. Why on earth wouldn't I be?

# Chapter Four

Lunch is a success.

The journalists leave tipsy, clutching goody bags and promising lots of press. I put the huge bill on my expense card, wave them off in their cabs, and collapse onto the backseat of mine.

At least, I hope it was a success, I tell myself, feeling the familiar pangs of worry as we start weaving through the traffic on the way back to the office.

My face aches from smiling. That's the thing about my job. It might look easy, sipping wine and nibbling on a grilled goat cheese and watercress salad, but schmoozing is hard work. You're on full alert the whole time. Trying to mix business with pleasure, trying to find the right balance between discussing your clients and discussing so-and-so's recent breakup.

"He did what? No! That's terrible! You poor thing. You should get away for a few days. Treat yourself to a spa weekend. *Speaking of which, I know an amazing one in Scotland that we just happen to do the PR for . . .*"

I make it back to my desk by around three, and spend the rest of the afternoon chained to my computer. Beatrice leaves at six on the dot. She has salsa on Mondays and is love with Pablo, the Brazilian instructor. Whenever she talks about him she puts on this really over-the-top Spanish accent, all very dramatic with lots of lisping and rolling of *r*'s, and starts tossing her hair around a lot, which is quite hard as it's a short blonde bob. I swear, the transformation is incredible. It's like she goes from this no-nonsense English Rose with sturdy calves to this tempestuous Latina seductress.

In fact, I could have *sworn* I saw a pair of fishnets in her handbag when she left. Bea in fishnets! The mind boggles.

Anyhow, as usual Beatrice (or should I say, *Be-a-treeth*) tries to "encourage" me, as she puts it, to leave the office with her by starting to turn off the lights while I'm still sitting here typing. Bea is not one to give subtle hints. Trust me, she would have pulled out the plug on my computer if I hadn't managed to throw her off my scent by saying I was just finishing up some paperwork for tomorrow's meeting and I'd be following her in five.

Of course I'm lying. And of course she knows I'm lying. But whereas normally she would have called me on it and waited next to me like a sentry to make sure I didn't do my usual trick of staying late, tonight the lure of Pablo and salsa is too strong, and she's out of the door faster than you can say *salida cubana*.

❧

Which means it's nearly eight by the time I finally put my computer to sleep, gather up my bags, and leave the office. And then, that's only because Miles has called twice from that new gastropub wondering where I am. I lie and say I'm just five minutes away.

Okay, make that ten.

Oh, all right then. Twenty.

"Sorry I'm late."

As I walk into the pub I spot Miles sitting up at the bar. He's reading the *Evening Standard* property supplement. He looks up and smiles and I feel a beat of pleasure.

"They've run out of the moules," he says pleasantly as I bend down to give him a kiss. He smells of aftershave and Guinness and his face is tickly with the soft blond fuzz that's sprouted since he last shaved, which in Miles's case was probably a few days ago. Miles has such baby-fine hair, he's in his thirties and is still trying to grow his sideburns.

"Aww, damn," I sympathize, sliding onto the bar stool next to him.

You see, this is what I love about Miles. He doesn't get annoyed that I'm late. No big argument ensues. He's just his usual calm, composed self.

"So what else looks good on the menu?" Shrugging off my coat, I reach for the bowl of olives and nibble off the salty flesh with my teeth. "Mmm, these are delicious."

Finally I can try to relax a bit. Have a drink. Some food. I rub my stomach. The knot that's been there all day feels as if it might be starting to subside.

"Well, the fish special sounds interesting . . ."

He squints myopically at the blackboard, his brow creased in concentration, trying to decipher the chalk handwriting. He looks so cute when he does that. Like a little schoolboy, not a successful thirtysomething property developer.

"Good choice."

A male voice next to me makes me turn around. Farther along from me, sitting up at the bar, is a man eating alone. He's got short, curly dark hair and is wearing little round glasses balanced on the end of his nose, which I can't help noticing is all bent out of shape.

"I'd recommend the fish." He gestures to his plate and smiles, revealing a faint Joaquin Phoenix–type scar running from nostril to lip, that's half hidden beneath his five-o'clock shadow.

"Hmm, no I'm afraid I can't eat fish." I shake my head.

"Oh, right, I didn't realize you were a vegetarian." He nods, and looks a bit embarrassed that he's said anything.

And now I feel bad. After all, he was only trying to be friendly.

"Well, I am, but I eat fish," I confess. "Only the thing is I already had fish this week, so I can't have it twice," I explain, and smile. "All that mercury."

We both look down at his plate again. The half-eaten salmon looks back at us.

There's an awkward pause.

"Well, I guess in that case there's always the macaroni cheese," he suggests, reading off the blackboard.

I shrug and wrinkle up my nose. "Dairy."

"Is that bad?" He looks puzzled.

"I have to avoid it."

He eyes me suspiciously. "Right," he says slowly, and suddenly I discern the corners of his mouth twitching slightly. I feel my guilt at being dismissive dispersing. Hang on a minute. Is he finding my food allergies amusing or something? Is he . . . I feel a prickle of indignation . . . *laughing at me?*

"I was told to by a nutritionist," I protest defensively, remembering the conversation I'd had with Dr. Bruce, Melody's nutritionist, when I was doing a press release for one of her books. I'd complained of being tired and she'd drawn up a long list of things for me to avoid.

I've been avoiding them for six months and I still feel exhausted.

"I'm not supposed to eat wheat or refined sugars either," I add, defensively. "I'm intolerant."

"You don't say?" he replies, clicking his tongue sympathetically, but his eyes give him away. Yup, he's definitely laughing at me.

Riled, I turn my attention back to Miles. "What are you getting, darling?" I say pointedly, putting my back to him. Honestly, it's not like I *asked* him to talk to me. He talked to me first!

"Well, actually I think I'm going to go for the Thai red curry . . ." he muses out loud.

"Oooh, yes, that sounds delicious," I agree, my voice a little louder than necessary. "I'll have that too."

Huh, that'll show him. Feeling a beat of satisfaction that I'm choosing something entirely different to his suggestions, I look up from the menu and try attracting the attention of one of the barstaff so we can order.

"God, it's really busy, isn't it," I tut, waving futilely at someone pulling a pint while Miles sits next to me, waiting patiently. "It's going to take forever to get served."

"Well, lucky for you, I've finished my break," says a now-familiar voice, and I turn sideways to see the man next to me getting up from his stool, empty plate in hand, lifting up the hatch to get behind the bar. At the same time as I notice he's wearing an apron. "Go ahead," he says, picking up a pad and pen.

Oh, no. I feel a mixture of dismay and relief. He works here.

"Well, I'd like the Thai red curry . . ." Miles is saying pleasantly.

"Righty-ho." He smiles, scribbling it down. "And for you?" He looks up at me and I could swear he's still got that amused look in his eye.

"I'll have the same. Please," I say decisively.

"You sure?" He cocks his head, eyes twinkling, pen poised.

"Absolutely," I say firmly.

"Okay." He sucks air in through his teeth and scribbles it down.

I watch him, feeling a tweak of irritation, but as he turns to ring it up at the cash register I suddenly have a thought. "Wait a minute, I'm sorry . . . does that have nuts in it?"

He pauses from punching in the total and looks up. "You're allergic to nuts too?"

My earlier twinge of irritation now goes up a notch to full-blown annoyance.

"Yes, very," I snap, looking at him tight-faced. "I could go into anaphylactic shock."

"She has to carry an EpiPen," adds Miles, overhearing our conversation and sliding his arm around my waist protectively. "A single nut could be lethal." He looks at me, his face suffused with concern. "Couldn't it, darling?"

I meet his unwavering gaze and for a moment I forget my annoyance and feel a rush of love toward him. Gosh, I am so lucky to have Miles as a boyfriend. He is so supportive and understanding.

"Wow."

Unlike some men, I think, flicking my eyes back to the barman, who's just standing there, barely keeping a straight face.

"Yeah, I know. Pretty scary, huh? It's life-threatening on a daily basis," continues Miles, thinking he's being genuine and not hearing the sarcasm in his voice.

Unlike me. Blatantly ignoring the barman, I pick up the *Evening Standard* and pretend to be engrossed in an article about house prices. Hopefully he'll get the message.

He doesn't.

"That's terrible. Every meal must be terrifying."

"I manage," I snap, from behind the paper.

"Yes, but we have to be extra vigilant," confides Miles. "Remember that time when we were having drinks at the Oxo Tower, darling? And you ate the pretzel that had been contaminated by salted peanuts . . ."

I feel a clench of irritation. And now it's directed at Miles. Honestly! Does he have to tell this guy everything? Can't he just ignore him like I'm doing?

". . . and it was pretty scary there for a moment, I can tell you. Poor Charlotte's throat swelled up, her lips went all puffy, and she got this horrible rash . . ."

*Oh God. Please. Shut up, Miles.* I shoot him a sideways look to silence him, but he's so absorbed in telling his story and defending my honor, he doesn't notice.

"Really? A horrible rash?" repeats the barman, looking over at me and pulling a face. "Ouch."

And you can shut up too, I think, throwing him the daggers.

"I mean, can you imagine? Using the same bowl for pretzels, that you earlier used for salted peanuts? Without washing it first?" Miles looks aghast. "I wrote a pretty stern letter to the management afterward, didn't I, Charlotte? Obviously they refunded our bar bill, but that wasn't the point—"

"Oh, look, there's a table free over there," I pipe up, suddenly seeing one open up in the corner of the bar. "Let's grab it before it's taken!"

Jumping up from my stool, I scoop up my bags and hurry over to it. Anything to get away from that annoying bartender. Honestly. Interfering like that. I look over at Miles and wave. Abandoned at the bar, he's looking a little confused as to where I've suddenly disappeared to. As he spots me he starts politely saying good-bye.

That's the thing about Miles, he's so polite and well-mannered. It's like when we have sex. He always asks permission and afterward he always says thank you, which I think is taking your pleases and thank-yous to the extreme, but that's a British private education for you.

Tucking the newspaper under his arm, he picks up the bottle of wine and glasses, and makes his way over.

"Don't worry, I've sorted it all out," he says, sitting down.

"Great, thanks." I smile, taking the glasses from him and pouring the wine. "So how's work?" I ask, changing the subject. Despite our false start, I'm determined to have a nice evening with Miles. We barely saw each other last week because we were both so busy.

*And* the weekend before that, come to think of it.

"Oh, you know, the usual." He shrugs, settling back into his seat and taking a draft of wine.

Miles invests in property—both here and abroad—and has what he calls "quite a portfolio." He's a real expert when it comes to house prices, up-and-coming areas, and mortgage rates. That's one of the reasons we don't live together. He says we should be sensible and wait till the market levels off before we, how did he put it? Ah, yes, that was it: *consolidate.*

I remember, because he got this meaningful look in his eye and reached for my hand, which is really unlike Miles as he never wants to hold hands. He gets all self-conscious at what he calls PDA, or "public displays of affection."

"I signed the Aquarius deal. They start building next month."

"Wonderful!"

"And it looks like I might be able to get investors for my other idea, so I think I'm going to fly up there tomorrow for a couple of days."

"Which idea is that?"

"The project in Leeds?" He raises his eyebrows as if to remind me.

"Oh, to convert that old warehouse into luxury flats?"

"No, that was Manchester." He corrects, frowning slightly. "Anyway, I don't want to bore you with all this, darling." Smiling, he rubs my hand lightly with his finger. "Let's talk about something else."

"No, please, continue," I say encouragingly. "It's fascinating."

Well, all right, perhaps "fascinating" is a *bit* of an exaggeration but it's important to show an interest in your partner's career. That's what a loving, caring, mature relationship is all about, according to a book I read recently called *Good Listener, Great Lover.* I read a lot of those types of books. They used to call them self-help, but that's so nineties. Now they're called self-awareness. In which case I should be super aware because I've accumulated stacks of them.

"Maybe later," he says, taking a sip of his wine and idly reaching for a section of the newspaper. But I can tell he's glad I wanted to know. Honestly, it's such a relief to finally be in a real grown-up and mature relationship. Two professionals, sharing a bottle of good red wine, eating a bowl of mixed olives, reading different sections of the same newspaper.

Flicking absently through the pages I feel a glow of contentment.

When I was younger I used to be so clueless about men. I was attracted to all the wrong guys and spent most of my twenties lurching from one disappointment to the next. So when I turned thirty I decided that was it. No more players. No more bad boys. No more disastrous flings and stormy relationships.

Six months later I met Miles. We were introduced at a dinner party and when he loosened his tie and stumbled over a polite hello, I knew I'd never have to spend another evening listening to Nirvana's "Smells Like Teen Spirit" being picked out on a Fender guitar, talking about commitment issues, or worrying about a roving eye. Here was a man I could trust. A grown-up with a successful career, his own flat in a lovely part of London, and an accent like Hugh Grant's. Plus, not one single T-shirt with a skull and crossbones on it.

I glance across at him now. Instead he's wearing a lovely cashmere sweater that I bought him for his birthday last year. He looks so adorable in it.

Taking a mouthful of wine Miles looks up and catches me looking at him.

A man with whom I have shared interests and can have a proper civilized conversation with.

"So?" he says, putting down his section of the paper.

"So?" I repeat, putting down mine.

Only, the thing is for a tiny moment I can't think what to say. It's like my mind's gone totally blank. How weird. Obviously my lack of sleep is really catching up with me; I must be completely overtired.

"I'm thinking of investing in another buy-to-let property abroad," he says casually.

Property! Of course. That's what we were talking about. How could I forget?

"Oh, where?" I ask interestedly.

"Well, I'm not sure yet . . ." he confesses, "but I was thinking about Dubai . . ."

"Wow, fabulous!" I exclaim. Sure it's a little boring, but as Miles always says, your property is your pension.

". . . Apparently there's a couple of off-plan developments that could bring in a really good yield."

"Really? That sounds really . . . um . . . interesting . . ."

It's just sometimes I don't always want to be thinking about pensions and retirement. I mean, okay, so I'm turning thirty-two in a couple of days, but it's not like I'm a hundred. Sometimes it would be nice to stop thinking about the future and just think about now for a change. Something spontaneous. Something fun.

"Two Thai curries and a mixed leaf salad?"

I look up to see the bartender hovering with two large plates.

"Organic, in case you should ask," he adds pointedly, shooting me a look.

"Yes, here please," says Miles, gesturing into the middle of the table. "We're splitting the salad. Is that okay, darling?"

"Of course." I smile brightly, ignoring the bartender. "It looks delicious!"

Honestly, what am I moaning about? This is great. Miles is great. Everything is great.

He passes me a napkin and impulsively I lean over to give him a kiss.

See. We can be fun and spontaneous.

Except my aim is off and I knock over his wineglass instead.

"Oh shit. Sorry—"

"Whoops, nearly," gasps Miles, catching it before red wine goes everywhere. "Phew, that was lucky." Placing it back upright on the table, he gives a little laugh. "That could have been a bit embarrassing, couldn't it?"

"Yeah—" I nod, catching the bartender's eye and quickly looking away.

And now I just feel like a total clumsy idiot.

There's a tiny pause, and I think about attempting that kiss again, but somehow the moment has passed.

"Mmm, this looks delicious, doesn't it?" says Miles, picking up his knife and fork.

"Yes . . . delicious." I nod, doing the same.

And turning our attention to the food, we both fall silent and start eating.

# Chapter Five

B riefcase? *Check.*
Laptop? *Check.*
BlackBerry? *Check.*

It's the next morning and as usual I'm rushing around my apartment, going through my itinerary to make sure I haven't forgotten anything.

Grabbing my keys I let the front door slam shut behind me as I race down the front steps. Scrambling into my car, I reverse out of my space and right into rush hour. Ahead I can see the signs for the diversion up ahead and as traffic starts merging into one lane, I resign myself to another long journey into work.

My stomach gurgles. No time for any breakfast again, and flicking open my glove compartment I rummage around. I keep a stash of energy bars in here, just for emergencies.

Okay, so they're not *just* for emergencies, they're usually my breakfast these days, when I *get* to eat breakfast, that is. I buy them then in bulk from the health food store. Finishing a phone call I tear open the wrapper and take a bite. These are full of oaty goodness and super delicious.

Well, okay, they're not *that* delicious. In fact, they remind me a bit of the food I used to feed my pet gerbil, but still, at least they're a lot healthier than a Twix, which is what I used to eat in my younger days.

I chew quickly as we crawl along the high street, taking advantage of the few moments of silence before my phone starts ringing. Still, at least I can catch up on my calls, I tell myself, trying to look on the bright side.

*It's that Beetle again.*

As I pull up at the lights I feel a jolt of surprise. *What a coincidence!* flashes through my mind as my eyes flick automatically toward the driver and I catch the briefest of glimpses. A split second. Barely long enough to see more than a flash of long dark curly hair before I'm blinded by the morning sunlight bouncing brightly off the windscreen. Then she's gone. Disappeared behind a sun visor. And I'm left staring at the car, feeling vaguely unsettled.

I peer closer.

And slightly bewildered.

I didn't imagine it. That really *does* look like my old car, I determine, my chest resting against the steering wheel, my brow furrowed as I squint in the sunlight. It's exactly the same, complete with animal rights sticker and rusting headlights. And bashed on the left-hand side from when I forgot to put on the handbrake and it rolled down the hill into the village and the farmer's tractor . . .

As the lights change and the Beetle drives past me, I gaze at it in stunned disbelief. That is *such* a coincidence I need a new word for coincidence. I mean, that's just *too* freaky. Unless—

Suddenly an idea comes to me. Maybe that's my old car! Yes, that must be it. It failed its inspection years ago on about a hundred different points . . . a vague English memory stirs: the mechanic calling it a death trap and telling me that the next time I put my foot on the brake pedal, my foot would go through the floor as it was so rusty. Dad very sweetly bought it off me to fix it and gave it to Mum as a run-around, something to use for taking the dogs on long muddy walks in the English countryside, until eventually they ended up selling it to someone.

Someone who must now be living in London. Someone who

must look a lot like I used to, I decide, feeling a flash of jubilant triumph.

*See.* I knew there had to be a rational explanation.

As I drive off I glance in my rearview mirror, but the Beetle has already disappeared. It must have turned off somewhere, I muse idly, sailing across the intersection. And to think I've been getting totally freaked out, thinking—

I catch myself. Well, let's just say I was thinking all kinds of silly nonsense.

❧

As usual Beatrice is waiting for me with an outstretched cup of coffee. "Morning," she trills chirpily.

"Morning." Scooping up my coffee I march over to my desk, turn on my computer, and start checking my e-mails.

"Any messages?"

"Larry Goldstein's people called to apologize that he's running late for lunch—so I've changed the reservation to two p.m.—but he's very excited about meeting you . . ." She beams and crosses her fingers.

My stomach flutter with nerves. "Anything else?"

"Oh, and Miles called."

I look up, surprised. Miles never calls me at the office; he knows how busy I am. Plus he was supposed to be flying up to Leeds this morning.

I feel a flicker of worry. "Is he okay?" I ask, going from zero to panic in less time than it takes to say "accident" and "emergency."

"Yes, fine," Beatrice replies breezily. "He'd just landed."

Immediately I relax.

"He said he tried calling you this morning but couldn't get through to you on your mobile . . ."

"Oh God, I probably forgot to turn it on," I groan, digging it out of my pocket. "I was in a bit of a rush this morning." I glance at the screen. That's funny, it is on. I must not have been getting reception. Like yesterday, I remember. "He should have tried me on my Black-Berry," I think out loud.

"He did. He couldn't get through on that either."

"Really? How odd." Puzzled, I now look at my BlackBerry. But no, that's on too, and there are full bars of reception.

"They're called dropped calls," says Beatrice knowledgeably. "Apparently they are a growing problem because of all the sheer volume of people using mobile devices. In fact, I read in *New Scientist* that the number continues to grow at an exceptional rate and it's been predicted that by 2010 there will be more than one and a half billion wireless device users worldwide . . ."

"Hey, Bea, what did Miles say?" I interrupt hastily, before I'm quoted the entire *New Scientist* report back to me.

But she's in midflow.

". . . Although technically for it to be a dropped call I think you have to be actually cut off in the middle of a call, rather than not be able to get through at all, but essentially it's all the same thing, too much phone traffic . . ." She trails off as she catches my eyes, and blushes. "Oh, right, yes, sorry, Miles . . ." Scrambling for her jotter pad, she solemnly reads, ". . . has just had word from a contact at an estate agent's that an amazing house is about to come on the market and he wants to make sure you'll be free to go and look at it with him when he gets back." She looks up, her eyes shining. "Are you two moving in together?"

"Well, we've talked about it," I say, suddenly feeling a bit awkward.

"Golly, how exciting."

"Uh, yes, it is, isn't it?"

To be honest I'm feeling slightly taken aback. It's one thing talking about it, but it's another actually going to look at houses. It suddenly all feels very real. And not some far-off distant plan we talk about every now and again over a bottle of red wine and a bowl of mixed olives.

"Apparently they can't get the keys until Thursday but fortunately I've already checked the diary and managed to move a meeting with the beauty editor of *Elle* so now there's nothing in the diary for that lunchtime . . ." Beatrice is chattering away. "So I called him back to confirm that you'll meet him there at one o'clock."

"Wow. Miss Efficiency." I laugh lightly.

"Well, I do try." She beams, handing me a Post-it note. "This is the address." I look at it, feeling slightly dazed. Beatrice has the neatest handwriting, and yet the address seems to swim in front of my eyes. I take a much-needed gulp of coffee.

"You and Miles are, like, the most perfect couple. That's the kind of relationship I aspire to."

"You do?" I look back at Beatrice, clutching the files to her chest, her face all wistful.

"Absolutely," she exclaims, nodding vigorously. "You're both so successful and attractive and you have these exciting designer lives . . ."

Hearing her talking about us like that I feel a beat of pride. I suppose we do really, I muse, imagining Miles and me in one of those glossy at-home shoots in *OK!*: *"Property developer Miles and partner Charlotte, owner of Merryweather PR, relax in their stylish new home and talk to us about property, pension plans, and . . ."*

Actually that doesn't sound very exciting now I come to think of it, does it? I try to think of something else. I mean, come on. We must do *something* exciting.

But my mind remains blank. It's too early, my brain's not working properly yet, I decide. Plus I've got other things on my mind. Speaking of which.

"Bea, would you get me the Goldstein file, please?"

"Oh, of course. Coming right up." Snapping out of her romantic daydream of me and Miles, Beatrice dashes over to her beloved filing cabinets.

Draining the rest of my coffee I make a start on my in-box—I've got thirty-three unread e-mails.

As for me and Miles, I'll think of something exciting later.

❧

"Another macchiato?" asks the waitress politely.

I glance at my empty cup. I've been mainlining caffeine all morning to make sure I'm totally clearheaded and focused for this meeting, but to be honest I think I might have overdone it. I feel more jittery and anxious than ever. "No, thanks," I sigh, "I'll just have some water instead."

It's lunchtime and I'm sitting at a table at the Electric, a chic private members club in Notting Hill, waiting to meet Larry Goldstein, the Hollywood cosmetic dentist famous for the whiter-than-white smiles of all the big-name celebrities, and owner of a hugely successful chain of Star Smile clinics in the US. He's over from L.A. to meet with PR companies to discuss launching the first Star Smile clinic here in the UK.

My body tenses and I realize I've begun shredding my business card. Despite my shiny-suited veneer, I'm really nervous. I'm up against some stiff competition, but if I can win this launch, it will give Merryweather PR a huge amount of international publicity and put us firmly on the map.

"Still or sparkling?"

"Definitely still," interrupts a voice with an American accent, before I can answer.

I look up to see an older man. Attractive in that square-jawed, classic kind of a way, he's wearing a pale blue Ralph Lauren shirt and his steel gray hair is swept back from his tanned temples, as if he just ran his fingers effortlessly through it while stepping off a yacht in Saint-Tropez. And not, as is more likely, a result of half an hour with a hairdryer and lots of product. He reminds me of Blake Carrington from *Dynasty*. In fact for a moment there I almost think it *is* Blake Carrington from *Dynasty*.

"Mr. Goldstein?" I ask, hurriedly sweeping the little scraps of business card confetti off the tablecloth into the palm of my hand. I stuff them into my tote bag under the table as I stand up.

"Well, I was the last time I looked," he says, laughing confidently.

"Charlotte Merryweather, from Merryweather PR," I reply, giving him one of my professional smiles as I go to shake his hand. "It's such a pleasure to meet you."

"Please, call me Larry." He grins. "And I assure you the pleasure's all mine." Taking my hand in both of his, he squeezes his fingers around my own.

"Okay, Larry it is," I say cheerfully, doing my best to appear like this super confident career woman with her own successful PR company. And not how I really feel, which is so anxious I can feel damp patches forming under my armpits despite wearing a ton of antiperspirant.

"Excellent!" He beams.

He's still holding my hand and I'm beginning to feel a little self-conscious. We break apart and both sit down facing each other. As first impressions go, he's much older than I thought he was going to be. When I Googled him his age came up as a vague late forties, but sitting here in the flesh it's obvious those photographs on his website are airbrushed, as he looks at least a decade older. Nonetheless, he's incredibly well-preserved. Evidently no stranger to Botox, his forehead is unnaturally smooth and his eyes look a little stretched, but apart from that, he looks normal.

Apart from his smile, that is.

As our waitress reappears with a bottle of still water and starts pouring glasses, I gaze at it transfixed. I'd grown unaccustomed to smiles like his after living the past ten years in the UK. These perfect white picket fence smiles are the preserve of Hollywood A-listers and

British reality TV stars who *think* they're Hollywood A-listers. It's slightly bizarre to see them again in a real-life setting. I mean, they're so *white*. And so, well, *big*.

"Carbonated drinks erode the tooth enamel," he's saying now, flashing me his blindingly white smile that has nothing to do with tooth enamel and everything to do with porcelain veneers the size of dinner plates. "Just a little tip."

"Oh . . . um, thank you." I nod, mentally striking another thing off my list. God, what next? Soon I won't be able to eat or drink *anything*. In fact, at this rate I'll be on a drip. "So, you're from Los Angeles?" I ask brightly, quickly brushing away the worrying image of me being fed saline solution intravenously. "I'm from the States too. I grew up in Illinois, but went to college in California."

"You did? Wow, I never would have guessed. You've got yourself some British accent there," he replies, still smiling.

It's quite incredible really. How he can talk and smile at the same time. In fact, he's rather like a ventriloquist dummy.

"Well, I have been here ten years now." I smile, a little self-consciously. "There's lots I still miss about the States, like the summers, and the Super Bowl and Reese's Peanut Butter Cups . . ." I laugh ruefully, "but I've been here such a long time, London feels like home now . . ." For a moment I think about when I first moved here, how new and different everything was, how different *I* was . . . "Have you visited London before?" I ask, quickly snapping back.

"Many times. London is one of my favorite cities. I always feel so at home here," he enthuses, taking a sip of water.

I stifle a smile of amusement. With his California tan and perfect white smile, Larry Goldstein couldn't look *less* at home among the gray-faced, wonky-toothed Londoners I'd come to know and love so well.

"Well, you certainly brought the good weather with you," I say, launching into my well-rehearsed patter for visiting overseas clients.

"So tell me, is this just a business trip, or do you have any fun things planned while you're here?"

"Oh, I'm hoping I'm going to have some time for pleasure." He smiles, resting his elbows on the table and leaning toward me.

For a split second I feel a little prickle of something, but I'm too busy focusing on making relaxed small talk to give it much thought.

"Well, there's a Frida Kahlo exhibition on at the Tate Modern that's amazing," I continue with a smile. "You should check it out."

(I only know this because Beatrice went last weekend and told me all about it. Obviously.)

"Oh, really? That sounds fascinating, I love Frida Kahlo. Tell me, what's your favorite painting of hers?"

Damn. All I know about Frida Kahlo is that she had an impressive unibrow and that Salma Hayek played her in the movie.

"All of them." I smile brightly. "They're all amazing."

"Spoken like a true PR person." He laughs smoothly, and fixes me with his gaze. For the first time I notice how blue his eyes are. They almost don't look real. In fact everything about Larry Goldstein is so perfect, it seems fake.

"Which is why I'm really excited about this lunch," he continues. "I've heard great things about you and your company."

"Why, thank you." I smile, relieved to be off the topic of Frida and onto something I know a lot more about: *work*. Taking this as my cue, I pull out my portfolio from my briefcase and open it up on the table. "As you can see from this portfolio of media coverage I've achieved for my other clients, this is the sort of thing you could expect from Merryweather PR . . . ." I turn it around so he can see it and start leafing through the pages.

"Mmm, yes, very impressive." He nods, looking at a full-color spread from the *Times*.

"Obviously it's impossible to guarantee anything," I continue. "But with such a strong brand as yours combined with my journalistic experience and intimate knowledge of how the business works, I think ours would be an incredibly successful and mutually beneficial partnership."

"Mutually beneficial?" he says, glancing up from my portfolio and raising his eyebrows, which, now I'm up close, I notice are plucked into two perfect arches.

"Yes. With the right media coverage in the right places we could raise your profile here in the UK. Let the public know who you are. What Star Smile stands for. And Merryweather PR has the expertise to do this. Being from the US myself, I'm a master at creating a UK presence for those looking for opportunities overseas."

I'm in my stride now and, I have to say, I'm feeling pretty confident.

But then I should be. I've spent weeks working toward this meeting, researching information, putting together ideas, making sure I've thought of everything. I'm totally 100 percent prepared for this.

"And you say you have an *intimate* knowledge of how the business works?"

He's looking at me intently and for some reason, I get this momentary nagging of deep discomfort. The same one as I got when he shook my hand earlier.

"Um . . . yes," I reply quickly, brushing it aside and swinging back into full professional mode. "That's something we pride ourselves on at Merryweather PR."

"How intimate?" Still holding my gaze, he leans his body farther across the table. Not a lot. Maybe only an inch, if that, but it's enough to make the discomfort I just brushed away come racing back again.

"Would you care to hear the specials?" The waitress reappears at the table, interrupting our conversation.

"Oh, yes, please," I reply, glad of the distraction.

"Well, for appetizers, we have an heirloom tomato salad . . ."

Focusing my attention on the waitress I listen to her going

through the list, until after a few moments it feels safe to sneak a peek across at Larry Goldstein. Only his gaze is no longer on me, but on the pretty young waitress. And now he's throwing her that great big shiny smile of his.

And I'm totally overreacting, I realize, feeling both relieved and a bit silly. It's no biggie. He's obviously just a bit of a flirt, that's all. Just humor him. And looking down at my menu, I decide it's time to concentrate on what I'm going to have for lunch.

## Chapter Six

Underneath the perfect suntan, I discover Larry Goldstein is actually a very smart businessman. Over our appetizers I run through my proposal and he asks lots of pertinent questions and seems genuinely impressed by both myself and the company.

"So tell me, Charlotte, how did you get started in the business?" As our entrees arrive he looks at me, eyebrows raised with interest.

"Well, my background is actually in journalism. I majored in literature at Stanford. Originally I wanted to be a writer . . ."

"A bit of wordsmith, huh?" He smiles, pausing from eating to study me with interest.

"Well, I try," I reply lightly, flicking back my hair under his gaze. "In fact, after graduation I moved to England with my parents, and my first job was for British Worldwide Press, a big London publishing company, as the editor of one of their magazines—"

"Wow." Larry Goldstein widens his eyes and looks suitably impressed. "That's amazing."

I feel myself blush slightly. "Well . . . it was a wonderful experience and gave me incredible hands-on training, but after a few years I decided I wanted a new challenge and turned freelance," I explain, trying to appear nonchalant at his compliment, while the little voice in my head whispers, *Keep it up, Charlotte, keep it up.*

"Brave girl." He nods approvingly.

"Fortunately, my risk paid off and I ended up having the opportunity to write for all the big-name glossy magazines and newspapers. Which, of course, is invaluable in terms of contacts now," I say, waggling my fork emphatically.

"Absolutely," he agrees just as emphatically and I feel a slight thrill. I don't like to get my hopes up, but things are looking very good. Very good indeed.

"But after a couple of years I just wasn't feeling stimulated or challenged enough. When I was presented with an opportunity to move into the exciting world of public relations, I jumped at the chance."

"And you don't regret giving up your writing career?"

"I've never looked back," I say with conviction.

"That's awesome," nods Larry Goldstein.

I smile modestly. "Well, I've been very lucky," I reply, turning back to my food.

Except the thing is, my life didn't happen *exactly* like that. Not word for word. But I've been telling this version of events to clients and journalists for so long now I've almost begun to believe it myself. After all, it's basically the truth. Sort of.

Okay. Let's cut the spin.

The *real* truth is this: I graduated from college and moved to England with big dreams of being a writer and applied for every job I could find. Nearly a hundred rejection letters later I finally got an interview with British Worldwide Press in London. That part is true. And I *was* an editor of one of their magazines.

The part I leave out is that they publish puzzle magazines, and the job was for an editor for their crossword magazine. Very glamorous. So, all right, it wasn't exactly *Vanity Fair* but it was a start. And everyone has to start somewhere, right?

Except there was just one problem:

*I totally suck at crosswords.*

Seriously. I honestly can't see the point of them. Plus, I can never get the clues. I mean, how am I supposed to know a ten-letter word for a coat of arms beginning with *e*?

*And why would I want to?*

But I was desperate. And broke. And living at home with my parents.

Thankfully, however, I got the job and moved to London, and for the next three years I made up crossword clues by day and partied around the bars and clubs of West London by night.

And in my lunch hours? I updated my CV and sent it out to every magazine and newspaper I could think of. Until one day it landed on the right desk, at the right time. A new lifestyle magazine was looking for a features writer. The money wasn't very much, the circulation even less, but a working writer? Me? It was a dream come true.

Unfortunately the dream only lasted six months before the magazine folded and I found myself unemployed and looking for another job. Only I couldn't find one. So I turned freelance.

*Freelance.*

It sounds so exciting and glamorous, doesn't it? Images of me rushing around with a laptop under my arm, writing in coffee shops, staying up till three a.m. smoking cigarettes in order to meet that deadline. How fabulous! I was going to be Carrie in *Sex and the City* before Carrie even existed.

But life isn't a TV show, and this Carrie wasn't wearing designer heels and being paid a fortune to write a witty sex column. Nope, this Carrie was pitching feature ideas to belligerent editors who never returned her calls, watching daytime TV in her pajamas, and worrying how she was going to pay the rent. And there wasn't even a *sniff* of a cosmopolitan.

This went on for months until a friend of a friend took pity on me and told me about a vacancy at a PR agency. The job involved writing press releases. So you'd still be writing, she reasoned. Well, if you can call a thousand words on shampoo writing. But it paid the bills. And it was only temporary. Just until I finished that novel of mine that I'd been working on in my spare time and sold it to a publisher in a furious bidding war . . .

I wish.

Because I never did finish it. I got sidetracked, got busy, and gave up. I'm not exactly sure why I didn't go back to it, but the truth is that bit by bit my dream of being a writer receded as the reality set in. I got promoted, became more successful, earned more money, and then set up my company. And it's true, I never have looked back.

Well, maybe sometimes. When I walk into a bookstore and pick up the first novel by a new author. Or read a fascinating article in a magazine, and think maybe, just maybe, that could have been me. If I'd stuck it out longer. Tried harder. Been a better writer. And for the briefest second the longing is almost palpable.

But then I brush it out of mind. I totally made the right decision. I mean, if I'd followed that route, I wouldn't be where I am today.

❦

Having lunch in a chichi restaurant in Notting Hill, on the brink of winning an important new account that will take the company to a whole new international level, I think, glancing at Larry Goldstein, who's looking at me thoughtfully.

"You know, Charlotte, I see a lot of myself in you."

"You do?" I reply, not quite sure whether to take that as a compliment.

"Very much so." He nods. "And after meeting you and hearing all about your company I feel very strongly that Merryweather PR might be just what I'm looking for."

Sitting across the table from him I smile reservedly, the picture of professionalism, but on the inside I want to punch the air with delight. I hardly dare think it, but it's looking very possible that all my hard work, and evenings spent suffering through his US TV show, *Celebrity Smile Clinic*, might just pay off.

"Well, as I said before, we'd be more than delighted to represent you here in the UK, Mr. Goldstein," I reply, unsure how I'm keeping my voice so calm.

He throws me a look and holds up his hand.

"I mean Larry," I say, smiling.

"In fact, the more I think about it I really don't think there's any point in seeing any of the other PR companies," he continues evenly, raising an eyebrow. "Do you?"

*The contract is mine!* flashes through my mind in neon.

"No . . . I don't think there is," I reply, just as evenly. I feel a burst of giddy excitement and do my utmost to contain it.

"Excellent. So we're agreed." He smiles, reaching underneath the table to smooth down his napkin.

Oh my God, I can't wait to call Beatrice and tell her how well the meeting went—

I feel someone's fingers sweep across my inner thigh.

*What the—?*

I jump and look sharply across at Larry Goldstein, but he's innocently winding spaghetti onto his spoon. I stare at him with a mixture of doubt and disbelief. Did I just imagine that? Did that not just happen? My heart thudding, I fidget self-consciously in my chair, pulling down my skirt and crossing my legs.

"Is everything okay?" Larry Goldstein looks over at me, his brow creased with concern.

"Yum . . . yes, fine," I reply politely, taking a gulp of water.

Well, what else am I supposed to say? Did you just stick your hand up my skirt?

Although, that's exactly what *young* Charlotte Merryweather would have said. When she never stopped to think before opening her mouth, when she said exactly what was on her mind.

I'm not some impulsive headstrong twentysomething with nothing to lose. I'm a thirtysomething professional woman with everything to lose. Like my reputation, and a really important contract, I remind myself. I can't just start hurling accusations and causing a scene in a restaurant. Just think of all the repercussions.

Sitting bolt upright, I take a couple of slow breaths and concentrate on composing myself. Plus, I could have easily made a mistake. Things aren't always what they seem, I tell myself, my mind flicking back to that incident at the lights. It was probably just the tablecloth brushing against my legs or something. In fact, the more I think about it, the more convinced I am that's exactly what just happened.

"Wow, the food is delicious, isn't it?" I snap back to see Larry Goldstein smiling amiably at me across the table.

"Yes, delicious," I reply, automatically.

Disconcerted, I turn back to my meal and continue eating. Only, my appetite has disappeared and I'm relieved when a few minutes later the waitress comes to take our plates away.

"Coffee, dessert?" she asks and I shake my head.

"No, I'm fine, thanks," I reply. My earlier, shiny delight at having won the account seems to have lost its sheen somehow. I know I should be over the moon, but I can't get that bugging feeling out of my head about what just happened. Or what I *thought* just happened, I correct myself quickly.

"Not for me either." He beams, leaning back in his chair and fixing me with a satisfied smile. "Coffee is the number one biggest tooth stain."

"Really?" I say faintly.

"So, now that's decided, let's get down to business." Pressing his manicured hands down on the tablecloth, he looks at me intently. "Figure out a game plan."

"Definitely." I perk up, relieved to be focusing back on business. I start running through the many lists in my head. "When were you wanting to make an announcement to the press? Obviously the sooner we get the word out there, the more time we will have to start generating press, building momentum . . ."

"Totally." He nods. "Well, let's see . . ." He glances at his iPhone. "I leave for the States next Wednesday. So how about Tuesday?"

I look at him in disbelief. *"A week from today?"*

"Is that a problem?" He throws me a look that leaves me in no doubt that if it is a problem, he'll find a PR company for whom it isn't.

"No, of course not," I reassure him, thinking of all the work I'm going to have to do, all the extra hours I'm going to have to put in to get things ready. I can already feel the pressure piling on top of my shoulders.

"Excellent." He smiles with the confidence of a man who doesn't have problems. He has shiny white teeth, a perfect tan, and a prime-time show on American TV. And he plays golf with Jack Nicholson, according to one of his press clippings.

"So you're up for the challenge?"

"Absolutely." I nod, sitting more upright and throwing my shoulders back. Honestly, what's wrong with me? I love challenges. And I want this contract. This is my big opportunity. "As I said before, Merryweather PR might be a smaller agency but that works in our favor because we can provide you a lot more personal attention," I say with renewed enthusiasm.

"I like the sound of that," he replies, a smile playing on his lips.

"So have you secured a location for the store?" I say briskly, forging ahead through my list.

"Almost," he replies, leaning back against his chair. "I've had a location guy scouting for the right space for a while now and we've narrowed it down to two. Usually I go with my gut on things"—he gestures toward me—"but in this case I'm not really feeling it."

"Maybe I could offer some input?" I suggest.

"That would be very welcome," he enthuses. "I'm flying to Brussels tomorrow for an international conference on the latest break-throughs in cosmetic dentistry, but I'm back the next day—"

"Great." I nod, pulling out my BlackBerry and scrolling through my diary. "What time were you thinking?"

"Well, I'm pretty busy all day with designers."

Suddenly I get a horrible feeling that I know where this is going.

"How about in the evening? Dinner maybe?"

I was *so* hoping he wasn't going to say that.

"It will give us a chance to get to know each other a bit more . . ."

I'm nodding and smiling as he's talking but I'm flashing back to a few moments ago. Did I imagine it? *Did I?*

" . . . It's important to make sure we're on the same page. Don't you think, Charlotte?"

I snap back to see him smiling smoothly at me and automatically I switch on my professional smile, but my mind's all over the place. I wanted this contract more than anything, but now—

Larry Goldstein is still looking at me expectantly, waiting for answer.

"Absolutely. Thursday evening it is!" I suddenly hear myself saying.

He breaks into a wide smile. "Excellent!" Picking up his water glass, he clinks it against mine. "That's a date!"

I smile brightly. I've got it! The contract's mine.

Oh God.

# Chapter Seven

I wave Larry Goldstein off in a cab and cross the street to where my car's parked at a meter. Checking the time, it appears lunch went on far longer than I expected, and I really need to get back to the office, tell Bea the good news, and—

"Lottie!"

A familiar voice behind me interrupts my train of thought, and I swing around. No one ever calls me that anymore except . . .

Squinting in the bright summer sunshine, I peer down the busy street. Past cafés spilling out onto the pavement, people drinking cappuccinos and eating pastries, shoppers laden down with designer bags, and a mother with a double buggy and aging cocker spaniel . . .

*"Nessy!"* I break into a grin. "What are you doing here?"

"I live here, you idiot," she counters jovially. "What are you doing here?"

Vanessa is my oldest friend. I met her the fateful day I went to London for the puzzle magazine interview. She was sitting on wall outside the office, smoking a cigarette and looking utterly cool. To a nervous little girl just off the plane from the States and wearing her mother's suit, she epitomized everything about London. Six feet tall and a platinum blonde, she was twenty-five years old and shared a place with some friends in Kensington. I was in awe of her.

I still am, really. Happily married to Julian, her handsome lawyer husband, she's a mother to two adorable children and lives in a big rambling house in Notting Hill, with a fridge covered in finger paintings and thousands of family photographs cluttering the walls. We lead completely different lives and don't get to see each other as much as we'd want to, but we're still incredibly close.

"I had a business lunch," I say, gesturing to the restaurant. "I was just going back to the office."

"Bollocks to that." She frowns, looping her arm through mine. "Aunty Charlotte is coming back to ours for a cup of tea, isn't she?" She peers into the double buggy where Ruby, aged three, and Sam, who's just turned one, giggle and gurgle respectively. "See, that's a yes—in case you needed me to translate," she says and I can't help laughing.

"Okay," I surrender. I know better than to argue with Vanessa. "But just one cup."

"One cup," she repeats innocently, and grasping the handles of double buggy and dog lead with one hand, and me with the other, she propels us all down the street.

❧

"God, I wish someone would stick their hand up my skirt."

I've just spent the last ten minutes telling her all about my weird "incident" with Larry Goldstein, and to be honest, this wasn't the reaction I was anticipating.

"Vanessa!" I gasp, horrified.

"Sorry, honey, only joking . . ." she apologizes breezily. "Well, sort of," she mutters, furiously chopping up something unidentifiable until it resembles an orange gloop. "Though I must say I've seen that Larry Goldstein being interviewed on *Oprah* and he's bloody handsome."

She rolls her eyes and makes a face.

"So what if he is? In a plastic sort of a way," I can't help adding. "That doesn't mean he can make a pass at me in a restaurant. It was a business meeting."

She pauses from feeding Sam a forkful of orange gloop, hand held suspended in the air. *"And?"* she teases. Distractedly she puts it in her own mouth. There's a loud squall. "Oops, sorry, darling," she coos, remembering herself. "Silly Mummy is hungry too." Hastily she shovels up another forkful.

*"And* that's not acceptable!" I admonish. "It's sexual harassment. Have you never heard of equality in the workplace?"

She screws up her forehead and pretends to think. "Vaguely. I'm a stay-at-home mother who lives in a world of bath times, tantrums, and dirty nappies. I gave up my job and my life to breed. Need I say more?" A fork in each hand, she smiles dryly, then continues alternating orange gloop and pasta between two hungry mouths.

"Yeah, but you love being a mum," I counter.

"True." She smiles, turning to me, her face lit up. "My kids are the best thing. I can't imagine life without them . . ." She breaks off uncomfortably as she catches my eye and the smile slips from her face. For the briefest moment, a look passes between us. "But I'm glad I waited until my thirties to have them," she adds quickly.

She glances away and there's an awkward pause.

I fill it by changing the subject. "Anyway you hated your job," I point out. Vanessa used work in the law firm next to my office. That's how she met Julian, her husband. "You said you couldn't wait to leave."

"True."

She nods, breaking into a huge smile at Ruby, who's laughing hysterically as she smears orange pulp on her brother.

"You threw a resignation party," I continue.

"And you couldn't come," she remarks, shooting me a look.

"I was on a deadline."

"When aren't you on a deadline?" she counters.

I open my mouth to protest, then close it again. Now that she mentions it, I can't remember a life before deadlines.

"Gosh, that was a great party . . ."

I look back at Vanessa, whose eyes have gone dreamy. "We had over a hundred people squeezed into the old house. I was pregnant and couldn't drink and so Julian made me Virgin Marys all night and we played UB40 on repeat to celebrate my unemployment, you know, UB40: unemployed. . . ." She smiles wistfully, her mind wandering back to that night over three years ago. "Anyway, it's not as if you're even certain this Goldstein chap even *made* a pass. It seems very unlikely. Like you said, you probably made a mistake—"

"True," I admit. In fact, the more I think about it, I'm almost certain I made a mistake.

"And you got the contract, which is what you wanted, isn't it?"

"True." I nod.

"So don't look so worried," she reprimands.

"I'm not," I reply, quickly uncreasing my forehead.

"Really?" Vanessa looks surprised. "That's not like you. Usually you worry about everything."

"I wouldn't say *everything*," I say, a little miffed.

"Darling, you worry about being worried," she points out, smiling.

"That's not true!" I say defensively.

"What about when we were celebrating your birthday and we bought all that champagne? And as we were about to open it you got worried the cork was going to pop out and blind someone . . ."

"Well, it could have," I protest, "I was just being careful—"

"Yelling 'Duck!' and diving for cover?"

I blush.

"Okay, so maybe I was a little overcautious, but those corks can be dangerous. They *can* take an eye out," I argue, but I don't think Vanessa is listening.

"And what about the time just before Julian and I married, when we went to that spa hotel for my hen weekend and we are all having fun by the pool and you lay in the shade and refused to join in because you were worried you were going to slip and bang your head and become paralyzed?"

"It happens a lot!" I admonish. "Haven't you seen *The Sea Inside*?"

"We weren't diving off rocks into the sea, Charlotte. We were messing around on inflatable rafts."

"Accidents can still happen," I warn her.

"On an inflatable raft?" she gasps incredulously.

The tea kettle boils and flicks off and she starts pulling out cups and looking for tea bags.

"Do you have any chamomile?" I ask.

"Only Earl Grey," she replies. "Go on, live dangerously," she teases, seeing my expression. "I remember the days when you didn't even know what herbal tea was, and you certainly wouldn't have drunk it. In fact, you wouldn't drink anything back then unless it was alcoholic."

I frown, ignoring her.

"So how's Miles?" she asks, throwing me a look as she reaches for the kettle.

Vanessa is not what you'd call Miles's biggest fan. She's never *actually* said anything, but she doesn't have to. The looks say it all.

"Great," I enthuse. "We had dinner last night at this really nice new gastropub."

"So when are you two going to *consolidate*?" she teases, reaching for the wet wipes and cleaning Ruby and Sam's faces.

I told Vanessa the story. Now I so wish I hadn't. She's never stopped teasing me about it.

"We're waiting for the property market to . . . uh . . ." Crap. I have no idea what we're supposed be waiting for the property market to do. I must have zoned out at that point . . .

". . . do something!" I finish vaguely, but triumphantly.

"Right," says Vanessa, raising an eyebrow, and I fidget uncomfortably. "And when will that be?"

I wrack my brains for some recollection of what Miles and I have talked about. We've talked about this for hours. Hours and hours and hours in fact. I must know the key point of that conversation . . . come on, think!

"Well, it's impossible to predict," I say finally, feeling pleased at how wise I sound. "But we *are* going to look at a house this week. Apparently it's just popped up on the market and it's amazing—" I'm quoting Beatrice, who quoted Miles, so that has to be right.

Vanessa looks impressed. "Where is it?"

"Um . . ." I pause. I remember looking at the Post-it Note with the address but for some reason I didn't take it in. "London," I reply brightly; then, before she can fire any more questions at me, I add quickly, "But anyway, we're not in any hurry to move in together. After all, this way we get to catch up on our sleep during the week, so on the weekends we can have lots of sex. It's the perfect arrangement really." I add this, though I'm not quite sure whether it's to convince Vanessa or myself.

"Sleep? Sex?" Vanessa wrinkles her brow as she passes the twins a couple of strawberries. "What are those again?"

I know she's joking, kind of; she says this kind of stuff all the time. But this time I detect an edge to her voice that I've never heard before.

"Well, that's the *idea*," I say, quickly backtracking.

There's a whole chapter in one of my self-help books about how a couple's sex life can suffer after the birth of their children. Apparently you can become highly sensitive about the subject of sex, so I should probably be sensitive around Vanessa. Just in case.

"Though if you want to know the truth, usually one of us ends up falling asleep in front of that riveting real estate show *Location, Location, Location*," I admit. Well, I don't want her feeling bad or anything.

"Before Julian and I had the kids, we were at it like rabbits," she replies matter-of-factly.

"You were?" I ask, my voice coming out all high-pitched. I look at her, feeling slightly shocked. Vanessa and I don't really talk about sex. We did a little when we were younger and having flings, but not once we got into real relationships.

"Oh, absolutely. We couldn't keep our hands off each other." She sighs, sinking down onto a kitchen stool and looking wistful. "We were always at it."

I feel a vague beat of both alarm and curiosity.

"Like, how often?" I ask casually.

"Oooh, I don't know—"

If she says three times a week, that's okay. Miles and I have been known to have sex three times a week.

Maybe once.

". . . every day. Sometimes twice. We used to like to get in a quickie before work," she confesses, and then blushes like a naughty schoolgirl at the memory.

Every day? *Sometimes twice?*

I'm sitting here in the kitchen, sipping my tea, and trying to remain all cool and collected but my jaw has pretty much hit the floor. For the last year I've been reassuring myself that all couples in their thirties are like Miles and I, having grown-up, comfortable sex in bed, on a Saturday night, with the odd scented candle and some massage oil. If I've remembered to go pick one up at the pharmacy along with the toilet paper.

But now this discovery that my best friend, i.e., *other people my age*, were "getting in quickies" and on a daily basis, at least before their kids came along, is a tad worrying. Especially since recently I've been consoling myself that it doesn't matter if Miles and I don't have this incredibly passionate sex life, because once you're married, you stop having sex anyway.

"Well, you know, it's like they say. It's quality, not quantity," I say hurriedly. "And Miles and I have really good quality sex."

As I say that, I realize I'm sounding a little defensive.

"Well, I'm glad someone is," she quips, pulling out a stash of coloring books and felt-tip pens for Ruby, while bouncing Sam on her hip.

"Do you want me to do anything—" I stand up.

"No, no, I'm fine." She smiles, stuffing loose strands of hair into her ponytail. For the first time I notice she's got roots, which is so not Vanessa. She's the kind of person who was getting them touched up the day before she gave birth, despite all those warnings about dying your hair when you're pregnant. "Nonsense," she pooh-poohed. "I didn't see Gwen Stefani with regrowth." Which I was kind of impressed with—I didn't know Vanessa even *knew* who Gwen Stefani was.

"What about another cup of tea?" I offer.

"Actually, I might have a glass of Pinot Grigio and sit in the garden," she says conspiratorially. "Fancy one?"

About to say yes, I suddenly remember I have to go back to the office before I can go home, and change my mind. Maybe alcohol isn't a good idea. Plus I'm driving. "Better not." I shake my head. "I've been drinking a bit too much wine lately. In fact, I might go on this detox my client Melody keeps recommending."

"Another one?" Vanessa looks at me, aghast. "But you just did one."

"That was so long ago," I refute hotly.

"It was last month. I remember because you came over for dinner but refused to eat anything."

"Oh, right, yes. That was the Lemonade Diet," I say, remembering.

"Is there a Coca-Cola Diet?" she quips drily.

"It's not that kind of lemonade," I retort, but I can't help smiling. "It's this special liquid made of maple syrup and freshly squeezed lemons. Melody kept raving about it, and it's in her new book, so I thought I should try it. And anyway," I add, "that was a cleanse."

Vanessa pulls a face. "And there's a *difference?*" Glancing at the empty wine rack she pads over to the fridge.

"A big difference." I nod. "A detox is cutting all the things that are bad for you out of your diet. Like, for example, wine and coffee and sugar—"

Tugging open the door of her huge stainless steel fridge, Vanessa pulls a face.

"And a cleanse means not eating at all. Though usually you supplement with juices," I add as an afterthought. "Though, not orange juice obviously. That's full of sugar, but you can do all green vegetables, like celery, and maybe some broccoli, and aubergine, actually no, that's purple . . ."

"Sounds yummy," she says sarcastically. Tugging out an opened bottle of white, she pulls out the cork and empties the contents into a wineglass. "Though I think I'll stick with grapes for now. They're green."

A few drops trickle out and she shakes her head. "Damn. That was the last bottle."

"I can step out for you if you'd like," I offer.

The door bangs, and I hear footsteps approaching in the hallway. George, the cocker spaniel, who's spent the whole time asleep in his basket, suddenly starts wagging his tail.

"I have a better idea. Why don't we both pop out?" she suggests.

"But what about the—"

I'm about to say "children," but there's screams of "Daddy" and Julian walks into the kitchen. Tall and handsome with thick curly dark hair and carrying a briefcase, he walks straight over to their chair and high chair and scoops them both up, much to their delight.

"Why, hello, you terrible twosome!" he whoops, smothering them in kisses and blowing raspberries into their bellies.

I watch fondly. Julian is so good with them, I think, and then I catch Vanessa's face and instead of a glowing smile at this contented picture of a happy family, she's got a pinched expression.

"You're home early."

Julian stops blowing raspberries to look up at Vanessa. It's almost the first time he seems to have noticed she's there.

"I'm afraid I'm not staying. I just popped back for a fresh shirt. I've got to have dinner with a client. Totally last minute." He pulls an apologetic face.

"Well, in that case, I'm going out for a few minutes," replies Vanessa.

"Out?" He frowns.

"Yes, Charlotte and I are going for a drink," she says, gathering up her handbag from the countertop.

"We are?" I say in surprise.

Still holding a child in each arm, he turns around and sees me sitting on a kitchen stool. I wave weakly, suddenly feeling like I'm in the middle of a domestic argument and wishing I wasn't.

"Oh, hi, Charlotte," he says, a little awkwardly. "I didn't see you there."

"Hi, Julian." I smile. "How's work?"

Julian is a big-shot lawyer and is always working on some case involving millions of pounds and high-profile clients. In fact, a couple of weeks ago I was on the elliptical machine at the gym and I saw him on one of the TV screens, being interviewed on the evening news.

"Pretty hectic; we're in court at the moment and the jury—"

Before he can finish, he's interrupted by Vanessa. "Ready, Charlotte?" She throws me a look. I have feeling it's more a command than a question.

"Vee, please, I've only just walked in," he says tersely. "I've got to leave again in half an hour."

"I won't be long," she says.

"Can't I just have a few minutes to unwind a little?"

That's it. She pounces on him. "*You* want to unwind a little. What about me? Do you never think I want to unwind a little . . ."

Sliding off my bar stool I start backing out of the kitchen.

"What am I? An unpaid babysitter?"

Julian's face sets sharp. He looks as if he's about to say something, but then reconsiders. "Okay, fine, go ahead." He sighs, and turns back to bouncing Sam and Ruby on each arm. "Right, who wants to watch SpongeBob?"

There are squeals of excitement as Vanessa throws him a scowl, before marching ahead of me out of the kitchen and through the front door.

## Chapter Eight

*SpongeBob* bloody *SquarePants!*" she grumbles under her breath. "Can you believe it?"

Outside she turns to me for support and I grapple for the correct reaction. Not easy, considering I have no idea what she's talking about.

"Can you bloody *believe* it!" she insists, her face tight with annoyance. Vanessa can look impressively scary when she gets mad. She gets this big crease down the middle of her forehead and her nostrils flare.

On second thought, perhaps I don't actually need to know what she's talking about. I just need to agree with her.

"Um, *no* . . . definitely not!" I say loyally, and then for good measure throw in a "SquareBob indeed!" Complete with a loud tut. See, I can do the loyal best friend thing. I don't even need to know what she's talking about.

"You mean SpongeBob," she corrects, glancing sharply across at me.

Shit.

"Yes . . . of course . . . that's exactly what I mean," I say hastily, trying to brazen it out, but I needn't have worried—she's not even listening.

"He knows I don't like them watching too much TV. The odd half an hour is fine, I mean, I'm not one of those women who won't let their children near a television till they're going to university . . ."

Instead she's ranting as she marches ahead down the street, bag bouncing on her shoulder, arms swinging by her side. I scurry alongside of her. Vanessa is six feet tall in bare feet and she takes giant strides. I can barely keep up.

". . . but it's not fair, I never get any time by myself. Okay, I know I agreed to stop working and be a stay-at-home mum, but it would be nice if he could take both of them to the park sometime. Give me a bit of me time. You know he's never looked after the both of them together? Sam is nearly thirteen months old . . ."

"So! Is there a place to get drink nearby?" I interject brightly.

Vanessa stops ranting momentarily and pulls a face. "You see, that's the thing. He knows we're not really going for a drink."

"We're not?" I look at her, confused.

"No. I'm not going to leave him to cope with both Ruby *and* Sam. It'll kill him. Well, maybe for ten minutes." She smiles wanly. "There's a minimarket on the corner. I'll get a bottle of wine and take it back home."

As we enter the air-conditioned, neon-lit frontage of the market, Vanessa makes a beeline for the wine cabinet and swiftly picks out a bottle of Pinot Grigio. I get the feeling this is not the first time she's made one of these wine runs. There's no meandering up and down aisles looking for the wine section, minutes spent looking at all the different varieties before making a choice. It's a professional, quick in-and-out job, and now we're at the cash register and she's pulling out her credit card.

"Oh, and I'll take a couple of these . . ." She plucks two family-size bags of M&M's and throws them down onto the counter.

Uh-oh. This really is not good. Vanessa started Weight Watchers last month and has been doing really well. The last few times I've seen her she's been all about points, points, points.

I look at the bottle of wine and the candy. She must have a whole week's quota in her hands right now.

". . . and a packet of twenty Marlboro Lights."

"I thought you'd given up," I say, trying not to sound like the disapproving, health-conscious, antismoking friend and sounding exactly like the disapproving, health-conscious, antismoking friend.

"So did I," she says grimly, signing her credit card slip and snatching her bags off the assistant, who looks rather terrified at the sight of an angry, six-foot-tall, wild-eyed woman who's already lighting up a cigarette despite the large No Smoking signs.

Perhaps this is not the time to give her a lecture on the dangers of smoking.

Instead as we're walking through the automatic doors and onto the sidewalk I'm wracking my brains for something to say. Something light. Something to distract her, like for example, "Look at that lovely painting."

As we start heading back to her house I pause in front of an antique store. In the window is a large oil-covered canvas.

Vanessa puffs agitatedly on her cigarette. "What, the one of a bullfighter goring the bull to death?" she says, puzzled. "You think that's lovely?"

Oh shit. I hadn't even looked to see what it was.

Now I look closer I see his large red cape flung wide, the swords in the bull's back, blood gushing from its neck. Ugh. It's horrible.

"But you're a vegetarian. I thought you'd hate it."

"I do hate it," I say hastily, shuddering with disgust. "But it's got some . . . um . . . interesting use of brushstroke . . ."

"It has?" she asks doubtfully. "Where?"

Oh fuck. Me and my big mouth.

"Um . . . yes, look here . . ." I step right up to the window and peer through the glass. Vanessa joins me. ". . . in the corner . . ." I gesture vaguely. "See? Okay, let's go now." I link my arm through hers and turn to lead her away, but she holds firm.

"Where? I can't see," she grumbles.

You know when you've started something you wish you hadn't?

"Over there," I say breezily, and then tug a little harder. But she's unbudgeable.

"I really can't see what you're talking about," she snaps, being all passive-aggressive.

"Oh, well, never mind, let's go," I cajole, noticing a couple of figures inside, standing in the shadows. One of them is an old man with white hair and a tweed jacket. Probably the owner, I think distractedly, as he picks up something and shows it to the *bartender from the pub*?

"Oh God, not him," I groan out loud.

"Who?" pounces Vanessa. I swear she has the reflexes of a cat.

"No one," I mutter, putting my head down and quickly turning away from the window.

"Where? Inside the shop?"

Vanessa is one of those people who if you say "don't look now," she'll look. And she'll make it sooo obvious she's looking.

"Oooh, *him*?" she exclaims, practically pressing her nose against the glass.

Shit, he's going to see me. He's going to turn around any moment and see my friend pressed up against the glass like one of those stuffed Garfields you see suckered to car windows. And me standing next to her like a complete moron.

He looks over. And sees me standing there like a complete moron. Fuck.

As our eyes lock, I feel a jolt of embarrassment.

"Oooh, he's nice looking," she's now cooing approvingly. And loudly.

*"Nessy!"* I hiss. Hastily pulling my eyes away I scoot a few stores

down along the sidewalk, out of his view. My heart is thumping. God, what's gotten into me?

"What?" she says innocently. Reluctantly, she gives one last look before following me. "So, come on, who is he?" she asks, catching up.

"Oh, no one, just some bartender I met the other night who was truly annoying."

"Are you sure? He looked kind of familiar. Actually I think he's the husband of one of the women at Ruby's playschool . . ."

"Really?" Unexpectedly, I feel a tiny wave of dismay. Which is ridiculous. Like I care if he's married or not.

"Umm, maybe not." She shrugs. "Oh, I don't know. I don't know anything anymore . . ."

She looks really sad, and I give her arm a squeeze. "Vanessa, are you okay?"

"Not really." She shakes her head. "I think Julian is having an affair with his secretary."

Boom. Out of the blue. Just like that. I glance across her, sharply, almost expecting it to be one of her black-humored jokes, but she's straight-faced. So *that's* what this is all about.

"No way," I say, leaping to his defense. "Julian would never do that."

"He's been working late at the office for months, and then one day I just happened to pop in to see him and I saw them together."

"Together doing what?" I demand.

"Nothing that would incriminate them in a court of law but . . ." Her voice trails off and she sucks hard on her cigarette. "It was their body language. I could just tell."

"You're imagining it," I say, shaking my head resolutely. "You're tired with the kids. He's working late. Your imagination is just running a little wild."

She looks at me doubtfully. "You think so?"

"Absolutely." I nod vigorously.

Reaching her house, we walk down the driveway and she plops herself on the wall. Hidden from the house behind Julian's Range Rover, she stubs out her cigarette and immediately lights up another. "I don't know . . . I'm sure I saw something . . ."

"I promise you, you're imagining it," I say, sitting down next to her. "Look, if it's any consolation I was at the traffic lights yesterday morning and for a moment I thought I saw myself in another car," I confess.

"God, at least I'm not that bad," she says, making a face.

"Well, obviously I didn't *really* think it was me," I add quickly. "I'm not *that* crazy, but even so it was very freaky. She looked just like I did when I was twenty-one."

"Twenty-one," sighs Vanessa wistfully. Blowing smoke out of her nostrils she stares into the middle distance. "If only I knew then what I know now."

"Like what?" I ask curiously.

"Like, smoking isn't cool, so don't start." She smiles ruefully. "Because in ten years' time you're going to find it hell to give up."

She lets the smoke exhale through her nostrils.

"And have as many lie-ins as you can manage, because once you have kids you'll never have another one. Oh, and wear miniskirts."

She says this totally seriously and I look at her in surprise. In my whole life I have only ever seen Vanessa in black trousers.

"But you've never worn miniskirts," I say.

"Exactly," she replies. "But I should have. I always thought my legs were too fat but I look at old photos of me and I was so skinny."

"So wear a miniskirt now."

"Are you kidding?" She laughs, staring dolefully down at her legs. "I'm too old and fat."

"Don't be silly, you look amazing."

"I need to lose at least twenty pounds." Finishing the cigarette she opens up the M&M's and pops one into her mouth. "I've got my weigh-in tomorrow, and I haven't even lost a single pound."

She looks so miserable there's absolutely no way I can tell her to put down the M&M's and back away.

"Maybe I should go on that Lemonade Diet you were talking about." She prods at her stomach as if it's a strange object that really shouldn't be there. "What can you eat on it?"

"You don't eat."

She looks at me agape, her hand moving on autopilot from packet to mouth, without taking her eyes off me.

"You just drink the lemonade . . ."

"For how long?"

"Umm, I think I did it for five days."

"Jesus, Charlotte!" she gasps.

"But I was a slacker and gave up halfway through. You're supposed to do it for ten."

"Ten days," she squawks. "Ten days!"

"According to Melody, my client, you can lose ten pounds."

She stops squawking. "Right, that's it," she declares, galvanized. "Sod counting points. Where do I sign up?"

I look at her uncertainly. Vanessa? *On a cleanse?* "Are you sure . . ." I say doubtfully. "You won't be able to drink alcohol . . ."

"I know, I know," she snaps impatiently, shoving the bottle of wine on the floor. "Is that it?"

"Well . . ." I hesitate, wondering how I can put it. "There are a few side effects."

"You mean, apart from being thin?" she dismisses.

"Well, yes . . ." I look at Vanessa, wondering how I can tell her. Even though we're old friends, I'm not sure how to put it. "*Unpleasant* side effects."

"Such as?" she demands.

I pause. Oh, what the hell. It's best she knows.

"Sharting."

There. I've said it.

"Excuse me?" Vanessa crinkles up her brow.

"It's the saltwater enema, you see, that you have to do in *addition* to drinking the lemonade," I begin, quickly explaining, but she interrupts.

"Charlotte, what on earth's sharting?"

"It's when you think you're going to . . ." I lower my voice. "Fart," I whisper tentatively.

"That's it?" She rolls her eyes.

"Well, no, instead, you actually . . ." I trail off. "You know."

"No, I don't know, you're not making any sense," she snaps impatiently.

"It's the two words joined together—" I wince. Oh God, this is hard. "Farting and—"

"Shit!" she says in horror, suddenly getting it.

Her jaw drops open and she clamps her hand over her mouth, and just when I think she's going to launch into a disapproving diatribe, she explodes into hysterical laughter.

"Oh God!! That is *so* funny!" she gasps between giggles. "*Sharting* . . ." Shoulders shaking, she's rocking backward and forward on the garden wall, letting out loud snorts. "That's the old Lottie I know and love! Coming out with something like that! It's the funniest thing I think I've ever heard!"

My laughter subsides. "What do you mean, the old Lottie?"

"Well, you know, you're a lot more sensible now, you don't say things like that anymore. Unfortunately," she adds, cracking up again.

I feel a twinge of discomfort. I'm not sure that I like that.

"Vanessa? Is that you?" Julian's voice calls from inside.

Immediately she stifles her giggles. "I should go," she says reluctantly, standing up and hiding her contraband goodies in her handbag.

"Yeah, me too." I nod, glancing at my watch. "I need to pop back to the office before I go home."

She gazes at me for a long moment. "We should do this more often."

"Definitely." I nod in agreement. "How about two weeks on Thursday?" I say, checking my BlackBerry.

Vanessa rolls her eyes. "Are you serious?"

"It's my first free night," I say defensively.

"What about your birthday?" she gasps.

Suddenly I remember. "God, I'd totally forgotten about that," I confess.

"Well, it's this Friday," reminds Vanessa, shaking her head. "Don't tell me you were planning to work?"

"No, of course not!" I try to look affronted, but it's a bit hard, considering I spent last year's at a conference center near Heathrow Airport. "I haven't planned anything."

"Honestly, Charlotte!" she gasps. "What happened to the girl who used to love to party?"

"She grew up." I try to smile.

"Well, the four of us will go out for dinner then," she announces, ignoring me. "You and Miles, and Julian and me. I'll get a babysitter. We can go to that gastropub you were telling me about." Smiling triumphantly, she gives me a hug. "Sorted."

"You make me laugh." I smile, hugging her back. In the whole time I've known her, I don't think Vanessa has ever taken no for an answer.

"You make *me* laugh," she retorts, as if I've just insulted her. "I haven't laughed that hard in ages. I nearly peed myself!"

I laugh and, waving good-bye, cross the street to my car and climb inside.

"Oh—and that's another thing I wish I'd known when I was twenty-one—" Standing on her front steps, she calls after me.

"What?" I ask, buzzing down my window.

She grins ruefully. "Start doing your pelvic floor exercises *now*!"

## Chapter Nine

S queeze and hold. Squeeze and—

Damn, they're really tricky, aren't they?

Forty-five minutes later, I've popped back to the office to pick up some files, and am now sitting in traffic on the way home, busily practicing my pelvic floor exercises. To tell the truth, I've never done them before. Of course I've *heard* of them, but sort of vaguely, like when I was flicking through one of the "older women's" magazines in the doctor's waiting room—you know, the ones that have ads for StairMaster and articles about how to reupholster furniture—and saw an ad for the Kegelmaster 2000. I remember because I thought it sounded a bit like the broomstick in Harry Potter, but instead it was a sort of dumbbell for *down there*.

Anyhow, I always assumed they were something you didn't have to worry about until you were of the age when you start shopping for hormone replacement drugs. In fact, to tell the truth, I'm not even sure how to even *do* one.

But after Vanessa's earlier near-miss I need to learn, I tell myself, feeling a little panicked at the thought of myself in adult diapers. As the thought flashes across my brain I squeeze hard and hold in a rictus of terror.

*And fast.*

Holding my squeeze I shift into first gear as the line of cars in front of me starts moving again. The traffic is still nightmarish due to the construction. It's going to be like this until next week, I muse, glancing at the large yellow Diversion signs. It's going to take forever to get home. Still, it means I've got plenty of time to do my Kegels. In fact, I've done a hundred already, I think proudly.

Though I can't really tell if I'm getting the right muscles. In fact, to be honest, I feel as if I'm just clenching my buttocks. I fidget in my seat as I approach the lights. Okay, let's try again. This time I'll count to five.

Concentrating hard, I try to focus in on *those bits* and squeeze hard.

*One, two, three, four—*

I'm interrupted by the shrill ring of my phone. I pick up.

"Hello, sweetheart," says an unmistakably rumbly voice.

It's my dad.

Abruptly I stop squeezing.

"Oh . . . um, hi," I gasp, feeling a flash of embarrassment at being caught doing my pelvic floor exercises by my father. Which is ridiculous. I mean, it's not as if he just caught me having sex—

Okay, scrap that image. That does not make me feel any better.

"I'm just calling to say thanks for the lovely flowers. They came yesterday afternoon."

"Oh, good." I smile.

"But you shouldn't have gone to any trouble."

"Don't be silly, it wasn't any trouble," I reply. And it's true, it wasn't. I just called up and gave them my credit card details, I reflect, feeling a twinge of guilt as I think of all the time and effort Dad's made for me over the years. "I'm just glad you liked them . . ."

In my peripheral vision I see a flash of orange and I'm suddenly reminded. "Hey, Dad, do you remember that old Beetle I used to drive?" I say, glancing quickly sideways. I can't see it. It must have already driven past, I decide, looking at the line of traffic streaming through the lights.

"God, we're going back years now. . . ."

"Nineteen ninety-seven," I say automatically.

"Aye, that's right. Good grief, you've got a good memory." He chuckles, sounding impressed. "Mine's like a sieve these days."

"Well, can you remember who you sold it to?"

"Now, that I *do* remember—"

I wait expectantly, my mind running through people I know in the village who he might have sold my old car to. Not that I've spent much time there in years, but for the life of me I can't remember anyone else having long dark curly hair. Actually, what about the girl that works in the fish shop? I suddenly remember. Actually no, that was more of a shoulder-length perm. Plus, if she's working behind the counter battering cod, what on earth is she doing driving around West London . . .

"We had it scrapped."

Startled by his reply, I'm momentarily blown off course.

"But I've seen it in London," I reply, quickly recovering.

"You can't have. It failed inspection so I sold it to a scrap merchant. I remember."

"I thought your memory was like a sieve," I remind him teasingly.

"I might have a bad memory, but senile I'm not," he grumbles. "I towed it there myself."

"Well, somebody must have fixed it up," I reply stubbornly.

"I saw it being crushed with my own two eyes."

He's so adamant that for a moment I almost cave.

"That's impossible," I argue.

"What's impossible is you seeing it around London . . ."

This has turned into another one of our arguments. Dad's wrong. And as usual he won't admit it.

"Dad, you're *wrong*."

"No, I'm not. *You're* wrong."

Ugh! I feel a familiar burst of impatience. This always happens. We go back and forth for hours and nobody ever wins, unless—

Suddenly I get a flash of inspiration. This time I'm going to prove I'm right. Slamming my foot on the accelerator I pull down sharply on the steering wheel and do a U-turn in the middle of the road.

*I'm going to follow it.*

". . . It's probably been made into tin cans by now," my dad is chuckling down the phone.

Damn. Where did it go? My vision is blocked by a large truck in front of me—then I glimpse it. Just ahead of me. A flash of orange turning down a side street. Trapped behind the truck I edge slowly forward until finally—

Signaling left, I pull off and shoot down a leafy, narrow street in hot pursuit. Just in time to see the taillights disappearing around a corner which leads under a railway bridge. Cursing under my breath, I race after it. It's a blind corner and as I zoom through the underpass I pop out onto a main road.

And there's the Beetle. Waiting at the pedestrian crossing. I pull out and up behind it. Now I can see the number plate as clear as day.

"See, Dad, you're wrong," I say jubilantly. "MUG 403P. That's my old plate!"

Ha-ha! Dad is going to have to eat his words!

Only there's silence on the other end of the line.

*"Dad?"* Frowning, I glance at the screen of my phone; there's no reception. How annoying!

Making a mental note to call T-Mobile and complain, I stuff it in the center consol and switch my attention back to the Beetle, which has pulled away from the crossing. For a moment I entertain turning around, going back the way I came. After all, I've seen the license plate now. It has to be my old car. There's no other explanation.

Then again, I have come this far. And I am kind of curious to find out who's driving . . .

Plus if I'm going to win this argument with Dad, I'm going to need hard evidence and I've got a camera on my phone.

A few minutes later we're zipping down leafy streets in Camden,

North London. What is now quite an expensive neighborhood of London was my neighborhood when I first moved here. Back when you could rent a room for fifty pounds a week, I shared a rambling terrace house with six roommates on a little dead-end street, tucked away behind the back of a church.

In fact this is exactly the same route I used to drive home, I realize as the Beetle suddenly hangs a left at a mini-roundabout with no turn signal. Jesus. Whoever she is, she's a terrible driver. She doesn't use her indicator at all. Or slow down over speed bumps, I curse silently, as she shoots off ahead of me and I take them slowly. Honestly! If she's not careful she's going to ruin the suspension on that car.

We turn a corner and I suddenly see the turning for my old street up ahead. It's like a blast from the past: *Kilmaine Terrace*. Wow, it's been years since I've been down here, I think, my mind flicking back to when I used to live there. There's never been a reason to. After all, it's a dead-end street, I muse, my attention switching back to the Beetle, which is still zipping ahead, until suddenly and without warning it slams on its brakes.

God, wouldn't it be funny if—

And swerves right into Kilmaine Terrace.

My stomach spasms.

You have got to be kidding.

As I watch the car disappearing down the street I feel a bit stunned. Talk about a coincidence. Flipping my turn signal on, I follow. The street looks exactly the same.

Large white terrace houses, several blossoming trees . . . my eyes dart forward . . . I used to live at number 39, overlooking the little square right at the end. I hang back as the Beetle zips toward it, the noise of its exhaust reverberating on the quiet street. It doesn't show any signs of slowing down.

*Don't stop outside number 39.*

A voice suddenly pops into my head.

*Any other house. Just not number 39. That would be just too freaky. Too weird. Too much of a coincidence . . .*

*Screech.*

The red brake lights snap on.

Right outside number 39.

I feel the hairs rise on the back of my neck. I take a breath. Then again, I reason, you do hear of bizarre coincidences. I once read an article about a woman who had three sets of triplets. And all three sets shared the same birthday. I mean, what are the odds of that happening? And yet it happened. This is exactly the same, I tell myself firmly. Well, sort of.

Hurriedly I pull into a space a few cars down, turn off the engine, and squint across the street. Damn, I'm too far away. I hesitate. Oh, what the hell, in for a penny, in for a pound. Grabbing my tote bag, I shove on my sunglasses and without even glancing in the Beetle's direction I briskly walk the few hundred yards to the little square at the end.

It hasn't changed a bit. Same patch of lawn, same flower beds, same little bench in the middle. I sit down and pull out my book, *Finding Yourself Made Easy*, and pretend to start reading, feeling a slight thrill. This is like being one of those TV detectives you see who are going deep undercover!

Either that, or I'm some sort of stalker.

Suddenly the sheer of absurdity of my situation hits me. *Charlotte, you're going to get yourself freaking arrested! What on earth do you think you're doing? Sitting here, spying on some innocent girl trying to parallel park and making a complete mess of it. Seesawing in and out of the space, banging bumpers with the cars on either side with reckless abandon . . . having a conversation with yourself . . .*

I look back into the car. Honestly, she's the worst parker I've ever seen.

*Just like you used to be, remember?*

Out of nowhere, I remember the time I tried backing into a space outside the local bar and somehow mounted the curb, sending customers scattering and drinks spilling. My parking used to be a family joke. I once curbed every wheel on my father's new Volvo, and I've lost count of the numbers of dings and scratches I put on cars over the years. Thankfully I've got better as I've got older, but when I was twenty-one I was terrible. I was used to driving on the right in the States, but when I moved here I had to learn how to drive on the left. Which was hard enough, but parking was even harder. In fact when I lived down this street I once backed up into a—

I hear the crunching of metal.

—*lamppost.*

Okay, triplets, Charlotte. Remember the triplets.

The engine cuts out and a door swings open. Loud music wafts out into the silent street: *Be Here Now* by Oasis. I feel a rush of nostalgia. Wow, I used to love that album.

*When I was twenty-one.*

My hearts start pounding.

Suddenly the stereo is turned off and a tanned leg appears, then another, revealing the shortest denim miniskirt you've ever seen, followed by a low-cut vest showing off a generous amount of cleavage. *God, what a hooker,* instantly flashes through my mind. Her hair is hanging in a dark, curly sheet over the side of her face and as she gets out of the car, she turns away from me and walks around to the back of the Beetle. "Fuck," she curses loudly, as she sees at her crumpled bumper. "Fucking bastard lamppost."

*And crass too,* I decide with disdain.

And to even *think* for a moment there I thought she somehow bore some resemblance to me. I mean. As if!

Feeling somewhat ridiculous, I stuff my book into my bag and stand up. I've seen enough. Okay, so she's driving my old car and living in my old street, so what?

She turns.

And I freeze. It's like someone just dropped a ten-ton weight on my stomach.

That can't be.

That can't possibly be—

As I see her face up close my mind goes into free fall. I'd assumed it was a trick of the light, a combination of not enough sleep and too much stress. But now . . .

Steadying myself on the railing I squeeze my eyes shut. My mind feels like that symbol on my iBook that whirls around and around when I've opened too many programs and my computer's overloaded, about to crash at any minute. Because this isn't a case of mistaken identity, a look-alike, a stranger who looks like I did when I was twenty-one. *I know her.* All five-foot-six, mini-skirted, scrunch-dried, black-eyelinered, suntanned, twenty-one-year-old bit of her.

I snap my eyes wide open.

*It's me.*

&

Suddenly I realize I'm clammy with fear. I have no idea what's going on here. And it's scaring the living hell out of me. This cannot be real. This can't *actually* be happening. I know that. With every single inch of my rational, sensible, thirty-one-year-old self. I know there is only one of me. That's an absolute. A truth that not even Dad could argue against.

Which means if it's not real, I'm seeing things. I'm hallucinating. *I'm losing my mind.*

As the door to number 39 slams shut and she disappears inside I snap to. Snatching up my bag, I set off down the street in a canter, my heels clattering against the pavement as I hurry toward my car. Okay, Charlotte, just calm down. You're going to go home, take a Xanax, and go to bed. Sleep this thing off. Maybe tomorrow even take the morning off work, get some rest—

Shit.

I've got another parking ticket! Reaching my car I see a familiar plastic envelope slapped on my windscreen. Fantastic. Snatching it up from under the wiper, I glare at it in annoyance. That's just ridiculous. I've only been gone five minutes. Ripping it open I scan the details.

> Car/Make Model: VW Beetle
> Offense: Parking in a controlled permit area
> Time: 6:28 p.m.
> Date: 21 August 1997

What? My heart pounds as I stare at it, the figures swimming before my eyes: 1997, 1997, 1997 . . .

My hands are shaking. No, that just can't be, that just can't be—

Panicked, I drop the ticket. And as it falls, fluttering to the pavement, I jump into my car, fire up the engine, and screech away from the curb. I need to get the hell out of here.

And fast.

# Chapter Ten

H i, Beatrice, it's me, Charlotte. I'm calling in sick."

"Oh my gosh, you poor darling. What's wrong?"

"I think I have a brain tumor."

"Sshhhh!" I hear a loud hiss and I glance across the waiting room to see the receptionist glaring in my direction through a potted fern. "Can't you read the sign? No mobile phones allowed in the doctor's surgery."

It's the next morning and I'm sitting on a hard plastic chair, surrounded by dog-eared magazines and lots of sick people, waiting to see my GP. Last night I got home, took a Xanax, and must have immediately crashed out, as I don't remember anything until six o'clock this morning when I woke up fully clothed on my bed feeling slightly groggy. For like a second, until—*boom*—what happened yesterday came rushing back to me and suddenly I was wide awake.

And worrying.

People always advise you to sleep on things, the theory being you're going to wake up miraculously clearheaded and full of answers. But I had slept on it. And I still didn't have answers. Just more questions whirling around and around in my head. So I did the only thing I could do: I canceled my morning training session.

And started Googling . . .

"Hallucinations" threw up 936,000 results. All of them terrifying.

If one website wasn't talking about serious mental illness, the other one was diagnosing brain tumors and showing all these horrifying pictures of a woman having the top of her head cut off. But that wasn't all. There were all these warnings about headaches and fatigue and irrational behavior.

Such as turning from a sane, professional thirtysomething into a crazy stalker.

Well, something like that anyway. To tell the truth I can't remember exactly, as I was in a sort of mouse-clicking frenzy—going from one link to another, reading one terrifying personal blog after another—until, convinced I had all the symptoms, I raced to the doctor's office, pleading to be seen without an appointment and explaining it was a life-threatening emergency.

That was forty-five minutes ago, I think agitatedly, checking my watch for the umpteenth time.

"A brain tumor!" Beatrice is exclaiming down the phone. "Oh my Lord, are you at the hospital?"

"Not yet," I whisper, trying to hide my phone in the collar of my jacket, away from the eagle-eyed receptionist. "I'm at the doctor's. But I'm sure he'll want to send me there for tests." As I say the word "tests" a bolt of panic rips through me and I have to fight to steady my nerves.

"That's what they did for my cousin Freddy," she says darkly.

"They did?" I feel myself grip the phone tighter.

"Oh, yes, it was the oddest thing; one day he banged his head and the next he started having all these weird smells. It was really quite alarming. Everywhere he went he thought he could smell chocolate, which sounds rather lovely in *theory*, but poor Freddy was quite frantic as he hates chocolate. In fact he doesn't have a sweet tooth at all, he's much more a cheese and biscuits type of person . . ."

"Miss Merryweather?" I look up sharply to see the receptionist staring at me with a sour expression. "The doctor is ready for you."

"Oh, wonderful, thank you—"

"Unless you'd prefer to continue your conversation outside."

Wedged underneath my ear I can still hear Beatrice chattering away.

". . . so you can tell he's obviously not from my side of the family, as you know me, I can never say no to a pudding . . ."

"Beatrice, I have to go," I hiss, and snapping my phone shut I smile gratefully at the receptionist as I hurry toward the doctor's consulting room.

"Come in."

As I push open the door I see Dr. Evans, my doctor, sitting in his black swivel chair behind a leather-topped desk. A grave-faced man with a white wispy comb-over and tortoiseshell glasses, he's jotting something down on his clipboard as I enter.

"Please, sit down." He gestures, looking up with an avuncular smile. Which sort of freezes when he sees it's me.

"Ah, Miss Merryweather," he says evenly. Putting down his pen he steeples his fingers together. "How nice to see you again."

Sitting down I smile shakily.

"And so soon," he adds brightly, reaching for my records, which are lying on his desk in a large blue folder. Opening it up, he begins flicking through. Admittedly the file is rather thick, bulging in fact, but like I always say, it's better to be safe than sorry. "So how is the rash?" he asks, referring to my visit last week.

"Oh, fine," I say quickly. "You were right. It was just my eczema flaring up again."

"And the 'sharp pain in the left ribs,'" he continues, reading from his notes.

I feel a flash of embarrassment. That was the week before. I went to a yoga class and in the middle of this really big stretch I felt a sharp pain and thought I'd broken a rib. I swear, it was really painful. In fact, for a moment I thought I might have even punctured a lung and begged Dr. Evans to send me for an X-ray.

"Um . . . actually, it's much better," I reply, tugging at an invisible piece of cotton on my sleeve.

As it turned out I'd just overexerted myself. A hot bath and some Tiger Balm and I was as good as new the next day. But of course I couldn't have known that, could I?

"So," he says evenly. "What seems to be the problem?"

I swallow hard, wondering how to put it, where to start, what to tell him first.

"I think I have a brain tumor."

My words come tumbling out before I can stop them and hearing my worst fear, out loud in the doctor's surgery, makes it suddenly real and I'm scared. Really scared.

Dr. Evans, on the other hand, doesn't flinch.

"I see . . ." Raising his gray tufty eyebrows, he scribbles something down on his pad. I crane my neck to try to see what he's writing, but of course it's indecipherable.

"And what makes you think that?" he asks pleasantly, as if he's discussing the weather.

I take a deep breath as my mind turns back to yesterday. "I've been having these hallucinations," I reply, trying to keep my voice steady.

He continues scribbling. "Can you describe them for me?"

I take a deep breath. "I saw myself at age twenty-one."

There. I've said it.

Only instead of the jaw-dropping, gripping-on-to-the-side-of-the-chair astonishment I'd been expecting, Dr. Evans's face relaxes and he smiles ruefully. "Oh, that happens to us all as we get older," he says blithely.

I look at him in confusion. "It does?"

"Indeed." He nods. "I fool myself into imagining I'm twenty-one again on many occasions, until I look in the mirror." He chuckles, flattening down his wisp of gray hair.

"No, you don't understand," I try again. "This was real," I tell him urgently. "Plus I've been having headaches," I add, clutching at my temples. "Terrible, agonizing headaches."

Well, okay, they're not *that* bad, but you always need to exaggerate a little when you see the doctor.

Dr. Evans glances sharply from his pad and looks at me, suddenly concerned. "So you have to lie in a darkened room?"

*See.*

"Well, no, not exactly—"

"Nausea and vomiting?"

I hesitate. A little bit of exaggeration is one thing. Bare-faced lying is another.

"Actually I'm usually fine after a couple of aspirin—"

His eyes narrow.

"Although sometimes I have to take three," I add hastily.

"Miss Merryweather, I need to ask you some questions."

"Okay." I nod, bracing myself.

"Is there any mental illness in the family?"

"Well, my dad's always saying my mom drives him insane." I smile, despite myself. Which quickly fades at the sight of Dr. Evans's stony face. "But no. Apart from Great-aunt Mary, who had a talking parrot," I add as an afterthought.

"Have you ever suffered a seizure?"

Immediately I have a flashback to last week when I opened my credit card bill, but I'm pretty sure that doesn't count. "No." I shake my head. "Never."

"Memory loss?"

"Well, I forgot my dad's birthday," I confess, glancing down at my hands in my lap that are twisting up a tissue. "But I've been really busy at work, and it just slipped my mind . . ."

Dr. Evans makes a scribble on his pad. "And how many hours do you spend in the office?"

"Um, six, no, eight, no . . ." I try counting up on my fingers. "A lot."

He makes another scribble. "Do you get eight hours of sleep?"

"Does anyone?" I quip wearily. Despite twelve hours of drug-induced sleep I'm still exhausted.

"Do you eat three square meals a day?"

I think about the breakfasts I skip and my lunches that I eat al-desk-o, not alfresco, and usually only have time to pick at. "Well, I wouldn't call them square exactly. . . ."

There's a pause, and then putting down his pen Dr. Evans stands up and reaches for his stethoscope, which he proceeds to press against my chest. He makes a little sound, "Uh-hum," then takes my blood pressure. "Uh-hum." Before taking a small flashlight and shining it into each of my retinas. "Uh-hum." Wordlessly he sits back down behind his desk.

I wait, bracing myself for his diagnosis. "Well, doctor?"

"It's as I thought." He nods.

"It is?" I repeat, my voice wobbling fearfully.

"You're suffering from stress."

"That's it?" I look at him in astonishment. "But I read on the Internet—"

I break off as he shoots me a stern look.

"Stress is a very serious complaint," he says gravely. "My advice to you would be to get more rest, try to relax, start eating a healthy diet, and cut down on caffeine, alcohol . . ." Closing my file, he stands up. "Oh, and one other thing."

"Yes?" I ask, all ears.

"Do you know what cyberchondria is?"

I feel a clutch of panic. "No, but is it dangerous?" I ask fearfully. Shit, what if I've got that?

"It's when someone self-diagnoses themselves from the Internet," he says, raising an eyebrow and shooting me a look.

I feel my cheeks flush hotly. "Oh, I see . . ."

"Stay off the Internet and I think you'll find your health will improve tremendously," he continues, fixing me with a beady eye. And opening the door, he holds out his hand. "Good day, Miss Merryweather."

❧

By the time I reach the office it's nearly lunchtime. Having raced around to the doctor's still wearing yesterday's clothes, I go home to shower and change before driving to work. Thankfully this time the journey is pretty uneventful. No weird sightings of Beetles. No hallucinations. No inexplicable events.

In fact, as I pull into the little mews where our office is tucked away, and walk across the cobblestones, I'm starting to think that maybe my doctor is right. Maybe I am just stressed. After all, stress can do weird things to you. I know, because I've read about it in my self-help books, cases where people have lost their minds because of stress. Who one day are living these perfectly normal lives and then next day—*boom*—they're found wandering around naked on a pier in Brighton, talking about aliens.

*But bumping into yourself? Aged twenty-one?* I mean, honestly. How ridiculous.

So that's it. I've decided. No more Googling. No more getting carried away. And no more ridiculous thoughts about my twenty-one-year-old self. Reaching the door to the office, I push it open. From now on I'm going to really try to relax and take it easy. Doctor's orders.

"Oh my gosh, thank goodness you're alive!"

As I enter Beatrice scrambles from her chair and rushes over.

"I was so worried . . . I haven't been able to stop thinking about you . . . and poor cousin Freddy. Because of course it dragged it all back up again, you know. The hospital visits, the tests, the alarming smells—" She clutches her pearls and stares at me, showing the whites of her eyes. "Have you had any strange—" She pauses, and swallows hard. *"Odors?"*

"Actually I'm fine," I say, trying to brush it off. "It was an . . . um . . . misdiagnosis."

"You mean . . . you're not . . ." Involuntary she grasps both my hands in hers, then quickly drops them with embarrassment. "Well, you just sit down and I'll make you a nice cup of coffee," she says, quickly recovering and darting over to the coffee machine.

"Thanks, but I think I might skip coffee this morning and just have some water. Oh, and do we have anything to eat?"

Beatrice looks taken aback. "Are you sure you're okay?"

"Yes, fine." I smile gratefully. Shrugging off my jacket, I sit down at my desk and flick on the computer.

"So what did the doctor say, exactly?" She starts busying herself in the small kitchen in the corner of the office.

"Oh, you know . . ." I say vaguely, opening my in-box. My heart sinks. I have fifty-seven unread e-mails. "I just need to take it easy."

"Well, all we have scheduled for this afternoon is the launch party for Exhale, that new spa around the corner. I spoke with the manager earlier and they might be interested in some PR." She smiles conspiratorially. "Plus, I'm sure there'll be lots of yummy canapés and champagne. That's what you need, a glass of champers," she advises sagely. "That always makes me feel heaps better."

"Bea, I'm not sure if I should be drinking alcohol—"

"Nonsense. Best medicine ever, Mummy always says." She passes me a bottle of Evian and a bran muffin.

"Thanks." I nod and turn back to my in-box. Sipping my water I start reading an e-mail from a magazine editor about some press for one of our clients.

"Everything fine?"

I glance up to see Beatrice still hovering around my desk.

"Yes, fine. Thanks." I smile.

"Super." She smiles back and begins fiddling with the photo frames on my desk. "So," she says, trying to sound casual and failing horribly, "is there anything else you want to tell me?"

"Um . . . no, I think that's everything," I say, shaking my head and turning back to my e-mail.

She doesn't budge.

"About what happened yesterday," she says pointedly.

Apprehension prickles. "Yesterday?" I repeat, a little nervously.

"Your meeting with Larry Goldstein!" she gasps finally, unable to hold her cool any longer.

"Oh, of course . . . right!" I fluster, my mind rapidly changing gears. With everything that's been going on the meeting had totally slipped my mind. Which is ridiculous considering it's been on my mind for weeks.

"I've been on tenterhooks ever since but I didn't *dare* call, and then I didn't hear from you until this morning when you were at the doctor's . . ."

"It went really, really well," I reassure her quickly. "In fact—" I smile, then blurt simply, "We got it."

Her jaw drops. "Oh my gosh that's just . . ." She trails off, words failing her momentarily, before coming alive again. "*Splendid!*" she gushes finally. "Simply splendid!" She beams at me, almost trembling with excitement.

Watching her reaction it suddenly throws my own into contrast. She's absolutely right. It *is* splendid. Though I'd probably choose to describe it as fantastic, I think, bemused by Beatrice's choice of adjective.

"I know, isn't it?" I enthuse, mirroring her excitement.

"Absolutely. It's amazing," she whoops, and then fixes me with a stern look. "I just can't believe you kept this from me," she clucks scoldingly. "When I didn't hear from you . . ." She arches her eyebrows and pouts. "Well, *you can imagine.*"

I swear, Beatrice has this knack of making me feel like a naughty schoolgirl sometimes.

"I know. And I'm sorry," I apologize swiftly. "I did pop back to the office later but you'd already left on an appointment, and then last night I didn't feel well—" I stop myself before I even go there. "And anyway, as you and I both know, until the deal's actually signed and we've made our press announcement . . ."

I'm referring to an incident that happened last year where we thought we'd won a big contract with a hotel chain. Only to discover they'd changed their minds and gone with a rival PR company just as Beatrice was cracking open a vintage bottle of Bollinger she'd had "lying around" at home.

As compared to normal people who have things like coffee cups and loose change lying around.

"Ah, yes, that was rather a waste of good champagne," she concedes, frowning. "Well, we'll keep the champagne on ice this time, shall we?" She smiles cheerfully, before adding, "So when do you want to schedule your next meeting? I'll need to check the diary and make sure you're free . . ."

The diary is our bible. We don't do anything unless it's in the diary. The keeper of which is Beatrice, who takes her job very seriously. Screwing up her forehead she begins jabbing at her keyboard. The calendar opens up on her computer and she peers at it intently. "What day were you thinking? You've got a window at eleven o'clock next Tuesday . . ."

"Actually we need to announce on Tuesday, so we've arranged to meet up on Thursday—"

"Thursday next week? Yes, I think that will be fine if I just juggle a few things . . ." She starts typing.

"No, *this* Thursday. *Tomorrow.*"

She gives a sharp intake of breath.

"Well, it's important to get the ball rolling. We don't have much time."

"Gosh, yes, absolutely." She nods, her face serious. "Well, it's not going to be easy as it's pretty solid, but I'll do it, you can rely on me." She turns back to the keyboard, a look of determination on her face. "Now let me see, you've got a ten a.m. meeting with Trinny from the *Guardian*; at lunchtime you're seeing the house with Miles; in the afternoon you've got meetings with some journalists from *Sainsbury's Magazine*—but if you'd like I can try to arrange that for tomorrow instead—"

"Actually it's tomorrow evening."

*"Evening?"* she repeats, her eyebrows shooting up.

"We're having dinner," I say, trying to sound all casual. "At his hotel."

"Oh." She's nodding, digesting this piece of information. "How very intimate. Though that's probably what they do in Hollywood," she muses.

"Yes, probably," I agree, brushing away my doubts.

Turning back to her keyboard she types: "Thursday. Evening. Dinner with Larry Goldstein. . . . Okay, you're all set." Grabbing her mouse she clicks Save with a flourish. "It's in the diary."

## Chapter Eleven

The rest of the day flies by—returning calls, talking to journalists, dealing with clients, until before I know it, the sunlight outside has turned golden. It's late afternoon and Beatrice and I are leaving the office to walk the few hundred yards to the newly opened spa.

Arriving, we discover the party in full swing, *spa-style*: soft tinkly harplike music is wafting from out of the concealed speaker system, a fountain made from a thousand-year-old Indonesian rock is gently trickling water, and dozens of barefoot staff are flitting around in togas, handing out lotus flowers and offering free treatments.

Casting my eye around the large crowd, I take a draft of ice-cold Moët and savor the sensation of bubbles fizzing on my tongue. I never would have believed it but it seems Beatrice's mother might be right about something. Okay, I wouldn't call it the *best* medicine in the world, and I wouldn't say I'm *heaps* better, but I have to admit, I've only had half a glass and I'm already I'm starting to feel a lot more relaxed about things.

"Canapés?" A waitress walks past with a large silver tray.

"Mmm, yes, please," I murmur. "What are they?"

"Quail eggs with tomato," she proffers brightly, passing me one on a napkin.

About to take a bite, I hesitate. "Are they free-range?"

Well, okay. Not that relaxed.

The waitress's smile fades. "Um . . . I'm not sure . . ."

"Oooh, those look yummy," interrupts Beatrice, helping herself to a couple. She glances at me. "What? You're not eating yours?" she gasps, staring incredulously at my untouched canapé.

"Actually, I'm not that hungry," I fib.

"Well, if you don't want it . . ." As the waitress moves away she swiftly takes it from me. "Mmm, this is a really good party, I have to say." She nods approvingly. Juggling her pile of canapés she takes a sip of champagne. "Are you going to try one of the free treatments?"

I glance at my watch. "I should get back to the office."

"Free five-minute facial?" offers a woman in a toga wafting past. She looks at me enquiringly.

"Oooh, Charlotte, go on, you should try one." Beatrice elbows me.

I shake my head. "I really need to finish up a press release . . ."

"It will only take five minutes," she points out, insistently.

Honestly, you'd never think I was the boss and she was my assistant. Then again—I hesitate—a relaxing facial might be just what the doctor ordered.

"Okay, why not? That sounds great." I smile at the therapist.

She beams back. Her hair's plaited neatly into cornrows and she has the kind of amazing skin that can only be inherited from an exotic heritage. And which is the envy of someone like me, whose entire family tree is made up of freckly skinned, mousy-haired generations from the north of England, or Illinois.

"Wonderful." Pressing her hands together, she does a little bow. "My name's Suki, and if you'd just like to come over to one of the chairs . . ."

Dutifully I follow Suki over to one of three large leather reclining chairs that are tucked away behind a small painted screen featuring a Zen-like landscape. Aromatherapy candles are burning and there's a large pot of bamboo in the corner.

It screams relaxation and inner peace.

Sinking into the soft leather I close my eyes as Suki takes off my makeup and presses a hot towel on my face. It smells of eucalyptus and I take a deep breath.

"Now, we're just going to open your pores," Suki's voice chants soothingly.

As she begins gently dabbing the towel against my cheeks, then slowly onto my forehead, and over to my chin, I can already feel the stress slowly trickling out of my body like sand through an egg timer. The doctor was right, I am really stressed.

"And then we're going to apply a cleanser to draw out impurities and clean pores . . ."

With Suki's fingertips gently massaging my face in circular motions I can feel myself drifting off. Gosh, this is actually quite lovely.

"Followed by a special mask made of clay minerals that will revitalize the skin and help balance out skin tone . . ."

Mmm, this is bliss. Sheer, unadulterated bliss.

". . . because you've got rather a lot of sun damage . . ."

"What?" Jolted out of my reverie my eyes snap wide open.

Clucking her tongue reprovingly, she continues massaging. ". . . all over your cheeks and forehead . . ." I stiffen. ". . . resulting in quite severe pigmentation and discoloration . . ."

*Severe pigmentation and discoloration?*

"But I always use sunscreen," I cry with alarm.

"Mmmm," she murmurs, and continues massaging.

"SPF 45," I say urgently, trying to sit upright. But she pushes back down firmly.

"Sshh, relax," she soothes. "You're very tense."

"And I never sunbathe," I protest, but I'm muffled by a hot flannel as she wipes off the cleanser and begins rubbing on a thick layer of clay. Actually this facial is getting a bit irritating.

"Eighty-five percent of irreversible sun damage is caused before the age of twenty-five," she intones. She stops sweeping clay across my temples and fixes me with a beady eye. "Did you sunbathe in your youth?"

My internal photo album produces a snapshot of me as a teenager in Illinois, slathered in Hawaiian Tropic in the backyard in summer, frying in the midday sun. Actually there's not just the one snapshot. There are whole albums full of them. From my teenage years in the States, right through to my late twenties here in London, I would dive into a string bikini at the first ray of sunshine. And don't get me started on the tanning salons . . .

"A little," I fib, under the beady glare of Suki.

"Well, that explains it." She nods, arching an eyebrow. "The sun is the skin's number one enemy. It causes aging, fine lines, wrinkles, sagging, loss of collagen . . ."

As she reels off a long list of terrible things I've done to my skin, I listen with horror. It's all right for Suki. She has skin the color of an iced mocha latte. She's never had to suffer the milk-bottle-leg syndrome that haunts every fair-skinned woman when it's time to ditch the trusty opaques at the end of spring. Or know what it's like to have a complexion that, without bronzer, prompts complete strangers to inquire about your health.

"Isn't there anything I can do?" I ask anxiously, clutching my face.

"Well, we do have some specialized laser treatments that could help." Suki passes me a leaflet.

I glance at the price list. "Five hundred pounds?" I gasp.

"And I'd recommend a course of five or six sessions."

Five or six? That means . . . Hurriedly I do the calculations. Oh my God, that's a fortune. I glance up at Suki, who's smiling at me brightly.

"Would you like me to book your first session today?"

"Um . . . I think I might wait . . ."

"Are you sure that's wise? We're giving away complimentary foot rubs as part of a special promotion . . ." She continues with her sales pitch.

I'm beginning to feel quite stressed. I only wanted a relaxing facial.

". . . and I would also recommend a whole new range of products to treat your damaged skin . . ."

"Excuse me, but I think the five minutes might be up," I interrupt as she draws breath.

"Oh, yes, so they are." She smiles, taking two cotton pads and wiping my face clean. "Well, if you change your mind." She hands me a card and a bag. "Here are some free samples for you to try."

"Great, thank you," I say, standing up with relief. Five more minutes and my credit card and I would have caved under the pressure.

Beaming widely, she puts her hands together and gives a little bow. *"Namaste."*

❧

After hastily reapplying my makeup in the bathroom, I find Beatrice on her third glass of champagne and chatting animatedly to a journalist. As with most launches, it's mostly press and industry people here, though as always there's the odd C-list celebrity with the prerequisite fake boobs and blonde hair extensions, posing for photo opportunities in a white spa robe.

"Oh, hi, Charlotte." Beatrice breaks off from her conversation as I approach. "This is Patrick." Throwing out her hand as if to say "ta-dah," like a magician when he does a trick, she looks at me, her eyes sparkling.

I know that look. She fancies him. And she's drunk.

Or as Beatrice likes to put it, "a little squiffy."

Patrick and I exchange pleasantries. He's wearing a blazer and checked shirt, under which I can see the outline of a white vest.

"He works for *Golfing Weekly*." She beams, playing with her pearls like some people play with their hair. She smiles eagerly at Patrick. "Isn't that exciting?"

Patrick chuckles in an attempt at modesty.

"So you're a golfer?" I ask, making conversation.

"I play a seven handicap," he says knowledgeably.

"Wow, that's amazing," coos Beatrice, leaning closer with what is supposed to be a surreptitious move, and is instead a clunking great big shuffle sideways. Subtlety is not Beatrice's strong point at the best of times. She hangs at his elbow, her face turned upward toward his shiny, pink one.

"And my wife plays a five handicap. So we like to make a lot of golfing trips. The Algarve's our particular favorite . . ."

"Wife?" repeats Beatrice, her mouth hanging open like a carp.

"Yes. She's semiprofessional," he adds proudly.

There's a beat.

"I'm sorry, will you ladies excuse me?" Patrick smiles politely. "I've just spotted a colleague." Excusing himself, he disappears through the party.

I glance at Beatrice. She looks crestfallen.

"Oh, well," she says, forcing a smile. "Never mind,"

I can tell she's upset, but she'll never admit it. Stiff upper lip and all that. In fact, Beatrice could probably plunge thirty thousand feet in an airplane, crash into the ocean, and find herself surrounded by man-eating sharks, and she'd still say "Oh, well, never mind" with a brave smile.

Polishing off the rest of her champagne, she plucks another flute from a passing tray. "So, tell me, how was the facial?" she asks, swiftly changing the subject in an effort to be cheery.

*Deeply disturbing,* I want to reply, but instead I settle for "Very educational" and pass her the bag Suki gave me. "I got you some free samples," I say, trying to cheer her up.

"For me?" Pressing her hand to her chest, she looks at me as if I've just given her diamonds. "Oooh, Charlotte, you shouldn't have!"

"Beatrice, they were free," I point out.

"Well, I know, but still . . ." Putting down her champagne glass, she dives on the bag and starts pulling out products. "A body lotion . . . foot scrub. . . . a moisturizer . . . oh, goody, I need a new moisturizer, I've totally run out of the Pond's cold cream Granny gave me."

She starts reading off the back label. "'Turn back the clock with this luxury moisturizer which erases fine lines with our specially patented formula, leaving your face looking and feeling ten years younger.'" She gives a little snort. "Well, that's nonsense."

"Mmm, yes, I know," I murmur absently. I'm still feeling perturbed about my facial.

"No moisturizer can make you look ten years younger. It's impossible."

"Mmm, yes . . ." Digging out my compact, I peer at my skin. It doesn't look that bad, but still.

"I don't care whether it's made of crushed pearls from the Adriatic or not . . ."

Hurriedly I start powdering my cheeks and forehead. "Mmm . . . I agree . . ."

". . . there's only one thing that's going to make me look twenty-one again and that's time travel."

Out of the blue I get the weirdest feeling.

"What did you just say?" I ask, abruptly zoning back in and snapping my compact shut.

"I said I don't care if it's made of crushed pearls from the Adriatic—"

"No, not that bit," I say quickly.

Beatrice frowns. "Gosh, I can't remember."

"You said something about being twenty-one again," I prompt, my stomach fluttering.

"Oh, yes, I was talking about time travel." She nods matter-of-factly. Putting the products back in the bag, she takes a swig of champagne. "Though strictly speaking if you *were* to travel back through the frontiers of time you wouldn't *look* like you were twenty-one, you'd *meet* yourself when you were twenty-one."

As she says that I suddenly I feel really light-headed. Dizzy almost.

"But you know Stephen Hawking says time travel isn't possible," she continues and then laughs. "Otherwise we'd all be run over from tourists from the future."

"Well, of course it's not possible," I scoff, quickly recovering. It must be the champagne, I tell myself, using a pamphlet to fan myself. And it is really stuffy in here.

"However, the theory of general relativity does suggest scientific grounds for thinking time travel could be possible in certain unusual scenarios," she adds as an afterthought.

I stare at her in disbelief.

"What? You're saying you *believe* in time travel? Come on, you're joking, right?"

"Actually no, I'm not joking," she refutes stiffly, pursing her lips. "According to the rules of physics, there are several ways it could be theoretically feasible. For example, there are some quantum physicists that believe every historical event spawns a new universe for every possible outcome, resulting in a number of alternate histories. . . ." She pauses to take a swig of champagne. "This is rooted in the many-worlds interpretation of quantum mechanics formulated by the physicist Hugh Everett in 1957, an alternative to the Copenhagen interpretation originally formulated by Niels Bohr and Werner Heisenberg around 1927."

*Um, hello?*

"Can you say that again, but in English this time?" I ask, completely lost.

"Think of it like this." Putting down her champagne glass she reaches over to a passing waitress. "Excuse me." She smiles, grabbing a handful of mini-quiches, before turning back to me and spreading out her napkin on the table. "Rather than a universe," she explains, placing a mini-quiche in the middle, "it's a multiverse." She continues dotting around several more mini-quiches around it. "And all these multiverses together comprise all of physical reality. The different universes within a multiverse are called *parallel universes*." She picks up a mini-quiche and waves it at me. "Imagine this is a parallel universe," she suggests, her face serious.

"Um . . . okay." I nod dubiously.

"It's existing at the same time as all these other parallel universes—" She gestures to all the other mini-quiches. "And you can travel between them. See?"

I stare bewildered at the mini-quiches, trying to grapple with the information. For someone who dropped physics in favor of creative writing, it's all rather confusing. Actually make that *very* confusing.

"But then of course there's the other theories, including traveling faster than the speed of light and moving large amounts of physical matter, which releases energy and can cause a crack in time. Or the use of cosmic strings or traversable wormholes," she says nonchalantly, helping herself to a parallel universe. Sorry, I mean a mini-quiche.

"A wormhole?" I repeat, my mouth twitching.

Well, I'm sorry, but I can't take this seriously. What next? *Star Trek*'s transporter?

"You know, like a portal." She shrugs. "Or some kind of tunnel that allows you to travel from one time"—with her finger she traces a line across the napkin—"to another."

Suddenly I get that weird fluttering feeling again in my stomach and a cog in my brain turns. No, but that's just crazy, I tell myself firmly, dismissing the thought before it's even fully formed. In fact, it's more than crazy. It's totally ludicrous.

"I know. Even I don't understand it properly," Beatrice soothes, misinterpreting my silence and patting my arm in consolation.

"And if I even try to explain it in more detail, I'm afraid your head will explode. Or implode, depending on what universe we are currently in and the particular wave-function-collapse laws," she adds, frowning. "Saying that, I loved *Back to the Future*, didn't you?" And draining her glass she smiles brightly. "Another glass of bubbly?"

## Chapter Twelve

Making my excuses, I leave Beatrice drinking champagne and sneak out of the party early. I drive home feeling unsettled, like on a hot summer's day, just before a storm comes when the air gets all charged and seems to prickle with electricity and anticipation. And you're filled with a strange mixture of excitement and apprehension, knowing something is going to happen. Waiting. Watching. Wondering.

It's another warm evening and as usual the rush hour is in full swing. Drivers with their windows wound down and elbows sticking out jostle for every inch of road, while on the sidewalks pedestrians scuttle like worker ants toward the underground. Following the signs for the detour I turn on the radio. A DJ's chirpy banter wafts out of my speakers, filling the space around with me with jokes and jingles and call-ins, and I listen, glad for the distraction.

For about thirty seconds.

Then, before I know it my mind is wandering back to the party like a guest reluctant to leave. Sidling over to my earlier conversation with Beatrice, her words replaying in my head.

"*. . . possible in certain unusual scenarios . . . parallel universe . . . moving large amounts of physical matter . . . tunnel that allows you to travel from one time to another . . .*"

My mind flicks back to yesterday. Driving past all the bulldozers moving all that earth, the detour, turning down that side street and going under the underpass, which I suppose is sort of like a tunnel . . .

Okay, that's enough. I screech my imagination to a halt. Like I said, it's totally ridiculous. So Beatrice does have some mind-bogglingly brainy physics degree from Cambridge, but time travel? Honestly, what next? UFOs and little green men?

*But what about the date on the parking ticket?* interrupts a voice in my head.

Stress, remember? I tell myself firmly. I was flustered and misread the date. If I hadn't dropped the ticket I could check it now, prove to myself I made a mistake, and that would be the end of it.

*And the fact she looked just like you did when you were twenty-one.*

Mistaken identity. Happens all the time. In fact, once I pinched Miles's behind when he was standing in line to buy popcorn at the movies. Only it wasn't his behind. It belonged to someone else's boy-friend, and believe me, that someone else wasn't very happy.

*And drove your car.*

Coincidence.

*Which was scrapped.*

No, it wasn't. Dad was wrong.

*And lived in your old house.*

For godsakes, what is this? An interrogation? Shut up, why don't you?

Rattled, I reach for the volume button on the stereo. Okay, that's it. I'm not listening to this nonsense anymore, I tell myself decisively, turning it up until the music is blasting out of my speakers. A little embarrassing because the roof is down, it's Avril Lavigne, and a few people are staring at me. Oh, screw it. So what? I'm going to listen to this song, and stare straight ahead and not even think about how she reversed into that lamppost just like I—

Shit. I've done it again.

I tug my mind back firmly, but it's like a restless child and I can't get it to sit still. Before I know it, it's wandering back again to play with those questions. I know there's a logical, rational explanation for all of it. I know that.

*And yet.*

Doubt flickers, like lightning on the skyline, momentarily illuminating a qualm lurking deep down inside of me. A secret, clandestine thought which zips fleetingly through my brain, whispering, *What if there's a different explanation? What if it's not stress? What if*—I brace myself, afraid of where this is going, but unable to stop it—

What if by some weird, freaky, unexplainable chance I really *did* see myself at the stoplight? If at that diversion my world collided with the world of my twenty-one-year-old self, driving to and from work in my old VW Beetle? And what if I had somehow managed to follow myself back to 1997?

These thoughts fire through my mind like an electric impulse. A split second and they're gone again. Vanishing almost sooner than they appeared. Even so, I'm embarrassed by their very existence and I grab hold of my overactive imagination by the scruff of its neck.

Honestly, Charlotte. That one glass of champagne really did go to your head, didn't it? This isn't *Back to the* Freaking *Future*. This is real life. My name's not Marty McFly. I don't drive a DeLorean. I'm Charlotte, I run a PR company and drive a Beetle. And let's face it, with the traffic in London, I can't have been doing more than thirty.

My attention is distracted by a street up ahead. I recognize that street. It's the one I turned down yesterday when I followed the old Beetle . . .

I look away quickly. Okay, enough of that. What was I thinking about? Oh, yes, stupid things. But I'm not going to think about those anymore, I tell myself, brushing them away firmly. I'm going to think about something else. Like, for example, when I get home I'm going to take the doctor's advice and run a relaxing bubble bath. Maybe even listen to that CD Mum sent me. Light an aromatherapy candle.

*Shall I turn off?*

A little voice pops into my head. No, of course not, I think sharply. I'm going straight home.

*It'll only take ten minutes.*

I hesitate, my resolve wavering. Which is stupid because, like I said, this is all nonsense. You don't drive down a street one day and discover yourself back where you were ten years ago. And I hardly think I need to prove that by driving down there again, do I? I muse, feeling a flash of amusement at the mere suggestion.

Plus, let's imagine for a second that it was somehow magically possible, *which of course it isn't,* the truth is I don't want to bump into myself when I was twenty-one thanks very much. I've left that girl behind years ago. Why would I want to meet her again today?

Like someone pressing play on a tape recorder I suddenly hear Suki:

*Eighty-five percent of irreversible sun damage is caused before the age of twenty-five . . .*

And get an image of me aged twenty-one sunbathing topless in my back garden, basting myself in Hawaiian Tropic and rotating myself on my towel like a pig on a spit.

Okay, I take that back.

Slamming on the brakes, I swerve right across the road and shoot off down the street.

❧

Five minutes later I reach Kilmaine Terrace and I'm already fast regretting my decision. It's one thing imagining doing something, it's another actually doing it.

*And what are you doing exactly, Charlotte?* pipes up that annoying little voice again.

I don't have an answer. In fact I'm going to have to take this secret with me to the grave. God forbid anyone should find out. "What did you do last night, Charlotte?" "Oh, I just drove back to my old house that I lived in ten years ago, looking for myself when I was twenty-one because my assistant told me that time travel is possible and I wanted to check it all out and see."

Stress or no stress, they'll be carting me off in a straitjacket. Forget Great-aunt Mary with her talking parrot, I'll go down in the Merryweather family tree as the unmarried career girl who went totally off her rocker. I can hear my mom now, "Well, it's not surprising, she lived in *Lundun,* you know," in her strong northern accent.

Turning down the street I head toward number 39, keeping my eye out for a tangerine orange Beetle. I scan all the parked cars. But no, nothing.

Well, what did you expect, you idiot?

I feel both foolish and relieved at the same time. And something else. A twinge of disappointment. Because as unthinkable as the whole fantasy is, there's the secret part of me that's fascinated by tales of the paranormal, that's watched every single episode of *The X-Files* (I had the *hugest* crush on David Duchovny) and loves the idea of it being possible. After all, let's be honest, who didn't adore *The Time Traveler's Wife*?

Abruptly my bladder twinges, interrupting my thoughts, and I realize I need to pee. Damn, it must be the dire combination of champagne *and* an empty stomach. I need to find a bathroom. And fast. There must be a bathroom around here somewhere . . .

Looping around the garden square I do another quick scan of the parked cars—not because I really think it's going to be there, but because I'm the kind of person who always goes back in the house to check I've turned off the gas—then, satisfied, whiz back down Kilmaine Terrace. I remember! The Wellington pub. It had just opened when I lived here, and Vanessa and I quickly became regulars. It's around here somewhere. I pull up at the yield sign at the end of the street. I think it's left. Actually, no, it might be right. I hesitate for a moment, my bladder twinging insistently.

Shit, where is it?

Then I have a flash of inspiration.

I know, I'll type the name into my GPS satellite navigation system, I think, very proud of my expert problem-solving abilities. This thing is amazing. I just type in the name . . .

That's funny.

I look at the screen of the system sitting on my dashboard. It's completely dark. I randomly punch a few buttons in, hoping it's going to magically spring back to life, and then give it a little shake. (My usual scientific approach to fixing electronic gadgets, which, surprisingly enough, usually works.)

But nope, not this time. The screen remains resolutely black.

My bladder twinges hard. Now of course I really want to pee. Damn thing, I curse, feeling slightly irritated. Oh, well, the pub's around here somewhere, I'll just have to try to go from memory. I swing a left and follow the road as it winds around the church. Now this is looking familiar. It should be on the right . . . I turn a corner. No, it's not there. What about the next corner . . .

As I turn right I feel a rush of happiness as I spot the familiar painted pub sign. Hooray! There it is. The Wellington Arms. Quickly parking, I dash out of the car and into the pub. God, it hasn't changed a bit, I muse, feeling a rush of nostalgia as I walk inside. Same scuffed floorboards on which are clustered lots of wooden tables and chairs, same large open fire that's all blackened and sooty from winter use, same chalkboards filled with scribbles describing today's specials and a large, extensive wine list, which I remember was a totally new thing back in 1997.

Wow. *It's like stepping back in time,* I muse.

Then catch myself and smile with amusement. No pun intended of course.

Despite it being only early in the evening, the Wellington is busy with the after-work crowd, and excusing my way through to the back of the pub, I hurry downstairs to the toilets. They're still in the same place, thank goodness, and I dash gratefully into an empty stall.

Thank God I've been doing all those pelvic floor exercises, I tell myself, finally relaxing my muscles. Boy, that's a relief.

I flush the toilet and go outside to wash my hands. It's all still exactly the same, and as I go to dry them under the fan I glance absently in the mirror to check my reflection. I must have looked in this mirror a thousand times when I was twenty-one: checked my hair was okay, my lipstick was fresh, reapplied my eyeliner. And now here I am, a whole decade later. For a moment I pause, lost in thought. It's strange. My life is so different now, I feel so different now, look so different now, it's hard to imagine being me back then.

The door swings open and I snap out of my reverie as another girl enters. Catching the door before it swings back, I scoot out of the bathroom and back up the staircase, fully intending to walk right out of the pub and drive home. But that was before I catch the pony-tailed bartender's eye. He cocks an eyebrow.

"So did you find it okay?"

I stop midstep, like a thief caught in his tracks. Oh God, is he talking to me? "Um . . . excuse me?" I feign innocence.

"The toilet," he says pointedly, giving me a look. A look that says, "I know your type, just waltzing in here to use the bathroom, without buying a drink. What do you think this is, a public toilet?" Trust me. It was that kind of look.

"Oh, yes, thank you." I smile awkwardly.

"Anything else we can help you with?"

"Just a cranberry juice, please," I hear myself saying before I can stop myself.

Honestly, Charlotte. You don't have to buy a drink if you don't want to. Just turn around and walk out. Who cares what he thinks? He's just a bartender.

But it's too late. He's already getting out the Ocean Spray.

"There you go." He passes me my drink. "That'll be a pound, please."

I'm pleasantly surprised. Well, I'm glad to see the prices are still reasonable, I think, digging out my purse. There's nothing worse than those fancy, overpriced bars these days that charge you £3.50 for a soft drink. But then this pub always was good value for the money.

"Thanks, great." As I hand over the money and take my drink I look around for a free seat. I scan the pub until finally, spotting an empty table, I dive on it gratefully. Excellent! Pulling up a chair, I sit down and am just getting comfy when—I wrinkle up my nose. Wait a minute. *Do I smell cigarettes?*

Just then, a blast of smoke wafts in my direction. I glance sideways. Sure enough, there, right next to me, is a couple smoking. *Inside!* Haven't they heard of the antismoking laws? "Um . . . excuse me. . . ." They both look over. "Would you mind?" I say politely and gesture to their cigarettes. Well, I hate to be one of those people who complain about smoking, but it's really bad for my sinuses. And really, I shouldn't feel that bad—after all, it is completely illegal to smoke in pubs.

"Sure. Go ahead, take one." He smiles, proffering his packet of Marlboro Lights. "Do you need a light?"

Oh, no, he's completely misunderstood me. "Um . . . no . . . thank you," I fluster, shaking my head. "I didn't mean . . . I meant . . ."

Watching him puffing away unfazed, I break off at a loss.

". . . my sinuses . . ." I gesture, sniffing a bit for emphasis.

"Right, yeah, summer colds. A bummer." He nods agreeably and drags hard on his cigarette.

I feel a sting of indignation. I can't believe it. The arrogance of some people! He's just going to sit there doing a still-life impression of a smokestack. And when I asked nicely and everything!

Picking up my cranberry juice I stand huffily.

"You should go sit outside, get some sun," he advises, slurping his pint.

"Yes, I think I'll do that," I reply tightly, and throwing my tote bag over my shoulder, I turn and stalk across the scuffed wooden floorboards toward the exit.

❦

Outside, the beer garden is already jostling with people crowding the few wrought-iron tables and chairs. This is just how I remember it: jammed-packed and buzzing with chatter. It's also still just as pretty. Vibrantly colored hanging baskets dangle from the walls scenting the air, and there's a lovely sycamore tree just around that corner. I can remember when they planted that tree, I reflect, casting my mind backward. It was nothing more than a skinny little sapling, but just look at it now!

Oh.

As it comes into view, I feel a pang of disappointment. It hasn't grown very much in ten years, has it? I thought it was going to be this great big spreading tree and I was going to sit underneath its shady boughs. I peer at the weedy little branches. If I didn't know better, I'd think it was still a sapling.

But then that shows you how much I know about gardening, I muse, spotting a free spot and plonking myself down with my back to the sun. No need to get any more sun damage . . .

I look around me. The crowd looks pretty much the same. Lots of cool, trendy people in low-slung jeans and floaty dresses, showing off summer tans and those Celtic armband tattoos that were so fashionable in the '90s. Thank goodness I never succumbed to *that* fad; you're stuck with them forever.

Resting my drink on the table I start rooting around in my handbag for my cell phone. I need to call Miles back. He left a message earlier today when I was at the doctor's, saying, "Nothing important, just checking in," which is what he always says whenever he calls. When we first started going out I thought that was really sweet—and I still do. Just maybe it might be nice if it *was* something important sometimes. Not scary important. Just *interesting* important.

I dial his number and I press the phone to my ear and wait for it to start ringing.

Except it doesn't.

Frowning, I look closely at the screen and notice all the bars have disappeared and I don't have a signal. *Again.* Irritation stabs. I called T-Mobile but they said there wasn't a problem with reception in the area. I don't understand it. I dig out my BlackBerry, but it's the same. No signal. I stare at in confusion. What was Beatrice talking about the other day? Oh, right, yes. Something about too many people using their mobile phones, I remember, glancing around me. Maybe she's right.

Except—

Wait a minute. That's odd. My eyes flick from person to person. Usually everyone is chattering away, handsets pressed to their ears, earpieces dangling, Bluetooth headsets flashing lights as they seemingly jabber away to no one. But now, looking around me, I can't see actually anyone using their phone.

Maybe they don't allow mobiles, I decide, feeling a little bewildered. Though I can't see any signs. Oh no, look, there's a couple of people on their phones. A few tables away I spot a guy chatting into his phone and as he finishes his call I jump up and walk over to him.

"Excuse me." He looks up. "Are you with T-Mobile?"

He looks at me blankly. "Sorry?"

"I saw you on your phone," I explain. "But I don't have any reception."

"Um . . . no, I'm with Vodafone and it seems fine." He shrugs, putting his mobile down on the table in front of him. I glance it. God, he must have had that phone for years; it looks really old-fashioned.

Still, it has five big black bars showing. Unlike my BlackBerry.

"Well, that's weird . . ." Confused, I peer at the bars on mine. Nope. They've all disappeared.

"What's that?" He looks at me quizzically.

I pause from doing my usual scientific approach of pressing every button and jabbing the screen. "Excuse me?"

"Is that a phone?"

"Oh, you mean my BlackBerry?"

"BlackBerry?" he repeats, as if it's a foreign-sounding word. "I've never seen one of those."

"Really?" I look at him in surprise. I assumed everyone knew what one was, even my mother. Then again, she does still call it "that thingamajig." "Oh, well, they're not that great. Trust me," I say ruefully. "Though they're useful for getting your e-mails."

"E-mails?" he repeats. "On a phone?" He laughs and shakes his head. "Yeah, right. Since when? You need dial-up and a computer for those."

Suddenly, I get this really odd feeling.

Okay, so now he's definitely pulling my leg, right?

But as I ask myself the question, my mind is already rewinding. I'm retracing my steps, away from the man with the old-fashioned cell phone . . . sitting back down and realizing hardly anyone is using a mobile . . . trying to call Miles with no reception . . . looking for shade and being surprised to discover the tree is still only a sapling . . .

Small, tiny things that seemed so inconsequential, so random, are magnifying in my mind, as if there's a camera zooming in for a close-up, and now it all seems so glaring, so obvious, so portentous. Talking to the man who was smoking . . . paying for my drink and thinking how cheap it was . . . walking into the pub and thinking how nothing had changed . . .

A shiver runs up my spine and despite the warmth I can feel goose bumps prickling, my heart quickening, my body tensing as if bracing itself for something.

And now the film is speeding up and I'm traveling back through time over the last two days and scenes are flashing before me: the traffic lights, my old Beetle, a girl who looks just like I used to . . . Faster and faster, they're being thrown out of sequence . . . the diversion . . . my old house . . . the date on the parking ticket . . .

"Oops, sorry."

A voice cuts into my consciousness as someone from behind bangs into me, yanking me back to reality, and spilling what's left of my cranberry juice down my shirt. Oh shit. I look down to see it covered in red, seeping splodges.

"Oh God, I'm really, really sorry, it was an accident . . ."

Digging out a tissue I start dabbing my shirt. Damn. It's white linen. I'm never going to get the stain out.

"I'm so sorry! Can I buy you another drink?"

"No, thank you—"

Except in the split second it takes for me to answer, something registers as not quite right. Something about her voice sounds familiar. . . . I stiffen. Hang on a minute. I twirl around, my heart thudding loudly in my chest, my breath caught tight in the back of my throat. Because I already know exactly who it is that's standing behind me. Even before I see her, I know who she is.

Our eyes lock. And in that instant, every single rational thought I've ever had flies right out the window.

*It's me.*

# Chapter Thirteen

For a moment nothing happens. It's as though someone has just pressed Pause on the DVD that is my life and said, "So tell us! What were you thinking *then*?"

Except I have no answer.

In books I'm always reading about people being rendered speechless, and I've always thought it an interesting concept, but one that was more figurative than realistic. After all, no one's ever *really* speechless, are they? You can always think of *something* to say. Even when I was dumped by Colin Channer in middle school with a blunt "I don't like you anymore," I found my tongue fast enough to reply with a "Well, I don't like you either, zitface."

Okay, so it wasn't going to win any awards for the most witty riposte, but at least I said *something*.

Unlike now.

Now I really *am* speechless. Lost for words. Struck dumb. This isn't a hallucination. This is real. And all I can do is stand here in stunned silence as I stare at myself. My younger, twenty-one-year-old self. In the flesh. Right there. In front of me.

*Oh fuck.*

I feel a thrust of panic and my mind starts swirling like a merry-go-round.

*Fuck-oh-fuck-oh-*

"Are you okay?"

A strong American accent stops me spiraling further and I snap back to see my younger self looking at me with concern. God, I'd forgotten how nasal my speech used to be.

"Um . . . yes," I fluster. "I'm fine . . ."

Which is a pretty big fat lie, for if there's one word to describe my situation right now it certainly isn't fine. Panicked? Maybe. Freaked out? Definitely. This close to losing it any second? Yup, that as well.

Bewildered, I glance down at my shirt with dismay. It's my favorite Nicole Fahri shirt and it's now splattered with cranberry juice. God, just look at it! I only bought it a couple of weeks ago and now it's totally ruined. Maybe if I take it to a dry cleaner's, maybe they can—

Oh, who am I kidding? I don't really care about my goddamn shirt. I'm just trying incredibly hard not to think about the small fact that I'm having a conversation with a girl in a skimpy top and silver eye shadow who just so happens to be me a decade ago.

As I look back up at her I wobble and nearly lose it.

God, this brings a whole new meaning to talking to yourself.

"It was just a bit of a shock," I say, trying to appear casual but it's as if the world has tipped on angle and I'm teetering on the edge, clinging on for dear life. "But no big deal." I shrug and laugh lightly, *while having to pretend everything is perfectly normal.*

But there's no reaction. My younger self is still staring at me, her smooth, wrinkle-free brow furrowed in concentration. As if she's thinking about something very, very hard. As if something's troubling her. As if—

Oh my God.

Suddenly, it registers.

Of course! Why didn't I think of this before?

*She recognizes me.*

As it hits me I know I have to pull myself together. No doubt she's going to be as freaked out as I am. Possibly more. In fact, I'll probably have to calm her down, being the older self. Act like a big sister. Tell her not to worry. That it will be okay, to stay calm and not panic, that we'll figure this out—

She opens her mouth to speak and despite my own feelings it's all I can do to stop myself from flinging my arm protectively around her shoulder and saying, "There, there, dear."

"Salt."

Or perhaps she's going to burst into tears. Or faint. Or have some kind of spaz attack. Or—

Hang on, rewind a minute. Did she just say . . .

*"Salt?"* I repeat, taken aback.

"Yes, that's right. And white wine." She nods, gesturing at my shirt. "I'm sure that will get the stain out. Though you'll probably need to soak it in hot water." She smiles apologetically.

What? She doesn't recognize me? *She doesn't know who I am?* I stare at her in shocked disbelief. But surely she has to. I'm her. I mean, she's me. I mean, we're the same person.

Fuck, this is confusing.

"I think we've met before," I try prompting.

Maybe she's in denial. Just like I was.

"We have?" Tilting her head on one side, she peers at me, and I can see she's wracking her brain. "Nope, I don't think so," she says, grinning, after a moment.

I swallow hard and take a deep breath. "It's me, Charlotte," I whisper, leaning closer.

Her jaw drops open with surprise and she clutches her chest.

I knew it. At last.

I brace myself, ready to do all the explaining. She's going to want lots of answers, lots of why, how, when, why, whats. Which will be quite tricky, as I don't have answers. But never mind, I'm sure I'll think of something. Just as Vanessa did when Ruby asked her why Daddy had a "thing" between his legs and she said it was a tail, like Mr. George, their cocker spaniel, had. Pretty inspired I have to say.

Although I don't know what Daddy will do next time they ask him to wag it.

"Oh, wow, what a coincidence," she gasps, her face creasing into a smile. "That's my name too. But my friends call me Lottie."

There's not a flicker of recognition. Nothing. It's like I'm a total stranger.

I stare at her with confusion. But how can that be? Unless of course this is all some crazy dream and I'm going to pinch myself and wake up to find Bobby Ewing in the shower.

I pinch myself. Nope. I'm still here. Or should I say both of me is still here.

"Sorry, I'm terrible with faces. Especially once I've had a drink." She gestures to her empty glass and laughs widely, showing off a mouthful of silver fillings.

God, I'd forgotten about those too. I had them all replaced about five years ago, after reading an article about mercury poisoning and freaking out. And my slightly crooked two front teeth straightened. And bleached. In fact my smile's completely different now. Like so many things about me . . .

And then, all at once, it dawns on me. No wonder she doesn't recognize me: not only do we look completely different now, but we are completely different. Of course I'm like a stranger to her. I *am* a stranger to her. She doesn't know me yet. *Me*, the person she's going to become in the future, in ten years' time. The person who no longer goes by her nickname of Lottie, but prefers Charlotte because it's more grown-up and mature. The person without silver fillings, long brown scrunch-dried hair, thick bushy eyebrows, and an American accent. We're not the same person at all: I'm not her anymore and she's not me yet.

I mean, for godsakes, does that look like my cleavage?!

Catching sight of it, I stare at it now with astonishment. My younger self is wearing a flimsy top which her boobs appear to be almost spilling out of. Automatically, I fasten a button on my shirt.

God, I'd forgotten how much heavier I was when I was younger, but then that's not surprising. I didn't exercise then and used to eat like a total scavenger. Now I work out and watch what I eat and I look and feel so much better.

"Um . . . nice top," I comment, as she catches me staring.

"Thanks, I made it myself." She grins proudly.

Yes, I know. From a handkerchief, I reflect, remembering how I thought it was an ingeniously creative idea at the time. Ten years later it's so revealing, I might as well have come to the pub wearing a doily. Seriously. What on earth was I thinking? *I'm practically naked.*

"Aren't you . . . um, a little chilly?" I suggest, resisting the urge to grab someone's jacket from the back of a chair and throw it over her shoulders.

"Chilly?" She laughs. "Oh, no, not at all. In fact it's really hot in here." Turning back to the bar, she starts fanning herself with a beer mat to cool down, her wrists full of bracelets chinking loudly as they start jiggling up and—

I stiffen. The bracelets aren't the only thing jiggling up and down. The handkerchief is made out of this thin silky type of fabric and—oh my God. *Is that a nipple?*

Suddenly I realize two things: 1) I'm not wearing a bra and 2) I've magically turned into my mother.

Right, that's it. This is too much. I'm getting out of here. Grabbing my bag I start to leave.

"Are you sure you don't want another drink?"

Having got the bartender's attention, Lottie suddenly turns to me, stopping me in my tracks.

"Ah, no . . . thanks, I have to go . . ." I say hurriedly, shaking my head and gesturing to the door.

"Oh, okay." She shrugs, and as she turns back to the bar I hear her ordering a half-pint of cider.

I feel an unexpected wave of nostalgia. Cider used to be my favorite drink before my tastes became more sophisticated and I started drinking wine, and for a moment I pause and glance back in her direction. Fiddling with her hair, she's waiting for her drink and chit-chatting with the person next to her at the bar, absently playing with her earring, laughing at some joke, chewing her fingernails, pulling faces, making different expressions . . .

I watch, completely fascinated. It's the weirdest feeling. A little like when I go home to see Mom and Dad and they get out the old home videos and we all sit on the sofa and hoot with laughter at our funny clothes and hairstyles. Only I'm not laughing. Glued to the spot, I'm transfixed. This is just so surreal. Did I really used to wear my skirts so short? And what's with all that big, poofy hair? And— hang on a minute—I watch as the guy next to her offers her a cigarette—*am I smoking?*

Deep down in my brain I can hear a voice yelling at me to get out of here as fast as my legs can carry me. Quickly! Go on, scram! Before you get stuck here in some terrible time warp!

At the thought a jolt of panic rips through me.

Okay, just stay calm. All you need to do is retrace your steps. You got here by driving through that diversion, so you just need to turn around, get back in your car, and drive back the way you came. And do not stop until you're safely back home and in your pajamas with a brandy and the boxed set of *Sex and the City.*

Well, that's always a guaranteed cure-all in any crisis.

I mean, this is insane, Charlotte. It's *insane.*

But it's also exciting, whispers another voice and out of nowhere I suddenly feel a tingle of adventure. Perhaps it wouldn't hurt to stay a little longer. Have another drink. After all, it's not as if this kind of thing happens every day, is it?

"Actually, Lottie . . ."

She looks over her shoulder and seeing me, smiles. "I thought you already left—"

"No, not yet. I've actually got some time to kill. So I was wondering—"

"Cranberry juice, right?"

"Yes, please." I smile and hold out a pound coin, but she pushes it away. "Don't be silly, it's on me," she protests.

I know she's broke, because I was always broke back then, and as she pays the bartender with what little she has I feel a glow of affection toward my own self. Which is *beyond* weird, but hey. At this point, beyond weird is beginning to feel normal.

"Try not to spill it this time," she jokes, as she passes me my juice.

"Thanks." I take it from her. "Oh, by the way," I add, before I can help it, "you get a stain out by soaking it in cold water."

"Not hot?" She looks at me in surprise.

"No, that sets it."

"Oh, man, trust me!" She laughs, pulling a face. "I guess I've still got a lot to learn."

I smile.

Actually, it's funny you should say that . . .

# Chapter Fourteen

Five minutes later, Lottie and I have decamped to the beer garden with our drinks. There's only one empty table so we end up sharing, and for a few moments we both sit there in silence, sipping our drinks, while I grope around for something to talk about. I feel absurdly nervous. Like I'm on a first date or something.

"So—" I finally say. "Nice . . . um . . . weather we're having."

No sooner have the words left my mouth than I feel myself cringe. God, Charlotte. *Is that it?* You bump into yourself aged twenty-one and of all the millions of things you could say you're chatting about the goddamn weather?

"Mmm, yeah, isn't it?" She nods, closing her eyes and tipping her face to the sun.

Triggering a flashback to Suki's lecture about sun damage . . .

"Agh, no, stop—" I blurt out before I can stop myself.

Jerking her head up, Lottie looks at me, startled. "Jesus, what's wrong?"

I hesitate. Oh shit. I really haven't thought this through, have I? I mean, what do I say now? You're going to ruin my skin? I have discoloration and pigmentation *and it's all your fault*?

"Um . . . there was a wasp," I mumble weakly.

"Oh crap, really?" Waving her hands around her, her eyes dart from side to side, looking for the invisible wasp.

"I think it's gone now," I add quickly.

"Really? Phew." Settling back in her chair she hitches her skirt even shorter and sticks her legs out into the full sun. "God, it's amazing, it's six thirty and it's still really hot, isn't it?" she enthuses, basking like a cat in the early evening rays.

"Yes, isn't it?" I nod, watching her helplessly while trying to block out Suki's voice, which is now ringing in my ears. "Um . . . are you sure you don't want to sit in the shade?"

*"The shade?"* My twenty-one-year-old self turns and looks at me with such horror you'd think I suggested she stick red-hot pokers in her eyeballs. "Why on earth would I do that? The English summers aren't the same as the ones back home and I've gotten so pale since I moved here. I'm trying to get a tan."

Trust me. This girl has a tan. She's practically mahogany.

"You know, I use this great fake tan—" I confide, but she cuts me off.

"Fake tan? Gross." She pulls a face. "No, thanks. I want a real tan."

I smile. Tightly.

There's a beat as I watch her put her face in the full sun again and close her eyes. God, this is ridiculous. I can't just sit here and do nothing.

"I have some sunscreen if you want to borrow it," I suggest, trying to sound nonchalant.

"No, it's okay." She shakes her head dismissively. "I don't wear sunscreen."

*I DON'T WEAR SUNSCREEN?*

Now it's my turn to look at her with horror as visions of all the skin care products in my bathroom cabinet swim before my eyes. Followed by visions of all my credit card bills. I've spent enough on miracle creams that promise to reverse the signs of aging, to make a dent in third world debt.

And no wonder, I realize, watching myself as I sizzle in the sun.

In fact, to be quite honest, at this rate, I'm lucky I don't look like beef jerky.

"Well, it's never too late to start," I reply, pulling out my sunscreen from my bag while simultaneously fighting the urge to grab hold of her and smother her in it till she resembles a polar bear. "Want some?" I ask, squirting a bit on my hand and rubbing it on my face.

"SPF 45?" she says, looking aghast. "No wonder you're so pale. No offense," she adds quickly.

"I'm not *that* pale." I frown, looking at the remnant of my spray-on tan. "And anyhow, sunbathing *is* really bad for your skin, you know. In fact, a tan is just the production of melanin . . ." I start quoting from one of the many skin care articles I've read on this subject. ". . . Which your skin produces to protect itself. So in fact you could say that a suntan is actually a sign that your skin is already damaged," I finish, quite impressed by how knowledgeable I sound. I hadn't really realized how much you learn as you get older, but as a woman, by the time you hit thirty, you've been exposed to enough magazines, beauty products, and mirrors to have become an expert in skin care.

"So what?" She laughs carelessly and tips back her face to the sun.

Only she hasn't hit thirty yet, has she? That version of me over there is still twenty-one, I realize, watching my younger self. I know nothing. I have no idea how much money I'm going to hemorrhage on this stuff in years to come, how many hours I'm going to spend daubing on creams and massaging in scrubs to achieve what I have right now, and what I'm taking for granted.

Frustration stabs. Was I really so clueless?

"You say that now," I persist, trying not to think of all the UVB and UVA rays that are right now attacking that perfect, peachy, freckle-free skin, sowing the future seeds of discoloration and pigmentation. "But you'll regret it when you're in your thirties."

"Thirties? Oh God, I won't care by then," she dismisses, slurping her cider. "I'll be old."

I flinch. "Thirties isn't old," I say tetchily and reach for my cranberry juice. I'm not actually a big fan of cranberry juice but it's chockfull of vitamin C and antioxidants. I take a virtuous sip. So much better for me than cider, which is just full of empty calories.

"Yeah it is," she retorts, and gives a little shudder, as if she doesn't even want to think about it. "It's ancient."

What? She's saying I'm *ancient*?

I feel a slam of indignation. I've been trying to be patient, but this is too much. I mean, honestly! I'm younger than Cameron Diaz! I shop at Topshop!

Admittedly only online, but still. *And* I have not just one, but *two* pairs of skinny jeans! How on earth can she think I'm ancient?

Because you did, reminds a voice in my head. You did, Charlotte.

And all at once then I remember a conversation I had when I was twenty-one. I was with a group of friends and we were all talking about the millennium, and how old we would all be, and when I realized I was going to turn twenty-five that year, I was appalled. I thought that was *so* old. And as for the few friends that would be in their thirties, well, that was just unthinkable. I didn't know anyone over thirty—apart from my parents—in fact, I didn't even *notice* anyone in their thirties. They were completely invisible to me.

Just like I'm invisible to her, I think, glancing at my twenty-one-year-old self sitting just inches across the table from me, oblivious to who I really am.

She catches me looking, and throws a hand over her mouth in horror. "Oh, sorry, I didn't mean you were . . ." She trails off and pulls a face. "Me and my big mouth."

"It's okay, no offense taken," I reply. "I was just saying. . . ." Absently I scratch my eczema on my elbow. "Besides, the sun will really make your eczema flare up," I can't help adding, moving even farther into the shade.

She frowns. "I don't have eczema."

I look at her in confusion. "You don't?"

"No, why did you think I did?"

"Oh, no reason." I shrug quickly. "It's just very common . . ." Puzzled, I try remembering when I got my first flare-up. It feels like I've had it forever, but actually, thinking back, she's right, I don't remember having it when I was her age. In fact the first time I got it was when I was really stressed out over an important deadline I was working on.

"What time is it?" I zone back in to see her gesturing to my watch. "I don't have a watch." She smiles in explanation.

"You don't have a watch?" I repeat in astonishment. It's unthinkable.

"No, I don't wear one." She shrugs.

Trying to absorb this shocking piece of information I glance at my own for the umpteenth time that day. "Um . . . ten minutes to seven."

She huffs. "Typical. She's always late."

"Who is?" I ask, but I already know. *Vanessa.* It has to be.

"My friend Nessy. She's supposed to meeting here for a drink, but she's never on time . . ."

Well, at least some things never change, I think, stifling a rueful smile.

". . . I'll give her another ten minutes, then I'm going home. I only live around the corner so I can walk there. Lucky since my car's in the garage being fixed." She makes a face. "I had a little bit of an accident."

Of course! The lamppost. That's why it wasn't parked outside the house.

"Which garage did you take it to?"

"Oh, just some place on the Harrow Road . . ."

"Barry's Motors?"

"Yes, that's it." She nods. "How did you know?"

Because they totally ripped me off, I remember grimly, but instead reply vaguely, "Oh, I took my car there once."

The details are fuzzy now but I'll never forget paying some ridiculously inflated bill because I was young and naïve and didn't know to question it. Then having to borrow money off Vanessa when I couldn't afford to pay my rent.

"When's it going to be ready?"

"They said next week sometime."

"Well, if I were you . . ." The irony hits me and I catch myself. ". . . I think you should take a male friend with you when you go back to collect it. Just to check they've done a good job," I suggest. "If you're anything like me you won't know the first thing about cars."

She smiles gratefully. "Thanks for the advice."

"My pleasure." I smile, stifling a yawn that's just appeared from nowhere.

There's a lull in the conversation and as I lean back in my chair I fight off another yawn. Suddenly I feel very tired. It's been a long day. The strangest, most bizarre, most remarkable day of my entire life, but now I can feel it all catching up with me, and I just want it to be over. I want everything to go back to normal.

A wave of tiredness engulfs me and, draining my glass, I reach for my bag. I need to go home and go to bed. And then, when I wake up tomorrow all this will have turned into one of those stories people tell at dinner parties that always goes, "You're never going to believe this, but—" Like that one Vanessa has about how she saw a ghost sitting on the landing when she was eight years old.

Although I have to say, I think bumping into yourself is *slightly* cooler than just seeing a paltry old run-of-the-mill ghost clanking some chains. But like I said no one's ever going to believe me. *I* don't believe me, and I'm seeing it with my own eyes, I muse, taking in my surroundings one last time.

"Hey, Lottie, I think I'm going to take off—" I stop dead as my gaze lands on a poster on the wall: *Shattered Genius, Playing at the Wellington, this Saturday: SOLD OUT.* There's a grainy picture of a band underneath and scrunching up my eyes I peer closer.

"Have you heard of them? They're amazing!"

Her voice grabs my attention and I turn to see her gesturing at the poster.

Quite frankly I have no idea, but I nod vaguely and concentrate hard on rummaging around in my memory. I'm so tired, everything's fuzzy, but I know it's going to come back to me any second.

"You know, I've got an extra ticket if you want to go. My friend Nessy was going to come with me but decided to see *Julian* instead." She rolls her eyes and smiles. "He's her new boyfriend and they're totally in love."

It suddenly strikes me just how friendly I used to be. I'd just moved down to London from the States and the city hadn't rubbed itself off on me yet. Now after being here ten years I tend to keep myself to myself—it's not that English people are unfriendly, on the contrary, it's just that people who don't know each other just don't behave that way here.

"Thanks, but I think I'm busy that night . . ." I reply, shaking my head. Seeing myself once is freaky enough, but twice? I don't think my sanity can handle a repeat performance.

"Oh, that's too bad," she sighs. "I can't wait. I love the lead singer."

"The lead singer?"

"Billy Romani." She nods excitedly.

As she says the name her face lights up like a department store at Christmas and I feel myself stiffen. I haven't heard that name for years, but now it's all coming flooding back. I had a crush on him for months and when we finally ended up spending the night together I thought it was the beginning of some great big love affair.

For about two days. Until I found out I'd just been a one-night stand and he'd already moved on to another girl and—

Pain stabs. Well, anyway, the details aren't important. Suffice it to say, at the time I was heartbroken, but of course I bounced back, and since then I've never given him or what happened a second thought. Well, maybe sometimes, on the odd occasion, I've wondered what if things had turned out differently between us . . .

But they didn't. And I'm glad. Still, it's nothing I dwell on. It was so long ago . . . "He's so talented, don't you think?" she's saying eagerly.

"Um . . . yes, sort of . . ."

Talented at being a total bastard, I think grimly.

A vague memory stirs. Wait a moment. Wasn't it after one of his concerts that I slept with him? I feel a clench of regret. God, if only I hadn't done that. If only someone had stopped me—

An idea strikes and all at once I feel a flurry of possibility.

No, surely I can't.

*Can I?*

Up until a moment ago I wanted everything to go back to normal, for this all to be over, but now . . . I hesitate, my stomach fluttering nervously as I know what I'm going to do. I knew before all this went through my head.

"Then again, I'm not *that* busy . . ." I hear myself saying loudly.

Because I might not know *why* this is happening to me, or *how* this is happening to me, but one thing's for certain: if I go to this concert, I can save myself from a broken heart.

Stirred up, I smile determinedly.

"How much do you want for that ticket?"

## Chapter Fifteen

That night I go to bed and have the strangest dream.

I'm with Doc Brown, the crazy scientist in *Back to the Future*, and we're driving along the freeway in the DeLorean. Only we're not traveling at the speed of light, we're going about 5 mph because of the diversion and now the car has changed into my old VW Beetle, and being an American, Christopher Lloyd can't drive a stick shift, so we swap seats.

But when I sit back down, I'm not in a car anymore, I'm in the Wellington pub and it's not the crazy scientist sitting next to me, it's Suki the facialist and she's wagging a finger at me, holding up a mirror so I can see my sun damage. Only when I look at my reflection my face is super smooth and blemish-free and suddenly I realize there is no mirror. It's me, aged twenty-one.

*And I'm sunbathing. Without any sunscreen!*

My tan is getting darker and darker, deeper and deeper, and I'm trying to stop myself before I turn into an old leather handbag, but I'm not listening. I'm smoking cigarettes and drinking cider and singing along to Billy Romani—

Hang on a minute, are you sure this is a dream, Charlotte?

Snapping open my eyes I tug off my eye mask and peer at my bedside clock: 2:00 a.m. Ugh. It's the middle of the night and I'm wide awake. For a moment I lie there, watching as the clock changes from 2:00 to 2:01, my mind replaying footage from the pub, over and over and over and over . . .

2:10 a.m.

Okay, that's enough. I've got to get up for work in less than five hours. I must fall back asleep or I'm going to be exhausted. I feel a gnaw of anxiety. Nothing worse than the pressure of knowing you have to go to sleep, to prevent you from falling asleep, eh?

Flopping back onto the pillow, I snap my eye mask back on. I just need to relax. Drift away . . . In the background the wave machine is set to "Relaxing Ocean Lullaby" and I listen to the waves rushing in, and rushing out, rushing in and—

This pillow is too hot.

I turn it over and place my cheek on the cool cotton. Ah, that's better. I squeeze my eyes closed again and try to fall asleep.

Then again, it's a little lumpy.

Hitching myself up on one elbow I bash it with my fist, pummeling the allergy-free feathers into submission, before flopping back down again. Right, okay. Sleepy time.

I wriggle down underneath my duvet. The wave machine is still whooshing rhythmically, the humidifier is still puffing steam—any minute now I'm going to be lulled into a drowsy slumber.

But first I have to get comfy.

I toss. Then turn. Then toss back again. God, is it me or is it really hot in here? I throw off my duvet and lie there relishing the cold air. Mmm, this is better. Much, much better . . . Though now my feet feel a little cold. And is that a draft? In fact, you know what, I'm actually feeling a little chilly. I tug back the duvet and strike a compromise by splaying my body half in, half out. Okay. Perfect.

I lie very still and focus on clearing my mind. Emptying it completely of all thoughts. Like, for example, me with bushy eyebrows, big hair, and that godawful silver eye shadow that I'd forgotten all about. Or me smoking and drinking and sunbathing and basically doing everything that's bad for me. Or me falling madly in love with losers like Billy friggin' Romani—

Oh God, this is useless. I'm a terrible sleeper at the best of times, but now? With all this stuff spinning around in my head? Not a flipping chance. Flicking on the bedside lamp I sit up and reach for my new self-help book, *Stress Is a Four-Letter Word.* I know, I'll read for a bit, I decide, turning to my bookmarked page: *"Chapter Two: Relax Your Mind."*

*"You're walking through a beautiful forest, the sun is shining, birds are singing as they fly gracefully overhead. Tilting your face to the sky you watch them, imagining what it would be like to be a bird . . ."*

A bird? What kind of bird? I know, I'll be an eagle. No, I can't be an eagle, they don't sing. What about a sparrow? No, too boring. A robin? Okay, I'll be a robin.

*". . . imagining what it would be like to be able to fly away, to soar away into the sky, higher and higher . . ."*

How high? I don't like heights. I get vertigo. In fact, I'm not that pumped up about flying either. Especially not after that nightmare flight I had years ago coming back from Spain. Oh my God, the turbulence was terrible, I remember anxiously.

Everyone was screaming, even the flight attendants! I swear, I thought I was going to die—

I snap the book shut. It's no good. I can't relax, I'm too restless. Only a few days ago I was living my perfectly normal life, my head full of perfectly normal things like deadlines at work, dinners with Miles, those extra five pounds I've been trying to drop since Christmas. But now everything's been shaken up and turned upside down and I'm not sure what to do about it.

Except agonize over it, of course.

Chucking down my book I clamber out of bed and tug on my nightgown. Feeling all agitated, I go into the kitchen, flick on the kettle, and go grab the soy milk from the fridge. But as I reach for the handle, I pause. Despite my portents about neatness, I tend to accumulate things on my fridge, like an out-of-date gym schedule, some photographs of Ruby and Sam, a couple of recipes that I've ripped out of magazines and keep meaning to try—one day—and magnets that read things like *The journey is not the destination* and *"Women are like tea bags, they don't know how strong they are until they get into hot water"—Eleanor Roosevelt.* Vanessa got me that one.

Only I'm not looking at any of that stuff. I'm noticing an old photograph, half hidden underneath a postcard sent from Mom and Dad when they went to Turkey. It's one of those big drunken group shots taken years ago at some party. Peeling it off the fridge, I look at it closely. The sunlight's faded it, bleaching out colors and washing out details, but I can still make out people's faces.

I smile nostalgically. There's me, right at the end wearing that now-familiar terrible silver eye shadow, and next to me is Vanessa. She's wearing black, as always, and has her arm draped around Julian, who's doing bunny fingers above her head. I smile to myself. Those two were always joking around back then, I muse, turning the photo over and looking at the date scribbled on the back.

*My twenty-second birthday party.* Wow, what a coincidence. I turn thirty-two on Friday, which means this photograph was taken nearly exactly ten years ago. I peer at the photo again, trying to jog my memory for details about it, but I can't remember. It was so long ago, I've completely forgotten.

The kettle boils and I pour the water onto the tea bag, absently watching the water turning a deep brown as my mind starts ticking over. What else have I forgotten? Who else has slipped my memory? How many other makeup horrors have I conveniently erased from my internal hard drive?

On impulse I abandon the tea and, grabbing a flashlight from one of the drawers, pad into the hallway. There's a little cubbyhole under the stairs that as I use as storage, and crouching down I pull it open and crawl inside. It's dusty and there are sticky, large cobwebs. Ugh, I'm terrified of spiders. I take a deep breath and try to remember the stuff I read in *Feel the Fear and Do It Anyway* about facing your fears. Even if they're black and have eight very hairy legs.

Trying not to think about spiders dropping on my head or crawling down the collar of my nightgown (and thinking *only* about spiders dropping on my head or crawling down my nightgown) I start rummaging through the boxes. I'm sure they're in here somewhere, hidden in all this stuff . . . Christmas tree decorations, an ancient tea set that was my grandmother's, old clothes that I'm keeping in case they come back into fashion. I hold up a pair of faded, ripped Levi 501s with a bandana for a patch on the knee. Well, that's the idea . . .

Aha—there it is. Behind a couple of dusty suitcases I spot a large, old-fashioned hatbox. Dragging it out, I carry it into the living room and plunk it on the rug; then, sitting cross-legged beside it, I tug off the dusty lid.

It's filled with photos. Now that we've gone digital no one hardly ever gets prints made anymore, do they? They're all kept on the computer—I've got the one of Miles and me at his birthday last year as a screensaver—but in the old days I used to be always getting film developed at Snappy Snaps in London, and putting them in albums. I've got dozens of them.

I start flicking through one randomly. And then another, and another, until I find what I'm looking for: an album containing pictures of me when I was twenty-one. With renewed curiosity, I open it and gaze at the photographs. I'd just moved to London and it's filled with a social whirl of parties, pubs, and picnics. Here's one of the many Christmas parties we had at Kilmaine Terrace, when I kissed Simon, who I worked with. I cringe. Boy, did I regret *that* in the morning.

Oh, and there's Vanessa and me drunk and dancing at the Notting Hill carnival—shortly afterward I was so drunk I fell into someone's bushes and twisted my ankle. I couldn't wear high heels for months. It was such a pain. Literally.

I turn a page. And here's me again in some horrendous patterned flare leg pants I bought from Camden Market. I shudder. I used to think they were so flattering, but looking at them now with the benefit of hindsight I realize they made me look like someone's sofa. God, talk about a fashion faux pas; I'd never let myself go out in those now—

I pause, the photo albums scattered around me. A seed of thought takes hold, starts to grow . . . if I can prevent myself from sleeping with Billy the wannabe rock star and save myself from getting hurt, why stop there? What about *all* the hundreds of mistakes I'm going to make, *all* the lessons I haven't yet learned, *all* the dumb, stupid stuff I'm going to do because I'm naïve and clueless and don't know any better?

Plus let's not forget all these other fashion disasters, I cringe, spotting another photograph. Only this time I'm wearing pleather pants that make my legs seem like they are encased in two shiny black trash bags. Enough said.

All at once it's as if everything seems to broaden, like being in the movies when the curtains pull back and the screen widens, and I can see the bigger picture. And it's not just about something specific, like the importance of wearing sunscreen, being warned about a sketchy garage, or staying away from a loser like Billy Romani, it's about everything. It's about all the coulda, woulda, shoulda's. It's about getting the one-in-a-zillion chance to hang out with my twenty-one-year-old self.

Like Vanessa said. If only you knew then what you know now.

*Well, now I can.*

I feel a rush of exhilaration and excitement, *potential*.

And suddenly it hits me. Just imagine. I'll be like Yoda! A wise master, teaching myself in the ways of the world, bestowing sage

advice and words of wisdom, giving myself the benefit of my experience and hindsight . . . I can see it now. I'll be fair but firm, wise but
approachable. Like Dumbledore in *Harry Potter*. Or Mr. Miyagi in
*The Karate Kid*.

But of course I shouldn't get too carried away, I think, catching
myself. After all, she has no idea who I am, so it's important I don't
appear like a know-it-all. I mean, I'm not going to give her a set of
instructions or dos and don'ts or anything like that. No, I'll just drop
a few subtle hints, gently lead her in the right direction, give her a bit
of friendly advice. I won't make a big deal of it at all.

# Chapter Sixteen

Okay, so I've made a list.

Fast-forward to nine the next morning and I've popped into a pharmacy before work. Armed with a basket, I'm navigating the busy aisles, on the hunt for a pair of eyebrow tweezers.

Well, if I'm going to do this properly I don't want to forget anything. So, I've just scribbled down a few random thoughts on a piece of paper. Nothing major. Just some things off the top of my head. So for example, first things first.

*1. Do not sleep with Billy Romani.*

I don't care how handsome he is. How charming he is. How amazing that thing was that he did with his tongue—okay, Charlotte, enough of the reminiscing. He's also a liar, a cheat, and a heart-breaker.

*2. Invest in property.*

My dad's motto was always "Buy, don't rent." Of course I didn't listen to him. Maybe now I'll listen to myself.

*3. Better still, invest in any of the following: Starbucks, Google, YouTube.*

Admittedly that might be a bit unrealistic. Especially considering

I used to barely have two coins to rub together at the end of each month. Plus I'm not even sure those things were around back then. But still, it's important to:

### 4. Think big.

And we're not just talking about you-know-what.

Though of course that's important, I reflect dreamily, my mind wandering off in all kinds of directions, until catching myself, I quickly glance back down at my list of instructions. Right, where was I? Oh, right, yes.

### 5. Start a pension.

All right, I'm just going to have to get the boring financial stuff out of the way first, so I can get onto the more important stuff on the list.

Spying the tweezers, I pounce on a super professional-looking pair made from industrial-strength stainless steel with "precision edges" for a professional finish.

Like, for example:

### 6. Pluck your eyebrows.

Look, I've got nothing against thick eyebrows, but it's one thing having sexy beetle brows like Brooke Shields in *Blue Lagoon*—and it's another having the unibrow of a *Star Wars* Wookiee. And while we're on the subject of grooming:

### 7. Do your bikini line.

I know for a fact I didn't have my first bikini wax until I was thirty. A fact I remember because it was *that* painful I still bear the emotional scars. Which means, down there I'm currently resembling a German tourist. *Nicht gut.*

Grabbing some Nair hair remover, I throw it in my basket.

**8. There is such a thing as too much eye makeup. So throw away the silver eye shadow.**
And while you're at it . . .

**9. Throw away the mousse too.**
Scrunch-drying is not a good look. Never was. Never will be.

**10. Nor should you try to lighten your hair with lemon juice.**
A) It doesn't work. And B) it attracts wasps.

**11. Start doing your pelvic floor exercises now.**
Remember Vanessa's advice? Kegels are like shoes, there's no such thing as too many. Reminded, I pause in the aisle to do a couple and notice I'm standing right by the sunscreen section. Like I said before,

**12. Wear a lot of sunscreen.**
I chuck in a couple of family-size bottles of SPF 45. Then a couple more. Well, better safe than sun damaged.

**13. Put down those snakeskin trousers and back away.**
Yes, sadly it's true. Last night I found the damning evidence. A photograph of myself vacuum-packed into a pair of skin-tight, belly-button-skimming, shiny, satin, snakeskin trousers. The word "mortified" doesn't even come close.

**14. Cancel that trip to Sicily in '98.**
It rained all week and I was forced to comfort-eat pizza and gelato.

**15. On second thought, don't cancel that trip. ☺**
Reaching the end of the aisle, I turn into the next one. There are

still a few things I haven't found yet, I muse, as I spot that rare creature: a sales assistant.

"Excuse me—"

For a moment I think she's going to pretend I haven't seen her and dart off into the back—a bit like Vanessa's cocker spaniel if you catch him sitting on the sofa—but at the last she seems to change her mind. "Yes?" she asks, turning. "Can I help you find something?"

"I'm looking for Nicorette patches."

Which brings me onto:

## 16. Stop smoking.

"Oh, I see." She nods briskly. "To help you with stopping smoking?"

"Oh, no, I don't smoke," I say, quickly putting her right. Before realizing by her confused glance that might not have been the best answer.

"Um . . . I mean, I don't smoke anymore," I correct myself.

She peers at me in confusion. "I'm sorry, I'm not sure if I quite understand . . ."

Welcome to my world, I think ruefully, switching my basket onto the other arm. I've thrown in quite a mountain of supplies and it's really pretty heavy.

". . . but I wouldn't advise wearing these unless you are suffering the withdrawal affects of nicotine," she continues, rather firmly.

Oh God, she probably thinks I'm one of those people who get high by drinking cough syrup, or something.

"Yes, absolutely," I agree in my most responsible voice. "Of course I won't. Unless I am. Which I will be."

Fuck. I'm digging myself a bigger hole here. I just know it.

She looks at me sharply, then, thinking better of it, says, "We keep the patches in our prescription section, just on the left."

"Oh, okay, thank you."

Hurriedly turning away, I'm heading toward the sign that says

PRESCRIPTIONS when I see a flash of suit and a familiar profile. Wow, that just looked like Julian, but it can't be, what he would be doing in this part of town? His office is on the other side of the city. I glance again to get a better look. But no, it's definitely Julian. A smile spreads over my face in readiness to say hello as I make my way toward him.

"Hey, Julian, fancy seeing you here!" I exclaim, tapping him on the shoulder.

He swings around like he's been shot. "Charlotte!" he gasps, clutching his tie to his chest, his eyes wide.

"Oh, sorry," I apologize, smiling. "Did I startle you?"

He quickly composes himself. "A little bit." He laughs awkwardly.

"So what are you up to?"

"Excuse me?" He looks at me blankly.

"In this part of town? I thought your office was in Chancery Lane . . ."

God, he's acting really weird. *Shifty*, almost. Which is ridiculous. It's Julian. What's he got to be shifty about?

"Oh, right, yes." He shakes his head distractedly. "I had a meeting close by."

"Snap." I smile, but he doesn't. "With a couple of journalists . . ." I trail off uncomfortably and absently glance down into Julian's basket. And there among the shaving foam and Gillette razors, I see them.

*Trojans. Extra large. Ribbed for comfort.*

Suddenly it dawns on me exactly why Julian is acting so weirdly. He's all self-conscious, as am I, I realize, feeling a flush of embarrassment. Which is silly—we're both adults here!

"Look, Charlotte, I'm running late."

I snap back to see Julian checking his watch.

"Oh, yeah, me too." I smile, blushing beetroot red. "Well, I'll see you tomorrow."

He looks at me as if he doesn't have a clue what I'm talking about.

"For dinner," I add, to jog his memory. "It's my birthday. Did Vanessa mention it?"

"Oh Christ, yes, that's right." He rakes his fingers through his hair and smiles apologetically. "Sorry, I've got a lot on my mind at the moment."

"Understood. Well, 'bye."

"'Bye, Charlotte."

I watch as he strides away down the corridor, his dark-suited figure causing a few turned heads from some girls by the makeup counters. Vanessa is such a dark horse. Haven't had sex for ages, indeed! Just wait till I see her!

And smiling to myself, I turn back to my list. Now where was I?

❦

"Morning."

Arriving at the office, I push open the frosted glass door expecting to be greeted by Beatrice as usual, but instead find her with head on her desk, fast asleep, drooling. As the door swings closed behind me, she flips upright like a jack-in-the-box.

"Oh . . . um . . . morning," she flusters, blinking frantically. Her keyboard is imprinted in her face, giving her this strange pink tattoo across her left cheek. "I was just . . . er . . . clearing up our database."

Strangely, "clearing up our database" is something Beatrice only ever does when she's suffering from a hangover. And even more strangely, it seems to be something she can do with her face on the desk and her eyes closed.

Hastily stifling a yawn she takes a sip of her Berocca vitamin supplement, which is fizzing merrily away on her desk. Lying next to it is her copy of *Vogue,* which she reads on the bus into work. Or at least that's what she wants people to think. And I used to think that too. Until I borrowed it one lunchtime and discovered her guilty secret: a copy of *New Scientist* tucked away inside.

"Are you okay?" I ask, looking at her with concern. Her rosy cheeks have a grayish pallor and her blue eyes are bloodshot.

"Yes, fine." She winces, massaging her temples.

"Because I've got plenty of acetaminophen," I offer, reaching for the family-size bottle I always keep on my desk.

She flinches at the noise. "No, it's fine, honestly," she whispers, getting shakily up from her chair and walking unsteadily over to the coffee machine. "Just a little delicate. I think it might have been those mini-quiches."

"Or the champagne," I add teasingly.

She looks at me, chagrined. "Oh dear, I did get rather sloshed, didn't I? I hope I didn't do or say anything silly."

Without warning my mind flicks back to last night and her speech about time travel and I'm tempted to share my secret with her. Maybe she can help shed some light on how or why this is happening to me. Either way, it would just be a relief to tell someone who won't think I'm going cuckoo for Cocoa Puffs. The theory being because Bea is already a little bit cuckoo for Cocoa Puffs herself.

"Well, there is one thing—" I begin.

"No, stop, don't tell me—" Putting out her hands to defend herself from what I'm about to say, she squeezes her eyes tightly shut as if she's going to be walloped by some great big embarrassing faux pas. "It's about Patrick, isn't it?"

"Patrick?" I stop my thoughts midtrack. "Who's Patrick?"

"The journalist I introduced you to," she reminds me. "You know, the super hot chap who was married."

Suddenly I realize Beatrice wasn't just sloshed. She was well and truly hammered. Beer-goggles, or in Beatrice's case, champagne-goggles, can be the only explanation for the slightly chubby, shiny pink-faced Patrick I met turning into a "super hot chap."

"No, why? Should it be?"

She blushes hotly, her neck prickling with bright crimson splodges, and, opening one large blue eye, looks at me woefully. "I'm afraid after you left I got rather . . ." She swallows hard. *"Flirtatious."*

"I see." I nod. Though I don't. Not really. Beatrice flirting is not an image that comes easily to mind.

"And then his wife appeared."

"Ouch." I wince.

"From nowhere. *Poof.* And she was there. Right in front of me. In a Pringle sweater."

"Ah, yes, the semiprofessional golfer, I remember now."

Beatrice hangs her head in shame. "I know it was terrible of me. I knew he was married. And I wasn't going to *do* anything, it's just—" She pauses and lets out a sigh. "Oh, Charlotte, do you think I'm ever going to meet anyone?"

She looks so utterly crestfallen, I really feel for her. "Of course you will," I say, giving her shoulder a squeeze. "You're sweet and kind and super smart—"

"But that's just it." She stops me. "When it comes to a girlfriend, men don't want super smart. They're looking for beauty, not brains."

"That's not true," I argue. "Look at . . ." I stall. Actually now I come to think of it, I can't think of anyone.

"See. You can't think of anyone, can you?" she accuses sadly.

"Of course I can," I protest, wracking my brains. Come on, Charlotte, come on. There must be someone . . . "I know! What about Miranda from *Sex and the City*?" I say triumphantly.

Beatrice gives me a look that could kill.

"What about her?"

"Well, she was a super-smart lawyer and she got Steve," I point out.

Now Beatrice looks more depressed than ever. "Exactly," she says, throwing me a doleful look and turning back to the coffee machine.

I'm about to argue, but think better of it. Actually, Bea does have a point. Okay, so Steve was a good guy, but he wasn't exactly hunky

Aidan or Mr. Big, was he? And he did have that really annoying, high-pitched nasally voice.

"Men want women who spend money on clothes and makeup and designer shoes, not three thousand pounds on a telescope," she continues, pouring out a fresh brew into two cups.

"Trust me, men don't care what you spend money on, as long as it's not their money—" I break off. "You spent three thousand pounds on a telescope?" I ask in astonishment (that's like six thousand dollars!!).

"Yes, I bid for it on eBay. Oh gosh, Charlotte, it's just amazing," she gushes, coming to life, her eyes shining with excitement. "It's Meade's all-new LX200R telescope with advanced Ritchey-Chrétien optics."

"Um . . . is that good?" I ask uncertainly.

Beatrice clutches her pearls and looks at me as if I've just asked if the red velvet cupcakes with cream cheese frosting from *Sprinkles* on the corner are worth trying.

"Nearly every observatory reflector in the world is a Ritchey-Chrétien, including NASA's Hubble Space Telescope!" she announces grandly, then breaks off, her face flushed with exhilaration.

Which quickly fades in the space of time it takes to snap your fingers.

"See, that's what always happens," she accuses.

"What always happens?"

"That expression."

"What expression?" I reply defensively.

"That blank look on your face."

Oh shit. Is it that obvious? "That's just how my face is," I protest hastily. "That's just how I look."

"That's not true," she pouts sulkily. "I have that effect on everyone. I start talking and people just switch off. Mummy advised me to go into PR, 'because no man wants a wife who's a scientist.' And she's right. Mummy's always right." Her large blue eyes start to fill up and she blinks rapidly, trying to fight back the tears, and grabs a coffee filter as a tissue.

"Mummy *isn't* always right," I argue hotly, then quickly catch myself. "I mean your mummy . . . *mom* . . ." I correct myself, ". . . isn't always right."

"You think so?" She looks at me doubtfully and twists the coffee filter in her hands.

"Absolutely." I nod firmly, then throw her a reassuring smile. "You just haven't met the right person yet."

"Like you met Miles," she says, looking at me meaningfully.

"Well, yes, like I met Miles." I nod, feeling a bit awkward as I realize that I've barely thought about Miles these past couple of days. What with everything that's been going on, my head's been full of other stuff. But now at the mention of his name I'm reminded that I'm seeing him at lunchtime to look at a house.

Out of nowhere, I feel a flutter of nerves. But that's just because I'm excited, I tell myself quickly. After all, who wouldn't be excited to go house hunting with their boyfriend?

"How did you know he was the right person?"

I tune back in to see Beatrice still looking at me.

"Oh, I don't know, lots of things—" I trail off.

"Like what?" she asks, eagerly.

Abruptly I get this feeling as if I'm onstage under the spotlight and it's my cue to say my lines. Only it's like I've got stage fright and I can't remember any of them. "Everything," I answer simply.

"Golly, that's so romantic," she sighs, and passes me my coffee. "You're so lucky, you know."

"Yes, I know." And it's true. I do know I'm lucky. I tell myself that every day. It's just—

"Ooooh! Someone's been on a shopping spree!" interrupts Beatrice. "Giving yourself a makeover?"

I snap back to see her looking at my bulging carrier bags with curiosity. At exactly the same time as I notice the Nicorette patches and several packets of condoms I threw in for good measure, balancing precariously on top.

"Um, yes, I suppose you could say that," I say, and quickly swooping on them I stuff them under my desk.

"Oh, what fun!" She beams, and hugging her coffee mug, she totters back to her desk.

Leaving me smiling uncertainly and wondering what exactly I've gotten myself into. For sure, the next few days are going to be a lot of things, but I'm not entirely convinced fun's going to be one of them.

## Chapter Seventeen

Hello, darling." At one o'clock I park outside a large redbrick Victorian house on a leafy West London street and find Miles already waiting for me by the gate, a huge grin on his face. "Isn't it just perfect?" He beams, sliding his arm around my waist so we can stand side by side on the pavement and look up at number 43 Andlebury Avenue. "Well?"

As he turns to me, his eyes shining with excitement, I realize I haven't actually spoken yet. "Gosh" is all I manage.

Miles smiles, his forehead furrowing. "Gosh?" he teases, his mouth twitching with amusement. "Is that it?"

"Well, no . . . I mean . . ." I trail off to take in the large windows, the black and white tiled path leading up to the front door, the shiny brass door knocker. It's a real, proper-looking, grown-up house. The kind of house in which you put down roots, raise a family, and live for the next thirty years.

"Are you sure we can afford it?" I blurt.

"Oh, I'm sure we can work something out," he says, like he always does, kissing my nose affectionately. "But let's not worry about that just yet, we haven't even looked inside!"

"No . . . yes, I mean, you're right." I nod.

I've never seen Miles so excited. Normally he's so levelheaded and moderate about everything, but today he's buzzing with eager anticipation. I feel oddly left out.

Why aren't I buzzing too? After all, I'm sure I'm going to love it, I can tell just from the outside, I decide, looking at the shiny navy blue front door and the large potted yuccas on either side. And we have been talking about moving in together forever now. It's the next step. It makes total sense.

"Mr. Richards?"

A sharp voice causes us both to turn around to see a gray pinstriped figure striding along the pavement. It must be at least eighty degrees today in London and as he hurries toward us, his jacket flaps open, revealing damp patches spreading out from under the armpits of his blue shirt.

"Benedict Meyers. Formans Realtors."

Jangling a huge bunch of keys, he shakes hands briskly with Miles.

"And Mrs. Richards?" Holding out his hand, he turns to me.

"Oh—no," I correct quickly, then blush. "I mean—"

"Not yet," jokes Miles, and we all share a polite chuckle on the pavement.

"Well, if you'd like to follow me . . ." The Realtor jangles his keys with authority and briskly sets about unlocking the front door, deftly disabling the alarm, and flicking on lights all while providing a running commentary: ". . . into the main hallway where, leading off to the left, we have the full-width reception room which opens into the breakfast room, offering a fantastic living and entertaining space . . ."

I walk slowly behind, trying to take everything in. I've always found house hunting to be slightly bizarre. It's like stepping into someone else's life. All this history, all these memories belonging to someone else, I muse, my eyes flitting across the photographs lining the shelves and trying to imagine them being replaced with pictures of me and Miles instead.

". . . and an actual working fireplace."

Looking up I turn to see the estate agent standing in front of a large exposed brick chimney.

"Wow, really?" I smile eagerly. Miles once told me that you're supposed to act like you're not that interested when you're looking at property, so you can haggle over the price, but I can't help myself. I've always wanted a real fireplace.

"Hmm, is there a gas supply as well?" interjects Miles, frowning slightly.

"Why do you need a gas supply?" I ask, puzzled.

"Real fires look lovely, darling, but they're a lot of work."

"But everyone loves a real fire!" I cry with dismay. "They're so romantic."

"In hotels maybe," he says firmly. "But not when you're shoveling ashes first thing in the morning. I used to have to clear out my housemaster's when I was at boarding school and trust me, it wasn't fun."

"Actually I do believe there is a gas hookup," the Realtor is saying, crouching down and pointing at something, "so if you prefer you could convert this quite easily."

"Hmm, right, yes."

I watch as Miles bobs down next to him, their heads bent together, neither of them listening to me.

"And you can get those very realistic gas fires these days, they almost look like the real thing."

"But we have the real thing," I protest loudly.

The Realtor and Miles suddenly both look up at me.

"Darling, I had no idea you loved real fires so much," he says, surprised.

"Well . . . sort of," I say, blushing slightly.

God, and now I feel like a bit of an idiot. I didn't mean to make such a big deal of it.

"My wife and I can never agree on anything," chips in the Realtor jovially. "Always an argument on everything."

"Oh, I'm sure we'll work it out," says Miles amiably. Straightening up he squeezes my shoulder. "We don't do rows, do we, darling?" he says proudly.

"No. . . ." I smile awkwardly.

"See. All sorted." Miles laughs, turning to the Realtor. "So, shall we move on to the kitchen?"

❧

We spend the next ten minutes exploring the rest of the downstairs and then move into the garden. I only have a tiny balcony at my place, and I've always dreamed of having my own real garden. This would be perfect, I imagine, wandering around the neatly trimmed lawn and looking at all the different flowers and plants that I don't know the names of. Still, I'm sure I could get a book about them, I decide, making a mental note to take a look on Amazon.

"Oh, and look, we could have barbecues," I say, spotting one by a giant fern. I try imagining Miles in a striped apron flipping burgers while I stroll around the garden, handing out glasses of home-made lemonade. Though to tell the truth I'm not sure when we'd have time to organize a barbecue with our busy schedules, I reflect, looking across at Miles. But he's not paying any attention to the barbecue or the garden. Instead he's staring distractedly up at the roof.

"As you know it's a three-bedroom property but there's a possibility of a fourth and even a fifth if you convert the loft," the Realtor is saying. "If you'd like to take a look."

"A loft conversion?" Miles seems galvanized by this news.

"Yes, a lot of the properties on the street have done that, and it gives you an extra bedroom. If you'd like to take a look inside . . ."

"Miles, don't you want to look at the garden—"

But it's no good, he's already gone back inside with the Realtor. I feel a stab of disappointment. I wanted to show him the little fountain, and the barbecue, and all those lovely plants. He didn't seem to notice any of it. Still, I suppose I can do that later, I tell myself, as I follow them back into the house.

Upstairs are two bedrooms and a bathroom, and I'm just taking a peek at the second when Miles joins me.

"Well, what do you think?" he whispers, out of earshot of the Realtor.

"I love it!" I whisper, as we walk inside the second bedroom.

"You do?" Miles's face splits into a relieved smile.

"Yes, it's gorgeous." I nod excitedly. "There's the lovely fireplace, and the garden . . ." Pausing to take in the dimensions of the room I'm suddenly hit by inspiration. ". . . and this room would be *perfect* for an office." No sooner has the idea struck than my mind is already working overtime. "We could put a desk over by the window, and there's plenty of room for a printer and everything . . ."

"I actually had another idea—"

"Oh, you mean put the desk against the other wall?" I frown, trying to picture it. "Yes, I suppose that could work."

"No, silly." Sliding his arm around my waist he pulls me close and looks at me meaningfully for a long moment. "I was thinking this room would be perfect for a nursery . . ."

"You mean . . . for a baby?" I falter.

"Well, what else do you put in a nursery?" He laughs, stroking my hair.

"Um . . ." I push my hair behind my ears and try to think of something to say. I suddenly feel a little panicked. One minute we're talking about moving in together, the next minute *I've given birth?* What happened to the stuff in the middle? We've just leapfrogged right over it. The proposal, me saying yes, the wedding?

Not that I think you have to be married to have a baby, and not that I don't want to have a baby—*one day*—it's just that we've never even *talked* about babies—well, once when we went to the christening of Miles's nephew (Horatio, which I thought was a bit mean—after all, he was only a little baby). It was on the drive home and we had one of those jokey, hypothetical arguments about what we'd call our children, which went something along the lines of:

Me: I like Tallulah for a girl.

Miles: Ugh. She sounds like a stripper. What about Tarquin for a boy?

Me: Yuck. He sounds like an idiot.

Back and forth, until we got bored and started talking about something else and forgot all about it. At least *I* did.

"So are you in a chain?" The Realtor reappears with blundering chirpiness and we break apart.

"Well, we'd be putting our own flats on the market but I can't see that being a problem; they're both desirable one-bedroom properties," says Miles authoritatively.

I glance at him sharply. *"We will?"*

God, this is all moving a bit too fast. I don't remember agreeing to that.

"Well, yes, of course, darling," says Miles. "We discussed it, remember? Consolidating our assets, selling our individual properties . . ."

"A wise decision," butts in the estate agent.

"Um . . . yes, I think so . . ." I say dazedly.

*Selling our individual properties?* That must have been at the bit where my attention wandered.

"It makes perfect financial sense."

"I know, it's just—" I falter, my mind slipping back to the conversation about the fireplace and Miles not understanding the magic of real fires. I don't know how to put it into words. I can't even make sense of it to myself, let alone to Miles. Or the Realtor, I notice, who's watching me intently for signs of hesitation.

"I have to tell you I've got several other interested parties chomping at the bit on this one," he warns. "In fact, I've already had a couple of offers over the asking price, so I reckon you'd have to make a really good offer to clinch the deal."

My stomach clenches. It's all suddenly very real. Buying a place together is something Miles and I have talked about over mixed olives and a bottle of wine, and it all sounded dreamy in theory, but until now I'd never really grasped what it entails.

"I guess I'm just a tad nervous," I confess.

"I know, darling." Miles smiles good-naturedly. "But don't you love this house? You've always said you've wanted a garden, and there's masses of room. . . ."

It's true. I am always saying that. Maybe Vanessa is right. Maybe I'm just worrying about nothing. I look at Miles. He's so handsome and smart, and he's found us this amazing house, and he wants us to buy it and move in together.

And I'm standing here dithering?

I grab ahold of myself. Charlotte, are you *completely* mad? What more do you want? What more could *any* girl want?

"You're right," I say, decidedly. Throwing my arms around his neck I give him a kiss. "Let's make an offer!"

## Chapter Eighteen

Back in the office I sit at my desk eating a salad and staring at the glossy real estate agent's brochure of the house. It looks gorgeous. It's got everything I've ever wanted: shiny wooden floorboards, big shutters, a garden with southern exposure. It's my dream house.

But even so, for the rest of the afternoon I can't turn off that nagging feeling in the pit of my stomach. Every time I start to work on a press release I find my mind wandering back to that moment in the bedroom when we talked about a nursery, or get a flash of Miles's excited face as we walked around the garden and he talked about extensions and planning permission and loft conversions.

As the digital clock on my computer screen flicks from 6:29 p.m. to 6:30 p.m., I put my computer to sleep. I've got my dinner with Larry Goldstein at seven p.m.

"Okay, I'll see you tomorrow," I say to Beatrice, who's hidden behind a barricade of files that are piled up on her desk. Her decision to reorganize the filing cabinets, at four o'clock this afternoon, not being one of her wisest.

"You're leaving?" Popping her head up above the mountains of filing, she looks at me with disbelief. "Already?"

"I'm having dinner with Larry Goldstein at Claridge's," I remind her.

She rolls her eyes. "Of course." She nods, then shoots me a

bright smile. "Good luck! And don't forget to order the chocolate profiteroles."

⤬

Arriving at Claridge's, I valet the car and hurry up the front steps. A uniformed doorman gets the door for me, and I smile appreciatively. God, I love Claridge's. It has to be the nicest hotel in London. I always dream about staying here. Once, after a night out in the West End, I suggested to Miles that we splurge on a suite and spend the night here, but he looked at me as if I'd gone nuts. Why on earth would we pay a fortune to spend the night in a hotel, when we only lived a few miles away?

I'm a little bit early so I cross the grand marbled lobby to where a couple of immaculately groomed receptionists are fielding telephone calls and queries from guests.

"Hi, I'm here to meet Larry Goldstein."

At the mention of his name a look passes between the two desk clerks. "Ah, yes, Mr. Celebrity Smile," says one, smiling brightly. *Too brightly*. I get the impression he's not the most popular guest at the hotel. "I'll call his room. May I ask your name?"

"Charlotte Merryweather. From Merryweather PR," I add out of habit.

"One moment."

As she dials up to the room, I take in the elegant lobby and try to steady my nerves. Several well-dressed guests are milling around and over in the corner there's a blond man wearing sunglasses and muttering into his cell. He looks a little like Daniel Craig. Actually I think it *is* Daniel Craig! Oh my God, just wait till I tell Miles! A real live 007. And he's *gorgeous*. Though of course Miles doesn't like Daniel Craig; he says having a blond James Bond is a travesty . . .

He turns to face me. Oh—it's not him at all.

I feel a sag of disappointment and, turning away, I stifle a yawn. God, I'm actually really tired. Right now I'd give anything to go home and crawl under the covers, but of course that's out of the question. This meeting is very important. I've already had a few e-mails from people in the industry asking if it was true that I've secured Larry Goldstein as a client, and a couple of journalists called today asking Beatrice to confirm the rumors that the first Star Smile clinic was due to open soon in the UK. As soon as the big press announcement happens next week, things will go crazy.

"Miss Merryweather?"

"Yes?" I snap out of my thoughts and look across at the receptionist.

"Mr. Goldstein's running a little late so he has invited you up to his room for drinks before dinner."

My heart thuds. *"His room?"*

"On the third floor. Room 35. The elevator is to your right."

Fuck. This is it. There's no escaping now. Gripping the handle of my bag, I walk nervously to the elevator. My palms have begun to perspire, and as the elevator doors open and I walk inside, I feel the familiar clench of anxiety in my stomach. Now, come on, Charlotte, I tell myself firmly. Stop worrying. He's just being polite and hospitable.

The doors ping open and as I walk down the dimly lit corridor I find his room. Nervously smoothing down my skirt, I tuck my hair behind my ears, and knock tentatively on the door. I hear footsteps.

I get a sudden image of Larry Goldstein greeting me in a slinky robe.

Gross, no. Stop it.

The door swings open and bracing myself I pin a smile on my face.

"Hi, Mr. Goldstein—"

Only it's not Mr. Goldstein. It's a woman with peroxide blonde hair wearing a bright pink velour Juicy tracksuit and clutching a small furry dog. At first glance she looks about twenty-five, but on closer inspection I realize she's older. Although I'm not sure how much. It's one of those weird situations when there are no visible signs of aging—no wrinkles, no eye bags, a perfectly taut neck—and yet somehow it's fairly obvious this is a woman nudging sixty.

"You must be Charlene!" she drawls, flashing a smile identical to Larry Goldstein's.

"Charlotte," I manage, trying not to stare.

"Well, come on in, come in," she demands, waggling her fearsome-looking acrylic nails at me.

I follow her inside, my mind racing. What's going on? Where's Larry Goldstein? My eyes sweep across the huge room, filled with antique furniture, a large flower arrangement, and dozens of bags littered everywhere embossed with designer names: Gucci, Prada, Dior . . .

"I'm sorry, we haven't been introduced . . ."

"Oh, look at those manners, so formal." She laughs gaily, then cradling her small furball in the crook of her arm, sticks out a diamond-encrusted hand.

"I'm Cindy. Larry's wife."

Larry Goldstein's wife? Well, that explains the smile. Two for the price of one, I realize, looking at her in astonishment. Not to mention a great deal of relief.

"Twenty-five years." She smiles proudly.

"Congratulations."

"I can see you're surprised." She laughs, patting her hair. "Most people are when I tell them."

"Oh, right, yes, because he doesn't wear a wedding ring." I smile.

"No, because I don't look old enough," she says sharply. "Larry doesn't wear a ring because he's a cosmetic dentist. His hands are his tools."

Fortunately before things get any more awkward the door opens from the en suite bathroom and out emerges Larry himself from a cloud of steam, like a superhero appearing from a swirl of dry ice.

Primped and smelling strongly of aftershave, he's on the phone talking loudly. "Yeah, Roger, I received the fax, the designs look awesome . . ." Seeing me he gives me a cheerful wave. "Yeah, my PR person's here right now so I'll run those ideas by her and get her take on it. Okay, later." He snaps the phone closed and turns his full attention to me.

"Hey, sorry about that." He smiles brightly, not looking very sorry at all. "So, I see the two of you have met." He walks up to his wife, puts his arm around her, and they both smile as if someone's taking a picture of them: Cindy, Larry, and the dog. It reminds me of when you see those official-looking photos of the American president and first lady.

"Cindy flew over to join me yesterday. She wanted to take in the sights, do some shopping . . ."

"Oh, I do love that Bond Street of yours," she enthuses. "And that Harrods!"

I'm presuming by her exclamation that's a good thing, but it's hard to tell as I'm watching her face but it's not actually moving, she's had so much Botox.

"It was the best mall I've ever been in! Much better than Macy's."

"Well, it's not really a mall—" I begin, but she doesn't let me finish.

"And the Egyptian escalator!" She rolls her eyes. "Who would have thought they'd have had escalators in the pyramids! I said to Larry, isn't that incredible? All those years ago."

I look at her in astonishment. Surely, she doesn't think—*does she?*

"Dirty martini?"

I turn to see Larry gesturing with a cocktail shaker.

"Ooh, my favorite," cries Cindy, her face lighting up. Which is impressive, underneath all that makeup.

"Charlene?"

"Actually, I better not—"

"Oh, I see. Twelve steps?" Cindy taps her nose conspiratorially. I look at her blankly.

"AA," she says, lowering her voice as if people might be listening. "All our friends are in it. In fact I was saying to Larry just recently that maybe we should join. They have some fabulous benefits."

"Oh, no." I shake my head. "I'm just driving."

"That's what they all say." She smiles, as Larry passes her a martini.

"No, I really am—"

But Cindy interrupts. "Don't worry. Your secret's safe with us." And pressing a manicured talon to her collagen lips, she says in a low voice, "Larry and I are the souls of discretion."

❧

"No wine for Charlene, she's in AA."

Throwing her hand protectively over my glass, Cindy hollers loudly at the waiter who's circumventing the table with a bottle of Cabernet Sauvignon. A few people at the next tables turn to stare. I feel my cheeks burn.

"Actually I'm not—"

"It's okay, honey. You don't need to explain," she whispers loudly, patting my hand.

That's it. I give up. My name's Charlene and I'm an alcoholic.

Two rounds of dirty martinis later and we've decamped to the restaurant downstairs. Cindy insisted on bringing Foo-Foo, her miniature Chihuahua, and after a tussle with the maitre d' ("No dogs are allowed, madam." "Foo-Foo is not a dog, she's my baby!") we're allowed to our table, under strict instructions that her "baby" stays in her Fendi handbag.

"So as I said, I'm really interested in hearing your views on the new space we're thinking of for the flagship Star Smile clinic," says Larry Goldstein, producing a folder and clearing a space for it on the table.

"Yes, absolutely." I nod, relieved to be finally getting down to business.

"I've just received a fax from the designers in L.A. and London, regarding the interior of the store. We're thinking organic, a totally new visual concept, very modern, minimalist, space-agey, sexy, but with all the latest high-tech equipment. A sort of *Barbarella* meets *General Hospital.*"

"Right, okay," I say, hurriedly trying to get my head around that.

"Obviously with the total refurbishment, we're hoping for a launch date of late autumn, though realistically it might be the end of the year—"

"But that's great." I smile. "That means we can really utilize that time to build up excitement and interest. Raise your profile here in the UK, *to an even higher degree,*" I add quickly, seeing his face twitch. "Launch the Star Smile brand. Get a waiting list going, involve some celebrities, really drum up the hype . . ."

"Exactly." He nods, looking pleased.

"And you said that you're still deciding on the exact location?"

"Well, we have a couple of spaces we're currently negotiating for, both in Harley Street; in fact I'd be interested in your opinion—" He takes out a piece of paper from the folder and slides it toward me.

"Of course." I nod, as my eyes scan it. It's floor plans for two of-fices, together with photographs and architectural drawings. "Right, I see. Well, they're both large spaces, and they've got all the amenities you'll need . . ."

"Hmm, yes, yes." He's nodding and sipping his wine.

"And of course Harley Street is a prestigious address and renowned across the world for the best in medical services—"

Larry Goldstein gives a smile of satisfaction. "Exactly, that's what the location scout said, which is why we've been working hard on securing premises there."

I hesitate. "But, if you don't mind me saying, it's a little—" I pause.

"Go on," says Larry Goldstein.

"Old."

"*Old?*" Up until this point Cindy has been petting Foo-Foo and drinking wine, but at the word she visibly recoils. Like a vampire that's just caught a whiff of garlic.

Larry Goldstein narrows his eyes and fixes me with a stern look. "But I was told it was the best," he says, his voice thick with disapproval.

"Well, it depends what your idea of best is," I say hastily. "The demographic that you're appealing to wants to know that you're not just the best, you're also cutting edge . . ."

He seems to perk up a little at the words "cutting edge."

"You're not *just* a world-famous cosmetic dentist," I continue, flattering his ego by dumping compliments left, right, and center. "Choosing the Star Smile brand is not *just* a medical procedure, it's a lifestyle choice."

He's nodding now, the corners of his mouth turned upward.

"And most people don't want to spend thousands at the dentist. The British don't like dentists, I can speak from experience—there's a little bit of a phobia of them . . ."

Larry Goldstein gives a slight shudder. "I've noticed."

"Going to the dentist is not something that's at the top of our list, but if you can make it into something appealing, something sought after . . ."

"Such as?"

"Well, think of having a Star Smile like having the latest designer handbag, or pair of shoes, or new car. *Then* you're getting closer to a winner."

"A winner," repeats Cindy approvingly from across the table. "We all want to be winners in life, don't we? It's like when you and I were in Vegas, honey—"

"So what are you saying?" asks Larry, ignoring her and fixing me with his steely gaze.

"That I think you should be based in a more fashionable location," I say, being truthful. I'm in danger of offending him by disagreeing with his earlier choices, but hell, this is what he's paying me for. "That you need a young, hip address. Somewhere celebrities are happy to be seen photographed, rather than to be seen trying to disguise themselves as they scuttle out of doctor's offices in Harley Street."

"Hmm, yes, I think you might be right." Larry nods thoughtfully. Suddenly galvanized, he whips out his iPhone and punches something in. "I'll get on my locations people right away."

I feel like giving myself a pat on the back. This meeting couldn't have gone any better.

"So are you thinking of visiting anywhere else while you're in London?" I ask, turning to Cindy. I feel a bit sorry for having left her out of so much of our conversation. But then again, she seems perfectly happy, I note, watching as she beckons the waiter over to refill her glass.

"Well, we did talk about Paris—" she says brightly.

"Oh, yes, you can go on the Eurostar." I nod. "Now we've got the high-speed link at St. Pancras Station it only takes two and a half hours."

"But then I said to Larry, 'Why bother?' We saw the Eiffel Tower in Vegas."

I look at her blankly. "Sorry, did you just say Vegas?"

"Yes, at the Venetian!" She frowns, as if I'm a bit stupid. "They have all the cities, there under one roof. Paris, Venice . . . And we went on a gondola. It was awesome." She takes a slurp of her champagne. "You should go."

"Um . . . yes, maybe I will," I reply.

"Okay, shall we order?" suggests Larry Goldstein.

"That would be wonderful," I say hastily, and picking up my menu I dive behind it.

# Chapter Nineteen

By the time I get home it's almost ten. Letting myself in, I dump my bags in the hallway and kick off my stilettos. My feet are killing me. Padding barefoot into the living room I flop onto the sofa and flick on the TV. I'll just watch a few minutes before I get started on the paperwork I brought home from the office, I tell myself, stretching out across the cushions and letting out a huge yawn.

God, I'm exhausted. I hardly slept at all last night. Or the night before that, for that matter. I was up half the night looking at photos. Speaking of which—I glance across at the albums still strewn across the rug and the piles of loose photos lying scattered all around. In my usual morning rush today I hadn't had time to clean up my mess, but I'd better do it now, before the cleaning lady comes tomorrow.

I love having a cleaning lady. That's one of the great things about being older, being able to afford the luxury of having a cleaning lady. Only the irony is I usually end up cleaning up for my cleaning lady— after all, I don't want her to think I'm messy.

Easing myself up from the sofa, I'm crawling around reorganizing the photographs when my phone rings. I glance at the screen. It's Beatrice.

"So did you get the profiteroles?" she demands as soon as I pick up.

"Excuse me?"

"For pudding?"

"Um . . . no . . . we just had green tea . . ."

"Just tea?" she exclaims. "Oh, what a shame! They're so yummy."

I check my watch. "Beatrice, did you just call me to talk about dessert? Because it is rather late. . . ."

"Oops, no, sorry," she says breathlessly. Beatrice is always breathless, even when she's sitting still. "I wanted to find out how the meeting went with Larry Goldstein and if you need any facts and figures, or anything really, ready for first thing tomorrow morning—"

My impatience turns to gratitude. There are assistants, and then there is Beatrice.

"It went really well," I tell her, wedging my phone underneath my chin so I can continue stacking the photos and putting them in the box. "He seemed really impressed with all my suggestions and ideas for the location for his new flagship store, and so we agreed to touch base on Monday for a final run-through before the press announcement."

"Oh, bravo!" she cheers. "So do you want me to check the diary and see when you're free? I have it right here . . ."

Like I said, Beatrice takes her job of looking after the diary very seriously.

"Okay, great."

I turn back to the photographs. There's so many of them, I still didn't look at all the albums, I muse, glancing at the ones left in the box. Idly I pick up a couple. Hang on a minute, what's this? One of them is smaller and leather-bound, and flicking it open I realize it's not filled with photographs, but with pages of my handwriting. Oh, wow, it's an old diary, I realize, fanning through the pages. And here's a couple more.

Digging them out of the bottom of the box, I spot one embossed with the date: 1997. My heart does a little leap. I wrote this when I was twenty-one.

". . . now obviously we'll need to juggle something around, so let's see, you have a nine a.m. conference call with the Cloud Nine people to discuss their new line of flavored water, then you've got a ten a.m. coffee with Katie Proctor, the journalist, followed by an eleven a.m. appointment . . ."

As Beatrice starts running through my diary I start reading my own from ten years ago. Here's the entry I wrote on the first day I moved to London, February 23, 1997. My eyes flick over my description of the office, my boss, meeting Nessy:

> . . . tall and blonde and smoking cigarettes by the fire
> escape, she seems really cool but a bit intimidating. She
> told me her name was Vanessa: "Which was created by
> Jonathan Swift for *Gulliver's Travels.*" I hope we'll be
> friends . . .

Smiling to myself, I thumb curiously to today's date. I wonder what I did ten years ago today. I glance down the page of swirly handwriting:

> . . . so exciting! All day I could barely concentrate.

Huh? I wonder what I was so excited about.

> . . . I've been looking forward to seeing the band all week
> and it was great! Shattered Genius was amazing . . .

Whoa, just one minute.

Frowning, I look again at the entry. I went to see Shattered Genius? But that can't be right, that's not till Saturday. I glance again at the date. Did I read it wrong? No, sure enough it's today's date: August twenty-third.

"Huh, that can't be right." I stare it, puzzled.

"What isn't?"

On the other end of the phone Beatrice sounds alarmed. "But it must be. I've already confirmed your three o'clock," she's saying anxiously.

"Oh, no, nothing. I was just looking at an old diary and the dates are different. I must have got mixed up . . ."

"But they will be different," she replies, sounding relieved. "Calendars are different from year to year."

Oh my God, of course. I'm such a dummy. I never even thought of that.

"The Gregorian solar calendar is an arithmetical calendar," she continues matter-of-factly. "It counts days as the basic unit of time, grouping them into years of 365 or 366 days. The solar calendar repeats completely every 146,097 days, which fill 400 years, and which also happens to be 20,871 seven-day weeks."

"Um, really?" I say distractedly, staring at the diary in my lap. So that totally explains it. Today is a Thursday, but when I was twenty-one, today *was* a Saturday. Which means—all once it registers—Billy Romani's band is playing tonight. Shit.

"Of these 400 years, 303—the 'common years'—have 365 days, and 97—the leap years—have 366 days. This gives an average year length of exactly 365.2425 days—or 365 days, 5 hours, 49 minutes and 12 seconds . . ."

Beatrice is forging on but I'm no longer listening. Instead my eyes are frantically glossing to the bottom of the page. Because there, in bold capitals, underlined twice and with four, no, *five* exclamation marks, are the words I'm dreading:

### SLEPT WITH BILLY ROMANI!!!!!

I take a sharp intake of breath. "Fuck."

Actually we did, the whole night, if I remember rightly.

"Charlotte?" says Beatrice uncertainly. "Is everything all right?"

No, I'm not all right. I'm not effing all right! I'm about to make a huge mistake!

"Sure, yeah, I'm fine . . ." My mind is whirring and I glance at my watch. Maybe I'm not too late. Maybe I can still stop this. Dropping the diary on the floor I jump up from the shagpile rug. "But I have to go."

"Go?"

"Um . . . yes . . ." I fluster. Music blares from the TV and I glance at the screen. "*Project Runway's* coming on," I blurt. "It's my . . . um . . . favorite show."

"It is? Oh, well, enjoy. See you tomorrow."

"You too." I hang up and look wildly around for my car keys. There they are! And scooping them up from the coffee table I grab the remote and flick off the TV.

Forget *Project Runway*.

This is Project Cockblock.

❦

Though I say I was a huge fan of Shattered Genius, I can't remember any of their songs. Not a single one. But I'm sure it's all going to come flooding back when I hear them tonight onstage, I tell myself, as I drive back through the diversion. Unexpectedly I feel a slight thrill. I can't remember the last time I went to see a live band. Actually, yes, I can. It was to see License to Thrill, a tribute band that did all the theme tunes to the James Bond films.

Reluctantly my mind slides back to that night a few months ago. Miles got the tickets. He's a huge James Bond fan. He's read all the Ian Fleming books about a hundred times and can quote the films off by heart. Which might drive me nuts if it wasn't for Daniel Craig and *those* swimming trunks. I could watch him forever. Though according to Miles, you have to prefer Sean Connery to be a true 007 purist.

Anyway, I like Shirley Bassey singing "Goldfinger" as much as the next person, but an aging trio from Manchester on keyboards, with a sequenced light show, was a bit much. Their big finale was "Nobody Does It Better," though frankly, I beg to differ. *I* could have done better. In fact, Great-aunt Mary's talking parrot could have done better. But of course I didn't tell Miles that. I didn't want to hurt his feelings so I raved on about how amazing they were.

Unfortunately that slightly backfired as he went and bought me the CD "because you love them so much." So now I always have to pretend to be listening to it whenever he's in my car with me.

Taking the same route as yesterday, I cut down the side street. Fortunately it's late and there's hardly any traffic on the roads so it's not long before I'm pulling up outside the Wellington Arms. As I turn off the ignition I hear a tuneless din wafting from inside.

Oh dear. Suddenly, that vague excitement I felt earlier is replaced with a resounding thud of trepidation and I have a flashback to me in a dingy club, full of cigarette smoke, while a band thrashes the hell out of the speakers. Actually maybe this wasn't such a good idea. Maybe I've forgotten all of Shattered Genius's songs for a reason.

Feeling my resolve wobble, I force myself to rally. Still, I can't turn back now. I'm here for me, remember. For Lottie, the twenty-one-year-old girl I used to be. And who right now is in that pub on course to get her heart broken by Billy Romani.

*Unless I rescue her.*

Resolute, I grab the handle and swing open the car door. As I step out onto the pavement I hear the muffled clash of drums, accompanied by a sort of strange wailing that doesn't sound quite human.

Okay, so it doesn't sound great, but it can't be worse than License to Thrill, I console myself, slamming the door and hurrying toward the pub. Plus, I used to be a fan of this band, remember? Seriously, how bad can they be?

Bad.

Very bad.

Like, truly terrible.

Pushing open the door of the Wellington I'm greeted by what sounds like an entire drum kit being thrown down the stairs, along with the drummer.

"Thank God—you made it!"

And Lottie, who spots me waiting unsurely in the doorway and rushes over. She's carrying a pint of cider and funnily enough, she's wearing those pleather pants that make her legs look like they've been vacuumed-packed inside a pair of shiny black trash bags. That said, her figure does look pretty fantastic, I think with surprise.

"Hi, sorry I'm late, I was—"

"You nearly missed the whole gig," she gasps impatiently, thrusting a ticket in my hand. "Come on, hurry up, they're about to do their unplugged version."

As the band falls silent she grabs my arm and charges back toward the small room at the rear of the pub. Packed with people, it's standing room only and as she pushes her way through the crowd toward the makeshift stage, Shattered Genius have disappeared offstage and a roadie is setting up a chair and microphone.

"So you really love this band, huh?" Reaching the front I turn to Lottie, whose eyes are glued eagerly on the stage.

"Well, I love the lead singer, Billy Romani," she confesses, sipping her pint.

Suddenly there's movement behind the stage.

"Oh my God, he's coming back on, he's coming back on," she gasps.

My chest tightens as I brace myself. I feel a mixture of anticipation and apprehension at the thought of seeing him again. After all these years I vaguely remember what he looks like, but to be honest it's all a bit of a lustful blur. Plus of course I tried my hardest to forget him.

In the commotion I get pushed behind Lottie, but she's wearing flats like I always used to, so in my heels I can see easily over her head. My stomach releases a cage of butterflies. Any minute now I'm going to see him again, and I have no idea how I'm going to feel.

And then, all at once, there he is, dressed all in black, and striding onstage with his guitar. Folding his six-foot-something frame into the chair, he pauses for a moment to take a swig from a beer.

And I feel absolutely nothing.

I stare at him in astonishment.

*That's him?* That's the man I used to be so crazy about? I was expecting to feel some kind of powerful emotion, desire, sadness, anger, *anything.* But instead it's just hugely anticlimactic. He used to seem so hip and cool and desirable, but now—

"He's wearing leather pants," I hiss, feeling an unexpected wave of amusement. The last thing I expected was to find him funny, but he looks like such a complete idiot I actually feel sorry for him! "And they're skintight!" I snort. Ha! This will definitely turn her off.

"I know." She nods, her eyes like saucers. "Sexy, huh?"

I look at her in confusion. This was not the reaction I was expecting at all. Why am I not snickering? Can it be . . . I hesitate, trying to get my head around this impossible thought . . . can it be true that once upon a time *I liked a man who wore leather pants?*

And with a lace-up crisscross fly, I notice with horror. I nudge Lottie quickly. "Look at his crotch!"

"Hey, hands off, he's mine," she giggles.

"No, I mean—" But I'm interrupted.

"This is a song I wrote about this crazy roller coaster called life." Billy Romani is drawling huskily into the microphone, his eyes downcast as if he's uncomfortable being under the spotlight.

Oh, please. If he's shy, so is Paris Hilton, I think, as he closes his eyes and starts wailing soulfully at the top of his lungs. On and on. Until finally, two encores later, it's all over and gratefully I steer Lottie back into the main pub, and to safety.

"Over there—" Spotting a couple of free seats we sit down.

Phew. Well, that was easy. All she has to do is finish her drink, then we can leave and put all this behind us.

"Hello, ladies, is this seat taken?"

*Damn it. I spoke too soon.*

We both look up sharply to see Billy standing above up, smiling lazily. But whereas before that smile would have melted me from a hundred feet away, now it's like I'm composed of super-Teflon or something.

"Yes!"

"No—"

We both speak at the same time. Lottie and I. Then we both look at each other. She makes a face as if to say "what are you *doing*?" and throws me a desperate look and all at once my heart goes out to her. Now he has zero effect on me, but back then I'd had a crush on him forever.

"No . . . no one's sitting there," she says hastily.

I watch her smiling tentatively and the longing is palpable. God, I really, really liked him, didn't I? I can see it in my eyes. That hopeful desire to be liked back.

And for a brief moment it all comes rushing back to me. The dizzy high I felt that night we spent together. God, it was amazing. I seriously thought he was "the one." Followed by the crushing low when I discovered he wasn't. But then I thought a lot of foolish things when I was younger, I reflect, glancing at him and wondering what on earth I ever saw in him. God, if only I knew then what I know now . . .

"Cool." Turning the chair around he straddles it and hugs the back of it. My eyes sweep across his shirt, open to the navel, and the crucifix around his neck that's resting on his smooth hairless chest.

I look back at Lottie, hoping to see her rolling her eyes sardonically or wanting to share a conspiratorial giggle, but no, her eyes have glazed over dreamily in the way men's do when they see a *Victoria's Secret* catalog.

"I'm Billy, by the way." He holds out his hand and I see a flash of silver in the dimness of the pub. Oh my God—is that? I peer closer. Just when I thought the lace-up leather trousers and crucifix was bad, it gets worse. *He's wearing a skull and crossbones ring.*

"I'm Lottie."

"And I'm Charlotte," I say, grabbing his hand before Lottie can. Shaking it, I squeeze his fingers just that little bit harder than necessary.

"Firm handshake you've got there," he quips as I finally let go. "You nearly broke my fingers."

Like you broke my heart, I'm tempted to reply, only I make do with an innocent, "Oh God, really?"

Stretching out his fingers, he turns to Lottie, who's sitting next to him, staring at him adoringly.

"So how did you like the gig?"

"It was awesome. You were really awesome," she exclaims, and then catching herself, blushes.

Gross. Could I be any *less* cool?

Billy Romani smiles appreciatively and, pushing back his shock of black hair which hangs lazily over his forehead, leans closer so that his face catches the light. It's just as I remember. The high, angular cheekbones, his dark doe eyes, the sultry mouth with the perfect cupid's bow. I have to say, despite the man-jewelry and leather trousers, he's still the sexiest man I've ever laid eyes on.

Which, of course, has somehow turned him into a total bastard.

"That's good to hear as we're working in the studio right now on the new album, trying to lay down some tracks. It's going to be really raw. It's a totally new sound. A combination of the spiritual meets the physical meets the metaphysical."

"Spiritual meets the physical meets the metaphysical?" I snort. He might be able to charm Lottie with this absolute nonsense, but he won't be able to charm me.

Unfortunately he's not paying any attention to me at all. I've suddenly turned into the ugly friend and instead he's focusing entirely on Lottie.

"You know, has anyone ever told you you've got really long eyelashes?" he's saying now, gazing at her intensely.

It's called mascara, dummy, I think, but my younger self just giggles flirtily.

"And you smell really good."

I look at him in disbelief. He did not just say that line. He did not.

"Thanks."

I glance sharply at Lottie. I can't believe I'm falling for it!

In fact, scrap "falling," I realize, watching myself flicking my hair around like I'm in a shampoo commercial. I've crash-landed right at his feet.

Shit. This is worse than I thought. I mean, just look at me! I'm a total pushover. There's a peal of girlish laughter and I see myself angling my body toward his. I swear, one more minute and I'll be nuzzling his chest. That's right. *Nuzzling*.

And I'm not even on a first date! Honestly. Charlotte Merryweather. I had no idea you used to be so *easy*.

"So, do you have a boyfriend?"

Fuck. I've got to do something. And fast. But what?

Panicked, I'm desperately wracking my brains when out of the corner of my eye I see him slide his hand on her knee and before I can stop myself—

"Hey!"

I'm "accidentally" kicking the table and Lottie's half-finished pint of cider is toppling over and landing all over his lap. Immediately they break apart and he jumps up from his seat.

"Oh God, I am so clumsy," I gasp apologetically.

Seriously, I should have been an actress. I'd definitely be up for an Oscar.

"Hey, no worries," he says, smiling tightly.

"I've got a tissue—" Lottie pulls one out of her bag and starts dabbing his crotch eagerly as he frowns at the puddle collecting at his feet.

"Hey, can you clear this up?" he hollers to a bartender who's collecting glasses from a table nearby.

"'Scuse me?"

As he turns I see it's the same bartender from the other evening.

"Oh, no, I'll do it, it was my fault," I begin quickly, but Billy Romani stops me.

"Hey, that's his job," he says cheerfully. "Right, man?"

I notice the bartender's jaw clench. "That's right." He smiles pleasantly, and grabbing a cloth, mops up the spill. "Accident, huh?" He winks, catching me watching.

"Um . . . yeah, absolutely." I nod, reddening as he walks away.

"Would you like another drink?"

I turn back to Billy, who's speaking to Lottie. But I'm undeterred. Cockblocking, I'm fast learning, requires a skin thicker than Simon Cowell's.

"Yes, please," I answer loudly. "I'll have a vodka tonic." Not that I'm drinking—I'm driving—but if there's one thing I've learned over the years it's that men hate nothing more than having to buy "the friend" a drink. "And can you make it a large one?" I smile sweetly.

He throws me a smile that's tighter than his leather pants.

"And for you?" As he turns to Lottie his smile transforms into one that Larry Goldstein would be proud of.

She blushes bright red. "Um . . . yeah, a cider, please."

"Coming right up." He smiles, and gets up.

As soon as he's gone, she turns to me excitedly. "So what do you think?"

*That he's going to sleep with you, promise you the world, then crush your soul,* I want to cry, but it's like it says in *How to Be a Good Friend,* it's important to be diplomatic when a friend asks for your opinion. Plus, I don't want to look like a total fruit-loop.

So instead I go for a more tactful approach with an ambivalent, "Hmmm."

"What?" She frowns in consternation.

"Oh, nothing." I shrug.

Which of course is the surefire way to make her insist I tell her.

"No, go on," she cajoles.

"Well, I didn't want to say anything—"

"No, tell me," she demands, just like I hoped she would.

"—but he's got a really bad reputation."

Lottie looks at me with both alarm and disbelief. "That's probably just people being jealous," she replies after a moment's pause.

I hesitate. I'm aware I'm treading a fine line here. I want to warn her off, but I don't want her thinking it's because I'm after him for myself.

"Before I met my *boyfriend*"—I say, emphasizing the word "boyfriend"—"I knew guys like him, and trust me, he's no good."

She looks crestfallen. "But he seems really cool."

"He *thinks* he's really cool," I correct her. "There's a difference. You need to go out with someone who's going to love *you,* not himself. Who understands you, who really, truly *gets* you . . ." All at once my mind skims back to Miles and our conversation about the fireplace. God, what is it about that stupid fireplace? It's not like it's super important or anything. "But who you can also trust to not let you down," I add quickly. Because for all Miles's faults, I know I can always depend on him, and that's really important.

Lottie nods, but I can see she's not thinking about loyalty and trustworthiness, she's thinking about attractiveness and coolness. Because when I was her age, that's all I thought about when it came to potential boyfriends. Speaking of which.

"And who doesn't want to be the next Kurt Cobain . . ." I say pointedly, remembering Rob, who slept with his Nirvana records. I start running through a few of the horrors I dated in my twenties. ". . . Someone who isn't an alcoholic . . ." That was Archie, the lawyer. I broke it off with him, but he was so drunk at the time, he didn't remember. "Here's a tip: if a man gets so drunk he passes out on the sidewalk outside the bar, leave him the number of the local AA, and lose him faster than you can say, 'Taxi!' "

Lottie laughs, oblivious to the fact she's got all this to come. Though with any luck she'll listen to some of what I'm saying and learn by my mistakes, I think hopefully.

"Oh, and someone who has ambition," I add, remembering Zac who lived in a tent in someone's back garden. Zac was tortured, and deep and angst-ridden, and talked a lot about the agony of life and having integrity and passion. And I agreed with everything he said, while secretly wishing that I too could be tortured. Unfortunately, the only thing that became enlightened was my wallet. With Zac I ended up paying for everything. "Someone with prospects," I finish emphatically.

"Billy's in a band," she replies eagerly.

"Exactly," I reply. "Never date musicians."

She throws me a puzzled look and laughs. "Don't be silly—"

"He's going to hurt you, Lottie," I warn, my face falling suddenly serious. Painful memories that I've buried deep inside of me begin rising from the surface, and I feel a sense of urgency. "Please, stay away from him."

"Hey—"

We're interrupted by Billy, who reappears empty-handed. "I thought we could get some booze and go back to a friend's house instead. Have a little after-party. There's a few of us going . . ." He looks straight at Lottie as if I'm invisible. "Fancy coming along and joining us?"

My heart thuds. This is it.

"Well?" He waits, hands on hips. "What do you say?"

*No! Say no!*

"Um . . ." Lottie glances at me uncertainly. I can feel her wavering. On one side there's me in her head telling her no, and on the other there's her groin telling her very much yes.

"Actually I really don't feel that well," I blurt desperately.

Well, I can't risk leaving this up to my twenty-one-year-old groin to decide, now can I?

"In fact I feel really nauseous. I think I need to go to the bathroom."

Lottie looks at me, alarmed. "Do you want me to come with you?"

"If you don't mind." I nod weakly.

Okay, so I feel a little mean, but like I said, it's for my own good.

"Sorry." Putting her arm around me, Lottie turns to Billy. "But no, thanks."

"No worries. Some other time maybe." He shrugs and, turning away, lopes out of the pub.

Watching him leave I stifle a small, yet victorious, smile.

*Not if I can help it.*

## Chapter Twenty

G reat. That's the first thing crossed off my list.
Sitting at my desk the next morning I unfold the crumpled piece of paper on which I've scribbled down my tips and advice, and taking a large black marker draw a line through:

1. ~~Do not sleep with Billy Romani.~~

I'm feeling really pleased with myself. Last night was a total success. After Billy Romani left I made a remarkable recovery, in fact, ten minutes later I was feeling well enough to drive and gave Lottie a ride home alone. Which partly explains my good mood. The other reason being because it's my—

"Happy birthday!"

I look up to see the door swing wide open with Beatrice attached to it, a bit like one of those magician's assistant's on a knife-throwing board. In her hands is a large cardboard box with *Sprinkles* written across it in large swirly writing.

"There's only two of us so I didn't buy a cake," she trills, her cheeks pink with excitement. "Instead I got the red velvet cupcakes with special frosting. Just wait, you're going to become addicted!"

What she really means is help! *I'm* already addicted. My name's Beatrice Spencer and I'm a cupcake-a-holic.

"You shouldn't have!" I smile with amusement.

"Nonsense," she says, setting the box down on my desk. "You missed pudding last night, so you deserve a treat." Flicking open the lid, she takes a deep, languorous inhale.

"Four?"

"Well, one's never enough," she says sagely, peeling off the wrapper.

Beatrice, it seems, has turned into a cupcake pusher so she can, quite literally, feed her habit.

"Mmm," she groans orgasmically, burying her mouth in the frosting.

I look at them, sitting there in all their red devilness, oozing dairy, wheat, and refined sugars, and probably contaminated with nuts from being near peanut butter–flavored ones. With all my allergies, I can't possibly eat them. Plus, I'm trying to be healthy.

Then again, I don't want to offend Beatrice, and a little bit probably wouldn't hurt, I tell myself, taking a nibble. And it *is* my birthday.

It's like a sugar overload. Soft, sweet buttery frosting and a rich, moist, velvety cupcake. Wow, I can see how Beatrice got hooked. Not that I ever would, I tell myself quickly, thinking about my private training session this morning and feeling a stab of guilt. Hastily I put the cupcake down.

"So what are you doing tonight to celebrate?" Surfacing, Beatrice looks at me. The tip of her nose is covered in cream cheese frosting.

"Having dinner with Miles and some friends." I take a swig of coffee. "Remember Vanessa and Julian?"

"Golly, no, I don't think so—" She taps her finger on her nose to think, then, discovering the frosting, licks it off hungrily.

"Here, look . . ." Tapping my keyboard, I click onto the photos on my computer until I find one of the two of them together.

"Oh, yes, I remember now." She nods. "He's a lawyer."

"Yes, that's right,"

"Jolly sexy," she adds.

"You think so?" I look back at the photo. I know Julian's attractive, but it's hard to see your best friend's husband as sexy. Especially when I know all about his personal habits, such as how he uses his nose-hair trimmer on a weekly basis and leaves all the little brown hairs around the sink.

"If he was single, that is," she adds hastily, obviously remembering her confession about flirting with the married guy a few nights ago. "I mean, I'd never find him sexy or anything *now*." She blushes bright red, and makes a start on her second cupcake. "So where are you going?"

"Back to that gastropub I went to with Miles on Monday."

"Oh, fabulous! What are you going to wear?"

Beatrice's interest in my wardrobe never ceases to baffle me. She has no interest in her own clothes and recently asked me, "Who is that girl I always see pictures of looking so unkempt?"

It was Kate Moss.

"My Chloé dress, the one with the little capped sleeves that Miles bought me for Christmas." Well, actually that's not strictly true. Miles bought me a gift certificate for a department store, but I never have time to shop these days, so instead I treated myself to a beautiful dress from Net-a-Porter online. Miles will never know I bought it from there.

Or how much it cost.

Trust me, I've long since learned to tell Miles that everything costs a fraction of the actual price, thus saving him from a heart attack and me from another financial lecture.

"Which reminds me, I have to remember to grab it from the dry cleaner's on the way home . . ." I'm interrupted by the phone ringing and glance at my watch. Nine a.m.

"That'll be the Cloud Nine people," remarks Beatrice, polishing off the rest of her cupcake.

As I go to pick up the phone I catch her staring at the cupcake that's left with a look of such longing that any moment now she's going to start salivating.

"Go ahead, Bea, have it," I tell her, reaching for the phone.

"Oh, no, I couldn't possibly," she protests, then without even a missing beat, "oh, well, all right then, if you insist." And diving on it she gives a little hiccup of pure, unadulterated pleasure.

❧

When I was younger my birthday was a huge deal. The year I moved to London I remember spending the whole day in constant celebration: taking phone calls from friends and family, opening presents from my coworkers, enjoying a boozy lunch at the pub with the rest of the office, before returning back to work sometime late in the afternoon to eat cake and sober up to get ready for the evening's celebrations. God, I used to love my birthday!

Now of course it's business as usual.

After my conference call, I dash over to the tearooms at Liberty, a beautiful old department store in the center of town, to meet Katie Proctor. Officially it's a meeting about getting promotional features for our clients in the newspapers she writes for, but unofficially it's a chance to catch up over iced lattes. Then it's back to the office to reply to e-mails—my in-box seems to fill up whenever I'm out of the office—before dashing out again to another appointment.

And another. And another. Until hours later I find myself sitting around a boardroom table with a lot of men in suits, discussing a campaign to raise awareness of "functional water" (which is basically flavored water that's supposed to be super healthy and costs £2.50 a bottle) while surreptitiously glancing at the clock on the wall. It's my last meeting, and it's running late. Really, *really* late.

*Like the dry cleaner's are closing late.*

Screeching into the curb, I jump out of the car and dash across to the sidewalk, but the shop's in total darkness.

Damn!

I stare in dismay at the Closed sign on the door.

What am I going to do now? My dress is in there. Along with everything else, I reflect, thinking about the huge pile of dry cleaning that had been growing over the past few weeks, and which I'd finally gotten around to dropping off a couple of days ago. That's the problem with expensive designer clothes, they're all dry-clean only. You can't just chuck everything in the washing machine like I used to. But of course that's because they're better designed, better cut, and made from much better fabrics, I remind myself.

Not that any of that is much good if I can't freaking wear them, I think, feeling a clench of irritation. Turning away from the shop I climb back in my car and look at the time. Even if I did have something to wear, I still wouldn't have time to go home and change now anyway, I realize. The reservation's for eight p.m. and it's ten to already.

Hurriedly I pull out my makeup bag and after a quick once-over with some lip gloss, blush, and mascara, I turn the ignition and pull out into the traffic.

❦

"Red or white?"

Entering the pub I'm greeted by Vanessa, who jumps up from the table and throws her arms energetically around me. "We can't decide and you're the birthday girl, so you get to choose!"

"Um . . ." Breaking free from her bear hug, I slide into my seat next to Miles, who stops munching on a bread stick to kiss me hello.

"Happy birthday, darling." He smiles pleasantly, then frowns. "I thought you were wearing the dress I bought you?"

"It's a long story," I roll my eyes, then I glance at the empty seat. "Where's Julian?"

"Working late," says Vanessa and we exchange looks. "He says to start without him and he'll be here as soon as he can." She grins cheerfully and anyone else would be fooled by her broad white smile, but I've known her too long. It doesn't reach her eyes. "So what's it to be?" she enthuses, changing the subject and passing me the wine list.

"Oh, wow." I look at the dozens of wines. I don't know much about wine. As I've gotten older I've progressed from cider to Liebfraumilch to dry whites and learned that if you pay less than a fiver for a bottle you're going to wake up with a very bad hangover, but that's about it. "What about this sauvignon blanc from Australia . . ."

"No, no, no." Miles clicks his tongue. He likes to think of himself as something of a sommelier. "If you're going to go for a sauvignon blanc, it has to be from the Marlborough region of New Zealand."

"Oh, okay then." I shrug.

"Though personally I think we should go for a nice full-bodied red."

"What about a Merlot?" suggests Vanessa, tearing off a chunk of bread.

"*A Merlot?*" repeats Miles, pulling a face.

"Oh, please, what is this? *Sideways?*" quips Vanessa, rolling her eyes.

"There's nothing wrong with trying to develop a palate," he replies, a little unnerved.

"She's only teasing," I say, rubbing his arm and shooting a glance at Vanessa, who's now burying her face in a bread roll. Vanessa and Miles have never seen eye to eye.

Not that they've ever actually admitted it, but they don't need to. They're like the human equivalent of oil and water.

"Not drinking yet?"

I look up to see Julian striding toward us. Carrying his briefcase and wearing a smart navy blue suit he looks very much the suave, successful lawyer that he is. "Happy birthday, Charlotte." He leans across the table to give me a kiss.

"We're still figuring it out," replies Miles, a little tightly.

"Well, as long as it's wet." He grins, lightly kissing Vanessa on the forehead with a "hello, hon" before turning to the table. "Sorry, work was insane."

"As always," mutters Vanessa, but if Julian hears her he doesn't react.

"I know, why don't we ask the waiter?" I suggest as a compromise and, closing the menu, I turn around to attract his attention.

Finishing up another table, he looks over. "Yes?"

Oh *God*, it's him again.

My heart sinks as I realize it's the same bartender who served us on Monday night. The one who thought my allergies were just *hilarious*.

"We'd like to order some wine, please." Julian smiles.

"What would you like?"

"I was thinking about a Pinot—" Miles begins, but is interrupted by Vanessa.

"But we can't decide," she finishes, throwing him a look.

"Well, I'd suggest the Rioja if you want a red, or the Sancerre if you'd prefer white . . ."

I'm sliding down in my chair, trying to hide between my menu, averting myself from his eyes. Hopefully he won't remember me.

"They both sound great," says Julian. "Why don't we have them both?"

"Excellent." He nods, then motions to the empty bread basket, most of which has been hoovered up by Vanessa. "More bread?"

"Um, no, not for me," mutters Vanessa guiltily. "Charlotte?"

"Charlotte doesn't eat bread," pipes up Miles before I can answer. "She has a wheat intolerance."

"Ah, yes, now I remember. The lady with the food allergies."

I catch the waiter's eyes and see they're twinkling with amusement.

"So, what's new, Miles?" asks Julian as the waiter leaves. Thankfully.

"Well, Charlotte and I put an offer in on a house yesterday—"

"You did?" Vanessa looks at me agog. "You never told me, Charlotte!"

"Didn't I? Oh . . . I was going to." Suddenly reminded, I feel an anxious twinge. "We haven't really had the chance to talk."

"Wow, that's exciting," says Julian, raising his eyebrows as if he's impressed.

"Yes, isn't it." Miles beams.

"I bet Mrs. M. was beside herself," Vanessa says with a grin, referring to my mom. She's known me long enough to know what my mother's like.

"I haven't told her."

*"You haven't?"* Miles rounds on me, shocked.

"Well, we don't know if we've got it yet, do we?" I say quickly.

"When do you find out if your offer's been accepted?" asks Julian evenly.

"Soon, I hope," replies Miles, turning to him. "It went straight to sealed bids, so we're just waiting to hear."

"Shall we order?" I suggest, trying to sound nonchalant. All this house talk is making me nervous.

"Not until I've given you your present," orders Vanessa, pulling out an envelope from her handbag. She hands it to me across the table. "And I don't want to hear any excuses about your being too busy."

I look at her quizzically and open my mouth to say something, but I'm shoo-shooed by her hand, so I tear it open instead. Out fall two Eurostar tickets to Paris.

"Oh, wow, Nessy! You shouldn't have!"

"I know." She grins teasingly. "But now you *have* to go away for the weekend and relax, otherwise you'll feel very guilty for wasting my money."

I smile back. She knows me so well. That's exactly what I would do.

"Well, Julian's money," she adds tersely. I know Vanessa hates that fact that now she's given up working, she doesn't have her own money to spend anymore. "And anyway, now I can live vicariously through you." She glances at Julian. "I can't remember the last time we went away for a weekend."

"We will," he responds, looking uncomfortable. "It's just that work's crazy at the moment. In fact, that reminds me, I'm going to have to go into the office on Sunday."

Vanessa's face drops. "But we were going to take the kids to the aquarium—"

"I know, I'm sorry, darling, we'll have to do it another weekend."

"Okay, now my turn." Seemingly unaware of the heated emotions going on across the table, Miles jovially interrupts. Vanessa and Julian fall silent, and all eyes fall upon him as he reaches inside his breast pocket and produces a small black velvet box.

A small black velvet *jewelry* box.

My stomach clenches and my heart starts thudding loudly in my ears. Oh my God, is that what I *think* it is? Is he going to do what I *think* he's going to do? I keep my eyes glued to the box in Miles's hands, too scared to look at his face. What am I going to say, in front of all these people? Well, yes, obviously. I'll say yes, right?

"Charlotte?"

His voice snaps me back as he hands me the box. His expression is serious, yet uncertain. I swallow hard. This is it.

*This is it.*

I take a deep breath, my fingers fumbling with the gold catch. My heart is racing. Everyone's eyes are upon me and I suddenly feel light-headed. As if time's slowed right down and the chatter and hum of the pub has gone all muffled, like watching a movie in slow motion with the sound turned down. The catch releases and with the breath caught in the back of my throat, I slowly open the lid.

*Pearl earrings?*

I stare blankly at them nestling white and shiny against the black velvet and almost want to laugh with giddy relief. Instantly I feel completely ridiculous. What on earth was I thinking? Of course he wasn't going to propose. Honestly, Charlotte, talk about getting carried away.

"Do you like them?"

I snap my focus back to the earrings.

"Miles . . . they're lovely . . ." I murmur, focusing on them properly for the first time.

"I thought you would," Miles is saying, his face suffused with pleasure. "They're just so you."

"You think so?" I feel a tiny voice of protest. I don't feel like someone who'd wear pearl earrings. Don't you have to be over fifty? Or be the queen or something?

"Absolutely! Try them on," he encourages.

Taking them out of the box, I slide them into my ears. I hold back my hair to murmurs of approval around the table. "Thank you, Miles, they're wonderful." I smile, ignoring my doubts and giving him a kiss.

So what if they're not me. It's the thought that counts, isn't it?

❧

The rest of the evening slips away over plates of delicious food, several bottles of wine, and the familiar conversations about careers, the housing market, and what antics Ruby and Sam are currently up to.

". . . I had to buy a new phone because Ruby was worried that he was lonely . . ." sighs Julian, finishing telling a story about how she decided to drop his cell into the goldfish bowl so that Boris the goldfish could call his friends.

"I think it was her way of getting you off the phone," remarks Vanessa dryly, as Miles laughs in consolation. "And pretty effective too," she adds, before making her excuses to go to the bathroom as the dessert menus are brought out.

"I'll come with you," I say, pushing back my chair.

"What is it with women going in pairs to the bathroom?" wonders Julian aloud as we get up from the table.

"So we can talk about you, sweetie," jokes Vanessa.

At least I think she's joking, but when we get into the restroom and I thank her once again for my present, she instructs, "Just make sure you eat lots of pastries and have lots of sex in Paris. Someone has to."

"Oh, come on," I protest. "I know what you and Julian are up to." Nudging her in the ribs, I smile knowingly, thinking of the contents of Julian's shopping basket.

"Up to?" she huffs derisively. "I don't have the energy to be up to anything. I'm exhausted. The only thing we're up to is arguing over who's going to get up and see to Sam when he wakes up crying for about the third time in the middle of the night."

"But I thought . . ." I trail off as I flash back to yesterday. Now I think about it, Julian did seem kind of jumpy. Nervous almost. As if he didn't want me to see him . . . my mind cuts back to Vanessa's comment about him having an affair with his secretary.

"Thought what?" asks Vanessa, and I see her looking at me quizzically.

"Oh . . . um . . . you looked closer, that's all . . ." Quickly I scrub that image from my mind. I'm being totally ridiculous, just like Vanessa was.

"I don't think so." She smiles wanly. "I've barely seen him this week. He's always at work. It's almost like we're two strangers. Like we don't know each other anymore . . ." She trails off, her shoulders slumped defeatedly.

God, I hate to see Vanessa looking so sad.

"I know what you need," I say cheerfully, changing the subject.

"A new husband?" She smiles ruefully.

"No, silly. A new lipstick," I laugh, digging a handful out of my handbag. "I know how you love your trademark red lipstick." I pass her one that's movie-star scarlet.

Vanessa's eyes light up. Since having Sam she seems to have stopped wearing makeup. She says it takes too long to apply. It's the same with her hair. Instead of blow-drying it straight, she now ties it up in a knot. "Oooh, where did you get these?" she says, pulling off the top.

"One of the perks of working in PR . . ."

"By the way, I meant to say—" She pauses to wand her bottom lip. "Is that the bartender we saw in the shop?"

At the mention of him all the cells in my body jerk to attention. It catches me by surprise. Why is it that someone so annoying can have this effect on me? "Unfortunately." I grimace, quickly brushing the thought away.

"Mmmm." Rubbing her lips together, she smiles wickedly. "I wonder what he's offering for dessert."

"Whatever it is, it'll be too many points." I smile back, and then cower as she punches me playfully on the arm.

❦

Five minutes later, a newly lip-glossed Vanessa and I make our way back to the table.

"Ah! Just in time," says Julian as we reappear.

"For what?" I ask, glancing around.

"Champagne!" announces Miles as the waiter appears with a bottle of Veuve Clicquot and four champagne flutes and sets them down on the table.

"Oooh, is this the bit where we start singing 'Happy Birthday' really loudly and embarrass Charlotte in front of everyone?" Vanessa grins.

"No, it's not," replies Miles, shooting her a look.

"Spoilsport—"

Next to me the waiter is deftly easing the cork out from the neck of the bottle and as he starts pouring the champagne into glasses I notice a small tattoo etched on the underside of his wrist. I stare at it for a moment, trying to make it out.

"It's a frog."

I snatch my eyes away only to meet those of the waiter staring at me, staring at him.

"Oh, right." I nod, feeling a hot flash of embarrassment.

"My mother's French," he explains, a small smile playing on his lips.

Is he making fun of me again? Is that supposed to be a joke?

"Isn't that offensive to French people?" I reply a little stiffly.

"You haven't met my mother," he replies evenly.

A look flashes between us and I suddenly feel all jittery. "No . . ." I manage, struggling for a witty comeback, but my mind's a total blank. "Obviously," I add lamely.

"I want to propose a toast—"

Miles's voice snaps me back and I turn to see him raising his champagne glass.

"—for Charlotte on her birthday."

Julian and Vanessa raise their glasses. "To Charlotte," they both cheer.

"And to our new house."

"Our house?" I swivel around to face him.

"I've been saving the best bit till last. The Realtor called earlier but I wanted to keep it as a surprise," he explains, grinning delightedly. "They accepted our offer. It's ours!"

"Ours?" I repeat, taken aback. So taken aback, it seems, that I've turned into an echo.

"Here you go," says a voice close to my ear, and I glance up to see the waiter passing me a champagne flute. "You're not allergic to bubbles, are you?" He throws me a look.

"Um . . . no . . . I'm not . . . thanks," I mumble, meeting those pale blue eyes of his, before quickly averting my gaze. "I mean, wow, that's great!" I try to exclaim, turning back to Miles, who's still grinning from ear to ear.

Raising his champagne glass, he clinks it against mine. "Here's to us!"

I smile dazedly. "To us."

## Chapter Twenty-one

We leave early.

"Babysitters," grumbles Vanessa, making an apologetic face as we stand outside on the sidewalk.

"If we're not home by ten, it goes into triple time," adds Julian, raising a rueful eyebrow.

"Crikey, I'm in the wrong job," chortles Miles, slightly flushed from too much champagne.

"No worries." I smile, giving her a hug. "I need an early night anyway."

Which is true. I do. Especially after last night. And it doesn't matter that it's my birthday, does it? I mean, so what? It's just another birthday. It's not like I'm disappointed or anything silly like that, I think, as we all say our good-byes.

Waving them off in a black cab, Miles and I walk to my car.

"Are you okay to drive?" he asks as I beep the lock and slide into the driver's seat. Miles doesn't own a car. He says having one in London is like throwing money down the drain and he's always nagging me to use public transportation, "Just think, with all the cash you save you could invest it in some bonds."

Which is true. I could.

Then again, I could also buy a fabulous new handbag.

"Because the number 72 goes straight from here . . ."

Miles has the bus timetable ingrained on his brain. On our first date he took me out for dinner, but he refused to take a cab to the restaurant—even though it was raining and I was wearing a new pair of shoes. A pair of nude suede strappy sandals.

Well, they *were* nude suede. A ten-minute walk to the bus stop and one packed bus ride later, they're now more of a sludgy gray and completely ruined.

"I'm fine." I nod, turning the ignition. "It's a five-minute drive. Plus, I only had a glass of wine."

"And champagne," he reminds me pointedly, clicking on his seat belt. He begins adjusting his seat with all the electronic levers.

"Oh, yeah . . ." I nod uncomfortably. Turning on my turn signal I pull out into the main road.

"Though you left most of yours," he points out, still fiddling with the levers. His seat starts whirring forward. Then backward. Then forward again.

"Well, I couldn't drink and drive, could I?" I say lightly, as I start negotiating the traffic.

"We could have caught the bus," he replies stubbornly. His seat reclines too far and he begins trying to hitch it more upright. "It goes straight from here."

"Yes, I know," I reply. I'm starting to feel slightly rattled. "You said."

Suddenly there's a loud crunch and his seat jackknifes backward.

"Miles, will you stop it!" I gasp impatiently.

"Stop what?" he replies innocently. "I'm just trying to get comfy."

"I know; it's just—" I break off and take a deep breath. I don't know what it is, but I feel all jumpy and on edge. "Sorry, I didn't mean to snap," I apologize quickly.

"I know." He smiles, and touches my hand affectionately.

I feel horribly guilty. What's wrong with me? Miles is being so sweet. Why I am behaving like such a grumpy old hag about everything?

"Don't worry, we won't be doing this for much longer," he says cheerfully.

"Doing what?" I ask distractedly, indicating right.

"Having to alternate between our flats every weekend," he says, as if it's obvious. "Soon we'll be in the new house."

"Oh, right, yes . . ." I clear my throat as my voice has gone a little bit grainy. "Of course."

"There'll be none of this back-and-forth. You in your place during the week, me in mine. Just think! We'll be able to spend every single night together."

He smiles at me excitedly, and I smile back trying to imagine spending every night with Miles. Waking up next to him every morning. Brushing our teeth side by side in the bathroom. Day in. Day out.

Forever.

I catch myself. For godsakes, Charlotte, I don't know what you're worrying about, I tell myself firmly. It's going to be fine. You love Miles, he loves you. It just means that you won't have to keep some of your clothes at his place, or have to double up on toiletries, or keep your underwear shoved in one measly little drawer.

Plus, just remember how annoying it was a few weekends ago when you left your mouth guards at your apartment and you woke up the next morning at Miles's with a headache from grinding? This way you'll have everything in one place.

Feeling more positive I pull up outside my home. And just think, poor Miles won't ever have to play squash again in my shorts, I reflect, stifling a giggle at the memory of his rather large thighs squeezed into my tight black Lycra running shorts when he'd forgotten his.

"I know; it will be great," I agree cheerfully, cutting the engine.

Then again, on second thought, that might be rather a shame . . .

Inside, I pick up the mail in the hallway. As usual I left early this morning before the postman arrived, and among the usual credit card bills and mortgage-related stuff there's a card from Mom and Dad. Right on time, as usual. Mom is amazing. She has this knack of knowing exactly when to mail a card to ensure that it never arrives a day early, or late, regardless of what the postal service is up to.

From the living room, I hear the TV blaring and, tearing open the envelope, I walk through to find Miles already ensconced on the sofa with the remote control in his hand.

"Did you record this week's episode of *Location, Location, Location*?" he asks, without looking up.

"Um, no . . ." I say vaguely, looking inside to discover a check and a note to "buy some proper food." I smile to myself. It's been the same every year since I was in college. I glance at my watch—they rang earlier but I was in a meeting—I wonder if it's too late to call them. Actually it probably is, I realize, with a pang of disappointment. My parents do everything early: "dinner" at twelve, "tea" at five thirty, then it's TV time and bed at nine thirty. I'll have to call them tomorrow.

"You didn't?" Miles frowns with dismay.

I tune back in. "Oh, sorry, I totally forgot—"

"Oh, well, never mind." He shrugs, flicking over the channels. "There's probably a film on." An old Clint Eastwood movie pops up on the screen.

"Actually I think I might go to bed," I say, propping my card up on my mantel.

"I'll be there in a minute," he murmurs, already totally engrossed.

Leaving him glued to the TV, I go into the bathroom, get undressed, and begin my usual nighttime ritual of cleansing, toning, and moisturizing. I have about a dozen different types of moisturizers. There's this gel I use for under my eyes which I have to dab on with my ring finger. A cream for my face that I'm supposed to massage in clockwise (or is it counterclockwise?) sweeping motions. And a lotion I'm supposed to use on my neck.

Opening my bathroom cabinet I survey the overflowing shelves. To tell the truth, I feel exhausted just looking at them. I have about a zillion products in here that promise to firm, smooth, brighten, and erase wrinkles and, despite the fact that none of them seem to make much difference, I'm always buying more. I can't help it. In fact, I just bought this new serum that's being hailed as a "miracle in jar." Apparently it's composed of particles of gold leaf and makes your pores magically disappear. I've never quite worked out *why* exactly I'm supposed to want my pores to disappear, but anyway the results are supposed to be amazing.

Quite frankly, for that price, they better be.

Slathering a few different things all over my face, I clean my teeth using my electric toothbrush and whitening toothpaste, floss, and finally rinse.

Done.

With the drone of the TV playing in the living room I gaze back at my reflection. My thirty-two-year-old reflection. Bare-faced, hair tied up in a scrunchie, and wearing my oversized flowery pajamas, I look about as sexy as, well, anyone wearing oversized pajamas with their head tied up in a scrunchie *can* look.

Suddenly, Vanessa's words about having sex with Julian here, there, and everywhere before they had children flash like neon in my mind. It's been over a week since Miles and I spent the night together, and even longer since we had sex. Admittedly we have both been stressed with work, and I know passion can fade when you're in a committed, long-term relationship, but that's why it's important to make even more of an effort.

Padding into the bedroom, I quickly slip on a satin camisole and shake out my hair. Hopefully this will spice things up a bit, I tell myself, spritzing my pulse points with perfume and dabbing a bit on my décolletage like they always tell you to do in all the women's magazines.

Turning on my bedside lamp I climb into bed. Then climb out again and flick off the main light. Ambient lighting. It's very important. I plump a pillow and arrange myself just so. Then wait expectantly. I can still hear the TV but I'm sure he'll be in any minute.

I wait a bit longer.

Should I maybe light a candle?

I light a candle. It's vanilla, musk, and jasmine and smells gorgeous. I inhale its aroma and fiddle with the straps of my camisole. I let one slip off my shoulder. Then both. Ugh, God, no, that looks too corny, I decide, shoving them back again.

I listen for any sounds of movement, but all I can hear is the TV. Restlessly, I glance at my watch. It's been twenty minutes. I hesitate, then call in my huskiest voice, "Miles? Are you coming to bed?"

Nothing.

I wait a few more moments, then raise it a notch. "Miles?" I call out.

Again, nothing. Just the sound of a gunshot on the TV and the wail of a police siren.

Oh, damn it. "Miles!" I yell loudly. "Can you hear me?"

But no, obviously he can't, as there's no answer, and so, giving up in frustration, I clamber out of bed and stomp into the living room. To find him lying flat out on the sofa, head lolled back, mouth open, emitting a faint, rattling snore.

I watch him for a moment, half inclined to wake him up and demand he have sex with me on my birthday. And then immediately think better of it. Miles is useless when he's had a few drinks. As if on cue he splutters slightly, rolls over, and nuzzles, snuffling into the cushion. Plus, whatever flames of passion I was trying to fan have now abruptly been extinguished.

So instead, I turn off the TV, cover him in a spare duvet, and go back to bed.

And lie there awake.

I glance at the digits on the alarm clock. It's only ten thirty p.m. And I'm in bed. On my birthday. God, if someone had told me ten years ago that I'd be in bed before eleven p.m. on my birthday I would never have believed them. Back then birthdays were all about partying and getting drunk and staying up till the crack of dawn. But once you're in your thirties, they're not such a big deal anymore, are they?

And like I said, I really do need to catch up on my sleep.

Flicking on the wave machine and humidifier, I blow out the candle and switch off the light. Pulling on my eye mask I close my eyes, but my mind has other ideas. *I wonder what Lottie is doing?* it whispers in my ear.

I don't know, probably partying, I think, trying to ignore it.

*Partying where?* it demands, a little louder.

I roll over restlessly. At my old house, I reflect, casting my mind back to the house party I threw to celebrate my twenty-second birthday. To be honest, my memories of it are vague. I was only reminded of it when Lottie mentioned it last night. Actually, she invited me. Which was slightly weird to say the least, but of course I couldn't go.

*But you can go now,* it says, putting an idea into my head.

Which of course I dismiss immediately. Honestly, how ridiculous. As if I'm going to get out of my nice warm comfy bed and go to a party. I've just had a lovely dinner with my boyfriend and my best friend to celebrate my birthday. I don't want to go to some silly party.

Then again, I suppose it could be kind of fun.

*A lot more fun than lying in bed on your own, unable to sleep, while your boyfriend lies snoring on the sofa,* pipes up that little voice inside of me.

I feel myself wobble.

But what about Miles?

*What about him? He's out cold. You'll be back before he wakes up.*

I hesitate, my mind ticking over. No, I can't. It's just too mad . . . It's insane . . . It's—

Oh, shut up, Charlotte. It's a bit late for all that, isn't it? And flinging back the covers, I jump out of bed and start getting ready.

# Chapter Twenty-two

Less than fifteen minutes later I'm in the car heading over to my old house. It's pretty amazing how quickly you can get ready when all your clothes are at the dry cleaner's and you don't have any choice of what to wear, I reflect, fiddling with the collar of my jacket, which is all tucked under in my haste to get out of the apartment.

Sure enough, Miles didn't wake up. I briefly considered leaving a note, or maybe even stuffing pillows in the bed to make it look as if I'm still asleep in there but a) this is real life, not *Shawshank Redemption* and b) unlike me, Miles is a really heavy sleeper even without all the wine and champagne. One time he even slept through the smoke alarm when I nearly set fire to the apartment with an aromatherapy candle—but anyway, that's a whole other story . . .

London is alive with Friday nightlife and it takes a while to cut across town, dodging black cabs that, with no given notice, will suddenly stop dead in the middle of the road to drop off or pick up a fare, and getting stuck in the heavy traffic resulting from the detour. And so, despite it fast becoming a familiar route, it's not until nearly midnight that I make my way through the diversion and finally turn into Kilmaine Terrace.

The street is lined with cars, and squeezing into a parking space without hitting any lampposts (see, my parking has gotten a *lot* better over the years, I think with a sense of satisfaction), I check my hastily applied makeup and climb out of my car. Then realize I don't have a present.

Shit. I can't go to a party empty-handed. Even if it's mine. Well, sort of, I think, scrambling through the glove compartment to see if I've got any of those freebie lip glosses left. Then I have an idea. I know! What about all those bags of goodies from the pharmacy that I bought yesterday? I was wondering how I was going to give them to my younger self without appearing odd, and this is the perfect solution.

Grabbing the bags out of the trunk, I smooth down my skirt and walk toward the house. A bunch of brightly colored balloons tied to the front door are bobbing in the warm summer night's breeze and I can hear the strains of the Verve's "Bittersweet Symphony" coming from inside.

Opening the gate, I climb up the front steps and then—for a moment—I pause, looking at my front door, my hand paused to rap the familiar brass knocker shaped like a dolphin. It seems like only yesterday since I had a key. Since this was my home. Where I lived, loved, dreamed—

"—Whoo-hooooo—"

Abruptly the door swings open to shrieking laughter and a couple falls out onto the doorstep. Heads rolled back in laughter, a can of Tennent's Extra and a cigarette in each hand, they're draped all over each other in what looks like an attempt to hold each other up. I jump back, before they knock me over.

"Whoops," they slur, then burst into drunken giggles and start making out in front of me.

I recoil. Oh dear. I'd forgotten what house parties used to be like in my twenties. Maybe this wasn't *such* a good idea after all.

They're completely blocking my way, so, clutching the bulging bags in my hands, I shove myself back against the hedge until they get tired of eating each other and untangle tongues.

"Sorry, we're just leaving," they apologize, grinning annoyingly.

"Oh, is the party over?" I ask, as another few people spill out of the house and squeeze past them, onto the sidewalk.

"I hope not," he says, turning to the girl draped over his shoulder and licking her face.

Ugh. Lovely.

"Charlotte!"

I whirl around to see Lottie standing on the doorstep.

She shoots me a huge grin. "Hey, I didn't think you were coming!"

"Well, I know, but . . . well, my evening got cut short," I finish in an explanation of sorts. "Anyway, happy birthday." I smile, thrusting the bags at her. "I'm afraid I didn't have a chance to wrap them," I add quickly, suddenly feeling embarrassed for handing her two plastic bags instead of an expensively wrapped present.

But if she minds, she doesn't show it. Instead her eyes go saucer-wide and a look of delight sweeps over her face. "Oh, fabulous, is all this for me?"

"Well, it's not that much—"

"All of it?" she repeats, in astonishment.

I had no idea she would be so pleased. She looks over the moon. And just about some stuff from the drugstore. God, I wasn't this thrilled when I got my new car, I think, looking at her delighted expression and feeling a curious mix of pleasure and envy.

"Uh-uh." I nod.

"Oh, wow, I can't believe it. You must have spent a fortune," she gasps, tugging out an Estée Lauder foundation that's the right skin tone, instead of that cheap stuff I know she wears that's bright orange. "That's so kind of you."

"Hey, don't mention it." I smile modestly. I'd forgotten just what a treat getting new stuff used to be, I muse, thinking about my own bathroom cabinet at home, stuffed full with unused products and feeling a bit guilty.

Still, it looks like my list has been a raving success so far, I think, with a sense of satisfaction.

"Anyway, I'd invite you in but everyone's getting ready to leave."

"Oh, really?" I feel a beat of disappointment. Damn, after all that, I missed the party. "I suppose it is pretty late. I guess I should be getting to bed too."

"Bed?" She stares at me, incredulous, then lets out a peal of laughter. "Ha-ha, very funny, that was a joke, right?"

Uh, no, I was perfectly serious.

"Yes, of course," I laugh uncertainly. "So . . . um . . . if you're not going to bed, where are you going?"

"Clubbing!" She whoops.

"*Clubbing?*" My smile sort of freezes. Oh fuck. I'd totally forgotten how I used to love to go clubbing, but now it comes back to me with the blunt force of a sledgehammer. Dry ice. Swirly strobe lights. Deafening music. "But it's a Sunday, isn't it?" I bleat hopefully.

"Yeah, but it's a public holiday tomorrow so they're having a special night, to mark the end of the summer. It's like Labor Day weekend in the States." She beams excitedly. "You're coming too, aren't you?"

"*I am?*" I squeak in a strangled voice.

Me? Clubbing? I don't do clubbing. Not anymore. I do Pilates, and yoga, and acupuncture when my back hurts.

"Of course, silly! You're invited."

I'm rummaging through my memory, as if it's a sock drawer and I'm feverishly looking for a pair that match. Only this doesn't match any recollection I have of this evening. But then again, it was ten years ago and I *was* very drunk. In fact, to be honest, every birthday till the age of about thirty is a bit of a blur.

For a brief moment I think about making up some excuse and going home, but before I have a chance she links arms and with a battle cry, yells, "Come on, it's time to *paaaartay!*"

And it's too late.
Help.

❧

The club is only a couple of streets away so we walk there—well, I walk—Lottie's wearing high heels for the first time since I've met her, and sort of half totters along the pavement in the four-inch heels, giggling tipsily. She's wearing a dress covered in tiny blue cornflowers that I bought from a flea market. I remember I had to haggle the stallholder down forever before I could afford it, even though it was only a few pounds.

Nowadays I can afford to shop for designer clothes, only what I can't afford is the time to *go* shopping, so I tend to do a lot of it on-line, and usually only twice a year—summer and winter. But back then I was always so broke most of my wardrobe came from charity shops or markets and I'd spend weekends when I first moved to London trawling through the racks at Camden or Portobello, looking for bargains.

Like that dress, which I ended up getting for half price because one of the straps was broken, I reflect. Though I never did get round to sewing on, I realize, glancing at it now and seeing it's still being held on by a safety pin. I feel a flash of embarrassment. Honestly, what was I thinking going out like that? Absently I glance down at my jacket and pick off a couple of bits of fluff from the lapels. Didn't I care?

Obviously not, I decide, looking back at myself puffing away merrily on a cigarette without a care in the world; I feel a rattle of disapproval.

Ahead of us I see a long line snaking around the corner, to which my first thought is

1.  Wow, look at all those people. I wonder what's hap-
    pening.

Followed by

**2.** Oh fuck. That's the line to get in.

Only Lottie doesn't appear to notice the line, and instead waltzes gaily to the front and beams at the bouncer. A huge, six-foot-something Jamaican man with biceps the size of watermelons and an impenetrable grimace. Horror trickles down my spine like icy cold water. Oh my God, what am I doing? *What am I doing?* I cringe, hanging back in mortified anticipation of the public humiliation I'm going to suffer when I get sent to the back of the line in front of all these people.

Correction, *all these kids*, I realize, my eyes sweeping over the parade of baseball caps, Celtic armband tattoos, and pierced belly buttons and realizing the average age is about twenty. Maybe even less, I decide, glancing at a group of rail-thin girls sporting microminis and what looks suspiciously like teenage acne. Before glancing back again at the bouncer who, at that very moment, is turning his hulking great frame toward Lottie, with the sort of slow-motion movement you get in those old dinosaur films, just before the helpless victim is about to get gobbled up by the big scary brontosaurus.

"Hi, there," she trills, puffing on her cigarette and grinning wildly.

Oh God, and now everyone's staring. I wince, hardly daring to look as I wait for the inevitable. Or not, I decide, my protective instincts kicking in. I'm supposed to be giving the benefit of my experience. Stopping her from making her mistakes. I can't just sit back and let this happen, I resolve, taking a step toward her and the thumping music that's pulsing out from the club.

"Hey, all right there, darlin'?"

And pause. Hang on a minute. Did he just say—

"Nice to see ya. How ya doing?"

Hovering just by her elbow, I'm staring in amazement at the bouncer, whose whole demeanor has now changed. Gone is the fearsome grimace. Instead he's grinning warmly at Lottie.

Um, hello, she's friends with the bouncer?

*I'm* friends with the bouncer?

"Awesome! It's my birthday." She's smiling as she stands on her tiptoes and plants a kiss on each of his cheeks. "And I really wanted to celebrate it in the club."

Oh my God. And I'm *flirting* with him to get in! What a floozy!

"Well, happy birthday!" he booms, letting out a deep rumble of laughter as he stoops down to accept her kisses, before lifting up the rope and standing back to let her pass. "You have a great evening."

"I will, thanks." She smiles, waving cheerfully as she sweeps past him and disappears behind the velvet curtain into the club.

Well, okay, perhaps she didn't need my help *that* time, I think as the rest of us follow one by one. And at least I didn't have to stand in line, I tell myself, trying to look on the bright side, but still feeling a sense of dread as I move forward, the music growing louder and louder, the base thumping harder and harder, the strobe lights shooting out from the gap in the curtain, until it's my turn to go in—

Abruptly my way is blocked.

"If you want to just hold it right there." Reaching in front of me, the bouncer replaces the red rope.

For a moment I look at him in confusion—what? He's not letting me in? Then it registers. Of course. He obviously doesn't realize I'm with Lottie.

"Excuse me." I smile confidently, as I get his attention. "I'm with the rest of the party," I explain, gesturing to those that have just gone in ahead of me. "I'm with Lottie."

The bouncer looks me up and down, his brow furrowed. "Sorry, luv." He shakes his head. "Not tonight."

My smile fades and I look at him uncertainly. "Lottie," I repeat, for want of something to say. "You know, scrunch-dried hair, major tan, safety pin on her dress . . ."

"I'm sorry," he repeats, only more firmly this time. "Not to-night."

I stare at him as it slowly begins to dawn on me. "Are you telling me you're not letting me in?"

"We're very busy tonight," he replies dismissively, before gesturing for me to stand to one side to allow more people to pass though into the club.

Blatantly. While I'm just standing here.

I glare at him angrily. "Excuse me, but you've just let all those people in," I say, somewhat obviously.

Sliding his gaze back to me, he looks me up and down.

"We also have a dress code," he grunts, gesturing to my outfit.

"What are you talking about?" I gasp in frustration. "I'm wearing a suit."

"Exactly," he replies, shaking his head sympathetically.

I feel myself blush hotly. Admittedly my dark gray pencil skirt with matching single-breasted jacket is not the *hippest* of outfits, and if I'd known I was going to go clubbing I would have worn something a bit more funky. Actually that's a lie. If I'd known I was going to go clubbing I'd be wearing earplugs. But even so. It's smart. It's classic.

For godsakes, *it's Prada*.

Behind me, I can hear grumbling that I'm holding up the line. I look at the bouncer in desperation. Oh God, I can't believe this. This is so humiliating. I'm half inclined to turn around and go home. After all, I've got no desire to go to his loud, stinky, sweaty club. In fact, right now, I couldn't think of anywhere I'd rather go less. Afghanistan maybe. The arctic in February, perhaps.

But I can't turn back now. Plus, even if I wanted to, my pride wouldn't let me.

Turning back to the bouncer, I take a deep breath. So he thinks I'm not cool enough, does he? He thinks that because I'm not some young twentysomething and flirting with him I can't get in his stupid club? Indignation stabs. Well, we'll see about that.

Reaching into my handbag I pull out my purse and count out five twenties. Okay, so I might not be young and hip enough anymore to pass the scrutiny of the doormen, but you see, that's one of the great things about being older. I don't have to be.

Like magic, the velvet rope disappears.

"Have a great evening," the bouncer tells me, standing back to let me through.

"I'll try." Smiling triumphantly, I waft right by him.

Because now I can afford to bribe my way in.

# Chapter Twenty-three

If you were to ask me to describe the Canal Club, I'd tell you to try this at home:

1. Turn up the thermostat on the central heating so it's about a hundred degrees and you're sweating profusely.
2. Turn on the stereo, choose a hip-hop CD (preferably one where all the tracks sound the same), and play on full volume so that you can't hear yourself speak and your eardrums feel as if they're about to explode.
3. Then turn it up even louder.
4. Put a tray of oil in the oven and turn it up as high as it will go so that everywhere fills with smoke.
5. Block up your toilet with toilet paper so that it won't flush.
6. Now squeeze as many people as you can into your living room.
7. Shut all the windows and ask them all to start smoking.
8. Charge a fiver for water.
9. And turn out the lights so you can't see a frigging thing.

"Oy, watch where you're going," yells a gruff voice in my ear.

"Oops, sorry . . ." I reply hastily, quickly removing my stiletto heel from someone's foot.

Trying to adjust my eyes to the smoky, strobe-lit darkness, I stumble around the club on the hunt for Lottie. I can't see her. But then again, that's not surprising, considering I can't see *anything*. Or hear anything over this thumping baseline. It's as if two of my senses just disappeared.

Resisting the urge to stick my fingers in my ears, I take off my jacket and begin squeezing, squashing, and shuffling my way through the droves of clubbers. The air is sticky and cloying with perspiration and I can already feel the beads of sweat pricking the nape of my neck as I move further into the sweltering heat. Jesus, it's as hot as hell in here.

*Because this is hell,* pipes up a desperate voice inside of me, as I'm jostled into a strange man's hairy armpit. At least I think it's a man. Like I said, it's difficult to see.

A fleeting image of my bed flashes across my brain. My warm comfy bed, with its pillow-top mattress, goose-down duvet, and plumped-up pillows. Me gently sinking into it. Just the sound of ocean waves and the faint puff of the humidifier. The scent of my aromatherapy candle, which has overtures of lavender and . . .

B.O.

Getting a really bad whiff of it I zone back in. Okay, that's it. I can't take much more of this. I remember that song: *It's my party and I'll cry if I want to.* Which is kind of apt, as, trust me, I might very well be doing just that if I don't find Lottie, I think desperately. Where the hell could she have gone?

Hurriedly extricating myself, I move deeper into the club. To the left I can make out a small bar and to the right are several sofas filled with dozens of entangled couples.

But no Lottie. I squint through the haze of cigarette smoke and dry ice, toward the small dance floor ahead of me. The odd strobe light sweeps back and forth, briefly illuminating the floor, which is covered in cigarette butts and blackened spots of gum. This is one of those places that if they turned the lights on it would send you running, screaming for the hand sanitizer.

And yet I used to love this place, I reflect, as blurry, long-forgotten memories of weekends spent here begin coming back to me. How *could* I? I wonder in amazement. What was there to love?

Reaching the edge of the dance floor I pause for a moment, my eyes flicking over the sea of bodies. There's a group of girls slap dab in the middle, dancing around a small pile of handbags, a couple in matching leather pants bumping and grinding over by the speakers. And then there's Lottie.

I feel a snap of surprise.

Me? *Dancing?*

I never dance.

Well, not anymore, I think, watching myself in fascination as I swing around near the DJ, shaking my hips to the music without any inhibition. Nowadays I have to be completely drunk to dance. I'm way too self-conscious to get out there otherwise. But look, there I am, shaking my thang for all the world to see and I'm not even drinking, I notice, seeing myself swigging from a bottle of water.

Speaking of which. Driven by my own thirst I make my way over to the bar to get a drink. Away from the dance floor it's a bit quieter, and spotting an empty bar stool, I plonk myself on it gratefully.

"Yes, what can I get you?"

I glance up to see a pair of pale gray eyes looking at me expectantly from behind the bar. For a split second my brain does that thing where you think you know someone and are about to smile and say hi, before realizing that you have no idea where you know them from, and stop yourself before you look like a moron.

"Um . . . yes, I'll have a bottle of water, please."

"Coming right up." The bartender nods and is about to turn away, when my curiosity gets the better of me. "Excuse me—"

He stops what he's doing.

"—have we met?"

He surveys me for a moment, then shakes his head. "Nope, don't think so."

I feel a flash of embarrassment. "My mistake. I just could have sworn I've seen you before."

"You probably have; I work behind the bar at the Wellington Arms."

"Oh, that must be it." My mind flicks back to last night. Speaking of, "Sorry about last night . . ."

He raises his eyebrows.

"I spilled a drink, you cleaned it up . . ."

"Oh, yeah." He nods, registering. "You were with the guy from the band. Billy Romani."

"Don't remind me." I roll my eyes, and he smiles.

"Not a fan then?"

"You could say that." I return a rueful smile. "What about you?"

He sucks in air between his teeth. "Not really my kind of music," he says diplomatically, but the way the muscle in his jaw clenches tightly makes me think it might not be a bad idea to change the subject.

"So . . . um . . . you work here too?" I ask, then immediately wish I hadn't, considering it's rather obvious as he's standing behind the bar.

But if he thinks it's a stupid question, he doesn't show it.

"Well, someone has to," he quips.

"You don't like it here?" I feel a sudden bond. So I'm not the only one suffering.

"Well, I wouldn't call it my dream job," he continues. "But I need the money and the experience. Plus the tips come in useful," he adds, and winks disarmingly.

All at once I feel myself blush like a schoolgirl and as he turns away to get my drink, I sneak a better look at him. Despite seeing him in the Wellington I haven't really taken much notice of him before. He's got a straggly ponytail and tie-dyed T-shirt, but even so he's actually really attractive, I register, trying not to look at his tanned, muscular arms and looking right at his tanned, muscular arms.

But only on a purely aesthetic level of course. I mean, it's not as if I *like* him or anything like that. I've got a boyfriend. A really wonderful boyfriend. And we're buying a house, we're moving in together.

Plus, he's still just a boy. Practically a baby!

As he leans over to pull a bottle of water out of the fridge, his T-shirt rides up and I watch his back muscles ripple. Quickly I glance away. God, it really *is* hot in here, isn't it? Feeling a trickle of sweat run down between the cups of my underwire bra, I grab a coaster and start fanning myself hard.

"There you go." Smiling, he passes me the bottle of water, his tanned forearm flexing as he reaches toward me.

"Thanks." I go to grab the bottle, but our hands collide and somehow my fingers get all tangled up with his. The bottle slips free.

"Nearly," he laughs, as he catches it deftly and hands it to me.

"God, I'm not usually so clumsy—"

As I look up and catch his gaze something very peculiar happens in my groin. What the—? I feel a flash of horror. Oh, no, I can't believe it.

*I've turned into a cougar.*

With my cheeks burning up like a furnace I quickly pay him. Honestly, what am I doing? Lusting after a bartender who must be ten years younger than me, at least. I mean, I'm practically old enough to be his mother. Well, okay, not his mother, but his older sister. His *much* older sister.

On the other hand, I mean, there's really nothing wrong with thinking another man is attractive, is there? And so what if he's ten years younger than me? Men are always looking at younger women. Plus, it's only *natural* to look. It doesn't *mean* anything. I'm sure Miles looks at girls practically every day.

Well, perhaps not *every* day, I think, quickly backtracking. But sometimes. Like, for example, at his bookkeeper Helen, who's small and busty and always wears tight Lycra tops. I'm a woman and *I* can't help staring at her cleavage.

Gulping back the ice-cold water I turn my back on the bartender and focus on the dance floor where I'm still dancing. But that's easier said than done.

"Amazing, isn't she?"

Hearing a voice next to me I turn sideways to find the bartender right next to me, leaning against the bar, his chin resting on his elbows. I look around for a moment, just to make sure he's talking to me, before asking, "Um . . . what's that?"

He gestures toward the dance floor, a faraway look in his eyes. "The girl in the dress . . ."

I feel a slight twinge of jealousy. Which girl? I think, following his gaze.

". . . with the little blue flowers . . ."

I look back at him in astonishment.

". . . She comes into the pub a lot . . ."

*Me?* He's talking about *me?* I look back at myself on the dance floor, through the swathes of gyrating bodies, and there I am, doing my impression of the funky chicken. He thinks *I'm* amazing?

"You think she's amazing?" I repeat incredulously. Maybe I didn't hear him right. After all, it is really loud in here.

"Totally," he sighs.

Nope. I heard him right. And that was a genuine sigh.

I turn back to my younger self, dancing away completely obliviously, while my older self tries to absorb this information. I don't think anyone's ever called me amazing before. I've had compliments like pretty, sexy, or attractive. But never *amazing*. Amazing is for superstars and celebrities like Angelina Jolie. Not Charlotte Merry-weather. And certainly not Charlotte Merryweather when she was twenty-one. Sorry, just turned twenty-two.

"Her name's Lottie," I say, still feeling a bit stunned.

"Oh, right." He nods. "Do you know her then?"

"You could say we're kind of related." I smile.

He looks at me in disbelief. "No way!" he snorts. "You look noth-ing like her."

I feel my smile slide off my face. Okay, so I know I look a lot dif-ferent now than I did ten years ago, but there was no need for that snort. I'm clearly a lot better groomed and a hundred times more stylish.

And let's not forget about those eyebrows.

"We've got the same nose," I point out stiffly.

He peers at me for what feels like just a little bit longer than is necessary. "Hmm, I suppose so . . ." he concedes, somewhat reluc-tantly. "Kinda."

I feel oddly miffed. And just a little bit jealous. Which is just ridiculous. How can you be jealous of *yourself*?

"So . . . tell me, why do you think she's so amazing?" I ask curiously.

"Oh, I don't know." He shakes his head. "She just is."

"But can't you be more specific?" I persist.

"I can't explain it." He shrugs. "It's just the way she is. I wouldn't change a thing about her."

"You wouldn't?" I look at him in disbelief.

"No," he says simply. "She's just—" He pauses, as if searching around for the right word, then finally finds it. "Perfect."

*"Perfect?"*

"The first time I saw her it was, like, boom."

*"Boom?"* I'm aware that I'm beginning to sound like my great-aunt Mary's parrot, but I can't help it.

"Yeah, boom. That was it. I'd fallen in love."

I look at him, bewildered. How could I never have known this? How could it be that there was someone going *boom* all over me and I was completely oblivious?

"Jeez, I sound a total soppy moron, don't I?" he says, misinterpreting my silence. He smiles self-consciously. "You must think I'm some kind of idiot."

"No, not at all," I protest, shaking my head. Quite the opposite. In fact, if it wasn't for Miles, I'd be in danger of falling for him. Ten years younger or not.

"So why don't you speak to her? Tell her how you feel?" I suggest.

He makes a face at the very notion. "I've spoken to her a couple of times, but I doubt she even remembers me."

No, I don't, I think, looking at him.

"She probably doesn't even know I exist," he continues. "After all, I'm just a barman, and just look at her, she could have anyone."

I feel a tug of regret. Oh God, why didn't I ever notice him all those years ago? He's so sweet and charming and such a nice guy.

Because you weren't interested in sweet and charming, Charlotte. You weren't into nice guys. You were into musicians and skateboarders and all the wrong guys, remember? I remind myself. He's right. You wouldn't have noticed a bartender with a straggly ponytail who wore tie-dyed T-shirts. He wouldn't have been cool enough.

"Well, I think she'd be lucky to have you." I smile.

He smiles crookedly and raises one eyebrow. "You think so?"

"Absolutely." I nod. "You're not *that* bad for a *barman*," I add jokingly.

He laughs. "You're not so bad either," he responds. "In fact, if you were ten years younger I might go for you myself."

"Ouch!" Affronted, I narrow my eyes at him.

"I'm joking, I'm joking," he protests, ducking away, chuckling. Grinning, he holds out his hand. "I'm Olly, by the way."

"I'm Charlotte."

I reach out and as we shake hands I notice something on the underside of his wrist. It's dark in the club, and I only see it briefly, illuminated by the light from the fridge, but there's no mistaking what it is. A tattoo of a frog.

My chest tightens. No, it can't be. It just can't.

*Can it?*

Abruptly my mind divides into a split screen. On one side is Olly with his ponytail, tie-dyed T-shirt, and hippy bracelets, and on the other is the waiter from the gastropub with his short curly hair, broken nose, and a scar that runs down his upper lip. That's impossible. They look completely different!

*But so do you,* whispers a voice inside my head.

All at once both sides merge and it's like two people suddenly become one. Oh my God, *that's* why he looked so familiar. Sweet, lovely boy toy Olly, who I have a bit of a crush on, is the bartender who thinks my food allergies are just *hilarious*. Who poured champagne tonight at my birthday and asked me if I was allergic to bubbles. And who annoys the living hell out of me.

I shake my head slightly, as if to clear it. It's him. They're one and the same person. Shit.

## Chapter Twenty-four

There you are!"

Feeling a hand on my shoulder I twist around in my seat to see Lottie bright-eyed and breathless from dancing. "I wondered where you'd gone!"

"Oh . . . hi," I manage. I feel like I've just been conked on the head with one of those cartoon hammers and I'm seeing stars.

"Propping up the bar, where'd you think?" quips Olly in an attempt to talk to her, but she's busy tying back her hair and doesn't hear him.

"Um . . . Lottie, have you met—" I make an attempt at an introduction, but she interrupts me by gushing excitedly,

"Come and dance!"

"No, no . . . I don't think so," I say, automatically shrinking back.

"Come on," she encourages, grabbing me by the wrist.

Then again, I don't really want to sit here talking to Olly now that I've discovered who he really is. It just feels too awkward. I mean, what am I going to say? How did you grow up to be so obnoxious?

Exactly.

"Well, okay," I acquiesce, "but just for one song—" Lottie isn't listening, though, she's too busy pulling me off my bar stool. And before I know it, I'm being dragged entirely against my will onto the dance floor.

Fuck.

It's like that dream where I'm walking naked through the halls of my old high school. Only this isn't a dream. It's a friggin' nightmare, I curse silently, looking frantically for an escape route in vain. But it's too late now, I'm stuck. Frozen like a rabbit in headlights. Or should that be strobe lights. Surrounded by dozens of gyrating bodies and there's nowhere to hide.

Feeling as though every single pair of eyes in the club are on me, I take a deep breath and try to move my feet, but I feel like they're encased in two heavy blocks of concrete. My arms, on the other hand, are like two ornaments that I don't know what to do with. I wave them around uncertainly and wiggle my elbows feeling mortified.

You see the thing is, I'm an absolutely horrible dancer. Some people are blessed with natural rhythm, but I'm not one of them. Remember that song by Gloria Estefan? "Rhythm Is Gonna Get You"? Well, it's never had much luck in finding me. At sports games I'm the only person in the whole stadium who claps out of time to "We Will Rock You." Try it, it's almost impossible. And yet I managed to.

That said, it doesn't seem to be stopping Lottie, I note, glancing across at her. Waving her arms around, she's bopping away, seemingly unconcerned by the fact that she looks like a duck. In fact, she's so unconcerned by it, everybody else around her seems unconcerned by it. In fact, I'm not sure anyone's even noticed, I realize, glancing around at all the other people on the dance floor.

Reluctantly, I tie my jacket around my waist and attempt to copy her as she gets on down. Only I'm older now and it's a lot harder to get back up again. *Ouch.* Feeling a twinge in my lower back, I grimace. This is torture. Thank God I don't have to suffer through birthdays like this anymore. So dinner tonight ended a little early, and Miles falling asleep on the sofa was definitely annoying, but a

nice low-key evening at a restaurant is a much better way to celebrate than being imprisoned in some hot sweaty club being forced
to dance. Relief rushes over me. Thank *God* I'm not twenty-one
anymore, thank God my clubbing days are over, thank God—

I stiffen, my shoulders back, my head up, like a meerkat. Until
now the music's just been a sort of blurring din that's been washing
all over me, but now I hear a couple familiar chords.

Hang on. Is that—?

It's like an injection of delight.

Oh my God, it is! "Ironic," by Alanis Morissette. I haven't heard
it for *years* . . . Oooh, I love this song . . .

Feeling a rush of energy, my hips begin wiggling involuntarily.
Then it's my waist. And now my shoulders. This is *so* great. I start
bopping away to the jangling guitar. I can't help it. My body won't
stay still. It's impossible. And *oh, wow*, I can even remember all the
words! Twirling around, my makeshift ponytail comes undone but I
ignore it, and tossing back my hair I begin singing along. Quiet at
first, then louder and louder.

And now it's the chorus and I've got my eyes closed and I'm
throwing my arms in the air and belting out the lyrics at the top of
my lungs. And in this moment I'm thinking about absolutely nothing. Nothing but dancing to this song. Losing myself in the chorus.
Leaving behind all my worries, totally letting myself go.

I feel great. Euphoric.

I feel . . . *someone grinding themselves up against my butt.*

Snapping open my eyes I whirl around and come crotch-to-crotch
with a man wearing a T-shirt that's four sizes too small for him, a
goatee, and a white man's underbite. He smiles at me lecherously.

Oh, no.

Oh no, oh no, oh no.

Still dancing I try edging away, but Mr. Bump'n'Grind is having
none of it. Putting on all the moves, he follows me around the dance
floor like my shadow until it's all too much and I yell in Lottie's ear,

"I'm just running to the bathroom," and I leave him and his thrusting crotch behind as I make a break for the ladies' room.

Phew.

Heaving a sigh of relief, I reach the safety of the ladies' and squeeze inside. As usual, there's a long line, but I really do have to pee after drinking all that water, and so resigning myself to a long wait, I lean against the wall. My feet are throbbing in their stilettos. They hurt before, but now after all that dancing, they're ready to murder me. I wince, tugging off one of the heels and releasing my foot like a cork from a bottle.

Rubbing my sore toes my mind slides back to the dance floor. Talk about a lucky escape. Another second longer and I'd have been pinned to the DJ stand by his crotch. I give a little shudder at the thought, which unexpectedly turns into a giggle. Well, I suppose he was pretty comical, I muse, replaying a clip of him in my head doing that weird pumping thing with his hips. And at least it was a good excuse to leave the dance floor.

But I didn't actually *want* to leave the dance floor, I realize, thinking about it now. It wasn't *that* bad. In fact, I was sort of starting to enjoy myself.

Oh, who I am kidding? I was having a total blast.

I catch myself smiling. It must have released all those endorphins or whatever they are, I decide, basking in my good mood. I mean, I never would have thought it was possible, but I had *fun* dancing. Sober! What a total shock.

And speaking of shocks—what about Olly! I'm still reeling from the discovery that this handsome, funny bartender and that really annoying waiter from the gastropub are one and the same person. I just can't wrap my head around it. Or the implications.

I mean, it's perfectly harmless having a crush on someone who's ten years younger than me. It's just a fun fantasy. Like lusting after Prince Harry (yes, okay, I admit it, but please don't tell anyone). But what happens when he's *not* a decade younger?

When he's the same age as me? When it's *real*. Does that mean it's no longer harmless? I feel a jolt of panic.

Which of course is completely ridiculous because I don't even *like* him now, let alone have a crush on him.

"'Scuse me, do you have a light?"

My thoughts are interrupted by a voice, and I stop rubbing my feet and look up.

Hang on, that sounds just like—

*Vanessa.*

Standing next to me with her peroxide hair and bright red lipstick, she waves her unlit cigarette hopefully and smiles her big toothy smile. God, it's good to see her. I feel a rush of affection and have to resist the urge to throw my arms around her and give her a big hug.

"Jesus—"

I'm suddenly aware of her peering at me, her brow creased in consternation, as if she's just noticed me for the first time.

"Excuse me?" I try to make my voice sound as normal as possible, but my heart is thumping. She knows it's me!

"Oh, nothing." She wrinkles her nose dismissively. "For a moment you reminded me of someone."

"I do?" I wait in anticipation, caught between fear and excitement.

She frowns a moment in confusion. "Hey, you're American!" she exclaims. "I thought I could detect a bit of an accent!"

Not knowing quite how to react, I raise my eyebrows and nod encouragingly.

"So's my friend Lottie." She laughs. "You actually reminded me of her for, like, a second. But actually you're nothing like her—"

I'm struck by a curious flash of disappointment. I know I've changed a lot, and *thank goodness* I've changed a lot, but surely I'm not a *completely* different person now, from the best friend she used to have then.

*Am I?*

"Oh, just ignore me," she continues shaking her head. "I'm all over the place at the moment. That's the problem with being in love." She rolls her eyes, but it's fairly obvious it isn't a problem. Far from it. "Do you know, someone once told me being in love is a form of madness, and it's true!" Letting out a snort of laughter, she starts digging around in her pink satin-quilted clutch, which is shaped like a strawberry.

I watch her. God, it seems so strange to see Vanessa with such a tiny bag. Now that she's had Ruby and Sam you never see her without one of those giant tote bags, filled to the brim with piles and piles of stuff.

"Damn, I could have sworn I had a lighter in here."

"Hang on, I think I have some matches." Sliding my hand into my jacket pocket, I locate some that I just took from the bowl on the bar. Now that everywhere is nonsmoking you don't see free matches anymore, and I always need them for my aromatherapy candles. I pass a packet to her.

"Thanks." She smiles gratefully, and lighting her cigarette, takes a long drag as we slowly shuffle forward. "Huh, this is taking forever," she complains, blowing smoke out her nostrils. "My boyfriend's going to think I've run off with another man—" Then leaning closer, she confides, "Well, he's not really my boyfriend *yet*. We've only been out three times, but I've already fallen madly in love with him. . . ." She smiles excitedly. "His name's Julian and he's studying to be a lawyer. . . ."

I listen in fascination as she gushes to *me*, a total stranger, like girls do when they're completely nuts over a guy and just want to tell anyone and everyone who will listen all about how lucky they are, how amazing it feels, and how wonderful he is. . . . And yet of course I know all this. I've heard it all before.

And yet.

As she keeps chatting away it suddenly strikes me just how different this Vanessa is from the Vanessa I saw only a few hours ago at my birthday dinner. To the Vanessa who stood next to me in another set of bathrooms talking about Julian.

She smiles dreamily, then giggles. "Or maybe *I'm* just crazy . . ."

Now she's all wide-eyed and excited, bursting with hope and happiness and this shiny new thing called love, but earlier tonight she seemed so resigned and unhappy, defeated.

I watch as she pulls out a compact and starts reapplying what used to be her trademark scarlet lipstick. Drawing two perfect arches of color on her top lip, and sweeping across the bottom with one deft flick of her wrist. She hasn't worn red lipstick in a while. In fact, tonight she wasn't wearing any makeup at all, until I gave her the lip gloss, I reflect, and her hair was pulled back in a clip. Apparently she didn't have time to take a shower when the babysitter was late.

But it's more than that. It's more than unwashed hair and the lack of mascara, it's like seeing a photograph which used to be in such vivid color slowly fade into black and white.

"Oooh look, there's a free one." She gestures ahead to an empty stall I hadn't noticed.

"Oh, yes . . . thanks."

Leaving her applying a fresh coat of mascara, I disappear inside. I suddenly feel incredibly sad. An awful lot has changed in ten years. And for the first time it hits me that perhaps not all of it is for the better.

## Chapter Twenty-five

It's three a.m. and I'm seeking solace on a sofa in a darkened corner. I feel like I've been here for hours. Days. Weeks almost. And now I'm bored and tired, have a headache, my feet hurt, and I want to go home.

But I can't. I have to stay and keep a watchful eye on Lottie, who at some point in the evening switched from water and has proceeded to get completely smashed on free birthday drinks. I'd forgotten just how drunk I used to get. At one point I actually started dancing on the table.

And in those heels. I don't know how I did it.

Rubbing my temples, my eyes do an automatic sweep around the club to check on Lottie's whereabouts and make sure she's not getting into any trouble (or falling off aforementioned table) when abruptly the music stops and the lights come on.

My heart skips a beat, hardly daring to believe what's happening. Oh my God, does this mean—hope holds my breath tight inside of me as clubbers begin leaving the dance floor and heading for the exit. Yes, it does! I almost feel like dropping to my knees and kissing the floor. The word "relief" doesn't even come close.

Halle-freaking-luyah. That's it.

*It's over.*

"Awww, what a bummer," slurs Lottie, emerging from the crowds, her face sweaty and wearing an expression of utter dismay. "I can't believe it's over. *Already!*"

"I know. What a shame," I lie, hastily grabbing my bag and throwing on my jacket. "Okay, let's go." I start racing out of the club, my sore feet suddenly coming back to life.

Outside, everyone is milling around on the pavement saying good night.

"Hang on, everyone, before you leave I want to take a photo," she yells, and producing a camera from her bag, she starts herding people together.

"No, you need to be in it, Lottie," yells someone.

I'm still standing by her side and she turns to me. "Charlotte, will you take a photo?"

"Of course." I take the camera from her with the intention of taking this as quickly as possible so I can get home, but as I look through the lens it suddenly hits me.

The familiar lineup. The clothes. The smiles.

Oh my God. This is the photograph. The one I have at home on my fridge. The one taken on my birthday.

*By me?*

My mind whirls in confusion. But how? That can't be. Unless—

"Come on, hurry up," yells someone.

Quickly I snap to. "Okay, everyone, smile!"

They all beam for the camera and as I press the button I look at Lottie, at my younger self, eyes wide, smile bright. There's a flash and the shutter clicks as I capture the moment forever.

❦

I offer to walk Lottie home. My car is parked outside her house. More importantly, she's walking like she just got her land legs and clearly needs an escort. I don't think she'd get home without me.

Linking arms we stroll back to her house. It's a balmy evening (or should I say early morning) and everything is quiet and slightly magical, as if the whole world is asleep but us.

Arriving at her house, she struggles with her house keys, and after dropping them on the floor three times, I take over. Deftly unlocking the door I haul her inside.

"I think I should make you a coffee, help you sober up a bit," I suggest, taking her through into the kitchen, which is in darkness. Flicking on the light, just a bare bulb hanging forlornly from the ceiling, the kitchen is suddenly flooded by a harsh hundred-wattage.

I freeze.

Sweet Jesus. There's been a robbery! Someone has ransacked the house!

Panic ignites. Oh my God, I need to call the police, quick! What if they've stolen lots of stuff? What if—God forbid—the intruder's still in the house? Panic fires up a notch, to terror. Shit, where's the phone—

And then suddenly I notice that my younger self isn't jumping up and down yelling, "We've been burgled!" On the contrary, she's leaning very calmly in the doorway as though nothing is out of the ordinary.

Because nothing is out of the ordinary, Charlotte.

All it once it registers. There hasn't been a robbery. And nobody has ransacked the house—*except the people who live here*. I huff in disbelief. Did I really *live* like this? My roommates and I were pigs! Actually no, pigs are most definitely cleaner. My eyes sweep around the room, across every surface littered with dirty mugs, half-eaten food, shriveled-up tea bags, and bowls with dried-on-cereal that it would take a hammer and chisel to remove, and finally land on the pile of dirty dishes. It's almost skyscraper in its proportions.

And what about the garbage? I glance with horror at the plastic trash can, its top off, the black garbage bag spilling over with empty cans, most of which appear to be Heinz baked beans.

*Then there's the smell.*

I look for a place to plop her down. A chair would be perfect, if each one wasn't piled with tons of domestic litter. Old dish towels, newspapers, and—oh God—is that a pair of panties?

I recoil at the sight of what appears to be a discarded G-string. Grabbing a wooden spoon with my free hand I loop the thong over the handle and quickly transplant them onto another pile. Clearing away a mound of mess, I drape Lottie on a chair.

Nearly gagging, I turn away and unearth the kettle, which I fill up (not an easy task as I have to wedge the spout between the faucet and the pile of dishes, a tricky maneuver that reminds me of a game of Jenga) and click on.

I turn back to Lottie, who's crumpled over, the side of her face resting on the dining room table, her eyes closed.

"Coffee won't be a minute," I encourage, trying not to let out a shriek as I look for a mug that doesn't have mold growing inside it.

"Ummmm . . ." she moans sleepily.

Somehow, in the space of a few minutes she's gone from euphoric life and soul of the party drunk, to falling asleep in her clothes drooling drunk.

"Maybe you should eat something too," I suggest.

"Mmmmm . . ."

Gingerly I tug open a few cupboards. Back at my place, my shelves are filled with packets of organic whole-wheat pasta, jars of sun-dried tomatoes, a bottle of virgin olive oil . . .

Cup-a-noodles.

I stare at them blankly. That's it?

I rummage around a bit. There's got to be something else, something aside from cup-a-noodles.

Oh, hang on! Ketchup. Nope. It's all congealed and lumpy around the top. Looks like it's cup-a-noodles or nothing, I decide, grabbing one in desperation and peeling off the lid. Mmm, very nutritious, I muse, looking at the freeze-dried dust in disgust. I dread to think how many additives and chemical preservatives are in there.

The kettle flicks off and I fill it up to the brim with hot water then turn back to making coffee. Forget freshly brewed espresso. Chipping away at the remnants in the bottom of the jar of Nescafé, I turn to the fridge for milk. But not, I have to add, without trepidation.

Bracing myself, I tug it open, and come face-to-face with more ice than we've got left in the arctic. Anyone who's worried about the polar cap disappearing would be greatly reassured by this fridge. Two triangles of butter, a half-used jar of marinara sauce, and an unidentifiable fossilized object that could be anything greet me.

Anything at all, I think, looking at it curiously.

Is this how I used to survive? On rehydrated noodles, ketchup, butter, and marinara sauce? I'm surprised I never got scurvy, or rickets, or something.

I think back to my list and hastily add to it.

## 17. Eat healthily.

"You know, you really should try to eat a balanced diet," I advise, spying a dog-eared carton of milk at the back and pouncing on it. "You're supposed to eat a recommended five servings of fruit and vegetables a day to lower your cholesterol and avoid the risk of colon cancer. . . ." I glance over at Lottie, but she's not listening. Crashed out on the dining room table, she's emitting a soft snore.

I give up on the dietary tips—for now anyway—and turn back to making coffee. I take a quick sniff of the milk. Well, better safe than—

Yuccckk.

It's totally sour; in fact it's gone past that and has morphed into some sort of solidified lump.

Jesus.

Hastily I put it back in the fridge (well, I would put it in the trash, but it's already spilling over). She'll just have to drink it black. It's better than nothing.

"Here you go."

I put the coffee and noodles in front of her, but she doesn't stir. She's out cold. I give her a shake, and she wakes up blearily, squinting in the light. For a moment she looks around herself as if not realizing where she is, then pounces on the coffee. "Mmm, thanks," she mumbles, perking up and taking a large gulp. Followed by a spoonful of gloop, I mean, noodles. "Yummy." She smiles, grinning up at me. "Want some?" She proffers the cup at me.

"No, thanks," I say hastily. "I'm not hungry."

"Suit yourself." She smiles, taking another forkful. "More for me."

Whatever, it seems to do the trick, and it's not long before she's revived enough to climb the stairs to her bedroom. I follow, partly out of curiosity, partly to make sure she doesn't slip and fall back down the stairs. I throw out an arm as she wobbles precariously on the top step. Phew, that was a close call.

"Well, here we are, home sweet home . . ." Cup-a-noodles in one hand, mug of coffee in the other, she bumps open her bedroom door with her hip. It swings open, revealing she's left the light on. Saving energy was not my big thing in those days. Neither, it would appear, was picking my clothes up off the floor.

Following her in, I stare at the scene that greets me. The only way I can describe it is this: Imagine emptying your drawers and tossing everything on the floor. Then, opening your closet, pulling everything off the hangers, and chucking those on the floor too. Add on top a few pairs of shoes. A coat. A few wet towels. And bingo, you've got my old bedroom.

"Make yourself at home." Lottie grins, kicking off her shoes and flopping cross-legged onto the Indian bedspread. I look around for somewhere to sit. The room is so tiny I can barely turn around. There's a small table and fold-up plastic chair by the window and I perch uncomfortably on the edge. The table is cluttered with books.

An ancient IBM computer takes up most of the space, and there's a pile of pages next to it.

"I'm writing a novel," she says, seeing me look at them.

"Oh, wow, I'd forgotten about that—" I murmur, remembering. Then catch myself. But Lottie hasn't heard me; instead, she's busily tucking into her meal.

"I haven't finished it yet, but I'm going to," she continues assuredly. "Right now I'm working at a puzzle magazine but I really want to be a writer. Ever since I was a little girl, it's always been my dream, I couldn't imagine doing anything else . . ." She smiles and takes another forkful. "What about you? What do you do?"

"Oh . . . I . . . um . . . I run my own PR company," I say.

"Wow, really?" Eyes wide, she looks impressed. "That's amazing. Your own company, you must be mega successful!"

"I wouldn't say mega . . ." I say modestly, but inside I feel a swell of pride at how well I've done. At how far I've come, I think, glancing at Lottie, sitting cross-legged on her rickety futon, in the middle of her poky little room, eating cup-a-noodles. "I bet you live in an amazing apartment, don't you? And you drive that amazing car . . ."

I smile as I remember giving her a ride home from the concert the other night, and her oohing and aahing about my heated leather seats. "Well, I like it—"

"You're so lucky," she sighs wistfully. "I'd love my own place and a new car one day. And some money would be nice . . ."

I smile, basking in her respect.

"So do you love your job?" she asks eagerly.

"Well, I don't know about *love* it," I admit, thinking about this last week. "There's a lot of stress involved—"

"Because it's important to do what you love, don't you think?" she interrupts, before I can finish. "Like my dad always says, you're at work a long time, you might as well do something you love, something you're passionate about."

I feel a jolt of uncertainty. God, Dad always does say that, doesn't he? To tell the truth, I've never been passionate about PR, not even close, but then how many people are passionate about their jobs? I tell myself in justification.

"True." I nod. "But that's also a little idealistic. Sometimes you need to compromise and focus on a career that will allow you to pay the bills and give you financial security," I reason. "Okay, so it might not be doing something you're truly passionate about, but it can still be challenging, fulfilling . . ." I can see I've got my younger self's attention and I feel pleased with myself. See. This is the amazing thing about being older. Having the experience. The hindsight. The maturity to know what's important.

"Ugh, no thanks—"

I snap back, to see Lottie making a face.

"Challenging and fulfilling," she repeats, as if the words taste nasty. "That doesn't sound like fun."

"Well, life isn't always about having fun," I reply, feeling a little rattled.

"Then what is it about?" she says simply.

Her question throws me. I open my mouth to try to respond, but I can't. I don't know how to answer that. Because she's right, I suddenly realize. What *is* it about?

I'm saved from replying by the sound of the front door being slammed.

"Oh, hell, that'll be one of the boys coming in," she groans. "Hang on a sec, I'm just going to run to the bathroom before they do—"

She jumps up and disappears out of the room before I've barely registered the front door slamming, and I'm suddenly reminded of what it was like sharing a bathroom with six other people. Waiting in line to take a shower in the morning, only to finally get in there to discover all the hot water is gone. Dashing, legs crossed, to the bathroom in the middle of the night and finding someone already on it. Listening out for the door to unlock so you can go in and have a nice, long, relaxing bath, then seeing one of the boys come out complaining about last night's curry . . .

"Sorry, what were you saying?" asks Lottie, reappearing.

I look up in surprise. I expected she'd be in there for eons brushing her teeth, flossing, rinsing, taking off her makeup, applying creams. I mean, the whole bathroom routine takes me forever. "Oh, was someone in there already?" I say, realizing and tossing her a look of sympathy.

"No." She smiles and flops back onto her bed. "All done."

*All done?*

I stare at her in confusion. What does she mean, all done? How can it all be done in about ten seconds? I'm in there about forty-five minutes.

Then I realize. She hasn't taken her makeup off.

"Um, aren't you going to take your makeup off?" I ask casually. I mean, every woman knows that your skin regenerates overnight and it has to be squeaky clean to soak up all those nutrients from all those creams you've slathered on.

I feel a stab of worry.

*Don't they?*

"Nah. I can't be bothered." She yawns, rubbing her eyes with the palm of her hand and smearing black eyeliner across her cheek.

I give a little inward shudder and, trying not to think of my poor skin, mentally add to my list.

*18. Always take your makeup off.*

Speaking of the list.

"You know, instead of renting, you really should think about buying your own place," I suggest, "then you'll have our own bathroom."

"Yeah, right." She laughs as if I've just cracked a very funny joke. "With what?"

"Your savings," I continue, bending down and picking up a wet towel. It's been bugging me ever since I got in here. Folding it up, I lay it over the back of the chair.

"I don't have any savings," she chuckles. "Apart from my overdraft. Actually . . ." She pauses, thinking. "I've got a three-hundred-quid overdraft and there's sixty quid left, which is like fifty bucks, so does that count?"

"No, that doesn't count," I retort quickly, suddenly feeling a bit like Miles must when I get confused about investment funds. At the same time, I can see her logic. Sort of.

"But you should start a savings account," I continue, reaching for another towel. "You don't have to put much in, just a few pounds a month, but it will all add up . . ."

Finished with the towels, I make a start on tidying up the rest of the stuff. Well, now I've started—

"And if I were you," I add pointedly. "I'd start a pension, and maybe invest. . . ." Putting some dresses on hangers, I start running through my list. "A little bit of an insider tip: if you can, buy shares in something called Google. . . ." Going off into a little fantasy land I start imagining how I'd spend all my millions. Though first of all I'd give a large chunk to my family and friends. Speaking of. My mind jumps to Vanessa, and her advice. "Oh, and before I forget, you must start doing your pelvic floor exercises—"

Suddenly I realize Lottie has gone silent, and I turn around.

"No, don't worry, they're not difficult—"

My younger self is completely fast asleep.

I stare at myself in disbelief.

No wave machine. No mouth guards. No aromatherapy mask. No humidifier. No blackout blinds. And with the light on. It's incredible. I obviously didn't suffer from insomnia back then, I reflect, feeling a tug of envy.

Gently I pull the bedspread over her and she mumbles something faintly in her sleep and turns over. I pause, watching her sleeping, then go to leave. My eyes sweep around the room for one last look, and land on the unfinished novel, sitting on the desk.

And it's never going to be finished, I sigh, suddenly feeling a beat of sadness. Because I threw away the dream.

I can't remember how long I stand there, reflecting, looking at the girl I used to be. Until finally, switching off the light, I leave her behind and close the door.

# Chapter Twenty-six

*B*ang *bang bang bang bang.*

What's going on? It's pitch-black and I'm trapped in a wooden box. I can't see, I can't move, all I can hear is this incessant—

*Bang bang bang*

Oh my God, I'm being buried alive. That's the sound of the nails being hammered into my coffin.

*Bang bang bang bang.*

I'm going to suffocate. I won't be able to get out. I'm going to die.

*Bang bang bang.*

Aghhhhh, let me out, let me out, *LET ME OUTTTTTTT!!!!!!*

"Darling, wake up, wake up—"

I snap my eyes open to find Miles shaking me by the shoulder.

"Wassup? . . . Wha . . . ?" I sit bolt upright and look at him, dazedly, trying to get my bearings. I'm in bed, and Miles is lying next to me, his face etched with concern.

"Sshh, don't worry. You were having a nightmare. You were yelling something about 'let me out, let me out.'"

"Oh . . . right . . . yes," I murmur, feeling a rush of relief. "Oh God, it was horrible, Miles, just horrible . . ." I flop back onto the pillow. "I was being buried alive."

He smiles reassuringly. "Well, don't worry, you're fine now, you're safe here with me." He smiles, stroking my hair which is stuck to my clammy forehead.

*Bang bang bang bang.*

I stiffen. It's that noise again! "What was that?" I gasp, sitting bolt upright again. See, I wasn't dreaming. It's real.

"Oh, that? Don't worry, darling, that's nothing." He laughs at my horrified expression. "Just the estate agent's putting up the sign."

"*Sign?* What sign?" I gasp, jumping out of bed and dashing to the window. Yanking off the curtain I stare out into the street. Just in time to see a man with a hammer giving a final thwack to the signpost.

"*For Sale,*" I murmur, reading the large red letters. My heart thuds.

"Well, what did you think it was going to say?" says Miles, jovially.

"Nothing . . . I dunno . . ." My mind is swirling in uncertain directions. "It's just . . . isn't it a bit *quick*?"

"Quick?" replies Miles, propping himself up against the headboard. "You can't be too quick when it comes to the property market, darling," he advises sagely. "Now our offer's been accepted it's important that the buyers see we mean business, and that means selling our own properties ASAP, organizing a survey, sorting out the joint mortgage and deposit . . ."

As his voice drones on I feel slightly light-headed. I rub my ears agitatedly.

"I think I'll make us coffee," I say, cutting him off as he starts talking about setting up a joint account. I suddenly feel claustrophobic, as if I can't breathe.

"Oooh, yes, good idea," agrees Miles. "I've got a bit of a hangover after last night. All that celebrating—" He looks at me, and I feel a twist of panic. "I must have crashed out on the sofa as it wasn't till the light woke me up, streaming in through the blinds, that I crawled into bed. Not that you'd remember," he adds, looking at me pointedly.

The twist of alarm tightens a notch. Oh shit.

After leaving my younger self asleep in bed, I'd driven back from my old house and arrived at my place just as it was getting light. Assuming Miles was still fast asleep on the sofa, I'd headed straight into the bedroom, which was in complete darkness because of my blackout blinds, and flopped straight into bed. But what if Miles had woken up while I'd been out clubbing? What if he'd come to bed and discovered I wasn't there? What on earth am I going to say?

My mind starts frantically flicking through a Rolodex of excuses. How on earth am I going to explain—

"You were fast asleep. Completely dead to the world," he continues, and I look at him in astonishment. "You were obviously exhausted. You're normally such a light sleeper."

He doesn't know! My body almost sags with relief.

"Must have been all the excitement about the house, hey?" He beams.

"Yes, absolutely." I smile uneasily. "It totally wiped me out." I do a show of stretching and throw in a faux yawn. Which turns into a real one. Actually I am still pretty tired. I can't have been asleep for more than a few hours.

"Do you want me to help with the coffee?" Misinterpreting my show of exhaustion, Miles starts to get out of bed.

"No, no," I say urgently. "You stay there. I'll get it."

"Hmm, I think I'm going to like this living together," he says, and looking pleased he slides back underneath the comforter.

Leaving him behind in the bedroom, I hurry into the kitchen and busily grab a bag of coffee beans, pour them into the grinder, switch it on, and reach for the espresso pot.

Then pause.

Hugging it to my chest, I lean against the counter and watch the coffee beans whirling around and around. Like all the kinds of strange, unfamiliar thoughts that are whirling around in my head.

I think back to last night. To all of it. My birthday dinner, Miles and the champagne, Vanessa and Julian, Lottie and the club, Olly the bartender . . .

At the memory of Olly my stomach does a little loop and I feel a flash of something—excitement—fear—foolishness—I don't know which. A scene cut from our conversation slides across my mind, down my spine, through my groin, and comes to an abrupt full-stop as my mind throws up an image of the waiter at the gastropub. Annoying, irritating, belligerent, *and the same person.* God, it's all gotten so complicated.

"There you are."

I twirl around to see Miles, standing in the doorway of the kitchen, wearing my bathrobe. It's too small for him and his pale arms and legs are sticking out from the cream waffle toweling, making him look rather comical.

"I wondered what had happened to the coffee."

I become aware of the noise of the grinder, still buzzing away noisily, and quickly turn it off. The beans have disintegrated into fine powder.

"I thought we could have our coffee and then go take a second look at the house . . ." he continues, reaching for the Weetabix. He keeps a box at my house. Apparently he's eaten them since childhood and can't break the habit. Not that he seems to want to. I've never seen anyone get as much pleasure from sprinkling a layer of sugar on top of the Weetabix, patting it down with the back of his spoon, carefully pouring milk around them ("like a moat," he once explained), making sure he doesn't pour it on the Weetabix directly as that would make them soggy, and then eating them with the kind of precision you'd expect from a brain surgeon.

". . . So we need to hurry up. I've arranged to pick up the keys . . ."

"Oh, um . . . yes, right . . ." I nod, feeling a familiar jangle of nerves.

Turning back to the espresso pot, I rub my ears distractedly. They're still itching. In fact, they're actually rather painful, I realize, leaning forward to peer at them in the shiny stainless toaster, which acts as a sort of mirror.

I get quite a shock. My ears are all red and inflamed, and there's an angry rash beginning to run down the side of my neck. Oh my God, it must be the pearl earrings. I'm allergic to them.

And all at once it's like the earrings are a sign. A sign that this isn't right. Buying this house. Moving in together. *Me and Miles.* I feel a jolt of fear and recognition. It's as if someone just unlocked a door inside of me that I've been too afraid to open. Because I know what's on the other side.

*I'm not in love with Miles.*

As soon as the thought pops into my head, I know it's been there for longer than I care to remember. I've just been avoiding it, ignoring it, pretending it wasn't true. Putting a PR spin on my own relationship, trying to convince myself that we are right for each other, that Miles is right for me. And it's only now that I've finally admitted it to myself.

Now I just have to admit it to Miles.

Like a drumroll, my heart starts thudding loudly in my chest as I turn to face him. He's sitting on a stool up at the counter, carefully cutting off a slice of Weetabix with his spoon, still talking.

". . . So there's lots of things we need to sort out, like for example, are they leaving the curtains and blinds because if not, we'll have to get those ordered and they can take at least four to six weeks. . . ."

I have to tell him. Taking a deep breath, I muster up all my courage. "Miles, I don't know how to say this, but I can't do this—"

"Oh, don't tell me," he interrupts, rolling his eyes. "You've got yoga."

I swallow hard. "No, I don't have yoga . . ."

"I mean, surely you can reschedule, this *is* very important . . ." he continues, turning back to his cereal bowl.

"Miles, you're not listening," I snap, then immediately feel guilty.

He looks at me in surprise. "What?" He looks confused. "Then what is this about?"

I hesitate. It's now or never. I have to just come out with it. "It's about us."

There. I've said it.

He looks at me for a moment, uncomprehending, searching my eyes for a clue, then nods. "Oh, I know what this is about."

I feel a curious leap of optimism. Maybe he feels this way too. Maybe it's not just me. "It's about last night, isn't it?" he continues, looking uncomfortable. "Me falling asleep on the sofa."

I look at him blankly for a moment.

"We didn't have sex on your birthday."

Oh my God, he's got it so wrong. So horribly wrong, I don't know what to say.

"Well, we can have it now if you'd like," he offers, putting down his spoon and standing up. "We don't have to pick up the keys and look at the house till ten—we've got time."

I look at him, standing there, in my bathrobe, his half-finished Weetabix lying soggy in the bowl, and strangely I don't feel very turned on. In fact, his offer of sex is so matter-of-fact, he might as well be offering to put out the recycling.

"Miles, it's not about last night, and it's not about sex," I say, quickly glossing over that bit. "It's about us. Me, this house, *everything* . . ." I flail my arms around. Miles is looking at me, his face uncomprehending. I'm hoping he's going to butt in, finish my sentence for me, guess what I'm going to say, but after two wrong answers, he's not going to, is he?

"I don't want to buy the house," I finally blurt.

He stares at me, his face a picture of astonishment.

"Why? What's wrong with the house?!" he demands.

"Nothing's wrong with the house," I reply quickly. "It's perfect. It's a perfect house."

"Well, then!" His astonishment has disappeared and he's looking annoyed now. "Look, Charlotte, I know you're nervous, but you're being ridiculous. What's got into you?"

"Nothing, it's just—" I stare fixedly at the floor. "Miles, I can't do this, I can't move in with you . . ."

There. Finally. I've said it.

There's silence. I drag my eyes upward. He looks stunned. Then his face sets, harder. "Can't, or *won't*?"

I swallow hard. "Miles, I don't want to do this. You're a wonderful person, but—" I falter a moment, not wanting to sound so cliché. But there's no other way to put it. "It's not you, it's me. I've been having doubts for a while, and I just never realized . . ." God, I'm really making a mess of this, aren't I? I swallow hard and continue. "But now, everything's sort of come to a head and it wouldn't be fair on either of us to continue—"

"You've met someone else, haven't you?" he suddenly accuses.

Every nerve in my body seems to jump and I look at him in shock. "No, of course not!" I protest quickly.

"Yes, you have," he continues "I just knew it. You've been acting really strange these last couple of days. Different. Ever since I got back from Leeds. So come on, who is it?"

"No one—"

Oh God, why is he asking me all these questions? And why am I feeling so guilty? I ask myself, thinking about Olly.

"Tell me who it is and I'll punch him." Curling up a fist, he shakes it menacingly. Only Miles could never look menacing. Especially not in my terry cloth bathrobe.

"Miles!" I gasp in exasperation, feeling the conversation veering wildly off course. "This isn't about anyone else. It's about me."

His chest deflates and, stuffing his fist in his pocket, he composes himself. "Look, Charlotte, I'm sure we can work this out. We always do," he says practically.

He's right. If we ever have a difference of opinion, we don't argue about it, we work things out. But that usually involves a compromise. And this time it's about more than a fireplace.

"No, Miles, we can't." I shake my head sadly. "We can't work this out. Not this time."

"Well, I think you're making a huge mistake," he snaps.

Guilt stabs. God, I feel like such a *horrible* person.

"We're going to lose out on a real steal with that house," he continues. "It's a great investment. How can you do this?"

Slowly it registers. Hang on a minute. He's talking about *the house*?

"Plus I've already arranged for the survey. That's at least seven hundred pounds down the drain, unless I can cancel it, but I doubt it, at such short notice . . ."

Obviously he's upset and just trying to distract himself. It's his way of dealing. After all men aren't like women, are they? I watch as he snatches his phone off the counter where it's charging and starts punching in a number. Then again, maybe he really *is* more bothered about the house.

"I'll call them now, see what I can do . . ."

"Miles, listen, I'll pay for the survey," I offer. "I'll pay for all the costs we've incurred so far. It's not important."

"Of course it's important, Charlotte," he snaps.

"No, it's not, it's really not." I shake my head. "It's just a house. We're talking about the rest of our lives."

"Just a house?" He laughs in disbelief. "I don't think so, Charlotte. It's in a prime location, it's a hot property—"

"I don't care if it's a hot property!" I yell, before I can stop myself. "I don't care if it's a prime location, or if we can get permission for a loft conversion, or if it's a great investment. I don't care if we drink a Pinot Noir or a Cabernet Sauvignon. And I don't care if I never see another episode of *Location, Location, Location*. Or talk about pension plans. Or listen to another James Bond theme tune as long as I live—"

I break off, panting. We both look stunned by my outburst.

"I'm sorry, I didn't mean to shout—" I trail off and spread my hands awkwardly. "It's just that I've been trying to convince myself. Going along with things. And I can't any longer. I've got to be true to *myself*, Miles."

"But you said you loved *License to Thrill*. I bought you the CD." He looks at me, his face hurt.

"I know, I'm sorry," I repeat again, only this time more softly.

"Me too," he replies stiffly, and putting the phone back to his ear, he turns away and stalks out of the kitchen in my bathrobe. "Ah, yes, hello. I'm calling about the survey . . ."

# Chapter Twenty-seven

Okay, so let's recap.

In less than twelve hours I've gone from having a boyfriend, buying a house, and being inches away from what my mother calls "settled." To having no boyfriend, no new house, and feeling very *un*settled.

Brilliant, Charlotte. Great move. One of your finest.

Feeling stunned, I plop down on the sofa and try to take in this sudden turn of events. I hadn't planned for any of this to happen at all. When I woke up this morning the first thing on my to-do list certainly wasn't "Must break up with Miles."

But once I faced up to the deep-seated doubts that have been simmering in the background for so long, it all unraveled so quickly. Like picking at some stitching, the whole thing suddenly fell apart. Right there, in the middle of my kitchen. And now I'm not sure quite what to do next.

Miles leaves, telling me he'll come back for his stuff later. I offer to drop it off with my car, it will be much easier than him lugging it on the bus, but he curtly tells me he doesn't need my help thank you very much, the number 47 goes right past his flat, and then he pointedly empties his pockets of my spare keys, and slams the door behind him.

He's angry and upset and I don't blame him. I feel awful. Terribly mean. Guilty.

But I also feel a huge sense of release.

I glance across at the coffee table, where the real estate agent's brochure of my dream house lies in all its glossiness. As I pick it up I notice that the nervous twist in the pit of my stomach, which I've been trying to persuade myself was just pre-moving-in-together jitters, has disappeared. Gone. Along with the dream life I always wanted, I reflect, looking at the full-color photographs.

At least I *thought* I wanted it. I flop back on the sofa, my head spinning. To tell the truth, I'm beginning to feel a little disoriented. Like I've been running a marathon these past ten years and now the finish line has vanished into thin air. I mean, if I don't want that, *what do I want?*

God, it's all a little too heavy for a Saturday morning, isn't it?

Scratching my inflamed ears, I let out a hippo-sized yawn. I haven't even had my coffee yet, I realize, closing my eyes. And I'm actually really tired. It was almost getting light when I finally rolled into bed, so I can't have had more than a few hours' sleep last night. I mean this morning, I think sleepily, snuffling into a cushion.

Then stiffen.

Eugh, what's that horrible smell? My nostrils wrinkle up in disgust. Yuck, it smells like stale sweat and cigarettes.

*That's because it is stale sweat and cigarettes.*

Abruptly I realize I'm smelling my hair. My normally swingy, shiny, glossy hair that smells of elderberry and jojoba and something suitably fragrant, now smells like an old ashtray and someone's armpit. I take another cautious sniff. Eugh, that's just gross. I spring up from the sofa.

I might not know what I want, but I definitely know what I need. A shower.

After giving my hair a through shampooing, followed by an intensive conditioner, I stay underneath the powerful twin showerheads for a long time. Eyes closed, face upturned, I relish the hot water blasting my skin. My mind flicks back to Lottie last night, rolling into bed, still wearing her makeup. God, imagine what her skin will look like today, I shudder, squeezing out a blob of special micro-dermabrasion crystals and vigorously scrubbing my cheeks. There's nothing worse than sleeping in your makeup. She'll look terrible.

And feel terrible, I muse, a vision popping into my mind of her drunkenly stumbling up to bed, noodles in one hand, a cup of black coffee in the other. Poor thing. I might not be having the greatest morning, but she's got to be suffering from the hangover from hell.

❧

Wrapped in towels I make coffee and then wander aimlessly around the apartment for a bit. I check a couple of e-mails. Pluck my eyebrows. Throw out all my rotting organic vegetables from the bottom of my fridge. Plump cushions.

The whole day stretches ahead of me. Weekends are always spent with Miles, and this weekend wasn't going to be any different. In fact, I purposely kept this weekend free from work and appointments so we could do lots of coupley things as I've been so busy recently. *Rebond*, as it says in my book about how to have a successful relationship. That didn't *quite* work out, did it?

Finished plumping all the cushions on the sofa and putting them all neatly on their corners, I look distractedly around me. I know, I'll call Vanessa, I decide, reaching for the telephone. No, on second thought, she'll be busy with the kids and won't be able to talk and we'll have one of those conversations where every third sentence is "No, Ruby, no, Mummy's on the phone." Plus, to be honest, she's got plenty of her own problems right now, without listening to mine, I reflect, thinking about our conversation last night in the ladies' room and feeling a wave of worry. I know, maybe instead I'll go for a run, get some exercise. Then again, my muscles are sore from dancing last night. I had no idea dancing was such a workout.

Maybe I'll—

I draw a blank. What *are* you supposed to do when you've just broken up with someone? I glance over at my bookshelves, bursting with self-help books, guides, and manuals. My eyes scan over the titles: there's everything there from *Stress Management* to *The Power of Positive Thinking*, but there's nothing there on breakups. Not even in my favorite, *Good Listener, Good Lover*. But then again, if you're both good listeners and good lovers you probably won't be breaking up, will you?

Grabbing my laptop, I log onto Amazon and punch in "breakup." A whole ream of books open before my eyes:

*Surviving as a Single. When Two Becomes One. You're Not Alone. Gay Good-byes* (I gloss over that one). *Getting Over It and Moving On* . . .

Clicking on one of them, I start reading a summary of what's inside:

> . . . it's important to mourn the end of a relationship as this will allow you to move on. Be kind to yourself. This will take time. You cannot rush this important healing process as you move through the various stages: 1) Shock and disbelief 2) Depression and grief 3) Anger and unfairness 4) Acceptance. At this final stage you are ready to now move on with your life, feel positive, and hopefully begin a new relationship. . . .

Hmm, so I suppose I must be in the shock and disbelief stage, I decide, clicking on the book to order it. Well, I'll need to read it, otherwise I'll forget all the different stages I'm supposed to go through. Though I'm not much looking forward to the depression and grief stage. I wonder if there's a way you can gloss over that bit—

Out of stock. This product will take 4–6 weeks to ship.

What? I look at the screen in annoyance. I can't wait four to six weeks to start mourning the end of my relationship! Those stages are going to take months, and I need to get started right now. Shutting the screen of my laptop, I get up from the sofa. I'll have to drive to Borders and buy the book instead.

Quickly I throw on some clothes and towel-dry my hair. I don't need to blow-dry it today. I'm not planning on seeing anyone. I'll just run to the store and hole myself up with the book until I finish it. I reach over to my bedside cabinet to put on my watch.

And freeze.

It's not there.

Flummoxed, I stare at the bedside cabinet: alarm clock, eye mask, aromatherapy candle . . . but no watch. But how can that be? I take my watch off every night before I go to bed. I'm as regular as clock-work, pardon the pun. It's always there.

But not today.

Fuck, where is it?

I know, maybe I forgot to take it off and it fell off my wrist when I was asleep. Clutching the ray of hope I fling back the duvet and chuck a few pillows around. But nope, it's nowhere to be found. Panic flickers. It was a present from Mom and Dad on my eighteenth birthday. It's engraved on the back and everything. It has such tre-mendous sentimental value.

Plus, it's my watch, for christsakes! I can't survive without my watch. How am I going to know what time it is? There's not always a clock to hand, which means I'll have to look at my BlackBerry every five minutes, and what if I have to turn it off in a meeting? Or it's at the bottom of my bag and I have to keep rummaging for it? Or—God forbid—I forget to charge it?

With spiraling panic I dash around the apartment on a desperate hunt. No copy of *Elle Decor*, inflatable exercise ball, or packet of organic coffee beans is left unturned. But it's nowhere to be found. I must have lost it somewhere, but where?

Okay, Charlotte, just calm down, retrace your steps, isn't that what they always say? Last night I was at my old house, then before that the club, and then before that the gastropub for dinner. . . .

Right, I need to start there. Grabbing my car keys, I dash for the door. I'll drive back to the pub and ask someone . . .

*Like the waiter.*

My stomach goes up and down like I'm on a swing.

Not that I want to see him or anything. I pause by the mirror. Well, all right, maybe a little, but only out of curiosity. Running my fingers through my hair I dab on a bit of lip gloss. To be honest, I wouldn't care if he was there or not.

He's not here.

Walking into the pub my eyes go straight for the bar. I feel a clunk of disappointment.

"Hi, can I help you?"

A shaggy, redheaded bartender pauses from wiping the bar and looks up.

"I wanted to speak to someone about my watch. I lost it last night and I just wondered if it was handed in—"

"I wasn't working last night, hang on." He smiles, putting down his dishcloth. "I'll get someone."

As he walks toward the kitchen I glance around the pub. Apart from a couple sitting in a discreet table in the corner, it's practically empty.

"Hey, Oliver," he calls.

My heart jolts. Olly—Oliver. That must be the same person. Oh my God, he *is* here.

There's a pause, and then, "Yeah?"

Suddenly I realize I'm very, *very* nervous. It's like my breath's got caught in my lungs and I can't breathe it out. Which is ridiculous. He's just a bartender.

*Except he's not just a bartender, is he?* pipes up a little voice inside of me. *He's Olly from last night.*

As he emerges from the kitchen, I see the redheaded barman saying something to him and pointing at me. He looks over. And for a brief moment I think I've got it wrong. He's not Olly at all, he doesn't look anything like him. He's much older, different, chunkier, I realize, looking at his baggy gray T-shirt. And for a brief moment I feel a sense of relief. I'm glad it's a mistake. I'm glad this bartender isn't Olly. This makes everything so much simpler.

And yet—

As he walks toward me my stomach does that weird swingy thing again.

His hair might be cut short, he might have a scar on his lip that wasn't there before, and he might now be wearing little round glasses, but behind them the pale gray eyes are the same. There's no mistake.

"Oh, it's you," he mutters, not smiling.

I falter. Well, that's a great start.

"Um, hi." I swallow hard. My throat has suddenly dried up. "I . . . uh, was in here last night."

"I know, I served you," he deadpans.

I'm getting the distinct feeling I haven't made as good as impression on him in my thirties, as I did when I was twenty-one.

"Um . . . yes, well . . . I lost my watch and so I was wondering—"

"Nope, nothing's been found here," he says, cutting me off before I've even finished.

I feel a snap of irritation. Has he even looked? "Are you sure?" I try again. "I mean, it could be underneath a table or—"

"Nope." He shakes his head. "'Fraid not."

I have to bite my tongue.

"Right, then," I say stiffly, hauling back my shoulders and meeting his eyes with my sternest stare. "Well, thanks for looking, and being *so* helpful. I'll leave you my card in case you do happen to find it." I take one from my purse and lay it on the bar. "Sorry to trouble you."

God, he's *such* an asshole. Talk about people changing. And not for the better, I fume, scratching my ears in agitation.

"What's wrong with your ears?" he says as I'm about to turn and leave.

"Nothing," I retort defensively.

"They're all inflamed."

"I had an allergic reaction to some earrings," I say, trying to force a casual voice.

He tries not to smile, but I catch the corners of his lips curl up in amusement.

Damn, why did I have to say that?

"The ones your boyfriend bought you?" he says evenly.

Triggering two thoughts: 1) That's none of your goddamn business and 2) *He was watching me.*

"He's not my boyfriend," I snap back, rattled. God, he's such a know-it-all.

"He's not?" He raises an eyebrow.

"I mean, not anymore." I'm beginning to feel all flustered. Like I've backed myself into a corner and now I can't find a way out. "We just broke up." I look at the floor, wishing it would open up and swallow me. Usually I think before I speak but for some reason I seem to have reverted to my younger self and my brain seems to have disconnected from my mouth.

"Hey, I'm sorry—" Dipping his chin, Oliver looks at me from under his heavy brows, his expression one of concern. "Are you okay?

I look up and meet his eyes. I don't know why but somehow I seem to want to pour my heart out to a complete stranger.

Only he's not, is he?

"Sort of." I shrug.

His mouth twists into a smile. "You know, I'm a really good listener. Working behind this bar I get to hear a lot of stories, get to dole out advice, not that it's probably good anyway. I'm a bit of an agony aunt."

I can't help smiling. "It's a long story." I can feel myself soften toward him.

"Well, I've got plenty of time. I was actually just about to knock off, go for a walk in the park, get some fresh air . . ." He looks at me questioningly. "Don't know if you're interested . . ."

I hesitate, then shake my head. "Thanks, but I should get going," I say, feeling awkward.

"Of course, I understand, you've got a better offer."

"No, it's not that—" I protest, then realize he's fooling around, relax.

At that moment there's a loud scuffling as a door opens at the back and in scampers a big scruffy black dog. With his tail wagging wildly, and a tongue lolling out of the side of its mouth like a long pink ribbon, he rushes up to me and starts trying to lick me all over.

"That's Welly," Oliver tells me, smiling.

"Hi, Welly, I'm Charlotte." I smile, patting his head.

"Looks like you made a friend." Squatting down he clips him onto his leash. "Leave the lady alone, boy, she doesn't want to come for a walk."

Watching them both I think about going back to my empty apartment, packing up Miles's things, reading that self-help book. After all, I can't go for a walk with someone I've just met. Except I haven't just met him, have I?

"Maybe some fresh air would do me good."

Smiling, he passes me the leash.

# Chapter Twenty-eight

We leave the pub and head toward the park, which is only a few streets away. Only today those streets suddenly seem to stretch out endlessly in front of me, like those roads I used to love to drive back home in the States, the ones that go on forever. Streets that need filling with conversation, I think, sneaking a look at Oliver, who's silently striding next to me on the narrow pavement, hands tucked deep into his battered jeans.

Anxiously I try to think of something to talk about. He obviously doesn't recognize me as Lottie from ten years ago, otherwise he would have said something by now.

I know, what about: *"Guess what, last night I went to the Canal Club and met you, only you were ten years younger, and you had a huge crush on me when I was ten years younger, but when I was ten years younger I didn't even notice you and when I introduced us, I completely ignored you."*

Right, Charlotte. You're aiming for casual small talk, not aiming to get carted off in a straitjacket.

"So, Welly, aren't you a handsome doggy?" I coo, resorting to the much safer option of talking to the dog. Welly ignores me and keeps sniffing the pavement. To tell the truth I'm not all that great with dogs. I love them, but I'm not what you call a dog person. I don't know how to do the clicky thing with my tongue and I couldn't tell a Labrador from a golden whatsit.

That said, this is pretty fun, I think, as he trots obediently alongside me. Maybe I could *become* a dog person.

"Yes, you are, you're handsome," I continue, as if Welly has re-
futed my claim.

Oliver catches my eye and I rub Welly's head casually, as if I'm a
pro at this. He stops at a tree and begins sniffing it enthusiastically.
"Does that smell nice?" I coo.

His tail wags excitedly.

"He's like me in the perfume hall at Harrods," I quip, glancing
across at Oliver.

See, I can even make doggy jokes too.

"Is that so?" he says evenly.

"Yes, in fact—" I break off as I glance down at Welly. Hang on a
minute, what's he doing now? He's stopped sniffing and is now sort
of squatting down low and—

I bend down to have a look. "Oh shit," I gasp, shrinking back.

"Yup." Oliver nods, his mouth twitching with amusement at my
reaction.

"Don't worry, I'll take care of it." He pulls a plastic bag out of his
pocket.

"It's okay, I'll do it," I protest quickly. I don't want him thinking
I'm some kind of stupid girl who's afraid to get her fingers dirty.
*Figuratively* speaking.

"Hey, don't worry about it."

"No, seriously," I insist. "What's a little bit of dog poo?"

He looks at me uncertainly. "Well, if you're sure." Shrugging, he
passes me the plastic bag. "Only Welly's been having a few problems
recently, his stomach's a little off . . ."

I glance down just in time to see the last of Welly's—

Oh dear Lord. My stomach lurches like a car with a failing clutch.
In fact I really don't think I can do this.

But you have to, I tell myself firmly. You can't lose face now.

Holding my breath, I bob down and start trying to scoop it up.

"Let me show you a trick; you see, you put your hand inside the bag . . ." he starts explaining.

Unfortunately he's a bit late for that.

"Ewwuuggh." He winces. Sucking the air between his teeth, he throws me a sympathetic look.

But I hold firm. Summoning up the same air of forced calm that I need to remove the spiders from my shower, which for some reason is where big hairy spiders like to hang out, I tie the ends of the plastic bag together and dump it in a nearby trash can.

There, done.

"First time, huh?" He smiles, looking at my shell-shocked expression.

I nod wordlessly.

He laughs. "It gets easier, trust me."

And he's right. It does.

❦

With the ice well and truly broken, the conversation flows easily between us as we enter Holland Park and the inner-city buzz gives way to a sanctuary of tennis courts, grass lawns, and flower beds laid out like a colorful patchwork quilt. It's a warm, hazy day and the park buzzes with the sounds of summer: children's laughter, music wafting from transistor radios, soccer balls being kicked.

After I've washed my hands thoroughly in the bathroom we meander through the serenely designed Japanese garden, walk over the bridge, and watch the majestic and fat orange koi swimming beneath. Welly crouches on his haunches, mesmerized by the fish, his nose almost touching the water.

"Wow, it's so pretty here, isn't it," I murmur, gazing around me.

"Yeah," agrees Oliver. "I come here a lot; it's one of my favorite places. You don't feel like you're in London. You can almost imagine you're in Kyoto."

"Have you been?" I ask with interest.

"Yeah, a few years ago, I spent a month traveling around Japan."

"Wow." I nod, feeling both impressed and envious.

"What about you?"

"The farthest I've been in the last few years is Yorkshire, where my parents live now. Too busy with work." I shrug in explanation.

"No one ever dies wishing they'd spent more time at the office," he replies. "Or whatever the saying is."

"Well, my friend did get me tickets for Paris for my birthday," I say defensively. "Then again I don't suppose I'll be going now," I add as an afterthought.

He furrows his brow questioningly.

"I was supposed to be going with my boyfriend," I explain.

"Did you guys have a blazing row or something?"

"No, we don't 'do' rows." I reply ruefully, quoting Miles.

"So what happened?"

Over in the distance, a peacock is fanning out its tail. I watch for a moment. "I'm not sure," I say, shoving my hands deep into the pockets of my jeans. "It just wasn't right. We weren't right. It's like everything was perfect, but it wasn't." I look at him, shielding my eyes from the sunlight. "Does that make any sense?"

"Emotions don't have to make sense." He shrugs, and we turn and keep walking. Squirrels scurry across our path as we zigzag through the flower beds.

"He didn't seem your type," he says after a moment.

"I know, that's what Vanessa always says—Hang on, how would you know what my type is?" I stop walking and turn to him.

"Well, he's nothing like Billy Romani." He raises his eyebrows.

It takes a moment for it to register, and then—

"You do recognize me!" I exclaim.

"People don't change that much." He shrugs in explanation, and starts walking again.

"I know, but I thought—" I stop myself. Actually, I'm not sure what I thought.

"I recognized you as soon as you walked in the pub on Monday night," he continues as we make our way toward the stretch of grassy lawn which is filled with picnickers. "To tell you the truth, I didn't think you remembered me," he says quietly, glancing at me sideways.

*I didn't,* whispers a small voice inside my head. And now I'm wondering how on earth that could have happened.

"I wasn't on your radar in those days."

"Oh, I wouldn't say that." I laugh nervously, and then catch his expression. God, he actually looks a little angry about it. I hope he's not holding some kind of grudge against me—A thought stirs. Wait a minute. "Is that why you were so mean to me in the pub? To pay me back for ignoring you ten years ago?" I blurt suddenly.

"I don't know what you're talking about," he refutes, but I can tell by the flash of color, I've hit the nail on the head. "When have *I* ever been mean to *you*?"

There's no mistaking the way he says that. It's abundantly clear he thinks I was mean to him.

"Making fun of my allergies," I retort. "Ridiculing me."

"Well, do you blame me? Come on, you've got to admit, they are a bit ridiculous," he snorts derisively.

"No, they're not," I snap, bristling. In the space of a few seconds, our conversation has jackknifed into an argument.

"So let me get this straight: you can't eat dairy, sugar, wheat, nuts, or fish more than twice a week." Counting them off on his fingers, he looks at me, eyebrows raised.

I feel myself reddening. Actually, when you put it that way, it does sound pretty ridiculous.

"So that means a ninety-nine ice cream with extra sprinkles and double fudge sauce is out of the question?" he demands, completely straight-faced.

Huh?

He motions to an ice cream van and I feel myself weaken. God, I'd love an ice cream.

"Absolutely," I manage, trying to stay angry.

"So if I get one, you're not going to get one too?"

We move toward the ice cream van.

As Oliver goes up to the window I grit my teeth. Boy, this is hard. "No, definitely not . . ." I shake my head decisively as he orders one for himself.

"A large cone with extra everything, please." He grins cheerily.

I shoot him a look. I'm sure he did that on purpose.

"Mmm, this is delicious." As the vendor passes it to him, he takes a large lick of ice cream. "Sure you don't want even a lick?" he asks, taking a bite. The bastard.

"No, I can't," I say stiffly, though I can feel my mouth salivating. "A nutritionist told me I'm intolerant, remember?"

"Oh, now, I don't know if I agree with that nutritionist." He cocks his head and looks at me. "I think you're pretty tolerant. What do you say, Welly?"

Welly wags his tail as if in agreement and I struggle to stifle a giggle.

"In fact I'd say you were *so* tolerant you'd probably agree to hold this ice cream for a minute while I go to the little boys' room."

"Oh, you think so?"

"Uh-huh." He nods. "And I think your tolerance levels are so high that even if the ice cream starts melting down the cone you'll lick it to stop it going all over your hand."

"Really?"

"Definitely." He nods, and thrusting it at me he walks away.

Leaving me standing there, feeling my anger melting away faster than the ice cream, which is now trickling onto my fingers in the hot sunshine. I shoot his retreating figure a smile. "You know what?" I mutter, curling my tongue around the cone and tasting the sweet vanilla. "Screw the nutritionist. I think you might be right."

❧

Emerging from the park we wind our way down the skinny side streets that lead into Notting Hill and Portobello, the world-famous market, which is brimming with stalls selling everything from flowers to furniture to fake you-name-it. Weaving our way through the throngs of tourists, we hit the main road and a row of shops and restaurants. Designer clothes, designer lingerie, designer cappuccinos . . . my eyes skim over the windows, until unexpectedly Oliver stops in front of an antique store.

"I just need to pop in here for a minute," he explains, reaching for a well-worn brass door knocker. Immediately Welly starts wagging his tail manically.

I suddenly recognize it as the one I walked past with Vanessa a few days ago when I saw him through the window. "Oh, okay." I nod, following him as pushes open the door.

Inside the store is dark and cluttered with all kinds of treasures in its dimly lit corners, and there's a musty smell of pipe smoke and furniture polish.

"Hello, anyone home?" calls out Oliver as Welly sniffs around, pressing his nose up against the legs of an old leather chair. Like he did with that tree. I feel a stab of panic.

"Hmm, there doesn't look like there's anyone around. Maybe I should make off with that rather nice French watercolor," he says in a low voice, pointing to a painting. "What do you reckon?"

I look at him in horror, then realize he must be joking. "Ha, ha, very funny," I whisper.

"No, seriously," he says, glancing shiftily around the shop. "Reckon I could get it under my T-shirt?" He picks it up.

Oh my God, he's not joking! I look at him aghast. Jesus. Olly, the nice bartender, a kleptomaniac!

And I'm his accomplice.

"What are you doing?" I hiss frantically, trying to tug it from him. "Put it down, put it—"

"Ahem." Someone coughs loudly and I look up to see an elderly man has appeared from the back, and is just standing there with a pipe in his mouth, staring at us.

"—*down,*" I finish, throwing a strangulated look at Oliver.

Rooted to the spot, my mind spins. How did this happen?! I was only looking for my watch and now I'm committing daytime robbery. Literally.

"So what've you got there, son?"

"A rather nice sunset by Claude Derbec . . ."

I close my eyes. This is all too much. I wait for the inevitable.

"Painted when?"

"Around 1870 I think."

*Wait a second.* I open one eye.

"Not bad, not bad at all."

I look at the old man. He's beaming and stroking Welly, who's lapping up the attention and returning it with giant sloppy licks on his hand.

"So you did learn something," he's saying, with a hint of pride in his voice.

"Well, I had a good teacher." Oliver is smiling.

Confused, I watch as they embrace.

"Hello, Granddad, how are you doing?"

"*Granddad!*" I repeat in astonishment.

And anger. I could kill him. I really could.

Oliver throws me a sheepish look. "Sorry. I couldn't resist. You should have seen your face."

I shoot him a look of fury. I want to throw something at him. But considering I'm surrounded by antiques, better to not, I suppose.

"And who's your lady friend?"

"Oh, hi, I'm Charlotte," I say, remembering myself. "Nice to meet you." I hold out my hand. He grabs it and hits my knuckles, in a hip-hop handshake.

"Granddad's a huge fan of Jay-Z." Oliver smiles, seeing my expression, then adds in explanation, "He's got teenage great-grandchildren. My sister's kids."

"So, tell me, what do you see in my grandson?" he's asking, looking at me.

I feel myself flush down to my toes. "Um—"

"She's not my girlfriend," jumps in Oliver, his cheeks going exactly the same color, under his stubble, as mine are. "We're not . . . you know," he says awkwardly, gesturing with his thumb back and forth between us.

"Ah, I see." His granddad nods, puffing on his pipe and surveying us both with interest, before demanding, "Well, why the hell not?" and letting out a loud, rumbling laugh. "Time you got yourself a girlfriend. You can't stay single forever, my boy."

Oliver looks as if he wants the ground to open up and swallow him, and I smile in commiseration. While paying absolutely no attention whatsoever to the little voice in my head which is gleefully whispering, *He doesn't have a girlfriend, he's single.*

"Charlotte and I just met," Oliver explains. "Well, actually we met a long time ago, but we've just . . ." He searches around for the right word, and I wonder what he's going to say. "Reconnected," he finishes.

"I see." His granddad nods again, raising his eyebrows, which scuttle up his forehead like two large white caterpillars. "How marvelous." He smiles. "Tea?"

He shuffles into the back to make tea, with Oliver offering to help, leaving Welly and me exploring. It's like the Old Curiosity Shop. Everything is piled high on top of everything else. A silver engraved pistol, a stuffed peacock, a mahogany table with two large carved claws for feet . . .

"Wow, you've got some amazing things," I exclaim, as Oliver and his granddad reappear carrying a tray on which are precariously balanced various mismatched cups and saucers and a teapot shaped like a man in a top hat.

"My Alice in Wonderland teapot," he says, observing me looking curiously. "A 1930s original. Hand painted, with no chips or cracks on the glazing, it's in perfect condition. One of only fifty sets ever made." He beams, flourishing it high in the air. A stream of hot tea pours forth from the Mad Hatter's prominent nose. "A real collector's piece." He passes me a teacup. "Milk and sugar?"

"No, I'm fine."

But it's too late, he's already adding both.

"What was that, dear?"

"Oh, nothing . . . thank you."

He smiles cheerfully and passes Oliver a cup. Then taking out a biscuit tin, he rattles it. "Shortbread finger?"

I hesitate, my eyes flicking over to Oliver, who's watching me with interest.

"Um, yes, thank you."

Well, he's such a sweet old man, I can't say no, can I? Plus I think the fact that I'd eaten nearly half of Oliver's ice cream by the time he emerged from the bathroom disproves the nutritionist's theory that I'm intolerant to wheat, sugar, and dairy.

"So how are you, Granddad?"

"Oh, you know." He waves his hand vaguely, a sad expression falling over his face. "I'll survive."

"Granddad's got to leave the store," explains Oliver, patting his granddad's arm supportively. "He's been here over sixty years, so he's finding things a bit difficult."

"Oh, no," I cry. "That's awful. Why do you have to leave?"

"Things move on, times change." His granddad shrugs, taking a sip of tea, his hand trembling slightly.

"It's got nothing to do with time moving on," Oliver says angrily. "His lease has gone up to something crazy, and he can't afford it anymore. He's being squeezed out."

"By *who*?" I gasp.

"Probably another overpriced coffee chain," tuts Oliver, not bothering to hide his disgust. "Or one of the big designer stores. They're all moving in around here now, taking over the neighborhood, trying to make it like bloody Knightsbridge . . ."

"Hey, now, there's no need for swearing," reprimands his granddad, shooting him a disapproving look.

"Well, I can't help it, it's disgusting. They have no respect for someone who made the area what it is. It's all about money. Profits."

"I was here during the Blitz, you know," remembers his granddad, turning to me. "My word, that was something, I tell you . . ." He pauses. His eyes shining he looks around at the walls, as if drinking in the memories.

"This shop has certainly seen me through some times. I met my late wife, Betty, here. She came in to buy a china teapot, yes, she did," he adds as if I don't believe him. "Ended up with a whole lot more than that," he quips, and laughs his rumbling laugh. "After she passed I thought about selling up, but to do what?" He shrugs his shoulders. "Antiques are in my blood, and look at me, I'm a bit of an antique now myself."

"But what are you going to do with all your antiques?" I ask, then immediately regret it. I don't want to upset him.

"EBay," he says simply.

"*EBay?*" Trust me, that was not the answer I was expecting.

"I've been having lessons from my great-grandchildren," he continues, dipping his shortbread finger in his teacup. "Apparently it's all the rage. I even have a PayPal account."

He flashes me a smile, and I smile back.

"It won't be the same, though," mutters Oliver.

"Ah, well, what can you do?" sighs his granddad with the calmness of a man who's lived through a lot. "Everything has to come to an end." There's a pause, as he looks at us both.

"You know, I've spent a lifetime dealing in expensive objects, but do you know what's the most valuable?"

"What?" we both ask with interest.

"Time," he says simply. "You can't buy back time, not for any price. There are no second chances. Every second is precious, so don't waste a single drop of it. It's priceless."

I look at him, absorbing his words. Is that what I've been given? A second chance?

"More tea?"

I turn to see his granddad looking at me. "Yes, thanks." And pushing those thoughts to the back of my mind, I hold out my cup. "That would be lovely."

# Chapter Twenty-nine

Two cups of tea and three shortbread fingers later, Oliver gets roped into helping his granddad pack up some of the heavier items for the imminent move. I offer my assistance, but I'm quickly rebuffed by his granddad.

"Gracious no, this is man's work," he puffs from behind a life-sized stuffed grizzly bear. Standing on its hind legs, it has its front paws outstretched and its mouth frozen in a silent snaggletoothed roar.

"Well, if you're sure."

Normally I'd feel obliged to argue with such a blatantly sexist comment, but in this case, perhaps not.

"One-two-three—*hup*."

With a loud grunt the bear is suddenly hoisted into the air and flung over Oliver's shoulder in a fireman's lift. His legs buckle.

"Jesus, Granddad, this thing weighs a ton—"

"Stop complaining, when I was your age I could carry one on each shoulder."

"What? There used to be *a pair*?" He grimaces, as a cloud of dust envelopes him.

"Aye, I sold Fred to a Japanese man in 1952, but there's only Ginger left now. . . ." He sighs wistfully, and strokes the scary-looking bear fondly as if it's a pet.

"Her name is Ginger?" I ask doubtfully.

"After the dancer." He nods proudly. "Both beauties, don't you think?"

"I think I'm going to collapse, that's what I think," complains Oliver, still trying to lug the beast across the shop floor.

Quickly sidestepping out of the way, I take it as my cue to leave.

"Okay, well, I better be going. It was nice to meet you." I go to shake hands with his granddad but he's having none of the formality. Grabbing hold of me, he plants a whiskery kiss full of shortbread crumbs on each cheek.

"Are you sure you wouldn't like a nice silver milk jug?" he suggests. "Or a set of horse brasses?"

"No, thank you." I smile as I'm released from his grip. I turn to Oliver, but he's still weighed down by a grizzly balancing precariously on his shoulder. "Well . . . um, 'bye."

I sort of hover awkwardly in the middle of the store floor, watched by the eagle eyes of his granddad and Welly, who both seem to stop whatever they were doing, be it sniffing the leg of a dining room table or dusting a horse brass.

Oliver pauses from grappling with the bear, and sticks his head out from underneath his wide roar. "Oh, hey . . ." He's all red-faced and out of breath. "You're leaving?"

If I'm not mistaken, he looks a bit dismayed.

Without warning, I feel a tweak of pleasure.

"Yeah, I'm going to walk back." I nod vigorously, feeling a bit flustered all of a sudden. "Keep looking for my watch . . ." I trail off and begin chewing my thumb nail. Before realizing and snatching my hand out of my mouth. What am I doing? I never chew my nails anymore. Not now that I have manicures.

"You know, I need to—"

"Retrace your steps."

"—retrace my steps."

We both speak at the same time, then laugh at the coincidence.

But the words aren't lost on me. I don't think they're lost on him either, because he gives me a look. Or am I imagining it?

I mean, I'm not exactly at my most lucid right now, am I? I've barely had any sleep, I've just broken up with my boyfriend, I'm probably experiencing a sugar high from all that ice cream and shortbread fingers, *and* I'm thinking all-sorts about a bartender I met ten years ago. One who's about to be suffocated by a giant stuffed bear.

I don't remember this being one of the stages I read about in the relationship book.

"Are you okay to walk back?"

"Yeah, fine, fine." I nod, hastily batting away his concerns with my hand. "I left my car at the pub."

"Do you have far to drive?"

"No, I only live five minutes away, by the church, Spencer Avenue," I blab. I've become all hot and jittery and feel the urgent need to go outside and get some fresh air.

"Well, if you're around, maybe pop in the pub later."

"Yeah, maybe—"

There's a pause.

"Well, it was nice meeting you." I turn to his granddad, who immediately colors and pretends to be engrossed in a pile of antique silver cutlery.

"Oh . . . you too, my dear," he says, feigning surprise as if he's just heard me and not just spent the last five minutes eavesdropping.

"Thanks for the tea, and good luck with Ginger," I add cheerfully, trying to sound all casual, and then, giving Welly a quick pat on the head, I stride purposefully out of the store.

*Correction:* bang into an eighteenth-century cabinet, bruise my knee, wrestle with the door, which appears to have stuck, finally manage to push it open, then forget to mind the step and sort of trip outside onto the sidewalk. I honestly don't know what's wrong with me. It's like I've suddenly regressed back into my clumsy twenty-one-year-old self, I think, as I quickly make my way down the street, my cheeks stinging with embarrassment. No, twenty-two-year-old self, I reflect, thinking of last night's birthday party.

After the dusty darkness inside the antique store, it's blindingly bright outside. In the rush this morning I didn't bring my sunglasses and squinting in the sunshine I spot a nearby stall selling cheap ones. I know, I'll buy a pair to walk home with, I decide, hurrying over.

There's quite a crowd. Clustered around the racks of glasses, people are jostling to try on all the different styles and vying for the small hand mirror in which to check themselves out. For a moment I nearly abandon the mission. This is why I buy my sunglasses at Harvey Nics. That and the fact that they're genuine designer glasses and have real UV lenses, I think disparagingly, managing to grasp a pair that is a copy of the latest style from Chanel.

Then again, these have UV lenses too, I notice with surprise as I pop them on. The stallholder thrusts a mirror at me, and I glance at my reflection. Of course when you put them on they're going to look real cheap and plasticky and—

Wow, these look fabulous.

I turn my head from side to side, feeling an old stirring of excitement. It's a feeling I haven't had for years but I recognize it immediately: the thrill of finding a bargain.

"Do you have any more of those she's wearing?" A woman gestures at me.

"No, that's the last pair." The stallholder shakes his head.

It's like a shot of adrenaline. I got the last pair! Which of course makes them even *more* of a bargain.

Digging out a ten, I quickly pay for my glasses and start walking back toward the park. What an absolute *steal*, I muse, checking out my reflection in every shop window I pass and feeling the bargain-hunter's buzz. I wonder if there's anything else I can buy. Maybe I should have a quick look.

Automatically I go to check the time, but of course, my wrist is empty and so I reach for my phone. I can see what time it is on there,

I realize, feeling for it in my pocket. Then I remember. It's in the car. I left it in the little center console . . .

As it registers, I feel a knee jerk of annoyance, but it's quickly replaced by something else. A flicker of freedom. Release. Liberation. As if a window of opportunity is opening before me and, like a schoolgirl playing truant, I feel giddy with excitement, as if I've escaped the confines of time, which are as real to me as any classroom walls, and I have a chance to play hooky from my life.

Normally, right now I'd be taking the shortcut back and hurrying home, but I don't feel like hurrying. But without my watch it's like time becomes this free-flowing thing, not divided into seconds and minutes and hours, to be ticked off, watched, kept to.

And so taking the long way home through the market I slow my pace down. It doesn't come naturally. My legs are programmed to trot briskly and my arms to pump up and down like pistons, but I force myself to stroll past the stalls and pavement cafés. To enjoy just *being* somewhere, rather than rushing from somewhere, to somewhere. Inhaling deep lungfuls of air, instead of my usual shallow breaths, I take a moment to just stop and look around me. And smile to myself.

For the first time in a long time, I can, quite literally, smell the coffee.

❦

I have no idea how long I spend meandering down Portobello, but I do know I keep stopping to lust over gold-hammered rings filled with a kaleidoscope of semiprecious stones from Nepal and to marvel at ingenious photograph frames made from the keys of old typewriters.

God, I'd forgotten how much fun flea markets can be, I muse, as I'm distracted by a yellow Indian blouse hanging from a nearby rail. Fluttering in the warm breeze, the tiny sequins sewn around the neck catch the sunlight and twinkle, like a dozen tiny stars, and before I know it I'm haggling with the dreadlocked stallholder and getting it for six pounds.

Six pounds! That's like nine dollars! Ha! It's incredible. No wonder I always used to buy my clothes from markets when I was younger.

Delighted with my shopping, I'm ready for the next amazing find and I don't have to look far. Next door is a small Chinese lady with dozens of racks filled with vintage clothes and, still on a high from my recent purchases, I rise to the challenge and try nearly everything on in the tiny makeshift changing room. A lot of it's horrible, some of it's worse than horrible, and then just as the buzz is fading, and my arms are aching, I find it.

An incredible blue silk dress with a plunging neckline that looks like something you'd see in *Vogue* for a month's salary. Plus it's totally unique. I'll never see anyone wearing another one.

Now I'm on a roll. Farther along is a stall selling secondhand shoes and almost breathless with excitement I grab a pair of gold stilettos. Ooh, these look fabulous, and they're such a steal, I tell myself, sticking my feet in—Ouch. The front pinches my toes. I try to wiggle them. Only now my foot's slipping forward. In fact, these are actually really uncomfortable. Plus the plastic heel is really ugly, I notice, looking at them in the mirror.

And freeze. What am I doing? Snatching my feet out of the shoes, I hastily put them back on the rack. My younger self might have taught me the joys of shopping for clothes in flea markets, but there's one I *have* learned now I'm older.

I make a mental note to add it to my list.

### 19. Cheap shoes suck. Save up and buy designer.

Because there are some things in life that are worth spending money on. And Jimmy Choos are one of them.

Happily slipping my feet back into my gorgeous sandals, with their full arch support and hand-stitched leather soles, I set off toward the park.

# Chapter Thirty

Only when I reach my car do I finally glance at the clock in the dash and realize how much time has passed.

And get the shock of my life.

Lord on earth, it's nearly six o'clock! That's six *p.m.* I stare at the electronic digits in disbelief. I've been wandering for *hours*. I didn't just lose track of time, I lost a whole afternoon! It just slipped away without me even noticing.

*Because you were having fun,* pipes up a little voice inside my head.

Automatically, I feel a sharp stab of guilt. I'm not supposed to be having fun. I'm not supposed to be rediscovering the thrill of flea markets, going on walks with cute bartenders, or getting whiskery kisses from grandfathers, I'm supposed to be mourning the loss of my relationship and looking for my watch.

Which is still missing, I remind myself.

I focus back on it. Where was I before I got sidetracked? Ah, yes, retracing my steps. . . . My mind spools back. If it's not in my apartment or the pub, then I must have lost it in the club—which will be closed now, I tell myself quickly, feeling relieved—or my old house.

Turning the ignition, I stick the car into gear and pull away from the curb. I'll drive over there now. Maybe it fell off my wrist when I was digging around in the fridge for some milk—I have a flashback to the unidentifiable foodstuffs lurking inside, and a shudder runs up my spine. On second thought, please, God, don't let it be in the fridge. I don't think I'm brave enough to stick my hand in there again.

Heading back toward the main road, I start heading north and it's not long before I see the now-familiar signs for the diversion. Though of course I don't see any workmen, I muse, filtering into the single lane past the large bulldozers and cranes that are sitting empty. Typical.

In the middle of cursing this peculiar habit of British roadwork to appear overnight in an explosion of orange cones and freshly dug holes, and then just sort of sit there for days on end causing huge traffic jams, my phone rings.

"Hello?"

"I tried you at home, but you weren't there," accuses the voice down the phone.

"Oh, hi, Mom," I say automatically. "Thanks for the card, and the check. I meant to call you last night when I got in but it was too late."

"So did you have a good time on your birthday?"

I think of last night. I'm not sure if "good" is the right adjective. "Yeah, it was, um . . ." I try to think of the right one, and settle on ". . . interesting."

"Any surprises?"

"You could say that," I murmur, remembering me at the club, on the dance floor, talking to the bartender, his tattoo—

"I knew it!" she gasps victoriously down the line, cutting off my train of thought. "I said it to your father. Didn't I say it to you, David? Didn't I?" She's hollering at my father, who I can hear grunting in the background. I can picture them now, her on the phone in the hallway, him in the living room trying to read the paper in peace.

"Knew what?" I say in confusion. Holding the phone out from my ear, I pull up at the traffic lights on the diversion.

"Now, now, don't keep us all waiting!" She laughs shrilly. She sounds almost giddy, and for a moment I wonder if she's been drinking. She has been known to have a couple of Bianco and lemonades before dinner. Or *tea*, should I say.

"Mom, I don't know what you're talking about," I say, a little bit more impatiently. Oh, good, the lights have changed. I put the car into gear.

"The proposal!" she gasps. "What other kind of surprise do you *think* I'm talking about?"

Suddenly it registers. When Mom said surprise, she thought— and I thought—

Oh shit.

My heart sinks. I have to tell her the truth. Only it's going to be like telling a lottery winner there's been a mix-up, and actually, they don't have the winning ticket.

"So?" Mom's voice nags from the other end of the line. "Are you going to keep your poor old mother in suspense?"

Deep breath. Here we go. "We broke up."

There's silence and then—

"What?" She's almost speechless with shock.

I quickly take advantage of the fact. "Actually I broke up with him. It wasn't right, Mom," I try explaining. "I thought it could work, I really wanted it to work, but it didn't, it couldn't, and when I stopped trying to convince myself and took a moment to really look at my relationship—"

She cuts me off. "Charlotte Merryweather. Have you gone mad?"

Taking the same shortcut as always and turning into the side street, I reflect upon the past week's events. Bumping into my twenty-one-year-old self, hanging out together at concerts, going clubbing, turning into a cougar, breaking up with my boyfriend . . .

"Quite possibly," I admit, whizzing past the parked cars. Maybe Mom's right. Maybe I have totally flipped my lid. Maybe I'm making a total and utter mess of my life and I'm going to totally regret this.

"What on earth has got into you?" she reprimands hotly. "I'm sure if you call him up now, he'll take you back."

"I don't want him to take me back," I exclaim. And if there was any doubt in my mind, it's extinguished by my reaction. "I'm not in love with him, and I don't think he's in love with me either," I add, remembering how concerned he was to be losing the house, not me.

"But he seemed so perfect for you."

"On paper, yes," I admit. "But not in reality. Miles is a great guy, but not for me, Mom. He just never really understood me—"

"And you think I understand your father?" she butts in. "Thirty-five years we've been married, and that man's still a mystery to me."

"Mom, that's different. You love Dad."

"But Charlotte—"

As I zoom under the bridge, the line suddenly goes dead. It takes a moment to register, and then—

Oh dear, we've been cut off. What a shame. And feeling a pulse of secret relief, I chuck my phone on the passenger seat and put the pedal to the metal.

❦

As I turn into my street, I spot my old car parked back outside the house. Well, I use the word "parked" loosely, but it's about three feet away from the curb, and has been left sitting at an awkward angle, as if someone was just driving along and got bored and abandoned the car in the middle of the road.

Which, now that I think of it, I was always wont to do, I reflect, pulling up behind the shiny new bumper. Obviously it's just come back from the garage, I note, turning off the engine. Hopefully she took my advice about taking a male friend with her to pick it up.

Climbing the steps to my old house I reach for the brass door knocker and rap loudly. There's the sound of footsteps and then the door swings open.

"Hi, it's me again—"

I'm expecting my younger self to be hung over. I'm expecting her to be suffering from the worst headache of her life. And I'm expecting her to look like shit.

What I'm not expecting is for her to be crying her eyes out.

"Oh my God, are you okay?"

Tears are streaming down Lottie's face, and her eyes are all red and puffy. In between gasping snorts, she nods vigorously. "Yes . . . fine . . ."

I was always a horrendous liar.

"Lottie, what on earth happened?" I ask anxiously.

Blowing her nose on a crumpled length of damp toilet paper, she looks at me with total despair. A fist of worry clenches my stomach. Oh my God, what it can be? She looks utterly distraught. Panicked, I start flicking through my stash of memories. I can't ever remember being this upset. What can it be?

"Billy Romani," she manages to hiccup, before dissolving into more heartfelt sobs.

At the mention of his name, I feel myself stiffen. Of course. *Now* I remember being this upset. It was when I discovered he'd started seeing another girl.

"What about him?" I demand, feeling like the protective big sister.

Her chest is heaving up and down and she begins stammering between hiccups. "He's been seen . . . with that pretty, rich girl . . . who looks like a rabbit . . ."

"Liberty the Trustafarian," I add grimly.

Her face screws up like a paper bag and she lets out a pitiful wail. It takes a few moments till she can speak, and then it's more of a stammer. "Apparently they are seeing each other. Apparently he's in . . ." She stops herself, as if unable to say the words "in love with her." She gasps, and then buries her head in her crumpled piece of toilet roll.

"He's in love with her trust fund," I console, putting my arm around her.

I'm rewarded by a brief smile, but then she starts sobbing again.

"Hey, come on, it's not so bad," I soothe, giving her a squeeze. "Look on the bright side, at least I warned you about him." I feel a swell of relief that I managed to do that. "I least you didn't go home with him after the concert. Now that would be much worse—" I break off as I see Lottie's expression.

"Oh my God, you did go home with him, didn't you?"

She nods mutely.

"After everything I said?"

"I know, but I thought—"

"You knew better," I finish.

Her face flushes.

My heart sinks. I should have known. I've always been terrible at taking good advice. It's my damned stubborn streak. And when I was younger, I was so headstrong. I always did exactly what I wanted. I never listened to anyone.

Not even my own self, I realize, suddenly feeling a burst of anger at Lottie for not taking my advice. I mean, how the hell am I supposed to help myself if I won't listen?

But it's not just her I'm angry at. I'm angry at myself. For not stopping her. For not being able to prevent her from making the same stupid mistake as I made. After all, isn't that what I'm here for? To protect her? To prevent her from doing all the things I wish I hadn't?

Regret stabs. I've let Lottie down. I've let myself down. I had the chance to put things right and I blew it. Feeling like a complete and utter failure, I glance at Lottie, her face puffy and blotchy with tears. And my anger vanishes as quickly as it appeared. Experience has taught me to stay away from players like Billy Romani, but it's also taught me compassion, I realize, feeling a rush of sympathy. After all, if anyone knows how bad she feels right now, it's me, isn't it?

"Do you want to talk about it?" I ask softly.

She glances at me with surprise, then, blowing her nose loudly, she nods and sits down on the front doorstep. I sit down next to her. Hugging her knees to her chest, she stares down at her bare feet. "After you dropped me off, I went back to the pub to see if he was still there," she says sheepishly.

"And was he?" I ask, although I already know the answer.

"Uh-huh." She nods. "He was still hanging around outside with the rest of the band. So I went with him to the party . . ." She trails off and falls silent for a moment as she thinks back.

As do I.

For me, that night seems like a lifetime ago, and it's hard to think about it without also thinking about everything else that followed. The pain of rejection, the embarrassment, the regret . . . But if I really try to, I can isolate that evening, focus in on my feelings, remember how I felt. Young, happy, *invincible*. God, I felt like a completely different person back then.

"It was amazing," she sighs, and despite herself, her eyes flash with excitement.

"I know," I murmur.

"You do?" She glances at me in surprise, her brow furrowed.

"I mean, I know what that feels like," I say quickly, correcting myself. "To have an amazing night with someone. Anyone." I add quickly.

She looks at me suspiciously. As if she could never imagine someone like me having an amazing night of sex with anyone, let alone a leather-clad rocker.

"Well, anyway, the next morning when I left he promised he'd call—he was doing a gig in Leeds that night, which is why he couldn't be at my birthday." She makes a face and takes another drag of her cigarette. "But it was all lies. He didn't have a gig at all. He was with that girl." Her eyes fill up again, and the tears spill over her eyelashes and down her cheeks. "How *could* he?"

Because he's a selfish, egotistical prick, that's why! I want to cry, but of course she's not going to take too kindly to that. I know, because when Vanessa said the same thing, we had a huge fight and I ended up defending him and stomping home in a huff.

But if I can't tell her that, what can I tell her? The truth?

I hesitate, contemplating how much I can say, when the phone inside rings, and a voice from the house shouts, "Lottie, it's your parents," and someone I don't recognize appears at the door, trailing a phone on a long, terribly twisted cord.

"Oh, thanks." She nods, taking the receiver, then glances back at me. "Sorry, this shouldn't be more than a minute . . ."

Now this will be interesting, I muse, watching as she presses the phone to her ear. "Mom! Hello, how are you?" she exclaims, a wide smile bursting over her face.

I look at her with astonishment. I don't know what I was expecting, but I wasn't expecting this. She seems so pleased to hear from her.

"Billy? No, he hasn't called . . ."

I'm aghast. What? I told Mom about Billy Romani? I can't believe it. I never confide in Mom about anything anymore. Certainly not anything to do with my love life.

"No, I'm fine . . ." reassures Lottie, before shooting me a look. "I'm here with a friend."

I stop staring, and manage a smile.

"Okay, well, give my love to Dad. And remember, I'm coming up next weekend anyway, so I'll see you then . . . yes, I'm really looking forward to it, we can go shopping together, I'll spend that check you gave me . . ." She laughs, and I'm sure I can hear Mom laughing on the other line. "Okay, 'bye, Mom! I'll call you tomorrow. Love you too."

She hangs up and turns to me, her face still suffused with a large smile.

I feel a twist of regret. I never have those conversations with my mom anymore. Nowadays ours are so abrupt, so much less intimate.

Like our relationship, I realize, trying to remember the last time we went shopping together. "So do you speak to your parents every day?" I ask curiously.

"Oh, yeah, we're really close." She nods without hesitation. "I'm lucky. Some people don't really get along with their parents, they never go see them or anything, but mine are great. They're really excited about me getting this job in London, and really supportive, but I know they really miss me. And I really miss them. . . ."

"That's great." I smile, but inside I can't help feeling saddened at how far I've allowed myself to drift from them. I hardly call them at all these days, and it's been so long since I even saw them. Guilt tugs, as I think about how I've neglected them and about Mom calling me in the car, asking about Miles. She still worries about me, even now, even if she has a funny way of showing it.

"Anyway, where were we?" Lottie looks at me expectantly.

"Oh . . . um." I try quickly gathering my thoughts together, remembering our conversation about Billy Romani, what I wanted to say, all the words of advice. There's so much, and yet part of me can't help thinking it's too late now. The moment's gone now, and so instead I think of the advice I just read from the self-help book on Amazon.

"At first you will be in disbelief and shock about what's just happened," I opine. "But that's normal after a breakup. Or encounter," I add, tactfully.

"Says who?" she asks, sulkily.

"I read about it in this really good book about breakups," I explain. "In fact, I was going to buy it today, but I got sidetracked—"

"Why were you going to buy it?" She frowns.

I hesitate. I don't really want to talk about it. But then again, what the hell.

"Because I just broke up with my boyfriend," I confess. Now I'm the one hugging my knees to my chest and staring at the floor.

"You have a boyfriend?" She sounds shocked.

"Did," I correct her.

"Wow." She looks astonished. "I mean . . . I just thought because you're older, you were probably divorced."

*"Divorced?"* I gasp. Jesus. I thought it was bad enough my mother wanting me to be married, but now my younger self has me pegged as a divorcée.

"Well, you weren't wearing a ring," she explains, looking remorseful.

"No, I'm not divorced. Or married," I add, just to make it clear. "I'm single."

The irony isn't lost on me. Here we are, sitting side by side, ten years apart, both single, and both talking about men.

Or lack thereof.

Some things never really change, do they?

"God, I'm sorry," says Lottie. "So what are you going to do?"

I think back to the article. "Well, it's important to mourn the end of a relationship, so you can allow yourself to move on," I say, quoting it from memory.

Lottie tucks her hair behind her ears and frowns. "What does that mean?"

"Well, it means you have to get closure," I explain. I've read a lot about closure. Closure is a big deal in self-help books.

*"Closure?"* she repeats, as if the word's part of a foreign language.

And I suppose it is to her, I realize. After all, at twenty-two, I had no idea about any of this stuff. Not like now, I think, feeling relieved at how much I've grown. Growing is a big deal in self-help books too.

"You'll need to spend time dealing with what's happened," I reflect, trying to use the benefit of hindsight. "But it's going to take time, so you need to be kind to yourself, pamper yourself, spend time with your good friends—" I'm talking about Vanessa. Even now, ten years later, she's always been there for me, whatever's happened. Just as she was back then. My mind flashes back to her sitting next to me on my futon, stroking my hair as I sobbed my heart out. She didn't have to say anything. Just knowing she was there was enough.

"But what's really important to remember is that you can't rush this important healing process . . ." I add, thinking back to the self-help book. I really do sound like Dr. Phil, don't I? See, at least I can be of some help, give some good advice.

"Why not?" she demands, arching an eyebrow at me.

An eyebrow, I suddenly notice, which has been aggressively plucked to within an inch of its life. She must have used those tweezers I gave her, I realize somewhat regretfully. On second thought, it wasn't such a good idea. I was aiming for Jessica Alba arches, not permanently surprised.

"Because it's a process," I repeat patiently.

"Balls," she admonishes.

I look at her in shock.

"That's just balls. Why should I have to go through a frigging process, while *he* goes out with another girl?" she gasps angrily.

"You're obviously at the angry stage," I say, trying to calm her down.

"But he told me he was falling in love with me!" she cries.

I raise an eyebrow. That's one thing I've learned in my thirties. Never believe a man who says he's falling in love with you, just as he's falling into bed with you.

"God! He's such a liar!" she shouts angrily.

"No, this is good, it's important to get your anger out." I nod encouragingly. "All these stages are really important in getting over something like this. First you go through shock, then depression, now anger—" I'm trying to remember all the different stages.

"I was just a one-night stand to him, and to think . . ." She lets out an angry howl. "I could kill him!"

"—and finally acceptance—"

She falls silent, and drags on a cigarette, staring off into the middle distance.

"This is the final stage. Once you reach this, you'll be able to deal with anything life throws at you . . ." I pause, thinking about my own life, what's happened in these last ten years since I was wearing Lottie's shoes. "You'll be able to move on."

"Actually, I do feel more positive."

"Really?" I smile, encouraged.

"In fact, I feel a whole load better."

"Wow, that's great," I say, feeling satisfied. Though to be honest, I actually thought it would take her a bit longer to go through the process, but I clearly have played an essential part. "And in time you'll feel healed enough to begin a new relationship!"

"Mmm, yeah . . ." She nods distractedly.

"Though don't worry if at first you're a little nervous."

"Mmmm . . ."

Hang on a minute—I suddenly get the impression she's not listening. "Did you hear what I just said?"

"God, he's really hot."

"Who is, Billy Romani?" I look at her, puzzled.

"Billy who?" she says pointedly, and then gasps impatiently as if to say "Keep up, Grandma." "*Him.*" She gestures with her head, and all at once I realize what's grabbed her attention. Across the road I spot a jogger. Bare-chested, with a body to die for, he's stopped running and is stretching out his muscles.

"God, he's gorgeous," she sighs lustfully.

"Lottie, have you been listening to anything I've just said?" I feel a snap of annoyance.

"Sorry . . . um." She turns to me, her eyes flashing and a big grin on her face. Her tears have miraculously vanished and there are two spots of color high in her cheeks. "You were saying something about stages?" she says vaguely.

"Yes, and it's really important," I remind her.

"Well, I'm sorry, but you can keep all that nonsense," she replies, looking back at the jogger. "Do you want to know my advice to get over a man?"

I look at her questioningly, then back at the jogger. Just in time to see him smile over, and her smile back, flirtily. All thoughts of Billy Romani completely forgotten.

"Get underneath another one."

# Chapter Thirty-one

As weekends go, this isn't up there with one of my best. My search of my old bedroom fails to give up my watch, which I now fear I might have lost in the Canal Club, if not some sort of time wormhole, and, leaving Lottie flirting with Mr. Bare-Chested, I drive home. It half crosses my mind to pop into the pub and say hi to Oliver, but it quickly crosses back again. What am I thinking? Don't be so silly, Charlotte. He was probably only being polite.

But then so was I, I tell myself defensively.

Instead I stay in Saturday night and pack up the rest of Miles's things, which plunges me further into gloom. To be honest, even though I know I've done the right thing, it's still deeply depressing. I console myself that we can still be friends. After all, we're both reasonable adults, we can be amicable about this. Like when celebrities split up and issue those joint press release statements, I think, remembering the one I did for Melody when she split up from her soccer player husband.

I set about concocting one as I clear out his sock drawer:

> Charlotte and Miles have made an amicable decision to separate. Their decision was made by best friends with a huge amount of love and respect for one another. Their relationship has ended, but their friendship continues.

They would request that the media respect their privacy at
this difficult time.

Sounds great, doesn't it? We sound so mature and laid-back about
it all. So cool. It makes you almost *want* to break up with your boyfriend.

In fact, by Sunday morning I almost feel cheered up, and am
imagining Miles and me doing Demi and Bruce–type dinners with
our new future partners. That is, until Miles arrives at my apartment
on Sunday waving an itemized telephone bill and demanding £7.38
"because it's the principle, and everyone has to be financially responsible," bitterly dumps two trash bags full of my stuff on my doorstep,
and then informs me in a triumphant voice that he's got tickets to see
the James Bond tribute band *License to Thrill*, and he's taking Helen,
his bookkeeper, who apparently is a *huge* fan (and has a huge cleavage) and who I know has always had a not-so-secret crush on him.

On second thought, perhaps forget the Bruce and Demi
dinners.

I lie awake on Sunday night, unable to sleep, mulling over recent
events in my head. I've made a complete mess of things. Miles now
hates me, and my younger self hasn't taken any of my advice. And
what's worse, I don't blame her. I mean, when it comes to love and
relationships, I've hardly got it figured out, do I? What was I doing,
thinking I could give advice about men? Maybe she does know better. What was it she said? Oh, yes:

*To get over a man, get underneath another one.*

Abruptly my mind throws up an image of Oliver. I throw it back
again like a hot potato. Honestly, as if. You can't go rushing from one
man to the next. Even if I *did* think he was sexy and wanted to sleep
with him—*which I don't*—he's not going to be interested in me, not
when I ignored him all those years ago. No doubt he's forgotten
about me already.

But that's fine. Meeting him again was definitely one of those weird, interesting coincidences, but I don't plan to make a habit of it. After all, aside from stumbling into that gastropub, it was ten years ago since I last saw him. Chances are it's going to be another ten years till I see him again, anyway.

❧

I wake up on Monday morning in a much better mood. It's like that saying: today's the first day of the rest of your life. So I've decided. Last week was full of surprises and all kinds of upheaval, but this week I'm determined to not have any more surprises. I'm going to put everything that's happened behind me. I'm going to forget about relationships and men and giving advice to my younger self and concentrate one hundred percent on my work.

And I'm going to need it. I've got a big week ahead of me. Despite it being a public holiday today, I still have to go into the office. Tomorrow's the press launch for Star Smile UK, and there are still hundreds of details to organize. Plus, I'm supposed to be "touching base" with Larry Goldstein some time today, so I really need to focus.

In fact, it's probably a really good thing I'm not going to have any other distractions, I decide, hurrying into my walk-in closet. The yellow sequined blouse I bought on Saturday catches my eye, but I brush past it and grab a pair of tailored cream trousers and a crisp white cotton shirt. A really good thing indeed.

❧

I arrive at the office feeling motivated and positive.

"Morning, Bea." Throwing her a large smile, I sweep up my coffee and stride over to my desk.

"Gosh, you're in a jolly mood." She beams, which is impressive considering she's working the public holiday too. But then, she insisted. She knows how important tomorrow's press launch is. "Good weekend?"

Briefly I consider telling her about Miles, then I see her shiny happy eyes, and I just can't do it. According to Beatrice, we're the perfect couple—I can't face telling her the truth. It would be like telling a child Santa Claus doesn't exist.

"Busy," I reply enthusiastically, swiftly sidestepping the issue. Well, that's not a lie. It *was* busy. "How about you? What did you get up to?"

"Oh, not much." She shrugs, pushing up her sleeves and folding her arms over her large bosom. "On Saturday I watched polo—my eldest brother, Toby, was playing—Saturday night I went to the opera with my friend Maddy, who has a box there, and then on Sunday it was Granny's birthday and we all had dinner at the Dorchester."

"Um, yes, you're right, just a regular weekend then." I smile teasingly. I love hearing about Beatrice's weekends. It's like reading the society pages of the *Tatler*. She lives in a completely different world to most people, and yet the thing I love the most about her is that she has absolutely no idea and thinks it's all terribly normal, darling.

"Which reminds me, I saw that friend of yours at the Dorchester."

Sipping my coffee, I start leafing through my newspaper. "Who?" I murmur distractedly.

"You know, your friend's husband. The one in the photo."

I stop what I'm doing and glance up sharply. "You mean Julian?"

"Yes, that's it. The one I thought could possibly be thought of as sexy, *but only* if he was totally single and definitely not married in any way, shape, or form . . ."

"Bea—"

". . . not even if it was one of those ceremonies that aren't technically legal in England, like a second cousin of mine who got married by some pygmy tribe in the Amazonian rain forest . . ."

"Beatrice—"

". . . poor Aunt Fi was so upset, though apparently they brought her back a lovely woven rug for the hallway—"

"*Beatrice!*"

She looks at me, startled, as if suddenly remembering I'm here.

"Sorry, you were saying?" She smiles brightly.

"No, *you* were saying. About Julian being at the Dorchester," I say, pointedly fixing her with a hard stare.

"Oh dear, have I said something wrong?" Anxiously she clutches at her pearls as if they can somehow protect her.

"No, of course not," I reassure her quickly. "But are you sure it was him?"

She eyes me warily.

"Beatrice, this is important."

"Absolutely," she says gravely. "I never forget a face."

My mind is scrambling around. I think back to his conversation with Vanessa over dinner on my birthday. He said he had to work. That was why he couldn't take the kids to the aquarium. So what was he doing at the hotel?

Business, I tell myself firmly. That's it, he was probably doing business with one of his posh clients. After all, I do it all the time. I'm always in hotels.

"And what time was it?"

"Umm, now let me think . . ." She tips her head to one side. ". . . Gosh now, it was after we'd had the petit fours, which were very good, I have to say; I'm not usually one for petit fours—too fussy, not big enough, I have to eat about a hundred—but these were absolutely deli—" She catches my expression, and swiftly catches herself. "But anyway, yes. It was after the petit fours, because Granny then fancied a brandy and I remember saying I'd have one too, but not before I'd gone to the loo . . ."

"Bea, is this story leading *anywhere?*" I gasp impatiently.

"Oh, most definitely." She nods. "Because you see, it was when I was going to the loo, that I went through reception and I bumped into him."

"Julian?"

"The very same. He was coming out of the elevator and we sorted of collided. He was very apologetic about it all. But there was something else."

"What?" I feel like some kind of detective in a TV series.

"He dropped his room key on the floor."

*"Room key?"*

My chest tightens. I can hear Vanessa's voice replaying in my ears: *I think Julian is having an affair.*

No, there's got to be a reasonable explanation. Maybe the meeting was in the room. In fact, that must be it. I mean, look at me, I met with Larry Goldstein in his room, didn't I?

"Uh-huh." Beatrice is nodding decisively. "I know, because I picked it up. Actually, it wasn't a room key at all, it was for the . . ." She lowers her voice to a reverential whisper. ". . . Oliver Messel Suite."

I look at her blankly. "What's that?"

"Only the most romantic suite at the Dorchester!" she exclaims. "It was Marlene Dietrich's favorite. Granny told me. Apparently they were good friends."

Okay, so now it's a business meeting in the most romantic suite at the Dorchester. Well, I suppose it's *possible*.

"And what time did you say this was?"

"I didn't. But I would guess it was quite late. Probably after ten."

A business meeting that runs until ten o'clock at night? In the Dorchester's most romantic suite? On a Sunday? When he told Vanessa he had to be at the office?

My stomach churns and flips over. I think about the condoms I spotted in his shopping basket. Vanessa's admission that they haven't slept together for ages. I have to admit, the evidence against him seems overwhelming.

"So come on, tell me." I turn my gaze back to Beatrice, looking at me, her eyes wide with curiosity. "Why all the questions? Didn't your friend Vanessa tell you they were staying there?"

"No . . . no, she didn't." I shake my head and force a smile. "She must have forgotten, she's terrible like that." My mind is whirling. I quickly grab hold of it. "Speaking of which, has Larry Goldstein called yet?" I say, swiftly changing the subject.

"First thing." Beatrice nods. "You're meeting him at twelve noon at a nail bar in Notting Hill." I throw her a quizzical look. "He has a manicure appointment at eleven," she explains. "It must be an L.A. thing."

"Or maybe because he's a dentist. You know, putting your fingers in other people's mouths," I suggest. At least I hope so. I hate to think he has manicures just for the hell of it.

"Oh, I didn't think of that." She beams. "And there was I, wondering what color of polish he'd be choosing, you know, whether he was a bright pillar-box-red man, or more a French manicure . . ." She breaks off and starts giggling. Then remembers herself. "Anyway, afterward he's taking you to see his new space."

Now she's got my full attention. "Oh, so he finally made a decision on the location?"

"Yes, and he said he was sure you'd approve."

"Really?" I feel a glow of pleasure. At least something's going right. "Where is it exactly?"

"He wouldn't say. He said he wanted to keep it as a surprise." Beatrice hugs herself. "Gosh, how fab, I love surprises, don't you?"

I feel a flicker of trepidation. What was that about not wanting any more surprises? First it was Julian, and now this?

Still, remember I've got to think positively, I tell myself firmly. Everything's going to be fine. In fact, it's going to be more than fine, it's going to be great. And looking at Beatrice, I smile brightly.

"Absolutely!"

# Chapter Thirty-two

Larry is having his cuticles trimmed when I arrive.
"Hey, how's it going?" He beams, flashing me his neon smile as I walk into the übertrendy nail bar, filled with ladies who do lunch and very little else. He's reclining on a massage chair, being attended to by two pretty therapists in white coats. One is doing his manicure, the other is massaging his bare feet.

"Hi, great, thanks," I reply, hovering uncertainly by the shelves filled with different bottles of polish and looking for a place to sit. This isn't the kind of venue I'm used to for a PR meeting, but then Larry Goldstein isn't my usual kind of client.

"Come on over and meet Andrea and Carla," he drawls loudly over the hum of small talk and clink of cappuccino cups.

I weave through the massage chairs toward him, carrying my briefcase and handbag, and making sure to hide my nails. I'm in desperate need of a manicure myself. "This is Charlene, my PR guru," says Larry Goldstein, gesturing toward me.

The two manicurists glance up briefly and smile. "Hiya," they both chirp in unison, before turning back to his cuticles and feet.

"Actually it's Charlotte," I correct him, smiling.

He laughs. "Whatever. It's all the same."

Actually, no, it's not all the same. How would you like to be called Leslie, or Lenny, or Leo? I feel like asking. But of course I don't. I remain perfectly calm, a professional smile pinned onto my face. This is an important meeting. Larry Goldstein is a valued client. And this is going to be a good week, remember?

"So, you've decided on the location for the new space?" I say brightly, moving right on to business and the reason I'm here.

"Andrea honey, can you just press a little harder on my left foot— yep, that's great—"

Satisfied, he glances over at me. "Sorry about that."

"It's quite all right." I smile evenly. "Now about the new space—"

"Did you know we have these pressure points on the soles of our feet? It has to do with the meridian lines. Like acupuncture. It's a way of rebalancing the *chi*—"

"Actually, yes, I do know that," I say briskly. "It's one of the basic principles of reflexology."

"See, she's not just a pretty face, is she?" he quips to his manicurists, who glance at me and laugh politely.

"But anyway, back to the new space—" *For the third time.*

"Clear varnish or just buffed?" interrupts Carla.

I curl my fingers into little fist balls.

"I don't know. What do you think, Charlene?" Larry stops peering at his fingers and looks up at me, eyebrows raised questioningly. "Clear or buffed?"

Okay, that's it. I give up. Trying to conduct a business meeting here is impossible.

"Buffed," I reply shortly.

He screws up his forehead. "You think so?" he asks, staring at his nails.

"Clear then," I deadpan.

"No, I think you're right, I'll go with buffed," he says after a moment's deep thought. "See, I always take my PR guru's advice. She knows best." He passes his hand to Andrea, who's waiting patiently. She reaches for her buffer. "Actually, before you do that, can we change the setting on this massage chair to pulse rather than vibrate?"

I watch as Andrea starts fiddling with the controls.

"You know, they do great herbal teas here," he says, casually glancing over at me. As if I'm not actually sitting here waiting for him, but simply passing the time of day. "You should have one." Settling back in his chair, he wriggles a little to get comfortable, then closes his eyes. "I'll be right with you."

*Right with you.*

Now, in my language that means soon, as in a few minutes, as in no more than five. Ten at most. In Larry Goldstein's language it means just over an hour of having his feet rubbed, his heels pumiced, and his hands wrapped in steaming cloths—apparently it's the special holiday pampering package—while flirting the whole time with Andrea and Carla, offering them discount veneers and tooth bleaching, and handing out business cards with instructions to give him a call.

It's past noon when we finally leave the salon.

"Everything okay?" As we step into the street, he turns to me, looking very pleased with himself.

"Absolutely." I smile back breezily, trying not to think about the last hour I've spent, drinking four cups of herbal tea, because as long as the client's happy, everything *is* okay. That's the basic rule of PR.

"So, are you excited to see the new space?"

"Very." I nod. *Finally.*

"Awesome, let's jump in a cab." He smiles, sticking out his hand.

"Are you sure you don't want me to drive? I've got my car on a meter . . ." I begin, but he's already flagging down a passing cab.

"No, this is the only way I travel when I'm in London. They're so cool." He beams as one pulls up at the curbside. "I'm thinking about getting one shipped over to the States. I can drive around Beverly Hills in it, instead of the Porsche. What do you think?"

I think you'll look like a complete idiot, I think, while saying, "Wow, yeah, that sounds like a great idea," as he holds open the door for me. "So, tell me. Where are we going?" I ask, climbing inside.

"Now that would be telling," he says, looking very pleased with himself as he slides next to me on the seat. Like really next to me. Like our thighs are pressed up against each other.

All at once I get that same feeling I got in that restaurant the first time we met. I can't be sure, but something feels off. A nagging air of discomfort. Is it just me or he squashing his leg right up against mine? Am I just completely imagining it?

I go for imagining it. Nevertheless, I cross my legs, in a maneuver intended to move my thigh as far away as possible from his.

"Just straight ahead, mate," hollers Larry to the driver, in a faux cockney accent that's even worse than Dick Van Dyke's infamous one in *Mary Poppins*.

I can see the cabbie grimace in the rearview mirror. Probably the only thing worse than pretending to be a cockney to a black cab driver, is giving them directions.

"American, are ya?" He nods gruffly.

"Is my accent that bad?" Larry Goldstein laughs jovially.

"Worse," growls the cabbie.

"Jeez, I love these guys," confides Larry, flashing a smile. I nod wordlessly. I'm not sure if Larry even understands the concept of sarcasm. It's as if those teeth of his are like a superhero's deflector shield which no irony can penetrate.

As the cab pulls away from the curb I wonder where we're going. Beatrice mentioned something about how I'd approve, so I wonder if he's taken my advice and gone for a hipper location . . .

Then again, he's really in love with the whole English tradition thing, and so he might have plumped for one of the grand suites in Harley Street, along with all his other peers—

"Right here."

The cab driver suddenly slams on his brakes, and we lurch to a juddering halt. I glance sharply out of the window to see we've only gone about a hundred yards.

"How much will that be?" says Larry Goldstein to the driver.

I look at him in puzzlement. I know everyone says people from L.A. don't like to walk but this is ridiculous. We've only driven down the street.

I turn to Larry Goldstein, but he's already climbing out of the cab to pay the driver, and, totally confused, I climb out after him.

"But I don't understand."

"It was all your idea, it's all credit to you," he's saying, as the cab drives off and we're left on the pavement. "You gave me the idea at dinner, telling me I needed to be in a more fashionable area, some-where a lot more hip, much cooler . . ."

I take in my surroundings. We're standing on Westbourne Grove, just near the junction with Portobello.

". . . somewhere that's filled with celebrities, the place to be seen . . ."

How funny. I was just here on Saturday at the market.

Larry starts walking slowly along the pavement, making sweeping movements with his arm, like a pioneer looking at the vista.

". . . and I thought back to our first meeting, how we met at the Electric at your suggestion, and how cool the location was. So I put in a few calls to my people right away and they managed to find this place. Of course, it wasn't without its problems, there's someone in there right now, but if you throw enough money at any problem, you can always make it go away . . ." He throws me a look that sends a shiver unexpectedly down my spine. "We just offered five times the rent, they couldn't refuse . . ."

"But what about the person who was renting already?"

"Business is business," he says, his voice steely.

"You mean they just have to pack up and move out?"

As I'm speaking I'm having this really, *really* horrible feeling; it's creeping over me, and my blood is running cold. I'm wrong. I have to be wrong.

"What kind of shop is it?"

We're still walking along, but my legs feel like heavy lumps of concrete.

"Oh, nothing special, some kind of junk store." He shrugs dismissively.

I feel myself stiffen in protestation as I hear his description. Nothing special! *Junk store!* Because I know what he's talking about. I know before I even look.

"So, what do you think?" he says, as he stops outside Oliver's granddad's antique shop and flings his arms out wide in a sort of *ta-dah* motion.

I think I'm going to be sick.

Right here on the pavement.

Desperately I muster composure from somewhere. "Um, it's great . . ." I manage to stammer.

"Just great?" His face drops with disappointment.

"No, I mean *amazing*," I gush, mirroring his own celluloid smile. *"Awesome,"* I add, with extra emphasis.

He looks finally satisfied. "I knew you'd approve." He beams, running his fingers carefully through his ice blue hair. "Just imagine"—he does this sort of arc-rainbow-like gesture in the air— "Star Smile."

Dismay washes over me. He's going to replace that lovely old sign with his tacky logo.

"So, shall we go in?"

"Excuse me?" I'm still reeling with horror at the thought that I'm responsible for Oliver's granddad losing his beloved shop, which he's been in for over sixty years; I'm still trying to register that and trust me, that's bad enough. *But now I've got to go inside?*

I get a flashback of Oliver's grandfather giving me a whiskery kiss on the cheek.

Oh my God, I can't. I just can't do it.

"Charlotte?"

I look at Larry Goldstein and at that moment I know this is it. My career's on the line. Either I go in that shop and get behind this, or I can kiss good-bye to my account with Larry Goldstein. And with it my chance of international expansion.

I can see the headlines now, hear the gossip among the rival PR companies who won't have any scruples about jumping in on this. It will be seen as a huge career mistake. Career suicide probably. And for what? A rival firm will take over and the deal will still go ahead. Oliver's grandfather will still lose his store. With or without me.

And I can choose to leave here. With or without a career.

I pause. This is what I've been working toward for years, and I only met his grandfather yesterday. It's business, remember? Not personal.

"Sorry." I smile professionally and throw back my shoulders. "I was just letting the anticipation build before I go in."

And then he's pushing open the door and I'm following him inside and as I step over the threshold, it's like crossing a line. I've made the choice. But the most frightening thing of all is the sudden realization that Larry Goldstein was right. I'm a lot like him after all.

Already waiting for us in the store is one of Larry Goldstein's design team and I spend the next few minutes trying to hide from Oliver's granddad by skulking behind Larry Goldstein, who's stalking around the store as if he owns it. Which I suppose he does.

"So we're going to rip out those windows and replace them with a big piece of glass," the design team member is saying now.

I glance with indignation at the windows. They're the most delightful old bow windows that have been there for years and add character to the place. They can't rip them out, it would be a travesty.

". . . And we'll have plasma screens, and concrete floors . . ."

As he continues talking I feel a rush of protectiveness. It's all very trendy, and übercool, and I know it will look amazing. But not here. Not in this store.

". . . pull down that old bookcase and totally renovate so that we create a loftlike space, all open-plan . . ."

Out of the corner of my eye I can see Oliver's granddad listening from the back of the store. With my hair tied up and still wearing my sunglasses, I look different enough from the girl he met on Saturday that I've already been here fifteen minutes and he hasn't recognized me. And thank goodness, I reflect, glancing at his face, which looks all pinched, and feeling a stab of shame to be part of all this.

"Totally." Larry Goldstein nods. "Though at the moment it's hard to imagine. I mean, this place just feels dirty, dark, cluttered . . ."

He's talking as if Oliver's grandfather isn't even in the store. Doesn't he realize how insulting he's being? I think protectively. He's been here sixty years. He loves this store. It must be like having your heart torn out.

"And, yeah, you're so right, those bookcases are just an eyesore . . ."

"Those bookcases date back to the turn of the twentieth century." Oliver's granddad finally says something.

"Really?" Larry Goldstein looks unimpressed. "Well, then it's time for a face-lift, isn't it?" He laughs. "Get into the new century. Actually, I was thinking acrylic floating shelves that you can suspend from the ceiling . . ." He turns back to the design guy as if Oliver's grandfather isn't important at all.

I glance at Oliver's granddad. His bright green eyes are flicking over Larry Goldstein, taking him in, absorbing him. Weighing him up.

Meanwhile I'm skulking in the back, trying to keep my head down.

"So what do you think—"

Oh, please, God, don't let him say my name, don't let him say my name.

"—Charlene?"

For the first time I'm relieved he got my name wrong. There is a God.

"Um . . . yeah . . . great." I nod vaguely, trying to hide behind a large grandfather clock.

"No other suggestions? About décor? Color? Design?" Larry looks at me, waiting for my input.

I swallow hard. "Well, obviously I'm bursting with ideas about this place, it's a total blank canvas . . ." I begin in my best PR spin. ". . . And I think we're all looking at creating at something clean, modern, and totally organic . . ."

I glance quickly at Oliver's granddad, who's now looking at me suspiciously.

". . . but obviously your design team will have all the ideas, they're the experts in this field," I finish quickly.

Shit, I've got to get out.

"Excuse me, Miss—" Oliver's grandfather motions to me.

I try to ignore him, but it's impossible. "Um, yes?" I say, dipping my head as I turn to him.

"Do I know you from somewhere? Your face seems familiar."

"No, definitely not," I say hastily. "One hundred percent nope. I've never been in here before." Fully aware that I'm blabbering, I continue, "But anyway, I think I just want to pop outside and have a look at the frontage again."

I lunge for the door. It's stuck again, but after struggling with it for a few moments, I manage to yank it open. "I'll see you outside, Larry," I say quickly. And letting the door swing closed behind me, I stumble outside onto the sidewalk.

# Chapter Thirty-three

Afterward, the design guy shoots off in his Mini Cooper and Larry joins me outside to wait for a cab to take him back to his hotel. He offers to drop me at my car, but I make an excuse and tell him I need the exercise—all two hundred yards of it—and I'll walk back.

"Good girl, firm up those glutes," he says approvingly as he pats me on the bottom.

I flinch. But it's done in that jokey, all-in-good-spirits kind of a way, so I know I can't say anything, otherwise *I'll* be the one that looks bad.

"So I'll add those finishing touches to the presentation this afternoon," I say briskly in my most professional voice. "I still need to finalize one or two things, but then we're all set for the launch tomorrow."

"Awesome." He smiles broadly.

"Unless, of course there's anything else you'd like to add?"

"Only that it's been incredible working with you on this," he says, and fixes me with those piercingly blue eyes. I swear, I'm sure he's wearing contact lenses. Nobody's eyes can be that blue.

I take a step backward. "Great, thanks. You too," I add, hastily returning the compliment.

"Let's hope this is just the beginning of things." His gaze is still fixed on me. In fact, he's not even blinking, I notice, feeling a little unnerved. "You know, we're both American, we're both business-people. We have a lot in common. I think you and I could go a long way together, Charlotte."

I don't know if it's because he says my name correctly for the first time, or just the *way* he says it, but I get a sense of unease that makes the hairs on my arms stand up and my body stiffen with apprehension.

"Oh, look, there's a taxi," I cry, changing the subject. Flinging out my arm, I start waving furiously. It's going the other direction, but it immediately swings a U-turn, and deftly pulls up alongside the curb. I feel a wave of relief.

"Um, thanks," says Larry Goldstein, giving me a peculiar look.

"No problem. It's all part of the service," I quip, slightly breathless from all that waving.

"Service? Are you sure don't want that *ride*?" Pulling open the door, Larry Goldstein looks at me, his carefully groomed eyebrows raised questioningly.

"No, I'm fine, thanks."

"Okay, well, we'll speak tomorrow, before the press launch." Jumping in the cab, he slams the door behind him, then pulls down the window. "I'm looking forward to it."

I feel a stab of apprehension, but I ignore it. I always get really anxious before a press launch, especially one done on such short notice. It's completely normal.

"Yes, me too." I smile brightly and, as the cab pulls away, I hitch my bags over my shoulder and stride out energetically on my power walk.

Which lasts about five seconds.

As soon as the cab disappears around the corner, I drop my bags on the sidewalk and flop onto a nearby bench. Resting my elbows on my knees, I bury my face in my hands and let out a deep exhale. It's as if I can feel the stress literally coming out of my pores. Oozing all over this bench and trickling onto the sidewalk in one great big sticky, gloopy stress puddle.

Right now I should be the happiest girl in the world. My newest, biggest client loves me. We've found the perfect location for the first UK Star Smile store. And the press launch is less than a day away. It can't fail. This is going to be a resounding success. It's going to boost my career into a whole new stratosphere. I'll get my picture in all the trade magazines. The business will get tons of publicity. More clients. And then there's Larry Goldstein's talk of Charlotte Merryweather PR taking on his contract full-time, not just in the UK, but globally. We'll have to expand, take on new staff, get more offices . . . God, it's everything I've dreamed of.

Except—

*Oliver.*

My mind flashes back to Saturday afternoon. Walking through the park with him and Welly. Laughing as he throws sticks and has to fetch them himself. Chatting about anything and everything. Drinking tea and eating shortbread fingers with his grandfather—

*His grandfather.*

I feel my heart plummet. I can't do it. I can't take away his shop. His livelihood. His life.

But then again, he was probably going to retire soon anyway, I tell myself comfortingly. I mean, he must be about eighty surely? I'm sure Oliver will understand. Though it's doubtful I'll ever be able to face him again anyway—or his grandfather, I think sadly.

"Beautiful day we're having, isn't it?"

A voice snaps me back, and I look up to see an old woman sitting near me at the other end of the bench. Resting her swollen ankles, her wrinkled face tilted to the sky, she's like a white-haired cat basking in the sunshine.

If she was there earlier, I hadn't noticed her. But then it could have been snowing, and I probably wouldn't have noticed.

"If you say so," I manage glumly.

Turning her head sideways, she looks at me. "Let me guess. It's a man."

"Excuse me?"

"That sigh. It nearly knocked me over." She smiles, raising her eyebrows.

Honestly. Why does everyone think a woman's woes are always to do with a man? "No, not at all," I say, a little indignantly. "I've got a problem at work."

"I see." She nods, but something in the way she looks at me tells me she doesn't believe a word of it.

"Well, actually, it's not really a problem at all," I add. "The client's really happy with everything, it's just—"

"*You're* not really happy," she prompts.

I glance at her. She says that so authoritatively it's almost as if she knows exactly how I'm feeling. But of course she can't possibly know. She's an old lady, with snow-white hair, a thick winter coat even though it's summer, and a walking stick, I muse, looking at her hand wrapped around it and noticing the sunlight catching a pretty emerald ring, shaped like a flower, next to her gold wedding band. She must be about eighty. What can she know about my life? How it feels to be me?

"Well, it's not as simple as that," I try to explain. "You see there are other people involved. Oliver and his granddad. And I'm the reason his granddad is going to lose his shop . . ." It's like now I've started I can't stop and it all comes spilling out. ". . . which means Oliver is probably going to hate me. Like he probably did ten years ago when I ignored him . . ."

For a brief moment I jump back to the moment when I tried to introduce Lottie to him, how she wasn't paying attention, how the whole time her entire head was filled with thoughts of Billy Romani.

"But that's not really my fault, because when I was twenty-one I didn't notice nice guys. In fact, it's only because a few days ago I went to my birthday party from ten years ago, and I was in my thirties, that I met him again, and he was in his twenties, that I got a second chance—" An image of Olly behind the bar in that tight T-shirt releases a butterfly in my stomach.

"And then of course, when I found out he was the waiter at the pub—" Suddenly I realize I've got completely carried away. I stop talking. At the other end of the bench the old lady is regarding me with a slightly bemused look on her face.

"Like I said, it's complicated." I shrug dejectedly.

But she just smiles and, reaching out her hand, pats my leg reassuringly.

"Life isn't complicated, dear. It's very simple, really. It's us that make it complicated."

~❦~

I decide not to go back to the office. I just can't face it. Instead I make a quick call to Beatrice to let her know I'll be working from home for the rest of the afternoon, and drive back to my place. Still, at this rate, at least things can't get any worse, I console myself, as I sit in traffic staring at the parking ticket stuffed underneath my wipers.

The shrill ring of my BlackBerry causes me to hold that thought as I click on my Bluetooth earpiece.

"Hi, Charlotte, it's me."

Oh fuck. They just did.

*It's Vanessa.*

A hand grips around my stomach. With everything that's been happening this morning I'd forgotten all about Julian, and my conversation this morning with Beatrice, but now it all comes hurtling back.

"Hey, Nessy, how are you?" I say evenly, forcing myself to sound as normal as possible. That old Scruples question is whizzing around in my head. *If you found out your friend's boyfriend was cheating, would you tell her?* I used to be always the first to reply "yes, absolutely" with the easy defiance of a twentysomething. Of course you'd tell your friend. It was a no-brainer. But now the stakes are higher.

Now they're sharing more than just CD collections, Domino's pizzas, and a futon. Now it's children, a home, a life together.

"Not great," she says, and I feel my stomach plunge.

Oh shit, she knows. I can tell in her voice. For a split second I feel a flush of relief that I don't have to lie—but it's drowned out by dread.

"Why, what's up?" I try to keep my voice steady.

There's a pause, and then—

"I found a receipt."

You wouldn't think those four words could have such an effect on me, could make my stomach hurtle into my sling backs and my hands grip my steering wheel, but they do.

"What kind of receipt?" I'm filled with trepidation. Whatever it is, it's not good. I mean, your best friend doesn't call you up to tell you she's found a receipt from Safeway, now does she?

"It's from Agent Provocateur."

First the condoms, then the suite at the hotel, and now *this*? My heart sinks but I quickly rally. Okay, let's think damage control here. I have to put a positive spin on this. And if anyone can do it, I can. A career in PR has to be useful for something.

"Ooh, lucky you," I gush, with about as much faux enthusiasm as I can muster. "Julian must have bought you some sexy underwear as a surprise."

"Yeah, right," breathes Vanessa. Something tells me she isn't too convinced. "In two sizes smaller than I really am? I called the store and gave them the bar codes. Trust me, if I can get in a size ten thong and B cup peek-a-boo bra, it'll be more than a surprise, it'll be a bloody miracle."

Fair point. I love Vanessa dearly and I think she looks great, but there's no way she's a size ten. And as for those boobs of hers—which make anyone like me, who has to make the most of their cleavage with a gel-filled bra, insanely jealous—they have never, and will never, see the inside of anything less than a double D cup.

"Maybe he got it wrong?" I argue. "Men are terrible about stuff like that. Miles always thought I was a size ten."

"You are a size ten, Charlotte."

"Oh, right, yes . . . well, you know what I mean," I say vaguely. Only I don't think she does—there's nothing but silence for a long moment.

"Sorry, I know you must be really busy, I'll go."

"No, it's fine, don't be silly," I say quickly.

"Really? Are you sure?" She sounds so grateful, I feel a twinge of guilt. God, am I always that busy with work that she thinks I won't have time to talk at a time like this?

"Of course, what's more important than my best friend, hey?"

No sooner have those words come out of my mouth than the line starts beeping and I can see another call trying to come through. It's Beatrice, but I ignore it.

"I just don't know what to do." She sighs. She sounds upset and I'm suddenly reminded of her at the club, standing in line for the bathroom, gushing happily about how madly she was in love with Julian. It makes me wonder how she got to this place, all these years later, where she's on the phone to me, worried he's having an affair.

"Why don't you ask him about it?" I suggest. "Be honest?"

"I can't. Then he'll know."

"Know what?"

The line is still beeping. I grit my teeth and continue to ignore it. It won't be anything important. It can wait.

"I wasn't snooping," she protests unprompted. "I was just doing the laundry and I found the receipt in his trouser pocket and—okay,

I was snooping," she confesses. I can hear puffing furiously on a cigarette on the other end of the line. "So no, I can't tell him."

"Look, it's not what you're thinking—"

*Or what I'm thinking.*

"Just you watch, there'll be a simple explanation."

The other line stops beeping. I feel relieved. Now I can focus properly on her.

"Like what?" demands Vanessa. "I find a receipt for lingerie that's not my size, but no lingerie. Believe me, I've looked high and low and it's not in the house. So he must have bought it for someone else."

"Um . . . maybe he was with a colleague, who suddenly remembered it was his wedding anniversary . . . and so they popped into Agent Provocateur to buy his wife a gift . . . but then the colleague realized he'd left his wallet in the office and so Julian stepped in and paid. Like the true gentleman he is."

Perfect, Charlotte, if I must say so myself. I just managed to turn that around and now Julian looks like a hero. Instead of a cheating lying bastard.

Which of course he isn't, I tell myself sharply. Because the more I think about it, the more I refuse to believe that Julian would do such a thing. Okay, so I know what it looks like when faced with the evidence, and I know we've all read about the pro sports players doing that kind of thing . . . and the politicians and the rock stars and the man next door who's a pillar of the community. But this is Julian. And although I know things between them haven't been great for a while, he loves Vanessa, I'm sure of it.

"Hmmmm." Vanessa sounds vaguely convinced. "I suppose it could happen—"

"Of course it could happen, I mean, there's tons of rational explanations—" I stop myself. Okay, quit while you're ahead, Charlotte.

"You think so?"

"Absolutely."

The other line starts beeping again. It's Beatrice. Again. She's nothing if not persistent. Only this time I can't ignore it.

"Look, Vanessa, I'm really sorry, but I'm going to have to go," I say reluctantly. "My assistant's calling and I have to get it, it might be something to do with the press launch tomorrow for Larry Goldstein's Star Smile UK."

"Oh, how is he?" she asks, suddenly perked up. "Made any more advances?"

"He's married!" I retort.

"Exactly," she quips dryly.

I ignore her. Though I'm glad to see she's got some of her black sense of humor back.

"Look, I'll call you later."

"I'll probably be divorced by then—"

"Vanessa!"

"It was a joke," she protests. "It's fine."

I know it's not fine. It's far from fine, but I don't know what to do. I've got the office trying to get through with something that could be urgent; my friend's marriage could be in serious trouble; and I'm responsible for robbing an old man of his beloved livelihood, ignoring his grandson when I was twenty-one, and, according to an e-mail received from Miles this morning, a seven-hundred-quid homebuyers' survey from the bank. That's a lot of dollars. And I *still* haven't called Mom back since we got cut off, I suddenly remember.

It's one thing after another. I feel as if I'm frantically rushing around, like those people you see who try to keep all those plates spinning, dashing from one to another to make sure none of them stops spinning and falls crashing to the ground. Smashing into a million little pieces.

Quickly saying good-bye to Vanessa, I switch lines. "Hi, Beatrice—what's up?"

And I can't let that happen. Because if I do, who's going to pick up the pieces?

## Chapter Thirty-four

By the time I pull up outside my apartment I'm emotionally spent. After spending twenty minutes calming down Beatrice, who was hysterical because of a mix-up over the caterers for tomorrow's launch, and sorting out the problem, I called Julian's secretary and left a message telling him to call me at home. I haven't yet worked out what exactly I'm going to say when he does, but I can't just sit back and do nothing.

Though boy, right now that's all I feel like doing.

Nothing. Nada. Zero.

Switching off my phones, I turn off the engine and, closing my eyes, rest my forehead on the steering wheel. For a moment I just relish the quiet. The sound of my own breath. The rise and fall of my shoulders. I just need to take a moment to calm down. To relax, like the doctor said. What is it they tell us to do in yoga—focus on the breath.

I focus.

*Deep breath in . . . and now exhale out. . . . Deep breath in . . . and now exhale out . . . Deep breath in . . .*

I concentrate on inhaling through my nostrils, then exhaling through them—I even put my thumb and finger on them, just like you're supposed to. I feel my chest cavity expand, and then slowly collapse. "As long as the breath can take you" is what my teacher always says, although usually at this point it is at the end of the class and I've nodded off in *savasana*.

Still, it seems to be having the desired effect, I realize, I am feeling a lot more calm. In fact, I think I might throw in some oms too for good measure.

"*Ommmm . . . ommmmmm . . . ommmmmmmmmm . . .*"

"Are you okay?"

A loud rapping on the window causes me to nearly jump out of my skin and I snap upright in shock. "Arggh," I yelp, cricking my neck in the process. Clutching at it in pain I turn stiffly sideways. "You stupid idiot! What the hell do you think you're—"

"Charlotte?"

And come face-to-face with Oliver. Stooped down on the pavement, his hands on his knees, he's peering in at me through the side window, a worried expression on his face.

Oh fuck. How long has he been standing there?

"Hey, are you okay?"

No, I'm not okay, I'm mortified. No, scratch that. I'm *beyond* mortified.

"Um, yeah . . . absolutely . . . thanks." I nod, and then wince sharply as a pain shoots up my neck.

"Are you sure?"

The shooting pain has now turned into more of a red-hot-poker stabbing agony.

"It's my neck," I manage to gasp.

"You probably pulled something."

"What if I've broken it?" I gasp, feeling a creeping panic.

"I doubt it."

"But how do you know?"

"Can you wiggle your toes?"

I wiggle them. "Yes."

"Can you wiggle your fingers?"

I wiggle them. "Yes."

"Now for the big test—"

I brace myself.

"Can you wiggle your ears?"

I try to wiggle them, but nothing. "Oh my God, no, I can't! What does that mean?" I cry in hysterics, twisting around to look at him.

And seeing him laughing. Killing himself on the sidewalk.

I feel my cheeks burn up. Oh God, I certainly walked into that one, didn't I?

"It means your neck's fine." He grins mischievously, and I can't help but smile back. Before it hits me again like an icy blow. *The store*. I've got to tell him.

"So—"

"So?" I manage, feeling my body stiffen as I brace myself.

"Well, now you're going to walk again, how do you fancy continuing our conversation without a car window between us?"

"Oh, right, of course . . ." I blush. Nerves are whooshing around in the pit of my stomach. I'm trying to think of the right way to break the news about his grandfather's store, but somehow I can't seem to find one.

Most likely because there isn't one, I tell myself. I'm just going to be honest and tell it like it really is.

"Actually I wanted to talk to you about something—" Releasing the door catch, I step out of the car, and am immediately accosted by Welly.

"Hey, down boy," instructs Oliver, and Welly immediately sits down. "Someone's pleased to see you," he says, and then smiles shyly. "He's not the only one."

The nerves that are swimming around in my stomach like tadpoles suddenly turn into butterflies. Maybe I don't have to tell him how it really is *right* this minute.

"So, what are you doing around here?" I ask, feeling all jittery, but this time it's in a good way.

"Oh, I was just in the area," he says vaguely. "I thought I'd take Welly for a walk . . ." He trails off and stuffs his hands in his pockets.

Those butterflies are going crazy in there.

"Well, now you're here, I suppose I *should* invite you in for a cup of tea," I say, doing my best to look unenthusiastic.

"Hey, no, I didn't mean—" he protests, then breaks off as he sees me smiling and realizes I'm teasing. "I suppose I asked for that."

"I suppose you did." I nod. "Hang on a minute." Turning back to the car, I reach inside for all my bags, folders, briefcase—

"Hey, do you want me to give you a hand with all that?"

"Oh, yeah, that would be great," I reply, leaning over the backseat and gathering up a big box of files. The top one is Larry Goldstein's and I suddenly notice on the front of it I've scribbled the address of the new store. My stomach flips. Shit. I don't want him seeing that. "If I *needed* you to help," I finish, reemerging with all the bags, the file pressed closely to my chest in a Beatrice move. "But I like to do things for myself . . . um, as a woman . . . you know, *The Female Eunuch* and all that . . ."

Oh Jesus, what am I talking about? I've never even read *The Female Eunuch*. He's going to think I don't shave my legs and go around burning my bras. But if he does, he doesn't show it.

"Fair enough." He smiles evenly.

I smile with relief. Phew, that was close. Still, like I said, I've got to tell him.

"Okay, well, this way," I say, puffing under the weight of all my stuff as I walk toward my apartment.

I've just got to find the perfect moment.

❧

I unlock the front door and step into the hallway. Oliver follows and lets Welly off his lead. Immediately he bounds off inside, racing through to the living room, leaving behind a trail of dirty pawprints all over the pristine cream carpet.

"Oh shit." Oliver throws me a strangled look. "Welly! Come here, boy!" he yells, whistling desperately. "God, I'm so sorry, I'll tie him up outside," he apologizes, looking mortified.

"No, don't be silly, it's fine," I say quickly.

"But your carpet—"

"Is totally impractical," I finish. "Don't worry." I shrug. "It's only dirt, it'll come off."

Hello? Earth calling Charlotte Merryweather? I freak out about the slightest bit of dirt on the carpet. I insist everyone takes their shoes off and if anyone drops so much as a *crumb* I'm there with the DustBuster.

But for some reason, the thought that Welly is scampering all over my cream wool carpet, leaving behind great big dirty pawprints, has no effect on me whatsoever. In fact, I feel almost *happy* that Welly is scampering around on my cream carpet leaving behind great big dirty pawprints.

Okay, I have been taken over by an alien.

*Or I've got a crush.*

My insides do a loop-the-loop.

And this time we're not talking a fantasy I'm-lusting-after-Olly-the-young-bartender crush, we're talking a certifiable I'm-lusting-after-him-now-that-he's-Oliver-and-all-grown-up crush.

*Shit.*

"So . . . would you like to sit outside?" I say, walking briskly through into the kitchen and opening the French windows that lead out onto the small wrought-iron balcony.

"Wow, it's so pretty out here," he says, approvingly.

"Thanks." I smile. "Though I can't take credit, I have a gardener to do the plants." I gesture to the medley of blue, yellow, and pink flowers that I don't know the names of that climb up trellises and spill over the balcony. "That's my contribution." I gesture to a string of lights that I've wrapped around a potted tree.

"I think your contribution probably makes it," he replies, his lips twitching with amusement.

"It does!" I laugh in protest. "Just you wait till it gets dark!" And then I suddenly realize what I've said and feel my cheeks prickle. That sounds as if I'm going to keep him trapped here until nighttime, doesn't it? Like I'm some kind of brazen hussy and I'm going to try to have sex with him or something.

Shit. I only invited him in for a cup of tea, and here I am thinking about sex. Except I'm not thinking about sex, I was thinking—

Oh, who am I kidding? I was thinking about sex.

"So, I didn't see you the other night—"

I snap back to see Oliver looking at me expectantly.

"I thought you'd stood me up again," he says, then smiles. "Just joking."

"Oh, no, I had to stay in and—" I'm about to say pack up all Miles's things, but I quickly change my mind. Then I really *will* look like some brazen floozy. Inviting a man back to her place when it's still warm from her last boyfriend. "I had to do some stuff," I finish, wandering back into the kitchen. Flicking on the kettle, I set about making tea.

"Yeah, me too," he says from the balcony, where he's taken a perch on one of my garden chairs. "I got back pretty late from my grand-dad's. There was loads to do, we were packing for ages."

The kettle quickly boils and, pouring water onto the tea bags, my hand trembles and I feel my insides clench with dread.

"Poor guy, he was pretty cut up," he continues, anger seeping into his voice. "And then to top it all off, he had some people over at his store today, talking about how they were going to rip the whole place apart."

Okay, this is it, I've got to let him know about Larry Goldstein, about the store, about me—My heart thudding loudly in my ears, I grasp the back of my neck, trying to brace myself.

"You know you should really put some ice on that." Oliver's voice makes me jump and I turn around to see him standing right behind me. "Your neck will feel a lot better."

"Oh, no, it's fine," I say quickly.

"You won't be saying that when you wake up tomorrow and can't move." Without further discussion, he tugs open my freezer. I watch wordlessly as he takes out the ice-cube tray, spreads out a tea towel, and lays it on top. Then deftly cracks out the cubes, and ties it up.

"You look as if you've done that a few times," I say after a pause.

"Yeah, well, I've had a few knocks in my time. I used to like to think of myself as a bit of a boxer, but I wasn't very good. I gave it all up five years ago when this happened." He gestures to the scar running across his top lip. "You know, I used to be pretty handsome before." He smiles ruefully.

"You're handsome now," I protest, then realize what I've said and blush like a schoolgirl. Until now I hadn't fully noticed just how sexy he is, but now I have, I can't seem to think of anything else. "Why, what happened?" I ask, quickly changing the subject.

"A mean left hook, twenty-two stitches, and a broken nose."

"Ouch." I wince. "Did it hurt?"

"Hurt?" he repeats, and looks at me as if I've affronted his masculinity. "I cried like a baby," he confesses.

I laugh, then wince as my neck twinges painfully. "Okay, now go sit outside," he orders, picking up the ice pack.

"But what about the tea?"

"This will only take a minute."

Without arguing I dutifully walk outside and sit down on one of my garden chairs. As he moves behind me I feel a stab of anticipation.

"Okay, you need to pull your top down a little," he instructs firmly.

Dutifully I pull down the collar of my blouse.

"No, more than that."

My heart beating fast I undo the top buttons and shrug it down, revealing my bra straps. It's hot in the afternoon sun and I feel a prickle of perspiration on my chest.

"Okay, I'm just going to move these—"

Gently he hooks his fingers underneath my bra straps and lets them slide down my arms. I can feel my breath quickening. My rib cage rising and falling.

"Where exactly is it sore? Here?"

I feel his fingers brush against the nape of my neck.

"Um . . . a little lower . . ." My throat has gone all tight and my voice comes out in a whisper.

I feel his fingers gently tracing underneath my hairline, down along my vertebrae, circling lower and lower. "Here?"

I can barely speak. "Yes, there," I manage.

A tingle rushes down into my groin. All the way down my legs. A tugging. Like a thread running between us. I never even came close to this with Miles. It's so erotic. I feel more excited than I've felt in years. If *ever*.

"Now this is going to be a little cold."

I let out a gasp as he presses the freezing-cold ice against my neck.

"Sshhhh," he murmurs, sliding his arm around my shoulders as my body gives a little shudder. "Hold still."

I do as I'm told and breathe in, sucking in the air between my teeth and holding it tight inside of me. Every sense seems to be on full alert. Every sensation. I can feel the cold ice melting against the heat of my neck, see the dark hairs of his arm wrapped around me, smell the scent of his body close to me, hear the sound of his breath close to my ear . . .

The moment is suddenly broken by the sound of my home phone ringing inside.

"Do you want to get that?" asks Oliver, his voice husky.

"No!" I cry before I can help myself. "It's, um . . . probably a wrong number," I add, my mind fumbling around for words, when all I can think is I don't want this to stop. I don't *ever* want this to stop.

The answering machine clicks on. I hear my voice on the outgoing message:

*"Hi, this is Charlotte Merryweather. I'm not here right now but if you'd like to leave a message . . ."* Followed by a beep.

"Hi, it's Beatrice, sorry to bother you at home, but your mobile and BlackBerry aren't switched on . . ."

"Oh, it's okay, it's just my assistant," I dismiss. It's probably about that goddamn press launch again, I curse silently, willing her to hang up. "It's nothing."

"Well, if you're sure—" he says quietly, running his fingers across my collarbone.

"I'm sure," I reply, feeling a tingle down my spine.

". . . and I just wanted to call you and say I'm so sorry for getting into such a frightful panic earlier . . ."

The icy water is dripping down my back. He moves the ice pack, sending a trickle down across my chest and between my breasts.

". . . and thank you again for coming to my rescue and sorting everything out with the caterers. You're a total star! But of course, you know that already. Oh, and by the way, Larry Goldstein's people called, just to say how delighted they are about the new space . . ."

I stiffen. Oh, no. *Oh, no*—I jump up. "Sorry, actually I think I do need to get this—" I rush through the French windows.

". . . and I have to say, Charlotte, what a brilliant idea of yours! Notting Hill is a perfect place for the first Star Smile clinic. Gosh, you are *so* clever. I can't believe you didn't tell me what you had up your sleeve," she chides loudly.

I race for the phone, but Welly is in the way, and as I lunge for it I trip over him.

"Oh, and apparently they're going to try to get the current chap out a bit earlier, so they can start the renovation as soon as this weekend. Apparently, there's loads to do. They mentioned it was a junk store or something and a frightful old mess . . ."

My whole body contracts with horror.

"So, just to confirm, the exact address for the press release is . . ."

I scramble for the receiver, but it's too late. Behind me I hear Oliver's voice in stereo with Beatrice's.

"One fourteen Portobello, London W11 69P."

Fuck.

"Anyway, got to run, *eeth* salsa tonight!"

The line goes dead, and there's silence. Frozen, I stare at the phone, my mind whirling. Until slowly, I turn around. Oliver is standing in the doorway, just looking at me. His face is white with shock.

"I can explain," I manage finally.

"You?" he says quietly in disbelief. "It was you." He's staring at me as if it doesn't make sense, his brow furrowed in confusion. "Granddad said he thought he recognized one of the people who came into his store. A girl. Blonde. I thought he was getting confused . . ." He trails off, his mind joining up the dots.

"Yes, it was me," I admit quietly, my whole body suffused with regret.

"You're the reason my granddad's lost his livelihood?"

His voice may be quiet but the accusation stings. "It's not like that," I say quickly.

"So what is it like?" he replies. There's an edge now to his voice.

"I'm in PR. I represent a client."

"But it was your idea."

"I might have made some suggestions about the location, but I wasn't specific—"

"So who's your client?" he demands, his shock fast giving way to anger. "Don't tell me, it's going to be another coffee chain," he gasps in disgust, before I can answer.

"No, he's a cosmetic dentist. He's going to open his first UK clinic: Star Smile." Hearing myself say it, it suddenly sounds ridiculous.

Oliver looks at me incredulously. "My grandfather's antique store—sorry, *junk store . . .*" he spits out angrily and I blush hotly. I've never used that phrase, it was Larry Goldstein, but suddenly by association I'm as guilty as he is. ". . . is going to be a fucking dentist's?"

"A cosmetic dentist," I correct, and then by the look on his face, wish I hadn't.

"I was going to tell you," I try again.

"When, exactly?"

"I don't know—"

"Before or after you spent the afternoon with my grandfather?" he says coldly.

A shiver runs down me and I'm suddenly aware that my top is still unbuttoned and bra straps are pulled down. I quickly shove them back up again, feeling vulnerable and foolish. "I didn't know until today. I just found out too. Look, I'm sorry—" I reach out my hand to touch his arm, but he wrenches it away.

"Yeah, I bet you're sorry," he retorts, his face set hard. "Sorry all the way to the bank."

"That's not fair," I exclaim. "You're being unfair!"

"*I'm* being unfair?" he cries acerbically.

"Well, it's not like I killed someone," I gasp, feeling a snap of impatience.

"You might as well have. It was my granddad's whole life."

All at once I feel a wave of anger. I feel guilty enough, without him attacking me. "How dare you stand there and judge me? You have no idea," I reply angrily. "You have no idea the pressure I'm under, or the impossible situation I'm in! I didn't mean for this to happen. I didn't plan it, but when a big client's involved there's a lot at stake. It's not just about me anymore, I have a job to do, a business to run, wages to pay—"

"Please, spare me the sob story," he says scornfully.

That does it. I feel a burst of renewed outrage. "Oh, silly me!" My voice rises, shrill and angry. "How could you possibly know what it's like to run a business?"

His eyes flash angrily. "What's that supposed to mean?"

"Well, how could you?" I gasp, my words tumbling out in a torrent. "You've never done anything with your life. You're still just a bartender!"

As soon as the words leave my mouth I want to stuff them back in.

But it's too late.

Oliver visibly recoils in shock, a whole range of emotions flitting over his features before, recovering, he looks at me, his jaw set hard.

"And you're a bitch," he says coldly.

It's like a slap in the face.

For a moment we both stand there in silence, our rib cages rising and falling, the air thick with insults and anger. And in that moment I wonder how we got here, how this happened, how I can turn it all back and start again.

But I can't. What's been said can't be unsaid.

"I think you should go," I say finally, trying to keep my voice steady.

He nods tightly. "Trust me, I'm already gone."

And with Welly following him, he turns and strides out of my flat, slamming the door behind him.

## Chapter Thirty-five

Grabbing the brass door knocker I hammer furiously. There's the sound of footsteps and the door is flung open by my younger self. Who takes one look at me and gasps,

"Oh my God, are you okay?"

This time there are tears streaming down *my* face. In between gasping snorts, I nod vigorously. "Yes . . . fine . . ."

Like I said, I've always been a crappy liar.

"What on earth happened?" she asks anxiously.

Blowing my nose on a crumpled tissue, I shake my head. "We had a huge fight . . ." I manage between sobs, ". . . he called me a bitch."

*"He called you a bitch?"* she exclaims. "Who did, your ex?" Her face flashes with fury. "Just you wait, I'll tell him a thing or two—"

"But I *am* a bitch," I sniffle, tears splashing down my cheeks.

"You're not a bitch," she protests indignantly.

"I am, I am." I'm wailing now, really quite loudly. In fact I'm making such a scene, a couple of people from next door have popped out to see what all the noise is about, and are now staring at me openmouthed. Which would usually be more than enough to douse me in self-consciousness and set me alight with shame, but not now. Now I don't give one iota that I'm making a total embarrassment of myself, I don't care if complete strangers are pointing me, all I care about is Oliver—

As the thought hits me, I freeze for a moment, stunned by my admission; then I let out an even louder wail.

"Why? Because you broke up with your boyfriend?" Lottie is saying, trying to calm me down by rubbing my shoulder. "By the sound of it he's a total idiot."

"I'm not talking about my ex-boyfriend," I hiccup, looking at her with puffy, red eyes.

"You're not?" She stops rubbing my shoulder. "Well, who are you talking about, then?"

"Oliver," I manage to gasp, before bursting into tears again.

Lottie looks at me in confusion. "I think you need to come in and tell me all about it."

"So, go on, tell me."

We're sitting upstairs in my old bedroom, only this time the positions are swapped and it's Lottie who's perched on the chair surveying me, while I'm curled up on the bed, hugging my knees and sipping from a cracked mug of black coffee that she made me. My old room's a total mess, in fact in the daylight it seems worse than ever, but while it bothered me before, now I find it oddly comforting.

"I don't know where to start," I sigh into my instant Nescafé.

"How about at the beginning," she suggests.

Tucking my hair behind my ears, I shake my head. "That's just it, I don't exactly know where the beginning is anymore. It's like everything's all tangled up together . . ." I pause, trying to sort through the jumbled reels of my life, trying to put things into some kind of order.

In the end I start with Oliver. Well, it seems as good a place as any. I tell how our paths crossed ten years ago, "But nothing happened between us, as I didn't notice him—although now I wish something had," I add regretfully, pulling at my tissue. "And then just out of the blue we bumped into each other again, and it seemed like something was *going* to happen between us, that maybe I was going to get a second chance . . ." I pause, reliving that moment a few moments ago on my balcony, feeling a twist in my stomach. "But then we had this big fight," I finish miserably.

"Don't tell me. He was a lying asshole like Billy Romani," she interjects angrily.

"No, not at all." I shake my head sadly.

"Then why?" She looks at me in confusion.

I think back to standing outside his grandfather's antique shop with Larry Goldstein. "I let my head rule my heart," I say quietly. "I told myself that business was business, that personal feelings don't come into it. I tried to rationalize—"

"You mean you ignored your gut instinct?" she says, translating.

I glance up at her, her words registering. I hadn't thought about it like that, but she's right. "I guess I've been guilty of ignoring a lot of things," I hear myself saying. "I ignored the doubts I had about my relationship with Miles. We were never right for each other from the beginning, but I tried to convince myself we were, because I wanted us to be. Just like I ignore that little voice inside of me that says I'm not happy. Because I *must* be happy. I've got the life I always dreamed of. I've got the lifestyle, a successful career, size ten thighs . . ." Smiling ruefully I hug my knees to my chest.

"And yet I can't help feeling as if there's something missing in my life." As I say it out loud, I realize I'm admitting this to myself for the first time. "But I don't know what it is. And the harder I look, the more I can't find it because there's just too much pressure and not enough time . . ."

I've bottled all this stuff up for so long that now it's as if I've lifted off a lid and it's all pouring out.

"It's like I'm always playing catch-up. I rush through my life exhausted and anxious and worried all the time. Not to mention hungry." I roll my eyes and make a face, remembering I haven't eaten since that energy bar at breakfast.

"But what's the point?"

"Sorry?" I stop talking and look at my younger self, not understanding.

"I mean, what's the point of worrying all the time?" She shrugs.

I stare at her, perplexed. Is that a trick question?

"Well, it's not about there being a *point* . . ."

"So why do it then?" she asks simply.

"Because—" I open my mouth to explain, only I can't quite think of one.

"It's a total waste of time." She shrugs, reaching for a pot of glittery nail polish and trying out a bit on her big toe. "If the worst is going to happen, it'll happen. Worrying can't protect you from that. And if it *doesn't* happen—" She raises her eyebrows. "Then you've missed out on all the time when you could have been having fun." Smiling brightly, she puts down the pot of glittery polish, picks up a bright purple one instead, and starts doing the other foot.

Meanwhile I'm looking at her in astonishment. How did I change from her to me? From this carefree person into someone who spends her whole time with a nervous knot in her stomach. What on earth happened to me?

But before I've even finished asking myself the question, deep down inside I know the answer.

Because you see, I haven't told Lottie the whole story. There's more. A lot more. I've just kept it buried deep inside of me for so long now, I'd almost convinced myself that none of it ever really happened. Almost, until a few days ago when I saw myself again with Billy Romani and all the painful memories came rushing back.

Of course Lottie doesn't know any of this. I haven't told her the real reason why I tried to stop her sleeping with Billy Romani. I haven't explained to her what really broke my heart. And how can I? How can I tell my younger self about the sequence of events that followed? About how I thought I'd bounced back, got over it, only to discover a few weeks after my birthday that something was wrong.

My period was late.

Well, you can guess the rest. Disbelief. Panic. Tears. I can still remember that moment as if it was yesterday, sitting on the toilet, looking at the two blue lines, feeling my whole world collapsing around me. I had just turned twenty-two years old and had no idea what to do. Emotions threatened to overwhelm me: anger for being so stupid, for letting this happen, for getting myself into this situation. And fear. An icy cold fear that had tightened its grip around my heart, leaving me scared and afraid.

The only person I told was Vanessa. She didn't judge me or admonish me, she didn't say anything, just gave me a hug and promised to be there whatever I decided to do. It was Vanessa who lent me the money and came with me to the clinic. If it hadn't been for her, I don't think I'd have got through it. But in a few hours it was all over and I consoled myself with the thought that now I could put it all behind me.

Except I never really did put it behind me. I don't think anyone ever does, do they? From that moment on it was as if something had changed inside of me. I'd crossed a line and I never crossed back. Of course I've changed gradually over the years, people do, it's all part of growing up. But if I look back, it's almost as if that was the moment the old Lottie disappeared.

A lone tear spills from my eyelashes and trickles down my cheek. Because it's only now I recognize I've never really forgiven myself. It was ten years ago but there are still times when I wonder if I did the right thing. In unguarded moments when I see Vanessa with Ruby and Sam, and I see how much she loves them, I ask myself if I made the right choice. Wonder "what if."

But now I know.

Because if spending time with myself and seeing Billy Romani again has made me realize one thing, it's that I completely made the right decision. We were so young, so wrong for each other, so not ready, we would have made terrible parents. We weren't even together—to Billy Romani I was just a one-night stand—and I couldn't have brought up a child on my own, I was still practically a child myself. I was silly, I thought I was in love, and it was an accident. It happens to millions of women. It happened to me. But now I need to finally accept that and stop blaming myself. It's like I said to Lottie, that day as she sat crying on her doorstep: acceptance is the final stage. I need to reach that to be able to move on.

And now I have.

"Hey, are you all right?" Lottie looks up from painting her toenails.

"Yeah." I brush away my tear. "I think so."

"You know you've got to stop worrying about the past and forget about the future and start living for the moment." Finishing painting them she wiggles them with satisfaction.

"I know." I nod, and smile ruefully. "But how?"

She rolls her eyes as if I'm a total moron, then realizes I'm completely serious and fixes me with a considered look. "Loosen up a bit more, be spontaneous, enjoy yourself."

"Enjoy myself?" I repeat, as if I'm speaking a foreign language.

"Like the other night on the dance floor." She does a little impression of what I can only assume is me dancing and feel myself blush. "You looked like you were having fun."

"Yes, I was," I admit. My mind spools back to dancing at the club. Walking through the park with Oliver. Eating shortbread fingers with his grandfather. At the flea market . . . I've had more fun in the last few days than I can remember having in the last few *years*.

"Here, I know what will cheer you up . . ." Jumping up from the table, my younger self scrabbles around in a spangly bag hanging on the back of the chair, and pulls out a Twix. "Chocolate." She pulls a delighted face and, snapping it in half, holds out a finger.

"Um, no, thanks." I smile, shaking my head. "I try not to eat chocolate."

"Seriously?" She stares at me agape. "God, no wonder you're so depressed."

And suddenly it hits me. Our roles have completely reversed. It's no longer me giving my younger self advice, it's her giving *me* advice. And I'm fast realizing that actually, I don't know better at all. About some things, yes—I glance at that terrible silver eye shadow—but not about everything, far from it.

Age and experience haven't made me this wise old master; it's made me this anxious, strung-out thirtysomething who worries about everything. Whose life is completely out of balance. Who's forgotten how to have fun. And who spends her life reading self-help books trying to find herself when she was here under her nose all along, I think, glancing at Lottie, and seeing this smart, confident, vibrant young woman.

Honestly, what was I obsessing about? She's going to be just fine, I suddenly realize. I can't wrap her up in cotton wool, I can't stop her making mistakes, just like I couldn't stop her and Billy and the inevitable result that will come from that. But you know what? I don't want to. There's a saying: what doesn't kill you makes you stronger. And yes, she's going to have some rough times ahead of her—but she's going to be okay.

*I'm going to be okay.*

Because it's true. There has been something missing in my life. *I* was missing in my life. I lost sight of who I was. I lost myself. And now here in this bedroom, I've found myself again.

"Actually, pass me some of that Twix?"

Oh, how I missed my sweet tooth.

❧

After polishing off the rest of the Twix, my appetite reawakens and I suddenly discover I'm starving. Lottie kindly offers me a cup-a-noodles, but I decline. While I might have had the right idea about a lot of things when I was younger, this definitely wasn't one of them. Instead I suggest going to eat at the pub. My treat.

Which seems like a great idea until we enter the pub and I suddenly see the young Olly.

I stiffen. With everything that's been happening I'd totally forgotten he'd been working here, and seeing him now brings my argument with Oliver whooshing back.

Apprehensively I walk toward the bar.

"Hey, how are you?" As he sees me, he smiles in recognition. "It's Charlotte, isn't it? We met the other night at the Canal Club."

"Yeah, hi, Olly." I smile awkwardly. It seems weird him being so nice, when only a few hours ago we were standing in my living room, screaming at each other.

"So how are things?" he asks cheerfully, and as I look into his familiar pale gray eyes, my insides pang.

"Great," I say brightly, forcing myself to look cheerful. If I felt bad before, now I feel worse. "And you?"

"Oh, I'm good." He nods, then pauses and plays with the woven bracelets around his wrist, as if he's got something on his mind. "Um, actually, I was going to ask you a favor," he says after a moment, and glances up at me nervously.

"Sure, anything."

Anything to try to make things up to you, I think, looking at him behind the bar and feeling myself almost sag under the weight of regret.

"Well, the thing is—" He swallows hard. "I'm cooking dinner tomorrow night for a few friends and I wanted to invite Lottie. Do you think she might come?"

He smiles nervously, his face infused with hope. And I know, right there and then, that this is my second chance. I might have messed things up but it doesn't mean Lottie has to.

"Of course she will," I reassure him.

"Really?" His face flushes with delight. "You think so?"

"Leave it to me." I smile. "Just give me your address."

"Oh, okay . . ." He scrambles for a piece of paper, as if barely daring to believe his luck. "Hang on, there's a notepad around here somewhere. . . ."

"Don't worry, use this." I dig a crumpled piece of paper out of my bag. It's my list of advice. Nineteen dos and don'ts. Funny, I never got to number twenty. "I won't be needing this anymore." I glance at it for a moment, thinking how much I got wrong, before passing it across the bar. "Just write on the back."

"Thanks," he mutters and, snatching up the pen, scribbles his address. "Tell her it's at seven thirty, and she doesn't need to bring anything. Just herself," he adds, with a small smile. He passes it to me.

"Consider it done." I smile back, slipping it into my bag.

"Now, what can I get you?" he asks. "Drinks are on the house."

I order two halves of cider and two packets of salt and vinegar potato chips as an appetizer—well, if I'm back on the chocolate it seems only fitting I might as well go the whole hog—and walk back to the table carrying a couple of menus.

"Hey, Lottie," I say casually, handing her the cider and chips and sliding into the seat next to her, "I'm going over to a friend's for dinner tomorrow night and I wondered if you wanted to come along?"

"Oh, yeah, that sounds cool." She nods, diving delightedly on the packet and ripping it open.

"But I'm going straight from work so I wondered if you could meet me there . . ." I continue, trying to sound as nonchalant as possible, hoping she'll take the bait. Because of course at the last minute I'm suddenly not going to be able to make it due to some "unforeseen problem at work" but by then she'll already be there.

"Sure, what's the address?"

Bingo.

"Here, I wrote it on a piece of paper," I say, digging it out of my bag and passing it to her. She sticks it in her pocket without even looking at it. Unlike me, who'd be immediately looking it up in my street map of London.

Or at least I would have in the past, I reflect, taking a sip of my cider. Mmm, that is good.

"So what do you think, Charlotte?"

"About what?" I snap back to see Lottie peering at the menu. "The fish and chips or the pasta? You've eaten here before. What do you recommend?"

I look at her, in her cutoff denim shorts that are too short, drinking cider and playing with a tendril of hair. She hasn't changed, she's still exactly the same as when I first bumped into her, and I'm glad. I don't want her to change. I want her to stay exactly how she is. How I was. How I'm learning to be again.

Well, maybe not the denim shorts.

Eating a handful of crisps, I take a large slug of cider. "Oh, I don't think you need any advice from me."

"Okay, well, then in that case I'll have the cheese nachos with refried beans and sour cream."

I glance at the list of ingredients. Dairy, wheat, fat, carbs, deep-fried, and not in the slightest bit organic, low-fat, or remotely healthy.

I throw her a big grin. "Sounds delicious. I'll have the same."

# Chapter Thirty-six

After what has to be one of the best meals I've had in eons, I drop Lottie at her house and return home to my apartment. Walking back into the living room feels like returning to the scene of a crime. The ice has now melted, leaving a soggy wet tea towel; two cups of tea, stone cold with a glassy film, sit untouched on the table outside; Welly's muddy pawprints have dried on the carpet.

Everything has moved from the present into the past. Wedging time in between Oliver and me. Pushing us ever further apart.

My chest tightens, but I don't let myself go there, and swallowing hard I look away, my eyes falling instead on the pile of folders sitting on my dining table. I've still got to put the last few finishing touches to tomorrow's press launch. After all, life must go on, I tell myself firmly, pulling myself together and beginning to clear up. I can't sit around wallowing about what happened, feeling sorry for myself. I just want to put today behind me and forget about it. Pretend it never was.

❦

I spend the next half hour tidying up my place, until every trace has been erased and it's like Oliver was never here. Only then do I sit down to do some work.

Turning my attention to the files, I open my laptop and click on the document I've been working on. Everything's been arranged. The press list has been drawn up. The invites have been designed and sent out. The venue's organized. The problem with the caterers is now fixed. The specialty cocktails have been decided upon (no champagne—bubbles play havoc with tooth enamel). The goody bags have been put together. All that remains now is to add the finishing touches to the speech I've been working on for the spokesperson.

That was my big idea. Getting a celebrity to be the spokesperson for Star Smile. Combined with a goody bag and free teeth bleaching, it's guaranteed to draw journalists and generate press. It's also an idea that Larry Goldstein fell in love with at our first meeting and which probably swung the account for me. Yet, even before I won the contract, I spent weeks beforehand drawing up a list of appropriate candidates, putting out feelers, approaching celebrities' agents.

Celebrities are renowned for having their teeth fixed. You'd be hard pressed to find a Hollywood A-lister who hasn't had a little help to achieve that perfect smile. Unfortunately, you *are* hard pushed to find one that will admit to it. Hence a batch of perfect-toothed, wrinkle-free, bee-stung-lipped celebrities who insist it's all down to Manuka honey and Pilates. Not, as everyone in the industry knows, their regular visits to the men in white coats . . .

Thus, after dozens of rejections, and just when I was about to abandon the idea, Beatrice suggested Melody. Well, we already do the PR for her line of diet books and health foods, she's always on the lookout for more exposure (translated: she's a total media whore), plus she's the nation's sweetheart, with just the right mix of glamour and girl-next-door. And let's not forget, she needs something to counter last week's scandal when she was caught eating Le Big Mac.

Sure enough, she jumped at the opportunity, I muse, reading an e-mail from her that's just popped into my in-box regarding the outfit she's wearing tomorrow. Plus of course, she's also jumped at the new promised set of veneers.

Which means everything is now finalized, I realize, turning my focus back on the speech. "Welcome, everyone, to the press launch for Star Smile UK, the brainchild of Larry Goldstein, or as he's been known in Hollywood, Mr. Celebrity Smile. Star Smile promises to offer the latest in tooth bleaching, the finest veneers, laser-gum con-touring . . ."

*I really want to be a writer.*

What? Where did that come from? I ignore it, and keep working.

". . . state-of-the-art cosmetic dentistry, to cater for all your twenty-first-century smiles . . ."

*Ever since I was a little girl, it's always been my dream.*

Lottie's voice flashes into my mind again, louder this time. For a split second I pause to listen, to reflect, then hurriedly brush it aside.

*I couldn't imagine doing anything else.*

It catches the breath in the back of my throat. It's true. I really couldn't imagine doing anything else. Not even slightly. But that was then—

Rubbing my temples, I force myself to sit upright in my chair and focus on the screen. Okay, I'll think about this later. Right now I've got to get this finished. Dragging my eyes back to the screen I begin reading over the rest of the speech.

". . . You too can have a celebrity smile. You too can dazzle with the stars. A Star Smile is the latest must-have accessory. Forget this season's Fendi; trade in your last-season smile, be it crooked, stained, or out of alignment—"

Ugh, that's not very sexy, is it? I need to vamp that up. Though God knows how I vamp up crooked, stained, and misaligned. I mean, please, I can't believe I'm even writing this kind of crap.

*Do something you love, something you're passionate about.*

Oh, be quiet! I gasp in frustration. That's all well and good, and I'm in total agreement with my younger self on that one, but I can't pull out of this now. It would be insanity. It would be career suicide—

And yet as I look back at the computer screen the words swim in front of my eyes, and I realize I'm doing just what I did before. It's like Lottie said. I'm not listening to my gut instinct. This isn't writing. This isn't what I wanted to do. This wasn't my dream.

*I'm writing a novel. I haven't finished it yet, but I'm going to.*

On impulse I jump up and go into my bedroom, where I reach down on all fours and peer under the bed. Underneath is the box of photos I found in the storage cubby, and tugging them out, I pull off the lid and rummage through the albums. I didn't even get to look at them all, I reflect, stacking them up on the floor. Along with another couple of old diaries and some ancient-looking birthday cards.

And then there it is. A thin pile of faded pages beginning to yellow around the edges.

My novel.

I stare for a moment at the title page, absorbing the feelings whooshing around inside of me. I feel suddenly emotional. It's like seeing a part of me that's been buried inside for so long I'd almost forgotten it was there. I swallow hard, tracing my fingers over the typewritten letters, then slowly I turn the page and begin to read.

❧

When I've finished, I stand up and walk back into the living room. I feel slightly euphoric. It's good. Better than good. Better than I ever remembered. Okay, so it's a bit long-winded in parts, and there's some clunky descriptions, but it's got something. Something that excites me. Inspires me. Makes me feel passionate again.

If there were any doubts before, now I'm left with none.

But first there's something I need to do.

I turn back to my laptop, close the document, and get onto the Internet. It's just a hunch, but I'm listening to my gut instincts at last . . . I hesitate, then type something into Google. Though who knows—I scroll down the page—maybe this time my instincts are wrong.

Then I see it.

I click onto the link and suddenly exactly what I suspected pops up onto the screen. My eyes skim through the text as I absorb the information, then I pick up the phone and dial. Far away across town I can hear it ringing, then someone picks up.

"Umm, hello?" mumbles a sleepy voice. It's Katie Proctor, my journalist friend.

"Hi, Katie, it's Charlotte. Charlotte Merryweather. Look, I'm sorry to call you so late, but I really need to ask you a huge favor . . ."

# Chapter Thirty-seven

---

## Merryweather PR invites you to the launch of Star Smile UK!

Join our guest host, TV personality Melody, and discover the exciting new London branch of the famous Beverly Hills clinic. Meet Dr. Larry Goldstein, known to all in Hollywood as Mr. Celebrity Smile, and learn how the latest state-of-the-art techniques can give you that A-list smile.

*We look forward to seeing you there.*
*Tuesday, August 28*
*Slide show and drinks 5–7 p.m.*
*The Charlotte Street Hotel*
*15-17 Charlotte Street, London W1*
*RSVP: Beatrice@MerryweatherPR.com*

---

O kay, so this is it.

Standing in the center of the private room we've hired for the launch, I sweep my gaze over the dazzling arrangements of white lilies, rows of sparkling glasses ready to be filled with the Star Smile martini (a delicious blend of vodka, lychees, and vermouth), and an elaborate centerpiece of sushi on ice, the snow-white rice gleaming under the lighting.

The theme, as you might have guessed, is white. To tie in with the idea of bright white Hollywood smiles.

Okay, I confess, my idea.

Still, it does look pretty impressive. I take a moment to savor the empty room. The journalists have already arrived, and after a welcome martini, were immediately ushered into the private screening room to hear a presentation by Melody and watch a short film about the Beverly Hills clinic. It's good background info. Plus everyone always likes to watch footage of Hollywood celebrities, don't they? Especially when they can say it's "for work."

I hear familiar music from the screening room. After having watched the film more than a few times, I know that's the cue that it's nearly over, and this room will soon be filled with hungry journalists.

"Mmm, this sushi is delish."

I turn around to see Beatrice swooning over a piece of sushi she's just stolen from a tray being held by one of the waitresses. I shoot her a look.

"Um . . . I mean, yes, it passed the test." She nods officially, straightening up. She smiles at the waitress, before turning back to me. "Well, someone had to make sure it tasted okay," she protests innocently. "We don't want to poison the journalists."

"Well, not all of them." I smile ruefully, and she giggles back.

For a brief moment I feel the tension that's been holding me hostage all day loosen its grip slightly, but then the door swings open and out comes Larry Goldstein.

He's deep in conversation with Melody, who's smiling at his flattery, and behind him spill out the journalists, their eyes blinking in the brightness.

Beatrice immediately launches into her meet-and-greet routine. I swear, she really should have been a member of the royal family:

"Why, hello, how simply wonderful to see you again . . ."

Meanwhile I glance anxiously at the clock by the door. It's almost six.

"Excuse me," I ask, hurrying into the lobby and over to the front desk. "Has a FedEx arrived for me? Charlotte Merryweather?"

The receptionist shakes his head and smiles brightly. "No, sorry."

My insides clench, but pinning on a smile I thank him and rejoin the launch.

"Charlotte, this is amazing—" I glance sideways to see a journalist from one of the UK's top beauty magazines. "And what a coup, getting the Star Smile account. I'd heard a whisper, but until I got the invite—" She raises her glass to toast me.

"Oh . . . thanks, yes . . ." I manage brightly, but my throat has gone dry. I spot Larry Goldstein over by the door, chatting to some journalists, and muster my courage. It's now or never.

"I'm sorry, but will you excuse me a moment?"

"Oh, sure." The journalist beams back. "I think I'm going to help myself to another martini . . ."

As she disappears, off I make my way toward him. I feel absurdly nervous. The palms of my hands have started to sweat, and I can hear my heart beating loud and fast in my ears, over the chattering din. Then suddenly, I hear Lottie's voice inside my head.

*Stop worrying. . . . What's the point? . . . If the worst is going to happen, it'll happen.* Drawing reassurance from that, I take a deep breath.

"Hi, Mr. Goldstein, could I have a word—"

He pauses from regaling his listeners with some anecdote, and turns to me. "Hey, Charlene, come and join us. I'm just telling these girls about the time I went in Tom Cruise's private Learjet—"

I smile politely and swallow hard. "Actually, it's really important."

"What can be more important than Tom Cruise's Learjet?" He

cocks an eye at the two pretty journalists, who titter into their martinis.

I clench my fists, digging my fingernails into the palms of my hands. Okay, here goes.

"My resignation," I say evenly.

He looks at me like I've just told him there are little green Martians in the room. Actually he'd look *less* shocked if I told him there were little green Martians in the room.

"Oh, I get it, it's not just the accent you've picked up, you've learned the famous British sense of humor," he laughs.

I swallow hard. "Mr. Goldstein, I'm actually quite serious. I'm afraid Merryweather PR can no longer represent you."

The two journalists stop giggling and look at me uncertainly.

Larry Goldstein on the other hand looks like he's just been shot. Grabbing me roughly by the elbow he marches me into the corridor outside. His head tips as if he can't quite compute what I've just said. "Say that again?" he demands. "I'm not quite understanding here."

Shaken, I pull my arm free and take a step back to regain my composure. "It was too late to call off the press launch at such short notice, and it would have also been unprofessional." I'm struggling to keep my voice steady. "And so I followed through on that commitment. However, I'm afraid we can no longer represent you or the actual launch of the Star Smile clinic in December, and we wish to formally resign from the account."

There. I've done it.

As my words register, his smile turns glassy and he pales underneath his tan.

"*You*. Are. Dropping. *Me*."

He points back and forth.

"Well, I wouldn't use those words . . ."

His face turns hard and he laughs scornfully. "I think you're getting a little bit confused, Charlene. I'm the one that drops people, not the other way around."

"You can call it what you'd like, Mr. Goldstein, but I'm firm in my decision. Merryweather PR will no longer be responsible for your public relations."

As the words leave my mouth his face puckers into a glare and it's suddenly as if the smooth veneer has fallen away and underneath is the real Larry Goldstein.

"Some nothing little agency is dropping me? Mr. Celebrity Smile?" His voice is almost a hiss, and his face is contorted with fury. "Who do you think you are? I'm offering you the chance to go global. To take on a big-name client. To further your career. To play with the big boys. To take your second-rate agency into the big leagues—"

"If you thought we were so second rate why did you choose us?" I fire back defensively.

"Because I thought I saw something in you. I thought you re-minded me of me. You were *hungry* for success."

I shake my head. "No, I'm not like you. I don't want the kind of success that comes from ruining someone's livelihood."

He screws up his face. "Huh?"

"The antique shop."

Even now he doesn't even register. And why should he? Business is business to him. He probably didn't even register what kind of store it was. He just saw it as an opportunity for him.

"The space you chose for your new clinic," I explain. "The space you threw money at to obtain the lease. The man had been in that store for over sixty years, and suddenly his rent was tripled. He's losing everything." I'm like Lottie now, the old me, speaking my mind, wearing my heart on my sleeve, putting my personal feelings first, and it feels good.

"Well, let me get out the violin," he says coldly, and I feel a jolt. Any doubt that I was doing the wrong thing vanishes in that very moment.

"I didn't expect you to understand," I reply calmly, then add,

"And as neither of us have signed the finished contract, it should be a simple parting of ways."

"Whoa—just one minute, little lady."

There's such vitriol in his voice, a shiver of fear runs down my spine.

"We might not have signed anything yet, but I know the law. There's legal binding here. I've got e-mails outlining your intentions to manage this account, the ideas we've discussed, the plans for the future." He looks at me, and it's like the gloves are finally off. "I'll haul you through the courts and sue your ass off. I'll take everything you own: your company, your house, your livelihood, every fucking thing—"

My heart thuds. This is what I was afraid of.

"Fine, go ahead," I reply evenly, trying to stop my voice from trembling.

I turn to leave, but he yells after me. "*You* can't just walk away from me like that. You don't know what you're dealing with here, Charlene. *I'm* the one who calls the shots." He's shouting now and his airbrushed tan has been replaced by a livid red flush.

"Honey—"

There's a high-pitched twang and his wife pops her head around the corner. With everything that's been happening, I'd totally forgotten her.

Holding a martini and her beloved Chihuahua, she smiles tipsily at him. "Honey, are you going to come back inside, the shrimp's sensational—"

"Get the hell outta here, Cindy, will ya?" he yells angrily. "Can't you see I'm talking business?"

Her face blanches and, as she scuttles away, he wheels around to face me.

"I'll ruin you. I'll tell everyone in the business that you were unprofessional, incompetent, that you weren't up to the job . . . I've got friends in high places, I'll go to the press . . ."

He's ranting now, spitting with fury, but I stand firm. I knew this would probably happen, but I was determined to go ahead anyway. I was determined to listen to my instincts.

"Excuse me, FedEx for Charlotte Merryweather?"

I whirl around to see the FedEx man appearing in the corridor. *Just in time.* I feel a rush of relief. My younger self might have helped me rediscover my dream, get my priorities right, and speak my mind, but my older self knows it doesn't hurt to take out insurance.

"The person at the front desk said I might find you down here. Said it was urgent."

"Actually it's for him." Signing for it, I gesture to Larry Goldstein.

"Huh?" Having stopped yelling, he looks at me, breathless and confused.

The FedEx man shrugs and passes him the envelope. Turning it over in his hands, he stares at it, a look of bewilderment on his face.

"I think you might want to open that," I instruct.

"What is this bullshit?" he snaps, finally finding his voice. "Because I can—"

"Sue me? Go to the press?" I finish, trying to keep calm, even though inside my heart is beating very, very fast. "I wouldn't do that if I were you."

Impatiently, he strips open the envelope, a scornful expression on his face. Which immediately disappears when he sees what's inside.

*"Jesus,"* he whispers, turning pale with shock.

Lottie accused me of ignoring my gut instinct, and when it comes to Larry Goldstein I'd been ignoring mine from that first meeting in the restaurant. I was sure I felt his hand grope me under the table, yet I dismissed it. Just as I dismissed the intense looks, the flirty innuendo, the uncomfortable feeling I got in the pit of my stomach. It was only later, when he turned to me outside the store and said, "if you throw a lot of money at things, they go away" that I knew for certain. Right then, that little voice inside of me knew—

But it wasn't until last night that I finally listened to that voice, and acting on my instincts decided to do a bit of research.

Because it seems I'm not the first. An entry in the *Santa Barbara Evening Post* in 1992 mentions the case of a sixteen-year-old who accused her then-dentist, a Dr. Goldstein, of groping her while she was in the dentist's chair. No further details were mentioned.

Which is why I called Katie Proctor. Being a journalist she's got access to all the international press databases and court transcripts. I asked her to do some investigation. My gut told me it was the same man, but I couldn't be sure. There must be hundreds of Dr. Goldsteins. And if it was, what had happened? Had he been found guilty? Struck off? Imprisoned?

Her inquiries confirmed my fears, and more. Because there hasn't been just one accusation against Larry Goldstein. Over the years there have been numerous complaints of sexual harassment—from former employees, from patients, from ex-mistresses—but in every case, all the charges were dropped after huge out-of-court settlements.

And you were right, his first name is Larry, Katie had said when she called me this morning to tell me she was FedExing over all the press cuttings, court transcripts, and documents she'd discovered.

Otherwise known as Mr. Celebrity Smile, I muse, looking at him. Although he suddenly looks nothing like his TV-personality self. His perfectly coiffed hair is now all mussed up, revealing a rather large bald patch, and he cuts a rather sad, pathetic figure.

"This is blackmail," he says finally.

"And you'd know all about that, wouldn't you?" I reply evenly.

He swallows hard, still clutching the damning evidence against him. "So what are you going to do?"

"Nothing," I say simply. "Good-bye, Mr. Goldstein." I start to walk away, then stop and turn. "Oh, and for the record. My name's Charlotte." And turning back I keep on walking. Somehow I don't think that's a name he's going to be forgetting for quite some time.

## Chapter Thirty-eight

By the time I reach the lobby my legs are jelly. I've been running on adrenaline since early this morning, but now that my face-off is over, I feel limp and drained. Steadying myself on the wall, I take a deep breath. I can't believe I did it. I feel a warm glow of euphoria, mixed with a shot of relief, not to mention disbelief. I did it. *I did it.*

I take a deep breath and close my eyes, and for a moment I just stay like that. Letting it all sink in. Letting my heartbeat return to normal.

"There you are!" I open my eyes to see Beatrice bursting through the doors. I'd already briefed her on what I was going to do. I thought it only fair; after all, I was putting the company at risk—and with it her job.

But if she'd felt any reservations, she didn't show it. Instead she'd given me a rib-crushing hug and replied rousingly, "I'm with you. Remember. We shall fight on the beaches, we shall fight on the landing grounds, we shall fight in the fields and in the streets, we shall fight in the hills; we shall never surrender."

I'd looked at her in confusion.

"Winston Churchill. Daddy's hero," she'd explained gravely.

"So how did it go?" she's asking now as she reaches me. "I just saw Mr. Goldstein leaving in a cab with a peroxide blonde and a yappy dog—"

"It went . . . well." I nod, searching for the right adjective.

She almost crumples over with relief. "Oh, thank goodness," she cries, before turning pensive. "So was he terribly angry?" Her voice is hushed and fearful.

"You could say that."

Beatrice takes a sharp intake of breath. "Honestly, Charlotte, you're my hero—"

"Oh, I wouldn't say that." I smile wearily.

"No, you are," she exclaims loyally. "You're like a superhero. Like Spider-Woman!"

"Spider-Man," I correct.

"Really? I could have sworn . . ." She frowns, then gives herself a little shake. "Anyway, chop chop!" She claps her hands together. "Let's go have a drink. There are a few martinis left, we need to hurry up and get them before the journos do—" She reaches out to link arms, but I shake my head.

"No, I think I'm going to go home," I say quietly, clutching my head, which is beginning to throb. "I didn't sleep much last night and I'm leaving early tomorrow."

And that's another thing. After hearing Lottie on the phone to Mom and Dad, it made me realize it's been too long since I saw them, too long since we just sat around watching TV together and chatting about nothing, too long to miss people. Which is why I've decided to drive up tomorrow as a surprise and spend a few days with them.

"Oh, absolutely, of course," says Beatrice, who's aware of my plans. "You run along." She gives me another hug, then, remembering herself, blushes. "I'll stay and hold the fort. Finish off the martinis." She tosses me a mischievous smile. "Well, someone has to." She stalks quickly away on her sturdy calves.

Leaving me alone in the empty lobby with just my thoughts. I feel slightly numb, dazed almost. Like in the lull after the storm, I think, wandering over to the cloakroom, where I'd checked my jacket. Because now it's over. And today is the first day of the rest of my life.

*Without Oliver.*

Once again I feel that familiar nagging ache. But it's not worry this time. I've been trying to block it out, but I can't, it's impossible. Just when I least expect it, his face pops into my mind. I can be driving in my car and I'll remember something he said, or walking down the street and that moment on the balcony will brush erotically through my head and I'll feel a tugging deep inside.

Ironic, isn't it? Ten years ago I didn't even notice him, and now I can't forget him.

Reaching the cloakroom, I zip open my bag and rummage around for my ticket. God, there's so much crap in here, I muse absently, while still thinking about Oliver. I'll probably never see him again. Never be able to tell him I'm sorry, that I quit the contract. And he's never likely to find out. Well, it's hardly front page news, is it?

Anyway, so what if he does? It's not as if I will have saved his grandfather's store. No doubt Larry Goldstein will just go ahead and get a different PR firm and it will be business as usual. Ultimately my stand won't make a difference to anyone. Not to Larry Goldstein, not to Oliver, and certainly not to his grandfather.

But it will, I tell myself as I pass my ticket to the attendant, make a difference to one very important person. It will make a difference to me.

"Excuse me, miss?"

I snap back to see the attendant shaking her head. "This isn't your ticket."

"It's not? Oh, sorry . . ." I dive once more into my handbag. Oh, there it is. I hand it to her with an apologetic smile, and she passes me back the wrong ticket. Only it's not even a ticket, it's just a scrap of paper. Wow, I really am out of it, I realize, as I glance at it.

At the untidy handwriting. At someone's address.

Olly's address.

My heart suddenly plummets. I must have given Lottie the wrong piece of paper. It's my stupid bag, it's filled with so much garbage— *The dinner party's tonight.* As the thought strikes, I feel panic grip me. Oh my God, if she doesn't get it, she's not going to know where to go. She's not going to turn up. *She's going to stand him up.*

Grabbing my bag from the counter, I make a dash for it.

"Miss, your coat, miss—" cries the attendant, but I don't stop. I just keep on running.

❦

Fifteen minutes later I'm back in my car hurtling though London. Zigzagging through other cars, jumping lights, speeding through speed cameras. Come on, come on, come on . . . I get caught up in the diversion again, and as I pull up at the lights I thump the steering wheel in frustration. I have to get there in time to give her the address. I can't let her stand him up.

But what if you already did?

As the thought fires through my brain I have a sudden flashback to yesterday in my apartment, explaining to Oliver why I didn't stop by at the pub.

*I thought you'd stood me up again. Just joking,* he'd said.

But he wasn't joking, was he? I *did* stand him up. I *didn't* get the address in time, did I?

The shrill burbling of my phone cuts into my thoughts and I glance at the screen: *Julian.* Immediately my mind swings like a pendulum, back to Vanessa and her phone call yesterday, the several messages I left with Julian's secretary telling him to call me back. I clip on my earpiece.

"Hello?"

"Hey, Charlotte, it's Julian, I got a message to call you."

I hesitate for a split second, wondering how I am going to put this, how I am going to broach the subject, then give up. "The game's up, I know everything."

"About what?" he replies innocently.

"Julian, don't try this with me!" I cry impatiently. "This is me you're talking to, remember. Your friend. I've known you too long, I can tell when you're hiding something."

There's a silence, then—

"Oh God, have you told Vanessa?" He sounds stricken.

"No, of course I haven't told Vanessa, but if you don't, I will."

The lights turn green and I start edging through.

"I was just waiting for the right time," he bleats.

"The right time?" I exclaim in disbelief. "Of course there's never going to be a right time!" I think about Vanessa and feel a surge of loyalty. "Julian, I can't believe you could do something like this!"

"Well, I had to do something," he protests. "I don't know if Vanessa told you but we've been having a few problems—"

"*Of course* Vanessa's told me," I cut off him. Honestly, do men really have no idea that girls tell their friends *everything*?

"And I admit, I haven't been exactly the best husband of late. Work's been a nightmare, *I've* been a bit of a nightmare . . ."

"You're using work as an excuse?"

"Well, no, it's not an excuse, I was trying to explain—" He breaks off. "Look, a colleague of mine just announced his marriage is over, he's getting a divorce; and when he told me it gave me the wake-up call that was long overdue—"

"God, I can't believe it!" I gasp furiously, not letting him finish. "You're all just horrible! And to think I always stuck up for you!"

"Well, um, thanks, Charlotte," he replies, only now he's sounding a little defensive. And no wonder, I think, hotly. "I'll take that as a compliment."

"A compliment! You bastard!"

There's silence.

"Charlotte? Are you all right?" he asks after a moment.

"No, I'm not all right," I gasp. "Vanessa loves you. She'd do anything for you. And you go and repay her by having a sordid little affair."

"An affair?"

I'm expecting him to be angry, sad, defensive . . . so I'm more than a little shocked when he suddenly bursts out laughing.

"You think it's funny?"

"I think it's fucking hilarious," he replies dryly. "Me, be unfaithful to Vanessa? She'd chop my balls off and eat them for breakfast. With ketchup."

I feel the stirrings of doubt. "But . . . I saw you at the pharmacy, you had condoms . . ."

There's a prickle of embarrassment on the other end of the line, then a deep sigh. "Okay, I confess. I'm guilty of planning to have sex with my wife, your honor."

"And my assistant saw you coming out of the Dorchester with a key to a suite."

"Yup, guilty of booking a suite for a dirty weekend with my wife."

I can feel the probable fast turning into the possible.

"And then there was the Agent Provocateur receipt."

"Yup, guilty of finding my wife sexy too, and buying her naughty lingerie."

I fall silent, absorbing it all. I'm getting the feeling I might have jumped to conclusions.

"I love my wife, Charlotte." On the other end of the line, Julian's voice turns serious. "When my colleague at work told me about his marriage falling apart, it brought me up short and made me look at my own marriage. It made me imagine for just a moment what life would be like without Vanessa in it, made me realize what a bloody idiot I've been, that I've been taking her for granted . . ."

As he's talking it slowly dawns on me that I've jumped to the wrong conclusion.

". . . and so I wanted to treat her, spend time together, get to know each other again. I know it's not going to work like magic overnight, but it's a start—"

I feel stupid and delighted all at the same time. "Oh my God, she's going to love it!" A smile bursts onto my face. "So when are you going to tell her?" I ask, turning off the diversion and zipping down my usual shortcut.

There's silence on the other end of the line.

"Julian?" I glance down at the screen on my phone and see it's blank. We've gotten cut off. Still, it doesn't matter. At least I know they're going to be okay now, I think, feeling a glow of happiness as I glance back up at the road—

And then all of a sudden everything seems to slows right down. As if I'm watching a film in slow motion—frame by frame—only I'm in it. Smiling as I'm lifting my head, catching the blur of color out of the corner of my eye, turning and seeing the truck heading toward me, hearing the horn blasting out, and pushing hard on the brake pedal. And now I'm opening my mouth to scream, knowing what's going to happen but knowing I can't stop it. I can't do anything.

All this in a split second and then—

*BOOM.*

Everything goes black.

# Chapter Thirty-nine

U ggh . . ."
Groggily I open my eyes. Everything is blurry. Kind of foggy. I can make out white shapes. It feels like there are weights on my eyelids. Slowly I flicker them open.

"Oh, thank the Lord! She's awake, she's awake!"

A shrill voice jolts me out of my wooziness and I flop my head sideways. And come eyeball to eyeball with Beatrice. White-faced.

"Charlotte, you've come back to us," she gasps, her voice tremulous with excitement.

Huh? Come back to us. What does she mean, *come back to us?*

"Bea, what's going on?" I open my mouth to ask, but instead, all I hear is sort of a weird croak. Hang on, what was that? "Where the hell I am?" I try again, but all I hear is a coarse rasp. I feel a jolt of alarm. Oh my God, is that me?

"Nurse! Nurse, come quickly!"

*Nurse?* Shit, where am I? A hospital?

I try to sit upright, and suddenly I get the most agonizing pains shooting through my body.

"Argghhhh," I yell out. And this time I really do yell out. Trust me, it's not a husky croak.

"Ooh, there, there, be careful now . . ." I see a figure in white coming toward me. For a moment I think I'm dead and it's an angel, but then I feel a pair of warm, plump hands easing me back down on the pillow and hear a strong Jamaican accent. "You've had a bit of a nasty accident—"

"Wha—?"

I look at her blurrily, trying to make sense of what's going on. I feel as if I'm trying to crank a brain into gear, kick-start it like my old car with a dead battery, pushing on the gas pedal until finally the engine fires. Only I'm pushing on the gas pedal in my brain, pumping it furiously . . .

"You lie still now," the nurse is saying, patting my arm gently. "I'll go see if I can find the doctor." And she disappears out of my range of vision.

Which is when it registers. I'm in bed. In a hospital. And I've had an accident.

It's hardly toppling dominoes, but it's a start.

"How are you feeling?" whispers a voice.

I glance sideways to see Beatrice still standing there. I'd forgotten she was there. Like I said, I'm a bit out of it.

"Um . . . I've been better," I manage to quip weakly. My eyes have managed to focus now and I notice she's got dark shadows under her eyes, and her usually neat bob is unkempt. She looks as if she hasn't slept for days.

"You gave us quite a fright," she reprimands with a small smile.

"What happened?" I manage, finally.

"You were in a car accident."

"*A car accident?*" I repeat in shock.

"A head-on collision with a truck." She nods gravely. "The truck driver got away fine. You came off slightly worse—three broken ribs, a fractured left shoulder . . ."

So that explains the pain, I realize, instinctively trying to move my shoulder and experiencing a sharp throbbing.

". . . a punctured lung . . ." she continues, counting my injuries off on her fingers, ". . . a gash across your left temple, which required twelve stitches . . ."

Automatically I reach up to touch my left temple and find a bandage. Suddenly I register how sore it feels.

"You've been in and out of consciousness for the last two days on morphine. . . ."

"Two days?" I look at her in astonishment.

"I've been on a round-the-clock vigil," she says loyally.

I smile gratefully.

"You've been very, very lucky, Charlotte."

I lie there in my hospital bed, trying to take it all in. The fact that I've been unconscious for two days, I've been in a head-on collision, I've broken bones, I could have died . . .

My eyes well up and without warning, I burst into tears.

"Oh, golly, here, take a tissue," soothes Beatrice. "It's the shock . . ."

I nod mutely and blow my nose with my good arm. "Sorry, I'm pathetic."

"Don't be such a silly goose," Beatrice scolds. "If it was me I'd be in floods. I mean, you could be dead, or horribly mangled, or disfigured beyond recognition and have to have one of those new face transplants I was reading about in *New Scientist*—" She breaks off as she sees my expression. "Not that *you* need a face transplant of course," she says quickly.

"I just don't understand—" I shake my head, groping my way back through the fog that's clouding my mind. At the press launch, finding the address, racing over to my old house, the diversion, the shortcut, Julian—

"According to the police, you were going the wrong way down a one-way street."

I stop blowing my nose and look at her incredulously. "What? But that can't be . . ."

"Apparently the One Way signs were obscured by the trees.

I've already put in a complaint with the council; it's a complete hazard."

I feel my certainty wobble. It doesn't make sense but thinking about it now the cars were always parked facing one way and I never actually saw any other cars use that side street except . . .

"No, that can't be right," I say with renewed certainty. "I saw myself—" I stop myself quickly. ". . . I mean, I saw a girl driving an old Beetle in that direction . . ."

Beatrice looks at me sympathetically. "I think maybe you're confused. That's one of the side effects of morphine, especially in the high levels you've been on." She gestures to the intravenous drip in my arm. "It can make you imagine all kinds of things . . ."

She's right about one thing. I am confused.

"It's a really powerful drug. I studied it at Cambridge," she's saying.

"I thought you studied maths and physics," I manage, feeling more befuddled than ever.

"Oh, I did, but I took a chemistry module just for the fun of it." She smiles brightly.

I look at her in disbelief. Yes, she really did just say that. That's not just the morphine talking.

"Morphine is the principal medical alkaloid of opium," she continues breezily. "And like other opiates, it acts directly on the central nervous system to relieve pain. However, one of the side effects can be incredibly vivid dreams. In fact the word 'morphine' is derived from Morpheus, one of the Greek gods of dreams."

"What? You're telling me I dreamed it?" I say disparagingly.

"Most probably," she replies matter-of-factly. "You've been murmuring all kinds of things in your sleep. Something about Lottie . . . Olly . . . clubbing . . ." She gives a little laugh. "That's when I knew you must be dreaming. I mean, *you, clubbing*? No offense, but when did *any* of us last go clubbing?"

Actually, now I'm thinking about it, it does sound totally implausible.

Wearily, I feel my eyelids droop. Having just regained consciousness it's all a bit too much and I feel as if my brain's about to overload with all this new information.

"But I wouldn't worry. It's perfectly normal," she reassures quickly. "In fact there are many reported cases of people experiencing wonderful dreams when taking morphine, including visions, hallucinations. Even lucid dreams."

My eyelids snap back open. "What's a lucid dream?" I ask, frowning. Then wincing as my temple throbs.

"It's when you feel totally conscious yet you're really completely asleep," she explains, helping herself to a mound of grapes next to my bed. "You're dreaming, but it's as vivid as 'real' waking life. You can go anywhere, meet anyone, do anything. It's a sort of virtual reality."

I suddenly remember the moment in the pub where I first met Lottie:

*Unless of course this is all some crazy dream and I'm going to pinch myself and wake up to find Bobby Ewing in the shower.*

"It's actually incredibly fascinating." She smiles.

I feel a creeping realization. What is she saying? What does this mean? That everything I thought was real *wasn't*? As the idea strikes, I feel my whole set of beliefs blown apart. Oh my God, does this mean that it really *was* all some crazy morphine-induced dream? That I didn't really meet my younger self? That none of it really happened?

"So what about the press launch with Larry Goldstein? Did I dream that too?" My mind is reeling. I'm trying to make sense out of all this, but I feel totally disoriented. It's as if all at once I don't know what's real and what isn't real. What to believe and what not to believe.

"Oh, no, that *certainly* happened," states Beatrice firmly.

"And did I—"

"Tell him where he could stuff his bleaching kit?" she finishes, giving me a small smile. "Metaphorically, of course."

I manage my first smile of the day.

"Speaking of which . . ." She tugs out a trade paper. "He released a statement, saying he's decided not to expand into the UK at this time, due to the economic climate, and he's going to concentrate on his business in the States . . ."

As she passes me the paper, I look at the short statement. So Oliver's grandfather's store will be saved after all, I smile, feeling a beat of pleasure. Followed immediately by a tug of sadness as I think about Oliver. I brush it away quickly. There's no point thinking about it. That's over.

"If you're still feeling a bit confused, I can run through last week's diary. It might make things a bit clearer for you."

I glance up from the newspaper to see Beatrice pulling her laptop out of its sleeve.

"I brought it with me so I could keep in touch with the office."

"Thanks, that would be really helpful." I smile appreciatively and make a mental note never to tease Beatrice about the diary again.

Balancing it on her knee, she tucks her hair behind her ears and squints at the screen. "Okay, so on Monday you had a meeting at the Wolseley, followed by dinner with Miles at some new gastropub . . ."

*That was the first day I saw myself at the traffic lights,* I think, before I can stop myself.

"Tuesday, you had the lunch meeting with Larry Goldstein . . ."

*And later that evening I followed myself to my old house.*

"Wednesday you had a doctor's appointment—"

"Because I thought I was hallucinating," I interrupt, suddenly galvanized. "But I wasn't. What I saw was real."

Beatrice looks at me doubtfully. "Hmm, well, according to his notes it just says you came in suffering from stress. The doctors here had access to your medical files after the accident."

I look at her dazedly. Waking up in the hospital and being told you've been in a car accident you *don't* remember happening is bewildering enough, but then being told that the stuff you *do* remember didn't happen, is totally freaking me out.

"Don't worry," soothes Beatrice seeing my expression. "I once dreamed I went to see the doctor and he asked me to get undressed so he could examine me, and when I turned around he'd turned into my great-uncle Harold!" She looks at me aghast. "Though that was probably more of a nightmare than a dream." Shuddering she hastily turns back to the diary. "Right, where was I? Oh, yes, then in the afternoon we had the spa opening—"

"And we had that conversation about time travel—"

Beatrice looks at me blankly. "Time travel? Did we? Golly, I was so drunk we could have been having a conversation with Brad Pitt and I wouldn't remember."

I feel a beat of disappointment. Maybe she doesn't remember the conversation. Then again, maybe it's more likely it never happened, I admit to myself reluctantly.

"Then on Thursday evening you had dinner with Larry Goldstein at his hotel."

"And went to see Shattered Genius in concert . . ." I say to myself.

"No, there's nothing in the diary about any concert. Plus I called you afterward, you were at home, remember?" She looks at me and I realize I'm thinking aloud.

"Then Friday was your birthday dinner."

"And afterward I went to Lottie's party . . ." I murmur.

"No, sorry." Beatrice looks at me sympathetically. "Nothing about that either."

Well, why would there be? I tell myself, but even as I think it, I know I'm clutching at straws. Beatrice is right. I've been mixing fact with fantasy, dreaming about last week's actual events and interspersing them my own imaginary ones about meeting my younger self, getting everything jumbled up.

Unexpectedly, I feel a deep pang of sadness.

"It just seemed so real," I sigh. "I really thought I met my twenty-one-year-old self, that I've been hanging out with her. I could have sworn—"

"Gosh, you did get a bang on the head, didn't you?" The doctor walks in and throws me a smile. "Don't worry, the effects of the drugs wear off in no time."

I feel my cheeks flush with embarrassment. Well, honestly. What was I thinking? Of course it was just a dream.

"Okay, so let's see how the patient's doing." Walking over to me, he consults my chart and looks pleased. "X-rays are great, your vitals are great." He nods, then, looking up, glances at my face. "Brow's healing nicely . . ." He smiles warmly and I realize he's probably not much older than I am. "We'll keep you in overnight, just to make sure everything's okay, but you should be out of here tomorrow . . ."

"And how long before my shoulder heals?" I ask, as he slips my chart back into its holder.

"You should start physio in a couple of weeks. But I'm afraid you won't be able to drive for a while . . ."

I smile gratefully. "Thanks."

"My pleasure." He nods. "Okay, so I'll check on you later. 'Bye, Charlotte. 'Bye, Beatrice." He smiles, glancing across at her.

"Thank you, doctor," she replies, blushing as a look passes between them.

Hang on a minute—I feel something slowly registering.

"Did I just see that look, or was I dreaming that too?" I say, once the doctor's left the room.

Dragging her eyes away from the doorway, she turns to me, her face flushed with delight. "Isn't he divine?"

I look at her in amazement. "You're going out with my doctor?"

"His name's Hamish," she says proudly, "We met when you were first admitted, and then we kept bumping into each other the last two days, by the coffee machine, in the canteen. He's been working nights, you know . . ."

"Now I know why you've been keeping a bedside vigil." I smile. She gasps in indignation. "No! I've been worried sick—"

"It was a joke, Beatrice," I say quickly, and her indignation immediately melts away into wistfulness. "I think I'm in love," she confides in a whisper. "He doesn't mind me talking about scientific things at all. In fact yesterday we had a fascinating discussion about X-rays and radiation—"

"But what about Pablo, the salsa teacher?" I tease.

"Oh, didn't I tell you! Oh, well, no, obviously." She catches herself quickly, then swallows hard, as if bracing herself to tell me some shocking news. "When I was at the salsa club on Monday night he introduced me to Julio, his boyfriend!" She looks at me, her eyes wide. "Apparently he's gay! Would you believe it?!"

"A gay salsa teacher? No, never," I say with irony.

"I know, golly, what a turnup for the books." She nods, wide-eyed. "But I'm so pleased for them. And they danced the fandango together, beautifully—"

"Oh, my goodness, she's awake!"

Beatrice's reverie is suddenly interrupted by the appearance of Mom and Dad who, on seeing me propped up in bed, look both shocked and delighted.

"David, she's awake!" repeats Mom, shoving her Styrofoam coffee cup at Dad's chest as she rushes over, arms outstretched. "Charlotte, you're awake!"

"That's right, I'm awake," I repeat, smiling affectionately. I feel a warm surge of comfort. God, I've never been more thrilled to see them.

"Oh, my little baby," gasps Mom, appearing by my bed, her face etched with concern.

"Your parents and I have been taking it in turns to keep up the vigil," interjects Beatrice, throwing them both a smile.

"We just popped out for a snack; your father was hungry," Mum begins explaining apologetically, while Dad waves a half-eaten sandwich sheepishly. "We got to London as soon as we heard about the accident."

"Well, if the mountain won't come to Mohammed . . ." Dad smiles, relieving himself of food and beverages on the chair next to the bed, and rubbing my cheek affectionately like he used to do when I was little. I feel a warm glow, the months I haven't seen them simply melting away.

"We've all been so worried, thank goodness you're all right . . ." continues Mom.

"I'm fine, Mom, don't worry," I reassure her. "And about the other day, I'm sorry about not calling you back—"

"Oh, don't be silly," she gasps, batting away my apology. "That's not important. All that's important is that you're okay." She squeezes my hand and our eyes meet. I don't have to say anything. I don't have to say how much I love her, or how I was going to drive up and surprise them both because I missed them. Because that's the thing about parents, you never have to explain, they just know.

"Give her a few weeks. She'll be back to nagging you for grand-children." My dad chuckles as Mom throws him a furious look. "Only joking, dear." He smiles, tossing me a wink.

"Well, I better go rally the troops," announces Beatrice, "unless of course you need more time alone."

"Troops?"

"Your visitors!" she exclaims. "Everyone's been so worried. They're all in the waiting room. Up until now it's only been family allowed—I had to bend the doctor's arm," she confides, smiling. "But if you're feeling up to it . . ."

"Oh, yes, of course." I nod, trying to sit a bit more upright. Wow, of course visitors.

As Beatrice disappears, I make an attempt to smooth down my hair, adjust my pajama top, then give up. Well, I've just been in a head-on collision, I'm hardly going to look my best, am I?

"So Sleeping Beauty's finally woken up, huh?"

I turn to see Vanessa striding into the room. I try to laugh, then stop myself. Ouch.

"That was some scare you gave us." She throws me a huge grin. "Julian was on the phone to you when it happened."

"And yes, before you ask, she knows about the surprise," interrupts Julian, appearing next to her.

"Surprise, bloody shock more like." She grins, punching him affectionately on the arm. "Still, he got one of his own when I told him my real bra size, didn't you, darling?"

He smiles sheepishly and wraps his arm around her waist, pulling her close. "I didn't know what your measurements were, so the assistant asked me which celebrity you looked like, so she could work it out. So I said, that's easy. Cate Blanchett."

Vanessa's face breaks into a grin. "Now I remember why I fell in love with you." She laughs and a look passes between them. A look that says things are going to be okay. "So how are you feeling, honey?" she asks sympathetically, turning to me.

"Like I've got the worst hangover." I wince, rubbing my temple, which has started to throb again.

She smiles. "Well, just as long as you're okay. When I think what could have happened—" Vanessa breaks off. "It really makes you realize what's important, doesn't it?" she says quietly, and I don't know if she's talking about me, or her, or both of us.

"Now I think Charlotte should get some rest," orders Beatrice, interrupting, and there's a murmur of agreement and lots of well wishes and promises to call. Mom and Dad give me a good-bye kiss. "Now, before we go, do you need anything? I can pop to the shop." Mum starts fussing, but Dad leads her out, promising to visit first thing tomorrow.

And now it's just me and Beatrice.

"I should be going too," she says after everyone's emptied out of the room. "I've got a hot date." She lets out a giggle.

"Thanks, Bea. For everything," I say gratefully.

"Don't be silly. All part of the service." She reaches for her coat and bags. "Oh, and by the way, I picked up your mail for you. Looks mostly like lots of get-well cards." Popping it on my bed tray, she disappears.

And then the room's completely empty and quiet, and I'm finally alone. Feeling suddenly exhausted, I sweep my eyes around the room, noticing for the first time that's it filled with flowers, and take a deep breath, letting everything sink in.

So that's it. It didn't really happen at all. It seemed so real and yet—of course, it couldn't *really* have happened, could it? I smile to myself. Because although a part of me is sad it was all just make-believe and that I didn't really meet my twenty-one-year-old self, I feel as if I reconnected with her somehow. Deep down inside of me.

Plus, let's face it, that was hands down the wildest dream I've ever had. It's certainly a change from the one where my teeth are falling out, I think, stifling a giggle.

My eyes fall back on the pile of cards, and realizing my fingers work okay as long as I don't move my left arm, I start opening them. There's one from Melody, with a big lipstick kiss, a few more from my clients, one from Miles:

> Sorry to hear about your accident. Get well soon.
> P.S. Did you take out that health and sickness insurance policy I told you about, because you will be able to claim.

I smile to myself and thank him silently. Trust Miles, I muse fondly, reaching for the next card. Then pause as I look at the envelope, which is covered in lots of different addresses and postmarks, as if it's been forwarded loads of times. Until finally it got my correct address, I note, noticing it's covered in all my old ones. Huh, how funny. I wonder what it is. I have just started tearing open the envelope when I hear a quiet knocking on the door.

I glance up. It's probably the nurse, come to check on me—

My heart nearly stops.

*It's Oliver.*

"Hi." He smiles sheepishly and hovers at the doorway. "I called your office; your assistant told me you'd had a bit of an accident—"

"Just a bit," I reply, my heart hammering in my chest. I feel absurdly nervous.

"I've heard hospital food isn't much good, so I brought you a dish from the pub—" He gestures to a tinfoil-covered plate he's holding. "Fresh wild-caught salmon, baby new potatoes, and grilled asparagus."

"Oh, um, thanks—" My voice wobbles a bit.

"I hope you havn't had your mercury rations for the week," he adds, and laughs nervously.

Then there's a pause and we both fall silent.

Which is bizarre, as there's just so much I want to say, I think, desperately constructing elaborate sentences in my head before blurting,

"I'm sorry—"

"I'm sorry—"

We speak at the same time, and then laugh with a mixture of relief and self-consciousness.

"Shall I toss a coin to see who can apologize first?" he asks, raising an eyebrow.

"Look, I didn't mean those things I said—" I begin.

"Neither did I," he interrupts. "How about we call it a truce. Start over?"

I smile, feeling a tiny ray of hope coming out from the black clouds that I've been living under ever since we had our fight. It's so good to see him actually standing here, to hear his voice again.

"So you got a lot of get-well cards, huh?" he says, gesturing to the pile in front of me.

"Oh, yes." I nod, looking down at the card in my hand, and tugging it out of the envelope. Only it's not a card. It's a parking ticket fine. I smile ruefully. God, can you believe it, those pesky parking tickets, they even find you in the hospital, I think, looking at it. Which is when I notice it looks really old and faded. Huh, that's odd—

I glance at the details.

Car/Make Model: VW Beetle
Offense: Parking in a controlled permit area
Time: 6:28 p.m.

My stomach suddenly goes into freefall.

Date: 21 August 1997

For a split second I just stare at, my thoughts frozen in shock, then it jerks back up to speed. So it did happen. It *wasn't* a dream. This is the parking ticket that I got the first time I followed myself. I dropped it on the floor but the council always keeps a record. They never let you get away without paying, not even if it was ten years ago . . . As the realization hits, I feel a huge smile splitting over my face.

"What is it?"

I snap back to see Oliver staring at me, looking puzzled. "Oh, nothing," I say quickly, trying to quell the delight that's rushing up inside of me. "Just a parking ticket."

"Crikey, I've never seen anyone so happy to get a parking ticket before." He smiles with amusement.

I laugh, my mind racing, my thoughts tumbling over each other, everything clicking back into place. And that includes me and Oliver, I realize, glancing across at him and noticing he's still standing by the door.

"Do you want to come in and sit down? Stay a while?" I ask shyly. "But you don't have to, obviously," I add quickly, wondering if he's just come out of politeness. "You've probably got to get back to work at the pub. . . ."

Oh God, if he says he has to go, I don't know what I'm going to do.

"Actually, I think I'll take the evening off," he replies. "Can't leave the patient on her own, now can we?" Smiling, he folds his large frame onto the plastic chair next to me.

"You can do that?" I say with surprise, feeling flushed with pleasure. "I don't want you to get in trouble with your boss or anything . . ."

"Well, considering I am the boss, I don't think that will be a problem." He smiles ruefully.

"The boss?" I repeat, puzzled.

"Yeah, I own the pub and the restaurant, and I've got another couple in London. Didn't I ever mention it?"

I'm staring at him in astonishment.

"But I'd really like to expand abroad one day . . . open some place in France, or Italy maybe . . ."

I suddenly blush bright red. And to think I called him just a bartender.

"No, I didn't know," I say, with embarrassment.

"I guess there's a lot we don't know about each other," he says, his eyes meeting mine. "Maybe when you get out of here, we can do some catching up . . ." His voice trails off and as we gaze at each other it's as if we're both thinking the same thought.

"Oh, by the way, before I forget—" He digs in his pocket. "I found this."

"My watch!" I exclaim. As he passes it to me, his fingers brush against mine. A spark runs all the way down my spine.

"It had rolled into a corner. I think someone stood on it."

As I look at it I can see it's broken. The hands have stopped. Time literally is standing still.

"I can get it fixed for you if you'd like," he says quietly, and I notice he hasn't let go of my fingers. I glance at them, and curling my fingers around his I look up at him, wanting this moment to last forever. "Oh, there's no rush." I smile. "No rush at all."

# Nine Months Later

*P*ardon, monsieur, combien?"

The market trader, an old man with a flat cap on his head and Gauloise cigarette welded to his bottom lip, smiles at me as if I'm a native speaker and just as I'm thinking that perhaps my pigeon French and nasal accent aren't so bad, he rattles off something in French that leaves me completely lost.

"Umm . . ." Digging in my purse, I wave a euro note hopefully. "It's okay?"

Okay, so I'm cheating. And trying to make it sound like French by making my voice go up at the end isn't fooling anyone, but I've really got my eye on that fabulous pair of dangly earrings.

The trader smiles and takes the note, then passes me the change and the earrings.

There's lots of smiling and nodding and I feel a flood of delight. See, we all speak the same language in the end, I think happily as I loop the earrings through my ears and give them a little shake in the mirror.

They dance back, the silver strands and small pieces of pink glass twinkling in the bright June sunshine. *So* much more me than pearl earrings, I think, feeling a burst of pleasure.

Waving good-bye to the vendor and saying *au revoir* (that's one phrase I do know) I continue weaving my way through the maze of stalls. Stalls selling everything from ornate jewelry and vintage clothes to handbags of every color, size, and description.

This is one of the best flea markets I've ever been to, I muse, consulting my guidebook again to remember what it's called. *"The most famous flea market in Paris is the one at Porte de Clignancourt, officially called Les Puces de Saint-Ouen, but known to everyone as Les Puces (The Fleas)."*

"Les Puces," I repeat to myself, breathing the smells from the food stalls: delicious aromas of sweet, sugary crepes, savory croque monsieurs, freshly brewed *café au lait* . . . my mouth starts watering. Mmm, I wonder if it's nearly lunchtime yet, I muse distractedly, wandering from one stall to the next, like a bumblebee bouncing from flower to flower.

In the old days, I would have known exactly what time it was. I would have already checked my watch a hundred times already today, but I don't wear a watch anymore. Plus, I can't look at the clock on my phone as I've left my cell phone back at the hotel, I think, picking up a raspberry pink silk dress that's caught my eye. I'm totally out incommunicado and it feels great. No ringing phones. No BlackBerry buzzing. No e-mails pinging. I can actually have a conversation that lasts more than a couple of minutes without being interrupted.

Though perhaps not in French, I reflect, resorting to hand gestures and facial expressions with the stallholder to try to explain I want to try a larger size.

But then I don't really carry my phone with me a lot these days anyway. I don't have to. Not since I made Bea partner and gave her full control of running the company. To tell the truth, I wish I'd done it a lot sooner. She's a complete natural and has hired staff, rented larger premises, taken on more clients. The business is doing better than ever.

And me? Well, I've taken a sabbatical to finish my novel. Though to be honest, I've enjoyed it so much that when I finish it I might just write another. Or try my hand at a short story. Or even a screenplay. Who knows? I'm not going to look too far into the future. I'm living in the moment, and right at this moment I'm doing something I'm passionate about. And now, if ever that little voice in my head asks me "am I happy?" I answer without a missing a beat. Yes. Utterly. I am utterly and deliriously happy.

The stallholder returns, smiling and with a larger size, and holding the dress against my body, I look at my reflection. Gone is the stressed-out, blow-dried, fully made-up woman I used to be; in her place is someone who leaves her hair to dry naturally, wears just a slick of lip gloss, and can't remember the last time she had eczema. I've also gained a bit of weight these past few months due to my more relaxed diet, but I think I look a lot better, younger even, as my face doesn't look as gaunt. Plus my boobs have gotten bigger, which is fortunate. You really need boobs for this dress, I decide, doing my best to haggle in French, before giving in and buying it for the original price.

But I don't care, that's all part of the fun of shopping at markets, I muse. That's one of the things I rediscovered from my younger self. At least I think I did. To be honest, looking back now I'm not entirely sure . . .

It's been nine months since my accident. My broken bones have healed, the scar on my brow has faded, and with it my certainty of what exactly took place that week before my car crash. Or didn't take place. I guess with the passage of time, the line's been blurred between what's real and what's imagined, what I believe and what I *want* to believe.

Looking back now, I'm not so certain I ever did really see my younger self that morning at the traffic lights. That I ever did get to spend a week with her, getting to know her and myself again. After all, let's face it, it all sounds completely crazy. *More* than crazy.

In the weeks that followed there were a few things that made me wonder if Beatrice was right, and maybe I did just dream the whole thing up. First of all the parking ticket got lost. When I came out of the hospital I looked for it, but somehow it must have got thrown away by accident, so I never got to check the date again. And I was a bit groggy when I woke up, I could have made a mistake, misread the date, gotten confused somehow.

When I was well enough to drive again, the diversion was gone and I never saw my younger self or the old Beetle again. Then, when I went back to my old house and knocked at the door, a young couple with a baby answered.

I continue walking through the market, my eyes wandering across the different stalls, still on the lookout for bargains.

But there is one thing that makes me wonder. When the police called me up to investigate the accident they told me the last time it was a two-way street was in 1997. According to traffic records, it had been made into a one-way street about ten years ago after a rather nasty car accident. "The records seem to have been lost, but I seem to remember it involved a truck and car," the policeman had informed me over the phone, "which is something of a coincidence . . ."

Which makes me think it did happen. Well, I like to think it did, but who knows? I was tempted to Google "morphine and dreams," but I remembered what the doctor said. I'm trying to kick my Google habit. I've been clean for nine months now.

So did I never really meet my twenty-one-year-old self? Was it all a figment of my imagination, a desire to find myself so deeply ingrained in my subconscious that I ended up literally *finding* myself? I don't think I'll ever know the answer. But one thing is for certain. I've changed. I'm not that strung-out thirtysomething I was before the accident. I've learned how to relax, have fun, take vacations.

"I ordered you a glass of rosé."

Reaching the little pavement café where we'd arranged to meet, I find Oliver already waiting for me at a table. Sunglasses on, sleeves rolled up, he's drinking a beer and examining the menu. Wherever we go Oliver examines menus, looking for interesting new combinations of flavors or unusual dishes.

"Thanks." I smile, giving him a lingering kiss as he curls his tanned arms around me and pulls me onto his knee. I take a sip of the chilled wine. "Mmm, delicious," I murmur, and I'm not just talking about the wine.

We're in Paris for the weekend. I finally got around to using those tickets Vanessa bought me for my birthday last year. We caught the Eurostar over on Friday and checked into this amazing hotel with its own spa and this amazing Michelin-starred restaurant.

Though to be honest we've spent most of our time in the bedroom, if you know what I mean.

"So what did you buy?" He smiles, then rolls his eyes. "Don't tell me, everything!"

I laugh and start to show him all my goodies. He oohs and aahs appropriately at my earrings, exclaims at my dress (even commenting on how it will match my new sandals), and doesn't laugh when I show him the vase I bought that's shaped like a guitar. Well, it seemed like a good idea at the time . . . But best of all he doesn't tell me I should have invested the money I just spent in my pension. And for that I truly love him.

But then there's a lot to love about Oliver. He's funny and kind and makes me laugh. And it doesn't hurt that I just can't seem to get enough of him. That's not to say we don't argue about things. Boy, can we argue. But it's usually over as quickly as it starts, and then of course there's the making up that comes afterward . . .

In fact I used to wonder why we wasted all that time, why it took ten years and a whole strange set of circumstances to bring us together again, but I've come to realize it's a good thing we didn't hook up when I was twenty-one—I wouldn't have appreciated him like I do now. And it wouldn't be as great. Which goes to prove, there are some things I've learned as I've got older.

Only now he's acting a little weird, I realize, as he sits back down across from me at the table and glances at me all shiftily.

"What's wrong?" I ask, throwing him a smile.

"Nothing," he says, smiling tightly and taking a big swig of beer.

Uh-oh. Something's definitely up.

I observe him for a moment, trying to think what it can be. I draw a blank.

"Shall we order?" I suggest brightly.

"Um . . . sure." He nods. "I'll have whatever you're having."

Right, okay. That's it. Oliver never has what I'm having; he always spends what seems like hours deliberating carefully over the menu, and then orders all these weird and wonderful combinations. And I'm just opening my mouth to tell him so, when he suddenly slides off his chair onto his knees.

Actually, *correction*: one knee.

I feel my breath catching in the back of my throat. Oh my God, is he doing what I think he's doing?

He looks up at me. I don't think I've ever seen him so nervous. "The first time I met you I fell in love with you at first sight," he begins, his voice wobbling, "but you didn't even notice me."

"I did," I try to protest.

But he interrupts. "No, you didn't—" And he smiles ruefully.

I blush. "Okay, I didn't."

"Then you stood me up."

"I didn't stand you up!" I cry. "Well, okay, I did," I admit be-grudgingly when I see his look, "but only because I didn't get the message . . ."

"And then I met you and I hated you." He grins.

"No, I hated you." I grin back.

"Well, I tried to hate you, but then when you cleaned up after Welly . . ." He wrinkles up his nose, and glances at the floor, and when he looks back up his eyes meet mine and he holds my gaze. "I fell back in love with you all over again."

Suddenly realizing my throat is dry, I swallow nervously.

"Charlotte, it's been ten years, nine months, and nineteen days . . ." Fumbling in his pocket, he pulls out a small antique jewelry box. "Will you marry me?"

As he says those words, my heart flips right over.

Wordlessly, he passes me the tiny ring box and as I open the lid I find nestled inside the most beautiful antique ring. An emerald, shaped like a tiny flower. And it's the weirdest thing, like I've seen it before. It catches the sun, glinting, and I suddenly remember. Nine months ago. The old lady, sitting on the bench. She was wearing this ring. But that's impossible, *unless*—

My mind reels.

Unless that was me. Years from now. My older self, talking to my younger self. What was it she said?

*Life isn't complicated. It's very simple, really.*

I gaze at the ring, a million different emotions whooshing around inside of me, then lift my eyes and look into Oliver's. And it's as if everything else disappears inside my head but the love I have for him. Suddenly it all makes sense.

"Yes." I smile. One word. How much more simple can you get?

Oliver's face splits into a huge smile and, slipping the ring onto my finger, he scoops me up and twirls me around and around, until finally dizzy he pulls me toward him and kisses me. Right there. In front of everyone. In the middle of a Parisian café. With everyone looking. But I don't care. I've never been happier.

My mind slides back to Lottie. Just think, she's got all this to come. She's going to love it. And although I've thrown the list away, there's one last thing I want to add, only this time it's a piece of advice she gave me:

20. Hold on to your dreams.

And saying a silent thank-you to her, I smile up at Oliver and wrap my arms tightly around him.

I'm sure as hell holding on to mine.

# ACKNOWLEDGMENTS

B ig, big thank-yous as always to my wonderful agent Stephanie Cabot and everyone at the Gernert Agency in New York; to my fantastic editor Sara Kinsella and the equally fantastic Isobel Akenhead and to everyone who's worked so hard behind the scenes at Hodder.

To my parents—I won't go into a teary Oscar speech, but I can't say thank you enough for your continued love and support over the years. I honestly couldn't do this without you. And to my sister, I'll just say thanks, Kel, for everything. (I had to keep that simple, otherwise it's going to run into pages . . .)

I also want to use this opportunity to mention my dear friend Mishky, who I don't see as often as I'd like, but who's always there on the other end of the phone with kind words and encouragement.

Huge thanks also go to Dana, fellow writer and dear friend, who managed to keep me just about sane while I zipped back and forth between 1997 and 2007 and being 21 and 31—trust me, time travel ain't easy—if wormholes do exist there were several moments when I wanted to throw myself down one . . .

Thanks also to Saar for all those hours spent brainstroming, cups of tea when I had writer's block, and never once complaining about having a dining-room table covered in calendars, index cards, and

Post-it notes for the best part of a year . . . And of course a big hug for my muse Barney.

I spent part of the time in England working on this book, and I want to say an extra special thank-you to Tricia and Matthew—two amazing friends—for their generous hospitality in allowing me to be a writer in residence in their lovely house in Wimbledon, which came complete with the adorable Mr. George. Thanks, guys!

And finally, if I could meet my twenty-one-year-old self, I'd tell her that she will make some wonderful friends in her life: one of whom will be called Beatrice. Thanks, Bea, for your continuing friendship, boundless enthusiasm, and insider knowledge about the world of PR. And for making me laugh. A lot. This book is dedicated to you.